APOCRYPHAN RISING

JOHN CORWIN

RAVEN
HOUSE

BOOKS BY JOHN CORWIN

THE OVERWORLD CHRONICLES

Sweet Blood of Mine

Dark Light of Mine

Fallen Angel of Mine

Dread Nemesis of Mine

Twisted Sister of Mine

Dearest Mother of Mine

Infernal Father of Mine

Sinister Seraphim of Mine

Wicked War of Mine

Dire Destiny of Ours

Aetherial Annihilation

Baleful Betrayal

Ominous Odyssey

Insidious Insurrection

Utopia Undone

Overworld Apocalypse

Apocryphan Rising

Assignment Zero (An Elyssa Short Story)

OVERWORLD UNDERGROUND

Soul Seer

Demonicus

Infernal Blade

OVERWORLD ARCANUM

Conrad Edison and the Living Curse

Conrad Edison and the Anchored World

Conrad Edison and the Broken Relic

Conrad Edison and the Infernal Design

Conrad Edison and the First Power

STAND ALONE NOVELS

Mars Rising

No Darker Fate

The Next Thing I Knew

Outsourced

For the latest on new releases, free ebooks, and more, join John Corwin's
Newsletter at www.johncorwin.net!

THE ABYSS UNLEASHED

During a recon mission of a Razor Echelon base, Justin and Elyssa uncover Xanos's new weapon.

The Apocryphan is building a portal device that could allow her to transport troops anywhere, including right in the middle of Queens Gate. The Eden forces have nowhere else to run, so Justin seeks the aid of allies to prevent the obliteration of the supernatural resistance.

They learn that a woman might be the key to salvation. She has the power to open portals between realms and from one place to another within realms. With her help, they could counter Xanos before the portal device is completed.

But first, they have to find this woman. She's been missing for years, presumably hiding from Baal and his minions in another realm. Justin discovers there might be a way to track the portals she's opened before. So he and the gang start off on their most dangerous mission yet: traversing unknown realms with the faintest hope of finding the one woman who might save them all.

That woman is Emily Glass.

CHAPTER 1

E nemy operatives in black uniforms patrolled the great crater of Thunder Rock. Thick forest interspersed with barren, rocky terrain surrounded the old granite quarry. The wards and illusion spells hiding Thunder Rock were gone, leaving the entire area visible to the naked eye for the first time in centuries.

Razor Echelon didn't like magic users. They'd eradicated wards and charms in their blitzkrieg against the Overworld even if it meant exposing secret supernatural places to the normal world.

Elyssa and I crouched on a nearby hill, the vantage point offering a clear view of the crater and surrounding area. A squad of soldiers on horseback patrolled the perimeter of the forest at a leisurely pace. They seemed supremely confident that nothing could threaten their grip on Overworld territory.

"Three minutes, give or take." Elyssa tapped the screen of her arcphone again to mark the latest passing of a patrol. "Getting past them will be easy."

"Yeah, it's the next part that I'm worried about." I looked to the south. Blackened earth, still torn and raw marked the last major battle fought on these grounds. It had been a feint, designed to keep Daelissa from marching her army straight through Atlanta. It had worked, but nearly cost me everything.

Scorching heat bites into my back. Elyssa yanks me from the line of fire. But another beam of Brilliance strikes her. Armor smokes. Flesh burns. Sizzling blood explodes from her chest.

I shuddered.

Elyssa gripped my wrist. "Stop thinking about it, Justin."

Banishing those memories wasn't so easy. "Daelissa nearly killed you here. Now we're right back to square one. Same damned place, different enemy."

"We're stronger and smarter than we were back then." Elyssa squeezed my hand. "Besides, we're not here to start a war. This is just recon."

I rolled onto my side and caressed her cheek. "Let's nuke them from orbit. Adam can hack a nom satellite, and boom!"

"Justin, pull yourself together." Elyssa's violet eyes flashed with an inner glow. "Thunder Rock isn't exactly at the top of my list of vacation spots either. So let's do this and get out of here, okay?"

I sighed. Nodded.

We'd finally made it back to Eden less than a month ago and discovered everything had gone to shit while we'd been away. Victus Edison had taken over and declared himself Overlord. With the majority of the Templars and other supers trapped in Seraphina, there was almost no one left to oppose him. But he hadn't counted on my sister, Ivy, being left behind. She'd overthrown him and freed the Overworld.

But Victus faked his death and came back again. Ivy wasn't around to stop him the second time. She'd been kidnapped and stowed in a preservation chamber by one of Victus's former minions. So Victus's son, Conrad Edison, did the job. Then he and his friends had found us in

Seraphina and brought us back to Eden. Unfortunately, Victus wasn't the last of Eden's troubles.

The Overworld had been whittled away by an international collective of anti-supernatural agencies known as Razor Echelon. They'd taken over dozens of pocket dimensions and waystations, converting many of them into prisons for supers.

They had weapons that could destroy magical shields, disintegrate demon spawn, and disable supers with high voltage electro bullets. They had tanks and missiles, spy drones, and thousands of operatives.

To top it off, they were owned and operated by a former god, an Apocryphan by the name of Xanos. And I was the one who'd freed her from the Abyss in a major battle against Daelissa.

Her first order of business was to wipe out all supernatural resistance so she could rule Eden. What came next was anyone's guess, but ultimately, Xanos wanted to recombine the realms back into one Earth.

Since the realms occupied the same physical space but existed in different dimensions, it wasn't hard to imagine what smashing them back together would be like. Some realms were small as asteroids. Others were nearly as large as Eden. Having so many heavenly bodies phase back into the same plane of existence at the same time would be nothing short of catastrophic. A billion living creatures would be snuffed out in an instant while the rest fought to survive the cataclysm.

It would make the war against Daelissa look like a cat fight in a Dollar General parking lot.

Xanos wasn't our only problem. Baal, the grand overlord of Haedaemos was taking over other realms with an army of dragons. He'd already driven us out of Seraphina, and it was only a matter of time before he set his sights on Eden.

The Overworld had to be united and strong before that day came. That meant Xanos had to go. That meant I had to put on my big boy panties and get over my Thunder Rock PTSD. It was time to man up and kick some ass.

Elyssa's eyebrow quirked. "Do you have to go to the bathroom?"

I blinked out of my thoughts and frowned. "Huh?"

"You've got this really constipated look on your face." Elyssa put a hand to my forehead. "Yeah, definitely constipated."

I snorted. "Very funny, babe."

"While you were having deep thoughts, I timed two more patrols." Elyssa nodded at another squad coming into view. She started the timer again. "Make that three. I think it's time to make a move."

"I've got on my adult diapers and my loins are girded." I cracked my knuckles. "It's go time."

"You know how much I love it when you gird your loins." Elyssa pecked a kiss on my cheek. "Let's do it."

We climbed down the steep backside of the hill and walked around it, keeping behind the trees. A wide expanse of rocky earth stood between us and concealment in the forest. Elyssa scanned the area then chopped an arm forward. We blurred across the field and into the forest.

Elyssa flicked on her arcphone and activated an app. A green line swept a circle on the screen--magical radar. "I hope it works this time."

"It better, or this'll be one short mission." I followed her through the trees, keeping a sharp eye out for more patrols. We hadn't gone more than fifteen yards when a blip showed up on the edge of the radar.

"Got something." Elyssa crept forward until the blip centered on the screen at the base of a tall oak. "It must be up there."

I manifested demon claws at my fingertips. "Allow me."

I clawed my way up the tree and reached a branch large enough to support my weight. I found the device about fifty feet up, a black box secured to the tree trunk by metal bands. I shielded my face and touched it. Amazingly, nothing happened. Most Razor weapons and devices self-destructed at the touch of a super. Apparently, these didn't.

My claws made short work of the metal bands. I tucked the black box beneath an arm and climbed back down. "Mission accomplished." I cocked an ear. "So far, at least."

Elyssa inspected the box and flicked a small toggle switch on the bottom. "I think it's off now." She opened another app with a map of the area. A horizontal line scanned up and down twice.

Scan complete.

The map shaded areas protected by the black boxes in red. We stood in a narrow slice of green barely wider than a person.

"That's it? Just an itty-bitty slice out of the pie?" I face-palmed.

Elyssa shrugged. "I'm afraid so."

"Well, forget sneaking our army through here."

In the past month, we'd checked out dozens of Overworld cities now controlled by Razor. Every one of them were protected by a perimeter of these black boxes. We knew they detected supers, but up until now we'd never laid hands on one.

Elyssa held her arcphone to the black box and let it scan the insides. We didn't dare take the thing back to headquarters until we knew more about it. "This is going to take a while. Let's do a quick recon of the crater."

I rubbed my hands together. "I can't wait to finally get a look at what they're up to." Razor's technology excelled at cock-blocking supers.

Our resident genius, Adam Nosti, was up to his ears in devices we'd stolen from Razor. He literally had to handle them with gloves because one touch from a super was all it took to make them self-destruct. Thankfully, most devices fizzled out instead of exploding, but there had been a couple that would have done serious harm if not for proper precautions in the lab.

Careful to keep within the narrow confines of the green zone, we crept through the woods and up to the edge of the old quarry. The first time I'd been here, Elyssa and I had been trapped inside with Kassallandra, the fiery redheaded leader of the Daemos. There'd been a lake in the crater back then, but Daelissa had drained it and opened it up the caves below to serve as a base of operations.

Razor apparently found the place just as useful as our old enemy had. It contained a control room full of arches they could use to invade other Overworld cities. The only disadvantage was the Obsidian Arch had been destroyed, leaving them only the smaller arches. That was why I was stunned when we peeked over the edge and down into the base.

A thick white ring segmented by black bands hovered vertically over the cavern floor. It spun slowly, humming like a generator building a charge. Dozens of figures in white coats stood around the ring. I took out my spectacles and zoomed in for a better look. An Indian woman with horn-rimmed glasses and a tablet caught my attention.

"Dr. Pari Sidana," I growled. "I guess she made it out of the prison somehow."

"That's the one who experimented on you when Razor captured you?" Elyssa said.

"Yep." I'd locked her up in the same chair she'd held me in. Even though Kalesh, my demon half, wanted to murder her in cold blood, I'd resisted the temptation.

The white ring spun faster, generating a blue vortex of energy in the middle. Lightning crackled across the vortex. Thunder rumbled, and a brilliant flash blinded me for a second. When my eyes cleared, the storm was gone, replaced by dark, rocky terrain. Stars dusted the alien sky, leaving little doubt that Razor had just demonstrated a new portal device.

I put the spectacles back to my eyes. The scientists cheered, high fiving each other. A group of Razor soldiers marched toward the portal. But before they reached it, another bright flash illuminated the ring. Thunder clapped again, and the portal vanished. The inside of the ring sparked violently and the contraption ground to a halt.

"This isn't good at all," Elyssa said.

"Why bother with a portal device?" I said. "They have a waystation full of arches that already do the same thing."

Elyssa shook her head. "Justin, that looked like a portal to another realm."

I wanted to see the downside, but I couldn't. "It's perfect. Now that we've finally figured out how to breach the perimeter of Razor strong-holds without them knowing, we can steal this tech from them. We can transport our army anywhere with it."

She bit the inside of her lip. "Maybe."

"Also, why does Razor want to go to other realms when they haven't even secured Eden?" I peered down at the now unhappy scientists scrambling like ants to repair the machine. "We can use this thing to fight Baal once we defeat Razor."

"You sound awfully optimistic." Elyssa pecked a kiss on my cheek. "That's nice for a change."

Kalesh wasn't the least bit happy. *We are doomed.*

"Yeah, my demon half is throwing another pity party, and his bad mood is starting to bring me down."

Elyssa rubbed my arm. "It's understandable, especially after what Baal did you."

I backed away from the ridge. "Let's get back to HQ with this info."

We backtracked through the green zone to the device we'd disabled.

Elyssa's phone had finished scanning its internals. She stared at it and frowned. "I can't make heads or tails of it."

I looked at her screen. The scan used a magical X-ray to approximate the insides of the box. I used my former expertise as a computer nerd to decipher what I saw. "Looks like a circuit board, wires, and some kind of crystal plugged into the middle."

Elyssa inspected the seams along the top of the box. "Safe to open?"

I shrugged. "Probably."

She produced a small knife from a hidden pocket in her uniform and pried along the seam. It popped open and she gingerly lifted it off. I noticed a thin, delicate wire attached to the inside of the lid. Before I could warn Elyssa, it snapped.

"What was that?" she said.

A red LED on the circuit board began to blink.

"If I had to guess, I think we just tripped an alarm."

"Damn it." Elyssa snapped hasty pictures of the insides, getting close-ups of the crystal in the center. "Thank god we didn't open it earlier or we wouldn't have seen the portal device."

I peered closer at the crystal. "That looks like aetherite. The same stuff they use in Seraphina."

"Might be a power source." Elyssa prodded at the wires inside then put the cover on the box. "Maybe we should put this back in the tree."

Shouts echoed in the near distance. I shook my head. "No time." I buried the box under some leaves. "Besides, I'm curious to see what they do if they think the box is missing."

"Think it might be booby-trapped?" Elyssa said.

"Considering they rig just about everything to self-destruct, I wouldn't doubt it."

We beat a hasty retreat up the hill we'd used earlier and peeked over the rise. The box we'd disabled was just at the edge of the forest, so we had a clear view. Six soldiers rode horses into view. They spread out and began searching the area. One of them hopped off her horse and clambered up the tree where the black box had been. She searched the branches and shouted at her comrades when she failed to find the box.

"Looks like Adam's cloaking app worked. The detectors didn't spot us." Elyssa pursed her lips. "I hope we got enough info about the detector for him to see how it works."

The soldiers spread out into a line formation and combed the forest out toward our position. A four-wheeled ATV drove up a moment later with two men in gray jumpers. One of them opened a laptop and began typing on it. The other climbed the tree and strapped another black box in place.

"Efficient." Elyssa sounded impressed. "I'll bet that guy on the laptop is tracking the other box."

"No. I'll bet he's about to hit the self-destruct because he doesn't know it's right in front of him under the leaves."

Elyssa's eyes brightened. "You think so?"

"I hope so."

"I've got to see this." Elyssa snuggled her shoulder up to mine as if we had front row seats and popcorn at the circus. She turned on her arcphone camera and aimed it below.

I looked through the spectacles for a front-row view of the technician. He held up a finger dramatically, a smirk on his face. That was when I knew for sure he expected to explode whoever made off with the black box.

His finger came down.

The earth beneath the front end of the ATV exploded. The vehicle flipped backward three times, sending the laptop guy cartwheeling through the air. He hit a tree and slid down it like a cartoon character. Burning leaves rained down. Horses screamed and bucked off their riders.

Elyssa and I covered our mouths and snorted with glee.

The laptop guy struggled to his feet and staggered away from the smoking ATV. The other technician in the tree dangled from a branch. A brown streak decorated the seat of his pants.

"He shat himself!" It was all I could do not to burst into loud laughter that would instantly give away our position.

Elyssa showed me the playback on her phone. "Shelton's going to enjoy this."

"Oh, I think everyone will." I eased back down the rise on my belly. "Maybe that'll teach them not to blindly blow up everything."

"Maybe they'll think the box fell out of the tree and the wire inside broke on accident," Elyssa said.

I shrugged. "With so many of those black boxes, you'd think false alarms would occur from time to time."

Elyssa pursed her lips. "Justin, that's a really good idea."

I blinked. "Uh, what's a good idea?"

"It's a classic!" She backed away from the peak of the rise before standing up. "And I don't think these bozos have the protocol to handle it."

"Yeah, it's genius." I gave her an expectant look. "So what the hell is my idea?"

"False alarms. Dozens of them." She opened the map and zoomed out to show the perimeter. "If we keep pinging them from all sides, they'll eventually think the system is bugged and ignore it."

"Or maybe they'll just keep doing the same thing they're doing now, no matter how many alerts they get." I brushed off my jeans and shirt. "Maybe they'll just stay on high alert all the time and we'll never breach their perimeter."

She bit the inside of her lip and went silent a moment. "Xanos would probably see right through our ruse anyway."

"Yeah, she's not stupid." I heard whirring, but it was so faint as to almost be a whisper. It took me a split second to realize the sound was coming from just over the rise. Before I could react, two black quadcopter drones flashed past overhead. Whoever controlled them must have spotted us because they veered back around and came at us.

They were different from the small, noisy ones we'd encountered before. They measured about four feet in length and width, and each had multiple gun turrets on the bottom. A loud electrical hum was all the warning I got before a bolt of blue electricity streaked toward me. I rolled to the side and narrowly avoided a trip to La-La Land.

Elyssa nearly dove into me as she avoided a blast from the other drone.

"I've never seen such big ones!" I summoned Brilliance and fired a beam of blazing white energy at the first drone. The attack splashed off magic-resistant armor in a shower of sparks.

"That's what she said." Elyssa rolled away from another electrical blast, smoothly drew her light bow, and fired an energy arrow. It didn't even leave a mark on the drone.

I dove away from two quick blasts and rolled to the side to avoid a third. Since magic didn't do the trick, I decide a low-tech approach. I found a hefty hunk of granite and hurled it. It crashed into a propeller and shattered it.

The drone wobbled, its other three propellers working overtime to compensate.

"You've got to be kidding me." Elyssa cocked her arm and threw a rock at the undamaged drone. It strafed to the side and the rock only glanced off the ring around the propeller. But that took it right into the rock I'd thrown an instant after Elyssa's. Mine nailed the drone dead center and sent it spinning out of control.

Another rock from Elyssa smacked the already damaged one and sent it spiraling out of view over the edge of the rise.

I nudged Elyssa. "What did Mary say to her little lambs?"

Elyssa frowned. "Say what?"

"Let's get the flock out of here!" I grabbed her hand and we ran for our lives.

Hooves thundered up the hill behind us, but not even horses could keep up with our supernatural speed. Elyssa and I reached another grove of trees where we'd stashed our flying brooms. We hopped on and zipped into the air.

But the fun and games weren't over yet.

Three black drones roared out of the quarry pit and came after us. If they'd been quadcopters, outrunning them would have been no problem. But these drones resembled miniature fighter jets. They even had cute little missiles attached under their wings.

I had a feeling they wouldn't be quite so cute when they blew us to bits.

CHAPTER 2

The fighter drones were too far away for me to hit with magic. We'd be within their weapons' range long before they were within mine.

"We've got to fly low through the trees," Elyssa shouted over the rush of wind. "It's our only choice."

There was a lot of forest between us and civilization, but I didn't know how effective it would be at saving us from fighter drones. On the other hand, we were guaranteed to get blown out of the sky without anything between us and the missiles.

As if to prove the point, each drone fired a missile. They streaked toward us, a trail of white smoke drawing a path to our doom.

"Dive!" Elyssa angled down toward the trees.

I willed the broom to full speed and shot into the canopy. A branch whipped my face. The next one nearly took off my head, but a quick barrel roll kept it attached. I aimed for the forest floor where the branches thinned.

I heard a massive boom. A shockwave washed over me and shoved my broom straight at a tree. I couldn't possibly stop it in time, so I pulled hard to the left. My stomach found a branch and the broom shot out from beneath me. The wind exploded from my lungs and I barely had the presence of mind to hang onto the branch instead of plunging painfully to the ground a hundred feet below.

Superheated air washed over my back. Just as suddenly, the hot wind reversed, and cooler air hit my face. I gasped for air, desperately trying to fill my lungs before my brain called it quits from a lack of oxygen.

I managed a breath and worked my way over to the tree trunk. I looked back and saw what was left of the tree the missile had hit. The top half was nothing but splintered ruins, much like other trees in the blast radius.

"Holy shit." I sucked in another breath. "What in the hell is in those little missiles?"

The drones roared past somewhere overhead. I couldn't see them, but they might be able to see me. For all I knew, they had thermal imaging or some magical means to spot me in the tree. One of the drones confirmed my suspicions, because I heard the tell-tale sound of a missile launch.

I'd never sprouted claws so fast in my life. I loosened my grip on the tree and slid down, shaving bark and leaving deep scars in the wood. The missile annihilated the top half of the tree when I was still twenty feet from the ground. The shockwave blasted me through the air. I hit the ground and skidded through the leaves until another tree stopped me.

Stunned and disoriented, it took a moment for me to get back to my feet. I ran in a lazy circle because I was too dizzy to manage a straight line. My broom lay on the ground a good distance from the tree I'd just fallen from. My body might have stopped in an instant, but the broom kept on going until it hit the ground.

I had no idea where Elyssa was, but she'd probably done a better job of dodging branches than I had. The jet drone circled overhead, a black silhouette in the gray sky. I retrieved my broom and inspected it. It seemed to be in one piece.

"Justin?" Elyssa's voice emanated from the comm pendant on my Nightingale armor. I tapped it. "I'm alive. Where are you?"

"I'm about a mile outside of the forest. The drone turned back. I guess Razor doesn't want to alert the noms."

I sighed with relief. "Thank god you got out. I had a little accident, so I'm still in the forest."

"Are you kidding me?" Elyssa huffed. "I thought you were right behind me."

I hopped on my broom and accelerated. "Don't worry, I'll catch up soon." *I hope.*

But it seemed my little drone stalker wasn't done just yet. Whoever was piloting the thing was probably a lot better at video games than I was, because the drone swooped down into the trees, weaving through them without missing a beat. The front cannon opened fire.

I opened up the throttle on the broom just in time to avoid a hail of electrified flak exploding in the air where I'd been. I veered hard right. The drone was going too fast to make the turn, forcing it to make a wide circle through the trees. Then it angled right back at me. The roar of another miniature jet engine sounded from ahead. The second drone dove into the forest and came right for me.

"Now you're just pissing me off," I growled.

Magic-resistant armor was excellent at dispersing magical energy. That meant all the destructive power I threw against the drones would probably be for nothing. Thankfully, I wasn't a one-trick pony. My Seraphim powers gave me access to not one, but four magical elements. Fiery white Brilliance was great for blowing things up. Cold ultraviolet Murk could be channeled into useful shapes and shields, while Stasis combined the two to make a field that absorbed all energy.

Clarity combined the first three but wasn't useful in a combat situation.

I could probably play ring around the rosy with the drones until the cows came home, but I was sick and tired of running. It was time to end the reign of terror from these mini-machines. Instead of dodging, I made a beeline for the drone in front of me. An orb of ultraviolet formed in my left hand. I channeled it into a curving shield and hoped the jet didn't fire a missile at this range since it would blow us both to bits.

The remote pilot apparently didn't care about preserving the jet, because it launched a missile.

"You bastard!" I channeled the Murk shield into a solid ball and blasted it ahead. I quickly channeled another shield in front of the broom just as the ball hit the missile. The shockwave shattered saplings and hurled leaves and dust into the air. Sharp splinters and debris crashed into the shield, sparing my face a catastrophic makeover.

Since I couldn't see anything, I swung the broom hard left. It was a good thing I did, because the drone slammed into a tree I would have flown past an instant later. The remaining missiles detonated. I pulled up hard. A wave of superheated air lifted me so fast, the broom spun upside down.

Cooler air tried to suck me back down into the forest. I wrestled the broom back under control and looked around for the other jet. I didn't see it anywhere, which meant it'd probably been destroyed by the explosion as well. Hopefully.

I extended both middle fingers back at Thunder Rock. "Suck it, you damned joystick jockeys!" I wanted to punch them both in their smug little faces until I broke all their teeth. I got my bearings and headed for Elyssa's coordinates.

My inner demon usually took great pleasure in my violent thoughts. But it remained quiet this time.

What, you're not even going to try to talk me into it?

My inner demon desired death and destruction. It had taken that path against my will many times before and caused me all sorts of problems. After fighting it almost constantly, I'd finally figured out how to control the urges. Then Baal planted a part of his essence inside my soul and my demon half took the upper hand again.

Baal's seed had grown and festered into a malevolent entity, a spiritual copy of myself that he transferred from my body and into my father's. My father's spirit was banished back to Haedaemos and his body transformed into my evil doppelganger.

The incident left my demon spirit heavily traumatized. So much so, that these days it hardly talked back to me. I could still manifest demon claws, and I had my demonic strength, but trying to spawn was a real struggle. I'd long dreamed of shutting up my demonic urges, but this was taking things too far.

You need a therapist.

No response.

I flew into a complex of abandoned warehouses at the edge of the forest and found Elyssa waiting next to a black sedan.

"Justin!" Elyssa wrapped her arms around me the moment I landed. "What happened? It sounded like they carpet-bombed the forest."

"The drones tried a pincer maneuver and blew themselves up with their own missiles." I shrugged. "No big deal."

She narrowed her eyes. "No, these new fighter drones are a huge deal. Every time I think we know about their arsenal, they spring something new on us."

"I mean, they already had ground-to-air missiles that homed in on magical energy. Why would they make little jets too?"

"Because these jets can be used offensively." Elyssa opened the car trunk and put my broom inside with hers, then hopped into the driver's seat.

I got in on the other side and closed the door. "I don't know how we're going to take back Overworld territories when we're up against that kind of firepower."

"I don't think any of us know." Elyssa slapped the steering wheel. "And it's frustrating as hell."

"That's not very comforting coming from our primary battle planner."

"Even my father is stumped." Elyssa looked like she wanted to cry. "It's like planning a war against the noms, except in this case, the noms have anti-magic tech that takes all our best weapons out of the equation."

"Well, let's just use rocks." I patted her leg and offered a reassuring smile. "They apparently don't know how to defend against those."

Elyssa sighed and activated the car's camouflage. She pulled back on a lever and took us into the air, then accelerated toward Decatur. "I guess we can be thankful Razor doesn't know about the Ranch."

"Or they don't care about it." The Ranch was the Templar compound that once serviced the southeast portion of North America. Now it was home to the remnants of the Templar legions.

Years of war in Seraphina had taken its toll on all the factions. The vampires, lycans, and Daemos were holed up in Queens Gate, one of the few remaining Overworld cities in our possession. We'd barely held off Razor once. I wasn't sure we could do it again. That was why Elyssa and I had started probing enemy territory, hoping to find a weakness we could exploit.

But so far, Razor's territories looked bulletproof. The only bright spot so far was that Adam's cloaking app seemed to have beaten the black box supernatural detectors. Unfortunately, it only worked on a small scale. It might get a small group past the detectors, but not an army.

Now that we knew every detector was rigged to go off like a bomb, that made trying to deactivate all of them very risky.

The Ranch, like everything else, had changed during our exile. The main house was gone, replaced by a four-car garage. The old church, an ancient structure moved stone-by-stone overseas and rebuilt precisely had been converted into a house. The best part was the huge purple barn with green trim.

I'll bet Thomas wants to cry every time he looks at that thing.

One of the first things Victus did after trapping us in Seraphina was to visit the Ranch and kill any remaining Templars. The battle had leveled the house and damaged most of the outbuildings. After that, the property sat vacant until the charms and wards expired, making it visible to noms.

Shelton had come here shortly after our disastrous arrival in Eden and discovered a nom had found the place and the magical goodies in the underground complex beneath the barn. Needless to say, the nom made quite a bit of money and used it to remodel the Templar compound into something straight off of HGTV.

"I'll bet Thomas loves the purple," I said as Elyssa landed outside the barn.

"It's lavender, and I think it's kind of cute." Elyssa sprang out of the car and spoke with a Templar guard for a moment, then hopped back in as the man opened the barn doors.

"Yeah, real cute. I'll bet the Templars adore it too."

"Say what you want, but I kind of like the new compound." Elyssa drove into the barn as the floor ahead dropped open to form a ramp into the underground garage.

There was still only a skeleton crew at the Ranch. Most of the Templars were holed up in the catacombs beneath Arcane University along with the rest of our original army. The underground mansion housed me,

Shelton, Elyssa, and most of our immediate families. Construction was underway aboveground to rebuild what had once been Greek Row.

Thomas had ordered the tunnels leading from the surface of London down into Queens Gate sealed to keep Razor from mounting another full-frontal assault. The Obsidian Arch waystation and all the arches inside were disabled by portal-blocking statues. The only arch in operation was the omniarch near the underground mansion.

But we were determined not to be holed up in Queens Gate forever. The pocket dimension was straining at the seams to hold all the refugees from other Overworld cities. Somehow, we had to release the pressure before the pent-up populace exploded into unrest.

A neon green Lamborghini, a white Tesla, and a bright red Ferrari were only a sample of the dozen or so exotic nom vehicles crowded into one corner of the underground garage. The nom squatter hadn't spared any expense when building up his collection. Back when I was in high school any one of those cars would've been a wet dream. But flying brooms, magic cars, and everything else in the Overworld made even the most exotic cars boring by comparison.

Elyssa parked the car, looked down at her lap, and sighed. Then she took a deep breath as if steeling herself and climbed out. I'd seen her do this a million times when she had to deliver bad news.

"Hey, your dad won't be disappointed with you. It's not your fault Razor has more gadgets than James Bond."

She nodded. "Yeah, but I really wanted to bring him something actionable, you know?"

Elyssa loved military jargon, so I spouted some of my own. "Well, let's give him recon intel on the opfor we can actionate."

Elyssa lightly punched me in the shoulder and laughed.

We walked across the wide garage and stepped into the levitator. The floating platform dropped us down to command level where we found

Thomas and Elyssa's hulk of a brother, Michael, staring at stacks of paper on the conference table.

Elyssa walked inside and put a hand on her brother's bulging shoulder muscle. "What's all this?"

It was one of the few times I'd ever seen Thomas actually look frazzled. He collected himself and stood up, tugging down on the hem of his black shirt. "Our days at the compound might be numbered."

Elyssa blinked. "Is an attack imminent?"

Michael shook his head. "It's even worse."

When these two sounded the doomsday bell, that meant things were really bad. "What's going on?" I asked.

"We had a visitor today." Thomas held up a letter printed on green paper. "The local tax office discovered we exist and that they have no records of us paying taxes. This is a court summons." He held up another piece of paper. "And this is a bill for millions of nom dollars for back property taxes."

Michael grabbed another stack. "And these are all infractions for not getting building permits, for not having livestock permits, and more."

Thomas dropped the papers. "I'm afraid this land is going to be auctioned off and sold, and there's not much we can do about it."

CHAPTER 3

My jaw dropped open. "How can they swoop in here and sell the land?"

Thomas shook his head. "They have no record of who owns this land, and we have no deed. The only reason we haven't been evicted already is because we convinced them there must be some clerical error."

"Then let's just magic all this away." I waved my hands. "Abracadabra. Make 'em forget."

"Too many people know," Michael said. "It's caused something of a scandal in the local government."

"We haven't had time to get the cloaking wards back up again," Thomas said. "Today, three government cars rolled in along with local police and bureaucrats. They invited the local news media as well to show they were taking care of illegal squatters."

"I don't get it." Elyssa tapped a finger on her chin. "We were gone for almost a decade, and a squatter sat on this land for about six years. How did they only just now discover us?"

Thomas pursed his lips. "That's a good question. The noms have developed most of the land around us. What used to be old houses and abandoned car dealerships are now high-priced townhouses. It's possible one of those developers did the research and discovered this land isn't even listed in the registry."

"Let's just forge some documents," I said. "It shouldn't be too hard using magic."

Thomas's comm badge beeped. He tapped it. "Yes?"

A female voice spoke. "Commander, there's someone else from the government here to see you."

His eyes tightened. "Very well. Invite them into the house and I'll meet them in a moment." He stood. "If you'll excuse me."

The voice in his comm badge spoke again. "Sir, they also want to speak with Commander Slade."

Thomas blinked. Elyssa's eyes widened. I flinched. Michael regarded me with a frown.

"How do they know about me?" I whispered, as if someone might be listening.

"Sir, I don't know," the female replied. "Shall I tell them to expect you?"

I nodded. Realized she couldn't see me, and said, "Okay."

"Very suspicious." Elyssa's eyes narrowed. "I don't think land developers are behind this."

Thomas tugged at the hem of his black shirt. "Then let's find out who is."

The four of us left the conference room and made our way back up to the garage. An electric golf cart hauled us across the wide space and up the ramp into the purple barn.

I patted the vinyl seats. "This is nice. Wish we'd had one of these a long time ago, because the walk from the levitator to the ramp is long."

"It's about the only thing useful left here by the squatter," Thomas said. "He sold nearly everything of value in the armory. We're nearly out of Nightingale armor, ASEs, and other vital tools."

"At least he kept records of his buyers," Michael said. "We discussed sending agents out to retrieve our items, but it's probably too late by now."

"Are we missing anything that could blow up a city?" I asked.

Thomas shook his head. "We don't keep anything like that on hand."

"The ASEs were the most sensitive equipment." Michael stared straight ahead at the house. "That surveillance equipment in the wrong nom hands would give someone a lot of power."

Thomas parked the golf cart next to a long black limousine. An ornate wooden door maintained the ancient aesthetic of the old church, now converted into a house. Thomas opened the door and stepped into a wide foyer of parquet floors and stone walls. He marched through without a second glance and went into an open space where a modern kitchen, den, and dining room all seamlessly connected. A wooden staircase with stainless steel handrails and cables led up to the second floor and the bedrooms.

I had to admit the modern design complemented the old-world feel of the stone walls and ornate floors. My problem was with the open design concept. There was literally nowhere on the first floor you could hide— no walls, no doors, nothing. Even the bathroom had sliding barn doors instead of a traditional latch door.

Thomas's eye twitched. I didn't know if it was because he saw the government bureaucrats sitting on the white leather couch in the den, or if it was because he loathed the makeover to a church that had been in Templar possession for hundreds of years.

A woman with gray hair sat facing away from us. Two twenty-some-things, about mine and Elyssa's age stood in front of her, fidgeting nervously. Their eyes lit on us and they said something to the woman.

She didn't even turn around or stand to greet us. Instead, she waited for us to walk all the way over and step around the couch.

When I saw her face, it was my turn to twitch. My heart went cold, and I whimpered like a frightened puppy. I wasn't the only one to lose their shit. I just didn't hide it nearly as well as the others. But judging from the green cast to Elyssa's face, she didn't want this to be happening any more than I did.

Thomas kept his cool as usual. "You reported us to the authorities, didn't you?"

The woman had a matronly look to her. She could be anyone's young grandmother, or even a mother to little Jimmy Delaney just down the street in my old neighborhood. But she wasn't a woman. She wasn't even human. Razor knew this woman as the Overseer. I knew her as Xanos, an Apocryphan. She could probably blow us all to smithereens right here and now.

Instead, she replied in a calm voice. "There are many ways to solve a problem, Templar. An army would spark panic among the noms, so I drew upon other resources. I can take this property by force, both directly and indirectly." She shrugged. "Every problem has many solutions."

Thomas narrowed his eyes. "I'd say we demonstrated a number of solutions to your army in Queens Gate."

I almost blurted out, "Sick burn!" and fist-bumped Thomas but decided I didn't want to piss off the Apocryphan just yet.

Xanos was apparently finished talking to Thomas, because she ignored his reply and looked at me. "I owe you a debt, Justin Slade." To anyone with normal hearing, her voice might sound normal. But my supernatural senses detected dozens of other voices speaking softly along with her normal one. When I'd first freed Xanos, I'd assumed she was an Abyssal demon, nothing more. I hadn't even heard of the Apocryphan in those days.

She'd resembled a humanoid figure with a single glowing eye and a vortex of black energy instead of feet. The voice with many voices had been more masculine and a lot more cryptic. It seemed Xanos had picked up some human traits in the decade she'd been free of the Abyss.

Somehow, I recovered my wits enough to speak. "That's great. Maybe you can gather your troops and help us fight Baal when he makes his move on Eden."

She didn't smile. "Baal will soon tighten the strings on the realms and gather them into one."

Even Michael looked startled by that statement. "Baal doesn't plan to merge the realms. You do."

Xanos didn't so much as glance at him. "Olympus was my home. My birthplace. I will rule the separate realms from there. As a reward for freeing me, Justin Slade will be given dominion over any realm of his choosing. He will answer only to me."

Naturally, I blurted a response without thinking. "So I could rule Eden?"

"If you so desire." Xanos stood and held out a hand. "You can see it to be true."

I tentatively touched her hand.

I fly past hundreds of worlds to reach Eden, the blue-green globe rotating slowly in the vastness of space. I speed through the clouds, down to a sprawling metropolis I don't recognize, and land atop a tower far taller than any other building. Hundreds of people gather on the massive rooftop, shouting and cheering my name. There are more than just humans in the crowd. I see Sirens, Seraphim, Fae, and creatures that resemble humanoid snakes. There are hundreds of species there, many that I can't name.

I raise my hands. The crowd roars my name. Elyssa stands by my side, eyes glowing with pride. My parents stand behind me, overjoyed to see me finally claim the throne I so deserve.

I rule the world, and it's the coolest thing ever.

The real world snapped back into place and I flinched at the calm, cold look in Xanos's eyes. The man and woman with her regarded me just as coolly. Apparently, they knew all about the Overworld.

I still felt the exhilarating rush of being king of the world. So much so, that I nearly took Xanos's hand and shook it to seal the deal. It took everything I had to curb my enthusiasm and take a reality check.

"I don't want to rule the world." It physically hurt saying those words. I knew it was true, but Xanos had some kind of magical persuasion that made me want to do nothing more than agree with her and wrap Eden up in a bow.

"You don't believe that, Justin." She held her hand toward me again.

I backed away. "No. You're using mind control or compulsion."

"Controlling a sentient mind is nearly impossible without destroying it." Xanos lowered her hand. "There are too many checks and balances. The soul and the ego are the controlling forces within."

I didn't buy her explanation. I'd seen mind control and it was never pretty. On the other hand, it certainly had destroyed the people it affected. "You did something to me."

"I showed you what will make you happy, even if you cannot admit it." Xanos motioned to her companions. "Jeff and Lisa once believed all humans were equal. That all were worth fighting for. But I showed them that millions of beings in Eden are inconsequential and can be discarded to make way for real progress."

"There's too much chaff, not enough grain," Jeff said. "We've fought for people all our lives, but the majority of them aren't willing to do what it takes to affect real change in the world. Xanos showed us the truth."

"We'll make this world a paradise," Lisa said. "But we need people like you, the ones who are worth something, to join us."

Elyssa waggled a finger at them. "You people are completely brainwashed. No one in their right mind would consider millions of people expendable."

None of the trio acknowledged Elyssa's response.

"Baal seeks to merge the realms." Xanos held out her hands helplessly. "I see no benefit to this. Diverse realms have created diverse beings. I will unite them. Governments will be reorganized. Societies will be perfected. Then we will expand our reach out to the multiverse and the expanses of our own universe. Somewhere in this vastness is the universal origin. Somewhere, there are definitive answers."

"Answer to what?" I said.

Xanos tilted her head slightly. "Where did we come from? Why are we here?"

"You've got to be kidding me." I shook my head like a wet dog. "You want to know the answers to life, the universe, and everything?"

"My first memory is of growing up with my siblings on Mount Olympus." A smile touched her lips but vanished just as quickly. "Our caretaker told us all that was wrong with the many species on Earth. How they warred, sought power, and never sought higher goals. My brothers and sisters were to bring them unity and enlightenment."

Xanos clasped her hands in her lap. "But we were given no guidance as to how this goal might be achieved. And just as suddenly, our caretaker vanished, leaving us to our own devices. My brethren became conquers. They fought for power over kingdoms, and even fought among themselves. Two of my siblings were murdered by the others. I wanted no part in their wars, so I kept to myself."

I really wanted some popcorn. Listening to a god recount history was totally epic, even if they had megalomaniacal designs on life as I knew it. I had some burning questions, but I let Xanos keep on talking.

"It became clear that my siblings had no better idea how to tame existence than anyone else. Our powers were great, and they believed that made them better." Most people might have frowned, but Xanos's face seemed unable to find the right expression, twitching, but remaining mostly passive. "That was when I knew our existence could not continue. It was better to destroy it all and start anew. So I fueled a war among all the kingdoms. When they descended upon Juranthemon in all their fury, I retreated to Mount Olympus that I might survive the apocalypse and watch it on high."

I couldn't keep quiet. "Instead, you got the Sundering."

"It achieved a similar goal. We and all the species were cast into separate realms. Thousands were killed. The result was peace."

"Only thousands?" I said.

"The world population was quite small at the time," Xanos said. "It was imperative to prevent it from growing out of control."

"So you nipped it in the bud."

She pursed her lips and considered that. "Yes, I see what you mean. I cut the bud from the plant to prevent it from growing seed and procreating."

Thomas and the others stood by quietly watching. They'd apparently gotten the message that this was between me and Xanos.

"What happened next?" I asked. I almost asked if I could make popcorn but didn't want to risk it.

"Centuries of peace. And then the greatest trick was played upon us." Xanos managed a smile, as if amused and even a bit impressed. "In our arrogance, we always made others do everything for us. Though my power base was small compared to the others, even I succumbed to this folly. After the Sundering, my brethren tried to find a way to reunite the realms. Posthanied forced the Sirens to find a way. They succeeded but kept many secrets from us. They used those secrets to trick us and cast us into the Abyss."

"How exactly did they do that?"

29

JOHN CORWIN

Xanos gave me an amused look. "It would not work on me anymore. We were ignorant in our arrogance. Vitania and her minions understood the true science behind the arches and used this knowledge against us."

"How do you know it wouldn't work anymore?" I said.

"The Abyss was supposedly cut off from everything, sealed beneath the infernal fount in the depths of Hell. The arch we traveled through to get there was destroyed, leaving no way out for all of eternity." Xanos shuddered. "But that was not even the clever part of the trap." Her lip curled into a faint sneer. "There was always a way out. I simply did not know how to open the door myself." Her sneer morphed into a smile. "So I recruited someone to help me."

In other words, me. I was the one who'd unleashed Xanos on the realms. And if what she told me was true, there was no way to trap her there again.

CHAPTER 4

"**F**reeing you from the Abyss isn't exactly something I'm proud of," I said. "Especially since you're hell-bent on world domination."

She didn't seem offended. "I have much more information to give you, should you choose to join me. The choice between me and Baal is stark. He wishes to merge the realms and rule what is left. I will preserve them and improve all life."

"Universal healthcare and everything?" I said.

"Do not mock the offer. It is upon my honor that I offer you this choice, for you gave me the freedom to seek this path."

I sighed. "If you owe me so much, why not just stop this senseless war against us and help us figure out how to make life better for everyone, even those you consider chaff?"

"Because that path leads nowhere." Xanos's lips flattened. "Those who contribute nothing are dead weight. Those who spread hate and negativity destroy the positive contributions of others. There are many who must be purged so that life can be improved."

I felt like this conversation was hitting a dead end, so I backed up to what she'd said earlier. "Look, Baal isn't the one who wants to combine the realms. He told us you're the one who wants to do that."

"Untrue." Xanos shook her head. "The Sundering improved life. I believe diverse realms will lead to the future I desire. But I have sensed the tug on the threads between the realms. I have caught glimpses of his great reach. Why Baal desires such an outcome, I cannot say. But he is too powerful for me alone. That is why you should aid me, Justin. You have proven yourself powerful and clever. Together we can stop Baal."

It was hard to imagine that Baal was more powerful than a god. But the fact that Xanos was here asking for help had to mean she wasn't back to full strength. A few thousand years in the Abyss had made her weak—but for how long?

I bit my lower lip and thought about her offer. I hated to admit just how tempted I was by Xanos's goals. Achieving enlightenment for all of life was admirable. But murdering millions was where her proposal became tricky. How did she judge who was dead weight and who wasn't? If she could see into the hearts of all beings and separate the pedophiles, murderers, misogynists, racists, and Nickelback fans from all the good people, then I could probably convince myself to go all in.

I could only guess how Xanos planned to make her utopia work. But since she was here, I decided ask her for specifics. "How will you separate the desirables from the deplorables?"

Lisa flinched as if she'd been thumped on the nose and answered. "We are forming an elite group of dedicated people we call the Enlightened. They will live secretly among the people and evaluate them as positive or negative. The evaluated candidates will then be judged by another Enlightened. If both Enlightened agree the person is a positive, then Xanos will pass final judgment to include or exclude them from Hearth. If they are negative, then Xanos will evaluate them herself before a final decision."

"What's Hearth?" I asked.

Lisa smiled proudly. "It's a term we coined for Heaven on Earth."

"So a secret group of people will judge every individual, then pass their recommendation to Xanos who will make a final decision?"

"That's it!" She bounced on her heels like an excited kid. "Isn't it wonderful?"

"Holy shit." I wanted to grab her by the shoulders and shake some sense into her. It was sickening seeing the mad fervor of someone happily trying to repeat the worst episodes of history. "Ever heard of Nazi Germany? How about Soviet Russia?"

Elyssa's lips peeled back in a horrified grimace, but she somehow kept quiet.

Lisa raised an eyebrow. "What do those have to do with the path to Hearth?"

"They both used neighbors and friends to spy on the little people so they could execute or imprison anyone who didn't agree with government policies." I slashed a hand through the air. "Do you know how demoralizing that is for people? How awful it would be to society as whole when people don't think they can trust anyone?"

"Just don't be an asshole," Lisa said. "Is it really that hard?"

"No, this goes way beyond that. You're forcing people to behave in a specific way. You want to take away their freedom and turn them into pansy-ass little slaves."

"They would be perfectly free as long as they contribute." Lisa's face turned red. "Why can't you see that? It's perfect!"

"It's perfect for the people in power." I turned my eyes to Xanos. "Shame on you. You know this scheme is anything but enlightened."

Xanos sighed. "So you reject my offer?"

I held up a hand. "I want to make a counter-offer."

She stared at me for a moment. Nodded. "I will hear it."

"Let's join forces. If Baal really wants to merge the realms, then he's the biggest danger to all of us. Let's defeat him, then we can discuss options for world domination afterward." I shrugged. "I mean, maybe there are some realms that would welcome your ideas with open arms. You rule the ones who want you and leave the rest of us to do our own thing."

If the past was anything to go on, Xanos would turn down my offer flat. Neither she nor Baal had any interest in making deals that didn't align perfectly with their goals. They wanted things their way and to hell with everyone else.

"I accept your offer of a temporary truce," Xanos said.

I stared at her blankly for a moment. "So...you agree to my terms?"

"I think it wise for us to step back and cease hostilities to see if we can arrive at an amicable agreement."

I certainly hadn't been expecting this. "You're agreeing to peace talks?"

"Yes." She offered a smile that chilled me to the bone. "During this time both sides will agree to halt any and all offensive activities. I believe we can reach an agreement that will allow us to defeat Baal and also achieve enlightenment for all species."

I was still in shock. I'd been rejected by Daelissa, Arturo, Kaelissa, and Baal when I tried to get them to agree to peace or an alliance against a greater threat. Those who sought power at all costs usually didn't care about making deals. Baal figured he had all the firepower he needed to take out the realms. Why he cared so much about recruiting me was a mystery, but now that he had my doppelganger, it didn't much matter anymore.

I rubbed my hands together. "Then let's start talking. We've got a conference room, we've got tea, and I think we even have cookies." I looked at Thomas "We do have cookies, right?"

His lips flattened. "Yes. There are cookies."

"Let's get an agreement ironed out today." I knew I was being overly optimistic, but Xanos's cooperation gave me actual hope for the first time in a long while.

"Today is perhaps a bit hasty," Xanos said. "Let's schedule our peace talks for seven days from now. For now, we will agree to a complete cease-fire. If that holds, then it means you are serious about reaching an agreement." She smiled. "There may be hope for the realms after all."

Lisa and Jeff looked happy enough to wet their pants. They hugged each other and squirmed with manic joy.

"Why one week?" Thomas said. "We need to know what your expectations are if we're to outline any sort of agreement."

"My assistants will create an outline and bring it to you," Xanos said. "I will tell you what is acceptable and what I won't budge on. That should make the process easier."

"Perhaps if we traded emissaries," Thomas said. "One of yours can stay with us and help us outline a proposal. You can do the same with ours."

"I don't think that would be productive, Templar." Xanos smiled at me again. "You have come far since the day you released me, Justin. I believe your horizons are endless."

"Well, if you really feel such gratitude toward me, how about a two-day delay instead of a week?" I held out my hands imploringly. "A week is a really long time to wait."

"A week is but a blink of the eye to one of my age." Xanos shook her head. "It will take time to formulate my requirements. Be patient."

Once again, my enthusiasm got curb stomped. I knew peace talks weren't easy or fast, but I didn't care for this weeklong delay. Since it didn't seem we could talk her into a shorter delay, I opted to sate my personal curiosity.

"When I first saw you, you looked only vaguely humanoid. Was that your true form?" Right now, she looked like that cool older aunt you could tell anything to. At least until you looked a little deeper into those matronly eyes and sensed something ancient and deadly looking back at you.

Xanos pursed her lips. "In a way, yes."

"Where did you come from?"

She shrugged. "Our caretaker never told us. She simply said we were the new gods who would restore creation."

"No pressure, huh?" I almost felt sorry for the Apocryphan. For a while we'd thought they were the original gods, but if someone made them, that meant there was a lot more to Heaven and Earth than we first thought.

Xanos took me literally. "No, it was a great deal of pressure."

I hoped she'd answer the final question, because it might not make me feel so awful. "Was I the only person who could free you, or could other Daemos do it as well?"

"I formed a personal connection with your aunt, Vallaena. I helped her banish many to the Abyss. But she refused to free me. Then you found me, and I knew you were the one." Xanos looked at her hands as if she couldn't quite believe she was here. "Now that I know the truth, not even Vitania can trap me there again."

She injected a lot of venom into that name, and who could blame her? Vitania was among the first of the Sirens. I'd only heard of her recently as a person who might have some answers about Baal. It also seemed she might know a great deal about the Apocryphan.

I simply nodded. "You're here to stay."

"It has been a pleasure finally speaking with you, Justin." Xanos touched my hand. "I look forward to our peace talks one week from today."

Once again, her touch sent a rush of giddy optimism crashing against my conscience. I didn't know if it was something she controlled, or if it was some kind of turbo-charged charisma. But it made things a lot clearer. Now I knew why her followers were so fanatical. It wasn't because she brainwashed them, but because the emotions she generated overwhelmed all logic. It meant people would do terrible things that contradicted everything they supposedly believed in simply because it made them feel good.

Humanity is a bunch of suckers.

I shook off the feeling. "So next Tuesday?"

Xanos looked at Jeff. She probably didn't bother keeping up with days of the week. He nodded. "Yes, next Tuesday."

Lisa reached into her purse and removed a handful of round yellow discs with smiley faces on them. They looked like pins, but without the actual pin. She pressed it to my uniform, and it stuck there, then she filled my hands with the rest. "Hand these out to show you support the cause!"

I blinked. "Uh, which cause?"

She pshawed. "Redeeming humanity, of course!"

I managed a fake grin. "Yeah, sure." I managed not to remind her what I really thought about Hearth.

Xanos nodded at the others, then led her small entourage to the limo outside. They all climbed in the back and the driver took them away.

I took off the pin and pointed at it, then put a finger to my mouth. Thomas nodded and held up a finger that told me to wait. He returned a moment later with a glittering black box. He opened the lid and I dumped the pins inside.

Elyssa scanned the pins with her arcphone, then swept the general area and nodded. Thomas closed the diamond fiber box and tucked it under an arm.

"I didn't detect any bugs," Elyssa said. "But they might just have something our magical scans don't pick up."

"Agreed." Thomas pursed his lips. "Why do I get the feeling this one-week delay is not because of peace talks?"

"It isn't." Michael opened and closed his hand, cracking knuckles with each flex. "Xanos needs time for something, and we just agreed to give it to her."

"I think our little expedition this morning triggered it," Elyssa said. "I think it has something to do with that portal generator we saw."

Thomas frowned. "Explain."

"We were able to look into the crater and saw a large white ring that generated a portal to another realm," Elyssa said. "Razor troops looked ready to go through it, but then it fizzled and died."

"Since the Alabaster Arches were disabled by Victus, there aren't many ways to reach other realms." Michael put a hand on his chin. "I can't see this affecting us in the immediate future."

"Me either," Elyssa said. "Unless there's an objective in another realm that will help Xanos defeat us."

"A distinct possibility." Thomas shook his head. "But since we've agreed to the cease-fire, there's nothing we can do to sabotage it."

Elyssa sighed. "She played us."

"Well, it's hardly playing us if we see the trickery," I said. "But I did stupidly agree to give her a week."

"No, you were smart." Thomas put a hand on my shoulder. "And you turned down the offer to rule an entire world."

Michael nodded. "Good man."

Compliments were rare from either of these two. Getting one from each almost made me tear up. I swallowed the lump in my throat and shrugged. "I mean, I kind of wanted to boss everyone around, but that's just too much work."

Thomas nodded as if he completely agreed. "Provided Xanos spoke the truth, she also gave us valuable intel."

"That's for sure," I said. "I don't know if we should trust her claims about Baal, or whether or not she could be trapped in the Abyss again. But if we're sticking to this one-week truce, then I want to use the time wisely by going to Iceland and finding Vitania. She's got to have some answers."

"That Siren could be the key to stopping both Baal and Xanos," Michael said.

"Supposedly, she has knowledge of Baal's origins," Elyssa said. "I don't know how that could help us, but at this point we need any help we can get."

I scoffed. "As usual."

She scoffed back. "All day, every day."

"Meanwhile, we've got other problems to deal with." Thomas started heading for the door. "Xander Tiberius wants to adjust the terms of the treaty he signed with us. He claims it's null and void since it was signed under duress."

I laughed. "Yeah, under duress from his wife!"

Michael walked with us outside. "We've monitored his sons Rhys and Devon. They've been speaking with individuals who are known as intermediaries of criminal groups."

"So what are they up to?" I asked.

"Nothing good," Michael said. "And we can't lose the support of Xander's Arcanes at this crucial juncture."

"Just great."

Things were never simple. I just hoped Thomas could hold things together while we tracked down information on Xanos and Baal. Because if we didn't come up with something at the end of the week, Xanos might have a nasty surprise waiting for us.

CHAPTER 5

"Holy farting Sirens!" Shelton shoveled a pancake into his mouth and muffled whatever followed that proclamation.

I bit into my bacon. "So, you're in, right?"

He chugged some orange juice to wash down the pancake. "Always. Besides, I hear Iceland is nice this time of year."

"The problem is, we have no idea where in Iceland to look." Elyssa consulted her arcphone then projected a holographic map over the table. "And the clock is ticking down to next Tuesday."

Shelton reached through the southern coast of Iceland and snagged more bacon. "Hot damn, it's nice cooking in my own kitchen again."

His wife, Bella, rubbed his belly. "You enjoy it too much," she said in her Colombian accent. "I think a trip to Iceland would be good exercise."

"We're not going to hike," Shelton said. "And you'd better believe I'm gonna eat a horse while I'm there."

Elyssa gagged. "Just because Icelanders think it's okay doesn't really mean it's okay."

Shelton shrugged. "When in Rome…"

"Eat spaghetti, not horses." Elyssa started highlighting beaches on the map but reserved a glare and scowl for Shelton every so often.

"What's the word from the Glimmer?" I asked Bella. My sister, Ivy, along with Conrad Edison and his group of friends, was trying to help the Glimmer Queen, Cora, revive her sleeping people. Apparently, her clone from the reflected world had taken over the Glimmer and put everyone to sleep a long time ago. Waking them up could be key to keeping the realms in one piece.

"No progress. Conrad believes there might be a relic of Juranthemon that could help, so he plans to ask Underborn for help."

Shelton grimaced. "Bad move. Underborn is gonna eat that kid alive."

"I wouldn't be so sure," Elyssa said. "Considering he beat Victus at his own game, I wouldn't put anything past Conrad."

"True, but Underborn is something else altogether." I hadn't dealt with the tricky assassin in quite some time, but he was on my short list of allies of last resort. "Underborn must know about the cosmic forces at work here. I'm surprised he hasn't approached us with one of his twisted plots to put a stop to it."

"My father put out feelers to both Underborn and Fjoeruss but hasn't had a response." Elyssa circled another coastal area on her map. "If it comes down to a war, I don't think we can count on them."

"They weren't too keen on helping us against Daelissa either," Shelton said. "But they came around."

It felt like everyone had scattered to the winds since the battle at Queens Gate against Razor Echelon. Mom was hunting for Emily Glass so she could bring Dad back from Haedaemos. Conrad and the others were in the Glimmer. The Mzodi had returned to Atlantis to help defend it should Baal make good on his threats to invade. As the last chunk of the original Earth, it was the only place that would remain safe should the realms be recombined.

Despite the looming threats, I enjoyed simple moments like breakfast. The underground mansion had been our replacement home after Daelissa destroyed the one aboveground. That had been the battle where Jeremiah Conroy sacrificed himself to save me, and where I'd first summoned Xanos. She hadn't escaped that time, but it had been close.

Now there was a new mansion, occupied by the former headmaster of Arcane University, Galfandor. The old man had been a prisoner of Xander Tiberius until our recent truce. Despite reopening the school, nothing in the Overworld was even remotely close to being normal. Until we solved our problems with Xanos and Razor Echelon, I didn't see a light at the end of that tunnel.

Adam came into the kitchen sporting a thick pair of glasses. His eyes looked huge through them. Apparently, the food did too, because he did a double-take when Shelton turned around. "Jesus, why is your head so huge?"

Shelton groaned and snatched the glasses of Adam's nose. "Gee, maybe because you left on your magnifying lens?"

"Ah." Adam took the glasses from Shelton, folded them, and put them in his shirt pocket protector. "Well, you'll be happy to know that I've delved a few more secrets from the weapons we stole from Razor."

"Oh?" I leaned on my elbows. "You know how they work?"

"The crystal Elyssa took a picture of is identical to the crystals that power Razor's rifles." He took a plate and piled on bacon and eggs. "Those crystals are, in fact, refined aetherite, or something very similar."

"You're saying Xanos has a way to get aetherite from Seraphina?" Shelton said.

Adam paused. "I don't think this is from Seraphina. I think she found a way to artificially produce it."

"Whoa." Shelton stopped eating a moment. "How's that possible? Aetherite requires extreme amounts of aether, incredible pressure, and energy to form."

The Mzodi, or sky fishers, mined aetherite from aether vortexes in Seraphina. Seraphim called them gems and used them to control nearly every aspect of life. The Mzodi enchanted the gems for specific tasks by encoding them with Cyrinthian. Adam and Shelton had learned how to decipher most of it, but they didn't have the same gift as the Mzodi did for enchanting them.

"Logic suggests the process would require too much energy," Adam said. "There are methods noms use to create diamonds from carbon. Theoretically, a similar method might yield this specific strain of aetherite."

Elyssa frowned. "So you're saying Razor, the anti-magic, anti-supernatural group, uses magic to power their weapons?"

"Yep." Adam nodded. "It's arcnology. That's how they pack so much energy into their ammunition. Their tank shells and electro-bullets are essentially filled with a charge from the aetherite."

"Like mini-crucibles," I said, referring to glass spheres we filled with aether and launched from catapults.

"Razor has primarily used non-lethal weapons." Elyssa highlighted another coastal zone on the map. "After our encounter with the drones at Thunder Rock, it's obvious they have an incredible lethal arsenal as well."

"Mini fighter jets." Shelton huffed. "Some tech nerd is having a lot of fun making weapons of war. And their so-called non-lethal weapons are still powerful enough to fry people. We need to come up with equal firepower of our own so they get a taste of their own medicine."

I looked at Elyssa's map. "What are you doing, anyway?"

"Looking at beaches." She zoomed in on the northern coast and scrolled along it. The satellite view showed snow-covered peaks and wide expanses of green. Then she zoomed back out to show the entire island. "I think that's all of them."

Shelton snorted. "Iceland is an island. The entire coastline is covered in beaches."

"Not really. The northern coast is mostly cliffs." Elyssa focused the view on the southeast coast. "Besides, I'm specifically looking for black sand beaches."

"Volcanic rock." Adam pushed a finger up his nose despite not wearing any glasses. "I've heard it makes for a very interesting beach."

"Melea described Vitania as the singer of the black sands," Elyssa said. "So I narrowed down the locations for those kinds of beaches. Hopefully, we'll be able to locate her."

"Ain't a lot of people in Iceland," Shelton said. "That'll make it easier."

"Still like finding a proverbial needle in a black sand haystack," Adam said.

Shelton sighed. "Stick to being the local genius." He clapped Adam on the back. "Leave the joke-making to the pros."

Elyssa grinned. "I thought it was very clever."

"Funniest thing I've heard all week," I said. Considering how the last few weeks had been, it wasn't exactly a lie.

"Thanks, guys." Adam smirked at Shelton and chomped on a piece of bacon. "I'm writing the jokes from now on."

Shelton snorted. He got up and took Bella's hand. "Let's get busy in the bedroom. I have a feeling we won't see each other for a few days."

Elyssa gagged. "Thanks for that imagery."

Adam turned to Bella. "Does Shelton manscape, or does he look like an escapee from the seventies?"

"Probably shaves his balls to make his junk look bigger," I said.

Bella giggled. "Since you're curious, I'll send you some pictures."

"Oh, dick pics." Adam grinned. "I can't wait."

I barked a laugh. "I'll bet Shelton blows up her phone with those."

Shelton scoffed. "Laugh all you want, but my junk is more than enough to satisfy my *mamacita*."

"Oh, it is." Bella blew him a kiss since she was too short to reach his lips without him bending over.

"Get a room!" Elyssa made shooing motions. "I can't take this anymore."

Bella smacked Shelton on the ass. "Get a move-on, *papi*."

He yelped and scooted out of the kitchen. Bella might be small, but she was a dhampyr like Elyssa, and as strong or stronger than most vampires. She was also old enough to be Shelton's many greats grandmother, but since most supers lived to be hundreds of years old, cradle robbing wasn't such a big deal in the Overworld.

I snuggled up to Elyssa. "Maybe we could get in some boom-boom time before we go."

She leaned over and nipped my ear. "I'll take that offer, mister."

Adam looked down at his bacon. It certainly wasn't because he was shy. Sadly, it was because the woman he still loved had broken up with him. Meghan Andretti had decided she'd had enough of Adam's constant adventuring with us and found someone who liked to stay in one place.

Meghan had saved a lot of lives in the time I'd known her. She was a good person, but also kind of a stick in the mud. She also didn't appreciate Adam's nerdy personality or how his big brain helped us save the world. I thought he deserved better than that.

I spared him the pity and opted to toss a piece of bacon at him. It bounced off his head. "Pork this."

Adam laughed. "I'll meet you guys in the omniarch room when you're ready."

I wasn't sure he'd wanted to come but was glad to have him along. "Maybe Vitania is looking for a boy toy."

He managed a chuckle. "The idea of having relations with a Siren is both alluring and terrifying."

AFTER THE RECREATIONAL activities were over, we packed our gear. The Templars were out of armored backpacks, and our Nightingale armor was in bad shape from the encounter at Thunder Rock. Thankfully, a vendor in Queens Gate kept us supplied with backpacks that had magical food preservation compartments and extra-dimensional space for things like tents and clothes.

I didn't like heading off on an adventure without armor, but it really couldn't be helped. I tossed in some rugged cargo pants and jeans and hoped it would be all I needed. Then Elyssa and I went downstairs where Shelton was busy stuffing tons of raw bacon into his backpack.

Elyssa laughed. "God, at least get an apple or broccoli in there."

"You'll thank me later," Shelton said.

"My arteries won't," Elyssa said.

We hiked out of the house and into the main cavern. A wide opening in the far wall took us into a corridor big enough for a herd of elephants to walk through. One end led to the Burrows, a maze of tunnels and chambers that once served as a dungeon. The other direction led to a room with the omniarch.

Adam waited outside, a Star Wars themed backpack resting on the ground beside him.

Shelton nudged it with a foot. "They custom make that for you?"

"Yep." Adam held it up proudly. "Turns out the owner of the shop is a movie nerd too."

A pair of Templars outside the room saluted us as we walked inside. They were there to manage requests to use the arch, but demand had been unsurprisingly light. There were too few safe places to go outside of Queens Gate. With Razor teams sweeping major cities for supers, no one wanted to risk being caught.

The black arch stood about ten feet tall and wide with a silver circle around the perimeter. This one was called an omniarch because it could take us anywhere in the world we could precisely envision. All we needed was a picture.

I hadn't been to Iceland before. I hoped we could find someplace secluded to open the portal so the locals wouldn't notice when we arrived. Flying brooms were still in short supply, but each of us had one. None of them were of the high-performance variety, but they'd do.

I glanced over at Elyssa. "Where to, boss?"

Elyssa looked at the map on her phone. "We'll start in Eyrarbakki and work our way down the coast."

"Ay what?" Shelton said.

"Eyrarbakki." Elyssa shrugged. "Hey, it's easier to pronounce than Eyjaf-jallajökull."

Shelton grimaced. "Sounds like your tongue is having a stroke."

Bella laughed. "I don't think I could say that if I tried."

Adam snorted. "Here's a fact: Scandinavian languages were invented wholly as a form of psychological warfare on anyone attempting to learn them."

Shelton grinned. "Ain't that the truth."

Elyssa struggled to find the image of a secluded alley in the town we were headed to, but the images online had nothing of that variety. "Well, hopefully no one sees us when we jump out of thin air." She knelt and sealed the silver circle, then focused on the arch. The air split vertically and widened into a gateway—a window to a place halfway across the world.

I stepped through. The world stretched ahead of me like the long hallway effect in a horror movie then just as abruptly snapped back to normal. An arch operator once explained to me why it did that. The arches formed a tunnel that connected one place with another, even though it was like looking through a window from either side of the portal. When a person stepped inside, they travelled so quickly, it distorted their vision for a fraction of a second.

I stood in a patch of scrubby grass behind a beige building. A quick scan of the environs confirmed there weren't any locals staring in shock, having witnessed a man appear from nowhere. Elyssa stepped through behind me. To me, it looked as if she just stepped through a door—no rubber band effect from this side. Bella kissed Shelton goodbye and he and Adam stepped through. The portal winked off, leaving us thousands of miles from home in a strange land.

Even though it was late spring, it was chilly in Iceland. Elyssa, Adam, and I wore black winter parkas. Shelton stuck to his wide-brimmed hat and leather duster. He tried to cover up a shiver when the wind blew.

Adam shook his head. "You could've at least worn thermal underwear."

"Pshht." Shelton flicked his wand in a pattern and wove a warming charm around him. "Magic beats underwear any day."

Adam grimaced. "So you're not wearing any underwear at all?"

"How 'bout I drop my pants and let you find out?"

"Keep your pants on, Shelton." Elyssa headed for the road. "We don't want to frighten the locals."

"Frighten them?" Shelton scoffed. "They'd get the show of their life if I free-balled it down main street."

I snorted. "I want to bleach my mind's eye just from imagining that."

Elyssa consulted the map on her arcphone. "There isn't much around here."

I peered at the screen over her shoulder. "There's a museum, a couple hotels, and a gas station. Maybe we could casually ask around at one of those places."

"What are we supposed to ask?" Shelton said. "Hey, you guys seen any mermaids around?"

"Melea referred to Vitania as the singer of the black sands." I shrugged. "Maybe people would know her as a singer."

Shelton scratched his head. "What, you think she's on tour here? Maybe the lead singer of a Scandinavian death core metal band?"

I scoffed. "Sirens don't do metal. She's probably best friends with Björk."

"Maybe she spends all her time singing on the beach." Adam said. "Maybe she doesn't even live on land."

"True." Shelton looked south toward the ocean. "There's a whole world under the sea and I doubt we're gonna find a singing crab named Sebastian who can help us find her."

Elyssa's eyebrows rose. "Someone's been watching *The Little Mermaid* again."

Adam guffawed. "Shelton and his cartoons."

"Hey, Disney movies ain't cartoons." Shelton straightened the collar of his duster as if it helped him regain some dignity. "I'm just saying it's gonna take a miracle to find this lady."

That sobered the mood in an instant.

Elyssa sighed. "Well, we've got to start somewhere." She looked back down at the map and began walking.

Our hunt for a needle in the haystack had officially begun.

CHAPTER 6

Most of the buildings along the main road were beige or gray, their exteriors made of corrugated steel. It might be good for surviving the harsh climate, but it wasn't the most stylish look in the world. The blasé choice of paint colors didn't help much either. Elyssa took a left into a restaurant and the rest of us followed. We walked through a small gift shop in the front.

Glass vials of volcanic rock, shark teeth, and other odds and ends filled the shelves. It was a lot like the souvenir shop in any seaside town, even sporting a few T-shirts with witty sayings on them.

Adam picked up a container of rocks and frowned at the price. "Wow. Two thousand krona. That's not cheap."

Shelton chuckled. "You actually researched the local currency, didn't you?"

"Of course." Adam put down the vial. "A little bit of research might save a lot of time and trouble."

A hostess appeared from a door behind the front counter. She glanced at me and Elyssa, but her gaze caught on Shelton and stopped there. She looked him up and down, a small frown on her face. "Americans?"

"Yeah, sure," Shelton said. "We're Americans."

"Why do you have brooms on your backpacks?" she said.

"We don't like dirty floors," Shelton replied. "Always keep a broom on hand."

I hadn't even thought about how our brooms might confuse noms. "We're professional street sweepers." The lame explanation escaped my lips before I could stop it.

Elyssa snickered and Adam looked like he was barely holding in laughter.

The girl seemed at a loss for words but finally found some. "Oh. Um, would you like a table?" She had a noticeable accent, but her English sounded perfect.

Elyssa regained her composure. "Actually, we were hoping you could help us find someone."

"You have friends here?" The hostess looked at Elyssa's broom again. "Will you be sweeping their street?"

Adam snorted so hard it sounded like he ruptured his nose.

Elyssa took a deep breath. "We heard there was a really good singer who lives in these parts."

"A singer?" The girl's forehead scrunched. "Old Jorgi sometimes brings his keyboard and sings at the pub."

Shelton barged into the conversation. "She's got big eyes and long hair that might be green or blue, and it flows around her head like she's underwater."

Elyssa groaned.

The hostess stared blankly at Shelton. "Not even Björk looks like that."

Shelton threw up his hands in surrender. "Well, I don't know what else to ask."

"Ever heard of the singer of the black sands?" Elyssa said.

"No, I'm sorry." The hostess leaned her elbows on the counter. "What else can you tell me about her?" Apparently, this was the most interesting thing to happen to her today.

"Ever heard the name Vitania?" Elyssa said. "Or Siren?"

"No, I'm afraid not." The girl quirked her lips. "It sounds like you're looking for a mermaid. Do they also need their streets swept?"

Shelton scoffed. "Man, you're just not gonna let this broom thing go, are you?"

"You people are strange, but I like it." She smiled. "Those brooms look like something witches would use, because bristles like those would barely sweep anything."

Shelton threw up his hands. "Fine. They're flying brooms and we're witches and warlocks." He glared at her. "Satisfied."

The hostess laughed. "Oh, more than satisfied."

Adam leaned to my ear. "I like this woman. She's funny."

I strained my brain, hoping to come up with another question that might help us find Vitania, but came up blank. Finding the Siren was going to be a lot harder than I'd hoped. It was likely she disguised herself to blend into the populace. And if she lived in the ocean, we'd never find her.

Elyssa's shoulders slumped. "Thank you for your time."

"Why do you sell rocks?" Adam said. "They're all over the place."

"You cannot legally take anything from Iceland unless it's specially packaged," the hostess said. "Customs would stop you."

Shelton smirked. "That didn't come up in your research?"

Adam shrugged. "I can't research everything." He put a glass vial of the black volcanic rocks on the counter and dug into his coat pocket for a thick leather wallet. "I'd like to buy this please. Do you take American credit cards?"

"Yes, of course." She smiled, happy to make sale to the weirdos and swiped Adam's credit card.

"Man, I don't even keep money on me these days." I patted my empty pockets. "Hell, I don't even carry a wallet anymore. Then we've got Adam who's probably got a Diner's Club card on him right now."

Shelton laughed. "Hey, at least he can buy us lunch wherever we go."

Adam put his purchase in his backpack. "I'm ready to go."

"I'm so glad we came to Iceland to pick up souvenirs," Elyssa said. She nodded at the hostess. "Thanks for your help."

"I hope you sweep all the streets clean." The hostess laughed and covered her mouth.

We went outside and stopped by the gas station. The old man inside seemed just as interested in our questions and our brooms as the girl, but he didn't know anything either. We stopped at the two hotels and museum in the small town without any luck. Elyssa even asked a few passersby on our way to the other end of town. The people were as friendly as could be. Every single one inquired about our brooms, but not a one of them had any useful information.

It didn't take us long to reach the end of town. We walked down to the beach, looked around to make sure no one saw us, then got on our brooms.

"Why the hell is everyone so interested in our brooms?" Shelton said. "Maybe I should camouflage them for the next town."

"I think it's kind of funny." Adam took out his phone and snapped a selfie. "Hey, want to get a group pic?"

"We didn't come here for sightseeing," Elyssa said.

"Yeah, but it's really pretty out here." Adam smiled hopefully. "Please?"

"Yeah, sure." Shelton coasted on his broom next to Adam.

Elyssa groaned but lined up next to the others. I hovered above Adam and hung upside down from my broom. "Cheese!"

The next town was even smaller than the first. We asked the same questions and got the same answers from the locals there. Every time someone asked about our brooms, Shelton told them we were headed to a witches' convention.

Þykkvibær was the next blip on the map. It was so small it didn't even have a store, so we went house-to-house. No one answered at the first three places. A young man in dirty underwear answered at the fourth. He glared at us and slammed the door before we even asked a question.

"Well, we know who the town asshole is," Shelton muttered.

A house with peeling blue paint and rust stains on the corrugated siding was the next-to-last house in the town. An old man answered the door. He only shook his head when we started talking, then called out in Icelandic to someone else in the house. A middle-aged woman stepped up to the door.

"I'm sorry, but Gunnar doesn't speak much English." Her eyes wandered over our brooms and stopped on Shelton. "Are you lost? We don't get many tourists here."

"We're looking for a woman who lives in these parts," Shelton said. "She's a singer and loves the ocean and the beach."

"Sounds like a dating profile," Adam muttered.

"A singer?" The woman spoke with Gunnar in Icelandic.

The old man chuckled and replied. The woman laughed at whatever he said, then turned to us. "Twenty years ago, Gunnar's friend, Oleg, swore on his life he saw a woman sitting on the Reynisfjara sea stacks late one night. He claims she was singing to the fish in the most beautiful voice he ever heard."

Gunnar grinned at us and spoke again.

The woman laughed again. "He wants to know if you're looking for a mermaid."

"That's what the brooms are for," Shelton said. "We're mermaid hunters."

The woman burst into more laughter and spoke to Gunnar. The old man laughed until he started wheezing.

Elyssa squeezed my hand. "My god, I think we actually found something."

"I think you're right."

We asked a few more questions, but Gunnar had nothing else to give. We asked for Oleg's address, but the other man had passed away a few years earlier. We'd have to make do with the needle we'd just found in the proverbial haystack. No one answered at the last house, so we moved out.

Reynisfjara wasn't the next stop on the map. There were several tiny towns along the way, but I didn't see any point to wasting time there. "Let's go straight down there and look around."

"Might as well," Shelton said. "We can always backtrack if we don't find anything."

"I'd prefer to be thorough." Elyssa studied the map, zooming in on the next one-horse town along the way. "There's a lot of coastline between here and Reynisfjara."

"Yeah, but it'll take us all freaking day to ask questions in every place we come across." Shelton flicked fingers across the screen of his arcphone. "Vik is a bigger town and it's right next to that beach. I say we head there and see if anyone else ever saw a woman on the sea stacks."

I clapped my hands. "Vik is a town name I can actually pronounce. That's gotta mean something."

"I'd love to get some pictures of the stacks," Adam said. "And there's a plane wreck on a beach along the way. You think we could get a group photo there?"

"Really, Adam?" Elyssa shook her head disapprovingly. "We're racing against the clock and all you want to do is play tourist."

"I mean, we're here. We might as well enjoy ourselves." His shoulders sagged. "Just stop and smell the roses for once."

"Well, hey." Shelton clapped the other man on the back. "You're right. We're always running from point A to point B, and everything in between is just a blur, right Justin?"

I nodded. "True. If we're stopping in every town, let's take the time to enjoy the local flavor too."

Elyssa narrowed her eyes and shook her head. "We're on a mission, not a joy cruise."

"Aw, c'mon, Commander Borathen." Shelton saluted. "Sparing a few minutes here and there isn't gonna end the world."

"It might." Elyssa huffed and threw up her hands. "Fine. Let's live a little, so long as Adam foots the bill."

Adam's face brightened. "Absolutely. All my money market accounts really did well while we were gone, so the sky's the limit."

We'd flown over water most of the time, but what little I'd seen of the inland mountains was impressive. The fields of moss-covered volcanic boulders looked like something you'd see on a newly terraformed planet. During our flight to the next town, Adam explained how glaciers carved flat plains across the island, leaving mountains that seemingly rose out of nowhere.

We made our stops in the next few settlements, but the residents didn't have any bread crumbs for us to follow. Then we headed for the plane wreck on the beach. It was literally nothing more than the remains of a fuselage on a flat beach, but apparently, people walked two miles from the nearest road just to take pictures at it.

We flew in low on our brooms from the south and walked the rest of the way. Then we joined the tourists for about twenty minutes. Adam gave us the complete history of the wreck and took enough selfies to shame an Instagram star. But he looked happy as a clam for the first time the entire trip. I had a feeling his breakup with Meghan had hit him a lot harder than he was letting on.

I hoped this mini vacay at least got him over heartbreak hump, but couldn't stop hearing the clock counting down in the back of my head.

"I don't know about you guys, but I'm starving," Shelton said as we walked south along the beach. "Let's hit Vik next and eat."

There wasn't much else between us and the town, so Elyssa agreed. We flew further out to sea so tourists on the beach wouldn't see us. Even from that distance, I spotted the sea stacks, sentinels of craggy obsidian jutting up from the sea at two of the black sand beaches along the way.

Vik wasn't huge, but it had a nice selection of restaurants. We went to two before Shelton found one that offered horse steaks. They weren't cheap either—over sixty dollars. Even the hamburger was twenty-five.

"Get anything you want," Adam said. "My treat."

Shelton got his horse steak. It looked like an ordinary beef filet.

Elyssa shook her head in disappointment. "I can't believe you're eating a pony."

Shelton put the first bite in his mouth and moaned. "My little pony is so tasty."

She scowled. "Might as well eat a baby seal while you're at it."

Shelton's face brightened. "Are those on the menu?"

Elyssa made a fist. "I'm about to put you on the menu."

Adam had two Icelandic hot dogs. They were long and covered in brown sauce, but he claimed they were the best hot dogs he'd ever had. I had to admit my hamburger was delicious too.

After eating his pony steak, Shelton ordered two desserts and a cup of coffee. He leaned back and patted his stomach. "Now that was a tasty horse."

Elyssa ignored him and finished her fish.

Adam got the check and paid for it. Elyssa used the opportunity to ask the waiter if he'd ever heard of a woman singing on the sea stacks. He had not.

Shelton's stomach gurgled loudly, and he shot out of his chair. "Potty time, folks. I'll be back." He made a beeline for the bathroom.

"I hope that pony gave him diarrhea," Elyssa said.

Adam stood. "I'll be in the souvenir shop. There were some really cool seashells in there."

Elyssa looked around the mostly empty dining area. "It's getting late. Maybe we should find a hotel and call it a night."

"Probably a good idea." I got up and headed to the souvenir shop. Adam was in the back corner of the shop staring up at shelves of seashells.

For such a small shop, they had a jaw-dropping assortment: conch shells the size of my head, huge clam shells that were big enough to serve as a storage trunk, and statues made of brightly colored coral. I admired an octopus made of white coral. Even more amazing, it looked as if it had naturally grown into that shape.

"Where do they get coral like this up here?" Adam touched a statue. "This is the kind of stuff you find in the tropics."

"Maybe they import it," I said.

Adam lifted a sapphire clamshell and held it up to the light. "I've never seen anything like this." He took it to woman at the counter. "Is this a real shell or is it manufactured?"

"They are all real." She beamed proudly. "The seashell lady sells us only the finest shells I have ever seen."

"Seashell lady?" Adam's forehead pinched. "Does she import them?"

The woman shrugged. "I don't know. She has the best shells in all of Iceland, but she doesn't leave her house very often."

"May I ask where she lives?" He traced a finger along the shell. "I'd love to find out what species of mollusk made this."

"She doesn't sell directly to tourists."

"I really want to ask her what made this shell." Adam offered her a reassuring smile. "How much is it?"

He bought the shell and got the address.

"Aren't seashells made from whatever is lying around?" I asked after he completed the transaction.

Adam chuckled. "They aren't made like bird nests, Justin." He poked a finger inside the opening of the shell. "Mollusks excrete calcium carbonate that hardens into the shell around them. I've never read about any of them that make such a vibrantly colored shell." He leaned in closer. "But that's not why I'm interested in paying the seashell lady a visit."

"Ah. You want to take her on a date."

He snorted. "No. I think the seashell lady might have all the answers we need."

CHAPTER 7

"**S**eashell lady?" Elyssa said from behind us.

We both nearly jumped out of our skins.

I put a hand over my heart. "A little warning next time, please?"

She'd scared us so many times with her ninja skills it hardly amused her anymore. "What's so important about shells?"

Adam handed her his prize. "I'm certain that most of these shells don't occur naturally, but I also don't think they're artificial."

Elyssa rolled it in her fingers. "Either they're natural or they're not, Adam."

"They're natural, but I think they're influenced by magic." He winked. "Siren magic."

Elyssa's mouth dropped open. "Of course. Why didn't I think of that?"

"Because you're too busy sneaking up on people," I said.

Shelton emerged from the bathroom and headed toward us. "Much better," he exclaimed.

"Did you wash your hands?" Adam asked.

"Nah." Shelton sniffed his fingers. "They don't stink too bad."

Elyssa gagged. "I hope to god you're joking."

"Maybe." Shelton noticed the clamshell. "Was I supposed to use the three seashells instead of toilet paper?"

Adam groaned. "As long as you wiped with something."

Shelton whistled. "That's one fancy shell. Where'd you get it?"

"Over there." Adam pointed out the display.

Shelton's mouth dropped open slightly when he saw the huge clamshells and coral statues. "Are those real?"

Adam nodded. "Yep, and we're about to go visit the seashell lady."

"Seashell lady?" Shelton narrowed his eyes. "You found a clue, didn't you, Scooby Doo?"

"I sure hope so." Adam flicked the screen on his arcphone and held it out so we could see a tiny red dot where a road ended at the beach. "Let's see what we can find."

It wasn't a long walk to the coordinates, but Shelton complained anyway. "I'm so tired of walking. Let's just fly. I don't even care if noms see us."

"Maybe you should've worn something besides cowboy boots," Elyssa said.

"My boots are just fine," he shot back.

"These boots are made for walking," Adam sang. "And that's just what they'll do. One of these days these boots are gonna walk all over you."

Shelton covered his ears. "My feet hurt bad enough without you killing my ears too."

I stopped walking and pointed at Adam. "Hey, I think we found the singer of the black sands already."

He bowed. "I'm here all week, folks."

"More like singer of my sandy ass," Shelton grumbled.

We finally turned onto the road leading to the beach. A herd of ponies watched us from their pasture. One of them whickered and came up to the fence as if expecting a treat.

Elyssa nudged Shelton. "The pony knows you ate his best friend. Look at how cute he is."

Shelton looked away. "No."

"Look at the cute ponies, Shelton!" Elyssa grabbed his shoulders and turned him.

"No!" He squeezed his eyes shut. "Don't make me look!"

Adam and I burst into hysterical laughter. Elyssa giggled.

Shelton turned away from the ponies and tried to scowl but couldn't stop a grin from spreading across his face. "I don't care how cute that pony was. He tasted delicious."

A canary-yellow cottage greeted us at the end of the lane. Unlike most of the houses we'd seen, this one wasn't made from corrugated steel, but wood and stone. It looked like a craftsman cottage one might find in the middle of an enchanted forest. An array of brilliant flowers and shrubs grew around the outside.

"Those are the first flowers I've seen this entire time," Adam said. "Do you notice how much greener everything here is than just a few feet away?" He pointed out some shrubs just down the road. "There's definitely magic at work."

Shelton waved his arcphone around like a scanner. "There's an aegis protecting this place. And it wasn't made by an Arcane."

I stopped in front of the door, hands trembling. "I'm a little nervous. This might be the home of one of the first Sirens."

"Or it might be the home of a crazy old lady who sells seashells," Shelton said.

"Sirens are no joke," Adam said. "Narine and her companions in Atlantis could put an entire army to sleep. We need to be very careful here."

"If she is who we think she is, then she already knows we're out here." I examined the door for a peephole. "The longer we stand out here, the more likely it is she'll think we're a threat."

"Just knock already!" Elyssa took a deep breath, stepped up to the door, and rapped on it. A moment later, a little old lady opened it.

"If you're tourists, I don't sell direct," she said without preamble. Then she started to shut the door.

She didn't look like an ancient Siren. Then again, Xanos hadn't much looked like a world-sundering god. "Vitania?" I said.

She froze. Her sea-green eyes locked onto me. "I'm sorry. Should that mean something to me?"

It was the eyes that gave her away. I could literally feel the weight of her stare. "Vitania, we really need your wisdom and advice."

Shelton put his hands over his ears. "Please don't sing us to sleep or kill us."

Adam piled on. "Vitania, you're our only hope."

The old woman's lips pressed together into a thin line. She stepped back and opened the door. "Enter."

I let Elyssa go first since she was the ninja, then I followed at a safe interval behind her to give her plenty of space to fight off any traps inside. But the interior was quite a departure from the cute outside. There was no foyer, only a family room sparsely furnished. A doorway to the right led to the kitchen, and a tight hallway to the left probably went to bedrooms.

Another old woman came out of the kitchen, a teacup in her hand. Bright amber eyes regarded us curiously. "Guests, dear?"

Shelton entered last and the first little old lady closed the door. She folded her arms across her chest and looked us over. "Two Arcanes, a Daemos, and"—she paused to consider Elyssa—"a day vampire with Seraphim magic inside her."

"How interesting," the other woman said. "Shall I prepare more tea?"

Shelton's jaw dropped. "How in the hell do you know what we are?"

"I have a divining charm around the doorway."

"So you're Vitania?" I asked.

Her wrinkled skin smoothed into the face of a woman in her early thirties. Sea-green hair hung past her shoulders, flowing around her as if underwater. Her almond-shaped eyes and olive skin gave her a slightly Asian appearance. Her gaze dispelled any notion that this woman was young.

Elyssa regarded the other woman. "Looks like my hunch was right. You're Lumia, aren't you?"

"What a bright one you are," the other woman said in something resembling an Italian accent. "Are you their leader, young lady?"

"Pretty much," I said.

The woman nodded. "I am indeed Lumia. I am curious to know how you could possibly know that."

Elyssa smiled. "We spent some time with one of your granddaughters, Thal."

"I do not know that name."

"She's Pyra's daughter," Elyssa said.

Lumia looked genuinely surprised. Her wrinkled skin smoothed out, and her height diminished until she stood about four feet tall. She was tiny and adorable like the other Fae we'd encountered, but I wasn't about to tell her that.

"Holy farting fairies," Shelton murmured. "We freaking did it."

Lumia's eyes narrowed. "I do not care for that mortal term."

Shelton blanched. "I—I'm sorry."

She smiled. "Perhaps you should leave the talking to your leader."

Shelton simply nodded.

Adam leaned toward me. "Dude, these are the original mothers of the Sirens and the Fae. This is epic!"

Vitania took Elyssa's hand. "Come. Let us get tea." She looked at the rest of us. "I suppose they can come too."

"Sounds wonderful." Lumia wove her hands in a pattern. Sparkling dust sprinkled around her and the house shifted. The wall between us and the kitchen vanished. The furniture melted into the wooden floor. A sapling grew where the kitchen had been, branches weaving into a long table. Red-capped mushrooms sprouted from the floor, a seat for each of us.

"Absolutely amazing." Adam knelt and ran a hand along the floor. "This entire house is formed from living wood."

"It's like the Glimmer," I said.

Vitania's eyes flared. "You know of the Glimmer and the Lyrolai?"

"I've met their queen and even fought alongside her," I said.

Understanding lit her eyes. "You are Justin Slade. Slayer of Daelissa. Protector of Eden."

I waved off her fancy titles. "No, *we're* protectors of Eden." I nodded at my friends. "Without them, I'd have died a long time ago."

Vitania raised an eyebrow. "Well spoken. We do not engage in the politics of the realms, but we do keep up with events."

Shelton couldn't keep his mouth shut any longer. "So what do you do then? Swim around and collect seashells?"

"Are you certain this one is of value?" the Siren said. "He seems a bit abrasive."

"He's a lousy conversationalist, but he pulls his weight," I said.

Lumia produced a kettle and teacups. She fluttered around the table on gossamer wings setting the table and pouring blue liquid for each of us.

"Is that blue milk or tea?" Adam said.

Lumia smiled. "It is tea, but I can procure blue milk if you desire."

He shook his head. "No, thank you. Tea is fine."

Vitania sat at one end of the table and Lumia took the other. We filled in the seats between.

The tea was dark blue and opaque, but it tasted perfectly sweet and slightly bitter. The opposing flavors really threw my taste buds for a loop, but it was the best tea I'd ever had.

Adam's eyes flared. "Wow. What's in this?"

"Dried seaweed from the deepest oceans of Aquanis and Aquilis," Vitania said. "Other herbs and spices Lumia grows in her garden."

Elyssa curled both hands around her teacup and looked first at the Siren, then the Fae. "Thank you for hosting us, Vitania and Lumia. We have journeyed here under dire circumstances to request information and possibly help that might protect the realms from disaster."

Vitania waved a hand. "Spare the formal talk, child. Tell us directly what you need."

"We are engaged in a war on two fronts. Baal, the grand overlord of Haedaemos, has already taken over Seraphina with a dragon army and will probably come soon for Eden." Elyssa took a sip of tea to let that sink in, then continued. "The mate of Altash, Lulu, came to us in Seraphina and told us that the first of the Sirens might know Baal's true name and give us power over him."

Vitania pursed her lips and stared off into the distance for a moment. She nodded ever so slightly. "There is much I once knew but have now forgotten. The Sundering nearly killed me and cost me many of my early memories. I remember fragments of the time before. Since then, I have kept a careful record of everything and stored it in my library. When one has lived so long, it is impossible to remember everything, even that which is important."

Hope drained from Elyssa's face. "So you don't know anything about Baal's origins?"

"I'm afraid I have no definite answers for you." Vitania tapped her temple. "At least not up here. There may be clues in the Great Library of Darya, but that is on Aquilis, and my people are not welcoming to strangers."

"The Grand Nexus and all the Alabaster arches were sabotaged," Elyssa said. "The only way we can get to other realms is with a special boat that can channel portals through Voltis."

A hint of a smile touched Vitania's lips, as if amused by this. "I am sorry I could not be of more help. For too long I tried to keep the realms on a steady course across unsafe waters. But it is impossible to stop everyone who seeks power. Baal is simply one more in a long line of those who desire power and will kill to get it."

"There is an entire universe to explore," Lumia said. "Hundreds of realms to see."

"And document," Vitania said. "The Sundering devastated the world, but it also created many wonders. New, amazing life sprang from the ashes of the old. Long ago, we gave up our kingdoms and rediscovered the joy of science. Once I have documented the realms, I plan to branch out into the multiverse."

Elyssa's eyes narrowed and she tilted her head, as if uncertain she'd heard something right. "How do you reach other realms? Do you have functioning arches?"

Vitania sighed. "Well, it seems in my advanced age I still let my enthusiasm run away with me."

"You brag, dear." Lumia smiled.

"I'm afraid I do." Vitania offered Elyssa an apologetic smile. "I have the ability to traverse realms without an arch."

"Huh?" I blurted. "Do you have an Obsidian necklace like Melea?"

Vitania's eyes tightened with anger. "Melea, that foul twit, still roams the world? I hoped she'd died eons ago."

"Well, kind of." I blew out a sigh. "Do you have anything you could give us that would allow us to travel the realms without an arch? We desperately need to stop Baal."

"Why bother?" Vitania took another sip of tea. "He will fail or succeed, and in time, another will desire power, then another, and another. It never ends."

"We can't just let him win," I said. "Besides, if he doesn't win, then Xanos probably will."

Vitania and Lumia gasped in unison. Vitania's teacup clattered on the table, but miraculously didn't spill a drop.

The Siren focused her full attention on me. "Xanos the Apocryphan?"

I nodded uneasily. "Um, she escaped the Abyss about a decade ago, and now she wants to rule the realms."

"How is this possible?" Vitania slammed the table with a fist. "She could not possibly know the truth!"

I gulped. "Well, it's kind of my fault. And Xanos claims she knows how you tricked her and that it's impossible to trap her again."

The Siren rose and glared at me with the anger of a thousand suns. "Then you will take her place beneath the infernal fount."

CHAPTER 8

Vitania's mouth dropped open inhumanly wide and her almond-shaped eyes widened enough to put an anime princess to shame. An eerie melody penetrated me to my very soul.

Maybe I shouldn't have admitted I set Xanos free.

It was too late now. Cold sweat broke out on my forehead and my hands trembled. Try as I might, I couldn't move.

A gentle voice from the other end of the table interrupted the song. "Let us not be hasty, love. This boy must have great power to free a soul from your prison."

The Siren's jaw relaxed, and her mouth resumed a normal size. "Tell us your tale from beginning to end that I may judge your fate."

A shuddering breath escaped my throat. *Holy shit! She's ready to banish me to the Abyss!* Kalesh seemed as shaken up as I was but didn't poke his head out of his cage.

Shelton raised a hand. "Hey, the kid's made mistakes, but he's got a heart of gold. You ain't got no right to judge him."

His poetic use of double-negatives didn't seem to sway Vitania.

"Tell us your story, child." Lumia poured herself a fresh cup of tea. "I suspect it is entertaining."

"And growing longer with every telling," Adam murmured.

Ain't that the truth.

I finished off the rest of the tea to sooth my dry throat and poured another cup. "I'll start from my beginning." I had the routine memorized by now. Hopefully I'd get some empathy points with my origin story. So far, this trip was looking like a complete disaster. Ending up in the Abyss would be a real capper to my career.

It took a good long while and two more pots of tea to spill my guts.

A loser nerd discovers his demonic powers and hilarity ensues. Well—not so much. The first time I'd unknowingly summoned Xanos had been to use her as a hellhound. That seemed to amuse Vitania a great deal.

"Oh, how furious she must have been, used as a lesser spawn." Vitania basked in the humiliation of the god for a moment before letting me continue.

The next two times I'd summoned Xanos was to fight demons. It was the second time she'd escaped. Daelissa's army had threatened to sweep through Atlanta. As a last resort, I summoned Xanos. She'd destroyed giant demons and golems, saving us from certain defeat, but controlling her for so long had nearly broken me. Our army survived. She escaped.

"It is not your fault, child." Vitania patted my hand, a mother soothing a frightened boy. "You used and humiliated that twisted demigod, and for that, I am happy. When you first probed the depths of Haedaemos for spirits, you did not realize your own power. You were able to open a quantum tunnel even beyond the infernal fount. I did not even know until a decade ago that it was possible for Daemos to do such a thing."

"I didn't even know about the Apocryphan at the time," I said. "Now she's threatening to destroy everything we fought for."

"And her spirit abides in a mortal body?" Vitania tutted. "That must be quite frustrating for her."

"Mortal body?" I frowned. "I thought Apocryphan could transform into any shape."

"No, but they can move their souls to other bodies," Vitania said. "They may also devour souls like Daemos." She scowled. "Monstrous things."

"Ah, so she moved her soul to a mortal body." It made sense. Her normal form looked like a black swirling tornado with a single red eye. "It's easier to remain hidden."

"Your Daemos powers allowed you to transport her soul to this world." Vitania nodded. "A mortal body is a necessity."

"Can all Daemos free Apocryphan?" I asked.

She shook her head. "While many have the strength to banish souls to the Abyss, very few can actually free spirits from there. Somehow, you created a quantum tunnel powerful enough to free her soul. Xanos must have realized what you did. There has always been a way out of the Abyss, but the Apocryphan did not know how to use quantum tunnels."

"I'm kind of lost here." I glanced at Adam, hoping he was taking this all in. "What do you mean by quantum tunnels?"

"They connect the realms, the multiverse, and everything." Vitania looked all around as if they were visible. "After the Sundering, the Apocryphan did not realize that the realms remained connected via these tunnels. Posthanied forced me and my people to find a way to bridge the realms. We discovered the quantum tunnels and divined the magic to connect them. But we could not make it so easy for the Apocryphan. So we delayed and sang stone into arches. We created enchantments so intricate and complex, that none would see the simple magic that actually opened the tunnels."

"This is astounding." Adam tapped away on his phone screen. "I've long theorized that there was more to the traversion tunnels than we understood but deciphering the enchantments on Obsidian and Alabaster Arches was impossible." He laughed. "I didn't even realize most of the code was a decoy."

"You are a researcher?" Vitania said.

Shelton snorted. "He's only the biggest nerd there is. Our resident genius."

"We wove a web of enchantments that would cause the entire arch to fail should one strand be broken." Vitania smiled fondly. "The Apocryphan in their hubris did none of the work. They knew nothing of the science behind the magic. Their ignorance led them to their eternal prison."

"Perhaps not as eternal as we'd hoped," Lumia said. She smiled at me. "I would hear more of your tale about the war. The second and third-hand rumors we heard weren't nearly as interesting."

Vitania nodded. "Continue your story, boy."

"Can I use the bathroom first?" My bladder was about to burst.

We took a short bathroom break then returned to the table. Lumia and Vitania somehow prepared snacks in the five minutes it took. There were fresh fish, oysters, and exotic veggies I'd never seen before.

Shelton wasn't impressed. "Got bacon?"

Both women made sour faces.

"I do not eat the flesh of land animals," Lumia said.

Shelton jabbed a thumb toward the pastures outside. "You don't sell those ponies out there for meat?"

"Of course not." Lumia's eyes gleamed dangerously. "Do not speak of it again."

Adam elbowed Shelton. "You gotta learn when to shut it, man."

Shelton held up his hands in surrender. "Yeah, yeah." He plucked a raw oyster and ate it. "Hey, these are damned tasty." He leaned over and spoke in a low voice to Adam. "Is it rude to ask for horseradish?"

Vitania patted my hand again and leaned back in her chair. "Please, continue your story."

So I did. All the way up to present time. It took less time than I'd thought because neither Lumia nor Vitania stopped me once to ask questions. When I reached the part about losing my father, it took everything I had not to tear up. Then I summed up the best I could to emphasize what would help us most.

"We need to know Baal's origins. We need to find Emily Glass so she can help me restore my dad to his body. Since sending Xanos back to the Abyss isn't an option, we need to know how to stop her. Can she be killed or imprisoned?"

The Siren and Fae remained silent and thoughtful even after I finished, as if digesting the story before speaking.

I took the time to polish off a few oysters and test some of the vegetables. Everything was tasty except some disgusting leafy greens that might have been kale.

Lumia finally asked a question but directed it at Vitania. "Why would Baal wish to recombine the realms?"

Vitania clasped her hands on the table. "I do not know."

"Do you think Xanos was telling the truth or just trolling us?" I said.

"Xanos would wield more power with the realms as they are," Vitania said. "Now that she understands traversing the realms is a matter of opening quantum gateways, she realizes that bringing them back together is pointless."

"If Baal truly means to recombine the realms, I think we must help the resistance," Lumia said. "Xanos can rule, for all I care, but I will not sit idly by while billions of living beings are snuffed at the hands of the demon overlord."

"I will not sit idly by and let Xanos achieve victory." Vitania's fists clenched. "She fomented the war among the Apocryphan, and I lost many loved ones because of it."

"Does that mean you'll actually help us?" I asked.

Vitania took a deep breath as if composing herself. "I will not fight, but I will help you find what you need." She clasped her hands again as if to keep them from curling into fists again. "I will search the Great Library of Darya and see if it holds any information on Baal. As for Xanos, only her mother would know the best way to stop her."

Elyssa perked up. "Her mother?"

The Siren didn't elaborate and moved on to the next point.

"Emily Glass is another matter. She was here many years ago, but she had to repay a debt to Fjoeruss and we have not heard from her since." Vitania shook her head sadly. "I hope the girl is okay."

"She was here? She owed Fjoeruss?" I'd only met Emily once and briefly. She and her boyfriend had stopped a demonic invasion around the time I'd been fighting Maximus and his vampire army. I wondered how she'd incurred a debt with Fjoeruss.

"I would dearly love to visit this library," Adam said to Vitania. "And it would be an honor if I could talk to you about quantum tunnels and other things you've learned about the universe."

She smiled at him and cupped his chin as if he were a little boy. "You are a bright one. So inquisitive. But it would be unwise for me to bring a mortal male to Aquilis. Someone sings the song of homecoming, and I fear my people prepare for war."

That sparked a memory of my conversation with Melea and Dolpha in

76

Atlantis. "Dolpha, a Siren in Atlantis, said there is a call. Does that mean all the Sirens are being called back to Aquilis?"

"Yes," Vitania said. "There are many great scientists and explorers among my people, often scattered to the realms. The song is sent through the quantum tunnels that all may hear it."

"Can you teach us how to use quantum tunnels before we leave?" I spread my hands imploringly. "It would be huge if we could travel the realms more easily."

Vitania gave me an appraising look. "I sense great power in you. You were able to breach the quantum veil on a spiritual level but doing so on the physical level is something else entirely."

Shelton scoffed. "If Sirens can do it, I'd bet dollars to donuts that Justin can."

"In fact, most Sirens cannot," Vitania said. "They require powered charms called scythera." She touched her throat. "The obsidian necklace worn by Melea was one such charm. They can only open tunnels to the realms they are specifically charmed for. The user simply fixes an image of the symbols and the destination in their head. But a scythera can only be used so many times before it must be recharged by immersion in an aether well."

"Can I at least try?" I said.

Vitania sighed. "Very well. But even Emily took several days before she could do it."

I jerked my head back like she'd slapped it. "Say what?"

"Hang on a minute." Shelton wiggled a finger in his ear as if cleaning it. "Did you say Emily Glass—a human with no Arcane powers—can open quantum tunnels?"

"She is far more than human." Vitania almost seemed proud. "And her power greatly exceeds even my own."

"Wow." Elyssa nudged me. "I guess finding Emily is a lot more important than we thought."

"That's amazing." Adam pushed a finger up the bridge of his nose. "You also mentioned something about Xanos's mother. Who is she?"

"She is someone we have not seen in many years." Lumia sighed. "I am not certain she would help you stop Xanos anyway."

"What's her name?" I asked.

"It's better you not know," Lumia said. "She is no one you'd want to encounter."

"As usual, we're an ass hair away from finding a solution, only to find out it's no good." Shelton puffed out his cheeks and blew out the air. "I don't even know why we bother. We always end up saving the world ourselves."

"Don't be such a Negative Nancy," Adam said. "We just found out we don't need Alabaster Arches to open gateways to other realms. If we find Emily, she could give us a huge advantage. We could find allies in realms we never even heard of."

I turned to Vitania. "What do I need to do to open a tunnel?"

She pressed her lips into a flat line. "I will be back." She left the kitchen through a doorway in the back.

While she was gone, I decided to press my luck with Lumia. "You looked shocked when I told you about finding Pyra and Thal locked up in Vokan's dungeon, but you haven't mentioned it since."

The Fae pursed her lips and looked down at her tea before responding. "Pyra had a child and it turned out every bit as stubborn and rebellious as she is. One might almost find it funny that Thal became an Unfae simply to spite her mother."

Pyra hadn't shown the least bit of gratitude for us saving her from Vokan's stasis spell. She'd been rude and unwilling to even discuss an alliance. I wondered if her mother was any different. "Would you be willing to help us form an alliance with the Fae?" I asked. "We need every advantage we can get against Xanos and Baal."

Lumia stirred the tea with a dainty finger. "Even though the humans of Eden were insufferable, I found the people of Utopia to be rather delightful. I marveled at their ability to question everything and seek scientific and magical truth. It was a mystery to me how they were so much better than their kin left behind in Eden."

"We wondered that too," Elyssa said. "Their society was almost perfect."

"The Utopians didn't have religion," Adam said. "They believed in logic and facts. That's why their society turned out so much better."

Shelton scoffed. "At least until Vokan came along."

"Pyra believed the Fae should remain in isolation," Lumia said. "I wanted to open talks with the humans and end the cold war between us. But Pyra threatened to leave and form her own kingdom with dissenters. She said all humans were inherently evil and should never be trusted."

"She ain't wrong," Shelton said.

Elyssa punched his shoulder. "Will you hush?"

I groaned. "So, there's no hope the Fae would ever help us?"

"There is little hope Pyra will help you. But my good daughter, Glacia, will help you if I ask."

Adam frowned. "The leader of the Unfae?"

A bright smile lifted the corners of Lumia's lips. "She is Unfae because she performed her duty. She did not want to kill, but she did what she had to do to save her people." Her nose wrinkled. "Pyra is spoiled and sick with her own self-worth. Because of Unfae like her sister, she has never known a day of strife."

Lumia looked up from her teacup and nodded. "I will speak with Glacia.

Since I am still the true queen, she and the Unfae will do as I ask. Some Fae may also answer the call."

"But will they fight?" I asked.

"Just because they will not kill does not mean they will not fight." Lumia spread her hands. "And if the enemy kills himself, that is not blood on our hands."

"Thank you so much." I wanted to give the cute little fairy a hug, but I didn't want to test the limits of our new relationship.

Vitania returned several minutes later with a tiny clamshell on a necklace. My hopes soared to new heights because I thought she'd brought me my very own scythera. The Siren must have seen the look on my face because she held up a hand. "Calm yourself, child. This is but the Quantum Codex—a directory of known realms."

The Quantum freaking Codex. Holy crap!

We were about to have the holy grail of quantum travel.

CHAPTER 9

Adam's fingers twitched and he licked his lips like a hungry dog. "I would love to take a look at the Quantum Codex."

Vitania smiled proudly. "I have refined it greatly. I finally took a year to add images, diagrams and in-depth details of the catalogued realms." She rubbed the top and the clamshell opened. A stream of water drifted out, globules clinging to each other and drifting apart as if in a weightless environment. Some globules spread into neat lines of Cyrinthian runes. Others formed little colored globes with land and bodies of water.

I'd learned Cyrinthian in Seraphina by having it implanted directly into my mind. Even so, I didn't recognize all the symbols in the list. It was an odd language, used by Arcanes for spellcasting, rituals, and enchantments. It had long been considered a dead language, the magical equivalent of Latin.

But when I'd visited Seraphina, I discovered it was the spoken and written language there. The Mzodi understood the deep complexities of the language, using it to create intricate enchantments in their gems.

Even Adam and Shelton had difficulty programming all the variations in their arcphones so they could decipher it.

Judging from the variety of unknown symbols hovering in front of me, it seemed I still had a lot to learn.

But each group of symbols in the list had several that repeated. I traced a finger beneath the last group of symbols. "Xhi budi tuan zot—I will to be a rift."

Vitania's eyes widened with delight. "Ah, you already know Cyrinthian?"

"Cephus crammed it all into my noggin." I tapped a finger to my temple. "Everyone else had to learn it since we were trapped in Seraphina."

Adam leaned in, mouth agape as he read the list. "These are truly archaic symbols. I've only seen them mentioned in ancient texts." He murmured to himself as he read them. "Judging by the position of the sholots, I think the first grouping of symbols is the name of the realm."

"You are a bright one." Vitania caressed his jaw again, a master petting her puppy. "It is a shame you're only an Arcane."

Adam didn't seem to mind her condescension. "Knowledge is power, but it's also pleasure."

"Yes!" Vitania clapped her hands. "Discovery is pure pleasure. When there is nothing new to find, I will be ready to die."

Adam peered at the first line. "This says, Aquanis, I will there to be a rift."

"Excellent." Vitania patted his head.

Shelton scoffed. "Jesus, dude. You're her new favorite pet."

Adam was too engrossed reading the next few lines to hear him.

"How do I use these symbols to open a portal?" I asked.

Vitania folded her arms across her chest. "Since you already know Cyrinthian, I assume you can reproduce these symbols?"

"Do I need to write them, or can I just will them into being in my head?"

A pinprick of light formed in front of Adam's nose. He cried out and dropped to the floor on his knees. Rolled onto his side and gasped for air.

Vitania tutted. "Dear boy, did you try to open a tunnel?

Adam retched up his supper all over the floor.

Shelton leapt back. "Christ Almighty, Nosti! What the hell were you thinking?"

I knelt down, doing my best to ignore the acrid stench of bile in the puddle of barf. "Adam, are you okay?" I gripped him around his waist and pulled him upright. Elyssa hoisted him to his feet, and we got him into a chair.

"He's white as a ghost," Shelton said. "Damn, I hope he didn't fry his circuits pulling that stunt."

Vitania smoothed back Adam's hair and looked at his pupils. "He's in shock. I can't say if he's further damaged or not."

Lumia sprinkled his head with dust. It sparkled gold and white for several minute, then faded away. "His mind is intact. He will be fine once his system recovers from the shock."

I gulped. "Is that what I have to look forward to if I don't have the power to open a rift?"

"It will not be as severe for you." Vitania put a hand on either side of my face and peered into my eyes as if inspecting a prize horse. "You might even be able to open a small portal." She released me. "We shall see."

I suddenly wasn't quite so eager to try.

"Oh, and yes. You may form the power words in your mind." Vitania looked sadly at Adam. "Just as he did."

Willpower and focus were key ingredients whether casting or channeling magic. I'd learned to control my demon powers through medita-tion. That in turn made learning spellcasting and channeling easier. So picturing the power runes and filling them with power wouldn't be the hard part. Giving them enough power to work would be the trick.

The real limit would be what my body and soul could handle.

I took a deep breath and steeled myself. The first set of symbols in the list seemed as good as any other, so I burned each one into my mind, channeling power into them as I went. It usually would've taken a matter of seconds, but I was dreading what might happen when I finished the last symbol and closed the circuit.

I reached the last one. With all my will, focus, and power, I spoke the words in my head and imagined a gateway tearing open in front of me.

Aquanis, I will there to be a rift!

The power levels in my body spiked. I suddenly felt as if someone plugged me into the electrical grid and flipped on the switch. Static electricity climbed up my body and I felt my hair standing on end. Heat flushed my skin and every nerve fiber in my body seemed to catch fire. I heard someone screaming in the distance and realized it was me.

A pinprick of light formed before me. It widened to the size of a peep-hole. *Open, you son of a bitch! Open!* It stretched to the size of my head. *Wider! Wider!* I imagined it the size of a doorway. It widened ever so slightly. Blue ocean waters rippled beyond the hole. A giant gray fish leapt from the waters and splashed back down.

And then I couldn't hold on anymore.

I released the power. The portal snapped shut. My knees turned to jelly, and I dropped to the floor. Nausea wormed up my throat. Somehow, I managed not to barf.

Strong hands gripped beneath my arms and pulled me off the floor. "I got you, baby," Elyssa whispered in my ear.

"Don't you always?" I slumped into a chair. My arms felt like lead weights, and my head bobbed back and forth on an unsteady neck. "How much power does it take to open a damned portal?" I said in a slurred voice.

"That was impressive." Vitania sat down across from me. "I would never have imagined you could open anything larger than my hand. Perhaps with practice you could actually create a usable rift."

"As long as they carry me out on a stretcher afterward."

"Opening a rift to another realm takes more power than opening one within the same realm." Vitania clasped her hands in front of her. "If you use the symbols for Eden and precisely picture your destination, you can open a rift to another location."

"Like an omniarch," Shelton said.

Vitania frowned. "Omniarch?"

"The small arches that open gateways anywhere you can envision," Shelton said. "But if you mess up, they'll open a portal to the Void."

"Ah, the global arches." Vitania nodded. "Yes, this works much the same way."

"So theoretically, we could build our own arches by enchanting them with the realm codes," Shelton said. "That would explain why every arch has a silver circle and is built on top of a major leyline."

"Precisely." Vitania looked surprised that Shelton had figured it out. "It needn't be an arch, but you will want to use peridotite as it's the only native stone that can handle the intense energy."

"Never heard of it," Shelton said.

"Plutonic, ultramafic rock," Adam said in a weak voice. "It occurs deep underground."

"Hey, buddy." Shelton patted him gently on the back. "Glad you're back among the living!"

"I'm an idiot." Adam feebly reached for a teacup and downed the contents with a shaky hand.

I knew exactly how he felt.

"He is correct," Vitania said. "Peridotite was used for the black and white arches. As it is formed deep underground, it naturally forms within leylines and can hold a charge better than any other native stones. We extruded several tons of it and took it to Alpha One, a small realm with no living creatures. The surface of much of the realm is covered in refined Peridotite that we sang into arches."

"Whoa. I think I've been there." I managed a weak grin. "I went through a broken arch in El Dorado, and it took me skipping across the universe. I saw a plain of obsidian and two Sirens singing an arch out of it."

Vitania raised an eyebrow. "This was recent?"

"Over a decade ago now." I inspected my trembling hands. "Any idea why they were building them in this day and age?"

"Perhaps my people are expanding their reach." Vitania frowned. "Or there could be an innocent explanation. I only communicate with a trusted inner circle and keep well out of politics."

Shelton looked up from his phone. "Why are Alabaster Arches striped black and white?"

"We simply changed the color a little to make the Apocryphan believe it was necessary." Vitania smiled. "Nothing more."

"I could talk to you forever," Adam said. "There's so much I could learn. Like, how did you destroy the Glimmer and create the Anchor Stone? How did you trap the Apocryphan?"

"I might enjoy having a pupil," Vitania said. "But it will have to wait."

"Are there male Sirens?" Shelton asked.

"Of course, but Tridents are not vocally gifted like the women." Vitania shrugged. "Their power is more physical."

"Do you think your people would help us fight Xanos and Baal?" I asked.

Vitania pursed her lips. "I believe they are already plotting. Otherwise, they would not sing the song of homecoming."

"I got a bad feeling about that." Shelton grimaced. "I hope the Sirens ain't planning a takeover of their own."

"Can you find out what they're up to?" I asked Vitania. "Maybe ask them to join our cause?"

"I will be lucky to get in and out of the library undetected, child." Vitania shook her head. "I did not leave the kingdom on good terms with the current rulers."

"You don't think we'd be safe if we visited on our own?" Elyssa asked.

"I cannot say for certain." The Siren made a sour face. "The current queen, Dactia, once sang an entire population to sleep simply because she thought they were ugly."

Shelton cringed. "She just left them that way?"

"Indeed." Vitania shook her head. "I would not risk a visit to her court."

"Who were the people she put to sleep?" I asked.

"The satyrs of Brin, a realm the size of a small island."

"Did anyone ever wake up the satyrs?" Elyssa asked.

"Dactia did not entwine the song of sleep with that of preservation, so I'm afraid all three hundred and twenty-one of the satyrs starved to death in their sleep." Vitania sighed. "I did not find out about it until it was too late."

Elyssa's forehead scrunched in thought. "Is there a song of awakening? A way to break a sleep spell?"

Vitania tilted her head slightly. "Why do you ask, child?"

"Queen Naeve—the fake one—sang the Glimmer folk to sleep and Cora can't wake them." Elyssa bit the inside of her lip. "Do you have a way to break the spell?"

"That would make for fine drama." Lumia smirked. "The elf queen has no love for the Siren who destroyed her kingdom to create the anchor stone."

"Yeah, but maybe this could turn things around." Elyssa shrugged. "We've got to try something."

Vitania's lips pressed together. "I will consider it, provided I make it back from Aquilis."

My teacup rattled ever so slightly, sending ripples across the liquid inside. I only noticed it because I was staring at it, still dazed from trying to open a quantum tunnel. It rattled again and again, a steady rhythm that seemed to get stronger with every passing second.

Elyssa was the first to say something about it. "Does anyone feel the ground shaking?"

"There's a geyser nearby that shakes the ground when it erupts," Lumia said.

"No, this is something else." Elyssa walked toward the front door.

The teacups rattled, stopped. Rattled, stopped. I imagined a tyrannosaurus rex charging down the beach toward us. Shelton ran to the door. Adam and I staggered to our feet and leaned on each other for support. Elyssa stepped outside into the dusk. Orange light lit her face. I poked my head out and saw where the light came from.

It wasn't the setting sun, and there wasn't a bonfire on the beach. But there were two massive fire demons storming down the beach straight for the house. They stood three stories tall with bodies made of molten rock. Giant horns curved from their monstrous heads and their four eyes glowed like suns.

Somehow, Baal had found us.

CHAPTER 10

Shelton took out a pair of spectacles and peered down the beach. "I can't see who's controlling the damned things."

"Who would dare such a brazen attack?" Lumia said.

"Baal would." My face heated with anger. "I don't know how, but that son of a bitch found out we were here."

Vitania pursed her lips. "Our location is no secret from Baal. I would not be surprised if he has spies watching us, especially after Emily's visit."

"Olivia certainly would have sold the information." Lumia tsked. "All because you thought it a good idea to bring her here."

"Let us not rehash that old argument," Vitania said. "Baal has never confronted us until now. One might assume he's only attacking because of our visitors. Surely he knows we can deal with his demons." She shook her head. "Then again, Baal does nothing without reason. If he's truly behind this attack, he wants to trigger a specific response."

Vitania hadn't given us much detail on the story behind Emily, but I was starting to think it had to be quite a doozy if Baal was involved.

"Are we certain it's Baal?" Elyssa didn't look convinced.

"Did you not say you have a truce with Xanos?" Vitania raised an eyebrow. "If the demons are not hers, then Baal is the only other option."

"Enough talking!" Shelton's eyes widened. "You realize those demons are gonna be here any minute, right? It doesn't matter who sent them. We gotta stop 'em!"

"Indeed." Vitania didn't seem the least bit worried. "Fire demons next to the ocean? What foolish game is this?"

Lumia closed her eyes and pressed a hand to the doorframe. "There are two individuals standing on the beach about a kilometer from here. They stand before two summoning patterns. Perhaps they might have answers."

"How the hell—" Shelton shook his head. "Did you look through the eyes of a bird or something?"

"I found a helpful crab." She opened her eyes. "I think someone should apprehend them before we engage the demons."

"Agreed." Vitania looked expectantly at Shelton and Elyssa. "Your friends are not up to the task. Can you handle this yourselves?"

Shelton nodded. "Easy, peasy."

"Shouldn't be a problem unless they have backup," Elyssa said.

"Wait. I want to help." I raised a trembling hand and nearly toppled over.

Elyssa steadied me and pecked a kiss on my lips. "Why don't you wait here, hot stuff?" She slapped my rear end and grabbed a broom. "Shelton and I got this."

They hopped on brooms and circled out to sea so they could flank the summoners.

Adam gripped the doorway for support. "My god, those things are huge. People can probably see them all the way from town."

"When do you plan on stopping them, Vitania?" The odor of brimstone stung my nose. "They're almost here."

"Now." Vitania began to sing. A dark hump formed several hundred yards offshore. Water receded from the black sands as if the entire ocean were being drained. With every foot of newly revealed land, the hump grew taller and taller. Then it began to roll toward shore, rising into a great wall that towered over the monstrous demons.

The demons looked at the oncoming wave, but did nothing to avoid it. Either their handlers were unaware of the situation, or they just didn't care.

"Something is wrong." Vitania frowned. "They are not even fighting their handlers to flee the water."

Adam held up his arcphone and ran a program. "I've seen fire demons, but these things are something else."

The wave crashed down with enough force to destroy a herd of elephants. Water hissed. Steam filled the air so thick it was impossible to see the demons. The fog swirled. Orange light flickered. A giant flaming hand fanned the air and the steam evaporated.

"Holy smokes." Adam tapped on his phone screen. "That much water would've extinguished ordinary fire demons."

"They are hellfire demons." Orange flames reflected in Vitania's eyes. "Water cannot quench their fire." For the first time since seeing the demons, she looked concerned.

"What about holy water?" I said.

"Do you jest?" Vitania looked at me like I was stupid. "They are fueled by the infernal fount itself. Summoning these creatures requires tremendous power and the ability to tap into the fount."

"Then how do we stop them?" I said. "Can you sing them to sleep?"

Vitania shook her head. "Not hellfire demons. The song does not reach them."

I grimaced. "Then what are we going to do?"

"That is a good question." Lumia fluttered about on her wings. "I cannot remember the last time I fought hellfire demons."

"What about Stasis?" I asked.

"That would slow them, certainly. But you're in no condition to work your Seraphim magic." Vitania shook her head. "Our only hope is that your friends disable the summoners. Then the demons will be forced back to Hell."

The demons were only fifty yards away, towering over the small cottage. Their every step left flaming footprints and molten black sand. One swipe from their massive claws would demolish the tiny cottage. Even if Shelton and Elyssa took out the summoners, the demons would wreak some serious havoc before their bodies disintegrated.

Somehow, we had to get them away from here—far away. But I was in no shape to lead them on a merry chase. I wouldn't even be able to sit upright on a broom in my condition.

But there might be another way.

"Vitania, can you open portals?"

She frowned. "Yes. I suppose we should use one to escape."

I shook my head. "I've got a better idea." I asked her a few questions and she gave me the answers I needed. Then I told her what to do.

Lumia smiled. "A clever plan, Justin. This will be fun." She sped into the air, trailing a glittery path of fairy dust behind her and flew right at the demons.

Giant maws of glowing orange teeth widened in anticipation of an evening snack as the small Fae darted toward them. She zipped up and down, back and forth, leaving a dizzying trail. The demons lunged eagerly toward her, but when she tried to lead them away, they reluctantly resumed their course toward the house.

"Well, Plan A is a bust," I said. "Let's hope Plan B fares better."

Lumia once again darted in front of the demons, casting golden dust in their eyes. The demons roared. Claws slashed the air. Lumia darted even closer. Too close. A paw swiped her from the air. She screamed. Her body split in half, entrails flaming.

"Jesus, no!" Adam reached a hand out as if he could save her.

"Holy shit!" I shouted. "They killed her!"

Vitania didn't lose an ounce of composure as the demons consumed their prey.

The demons reared back their heads and roared to the skies. Orange flames jetted from their throats. They were so happy they didn't even notice what happened right under their feet. A portal twenty feet in diameter swallowed the first demon. Before the second could react, another opened beneath its feet and it plummeted.

With a sneering glare, Vitania made a clenching motion with her hand and the portal closed before the demon was all the way through, cleaving its head off. A strangled roar cut off and the orange flames died, leaving nothing but cooling stone in the shape of a grotesque head.

Lumia landed lightly next to Vitania. She patted the Siren's bottom and grinned. "Did you enjoy my performance?"

"What the hell?" Adam wiped tears from his eyes. "I thought you died!"

Vitania leaned down and kissed the other woman on the lips. "Spectacular, my love."

"Holy shit." Adam slumped against the door frame, hands trembling. "I thought she died. Why didn't anyone tell me that part of the plan?"

I was still in shock myself. "I didn't expect that either." I barely remained standing.

"How darling." Lumia knelt next to Adam and kissed his forehead. "You were really so concerned about my wellbeing?"

"I don't like it when good people die." Adam wiped at his face. "I'm glad you're okay."

"I created a dust illusion of myself," the Fae said. "It is a solid illusion that can be very convincing for a short period of time."

"It had me convinced." Adam blew out a shuddering breath. "Where in the world are Shelton and Elyssa?"

The faint susurrus of flying brooms caught my ears a moment later, and our friends circled in for a landing.

"What happened?" I asked.

"We landed behind the summoners and sneaked up on them," Shelton said. "But they were fake! Freaking store mannequins."

"Where are the demons?" Elyssa said.

"I sent them to Aquanis," Vitania said. "That should break the bond to their summoning patterns, and there's little they can do in the ocean depths until their bodies lose cohesion."

"Didn't you kill that one?" I pointed out the cooling stone head.

"Only that part of it," Vitania said. "The larger part survives and regrows whatever was lost. But it will have little time to regrow a head before it's banished back to Hell."

"You've said Hell twice," Adam said. "I take it that's not the same as Haedaemos?"

"It is a part of it," Vitania said. "Hell was once a physical place, and there was no Haedaemos. The Sundering changed all that."

"I'd really like to know who pulled off this stunt." Elyssa looked at the sun setting on the horizon. "Baal's infernus bodies can't summon demons as far as I know. Can Daemos summon hellfire demons?"

"Older, more powerful Daemos, yes." Vitania tapped a finger on her chin. "But I thought all the Daemos fought for Eden."

"There might be a few who don't." I hadn't given much thought to it until now, but House Wakahisa hadn't come to Seraphina with the rest of the army. In fact, they'd tricked Ivy into staying with them, probably at the behest of Victus Edison. Ivy didn't remember much about what happened before she ended up in a preservation chamber in an infernus foundry. But it stood to reason that Yuuki Wakahisa knew we were back. And they knew they wouldn't be welcomed back into the fold.

Elyssa said what I was thinking. "House Wakahisa worked with Victus Edison, so it's likely they've formed an alliance with Baal to protect themselves now that we've returned."

"There are other possibilities," Vitania said.

"Do you think—" Lumia abruptly looked up and shouted, "watch out!"

Vitania's mouth dropped open and a sonic wave shattered the air. I didn't know what in the hell was happening, but I knew it couldn't be good. Something outside exploded and the entire house trembled in the aftershock.

"Someone's firing on us!" Elyssa's light bow appeared in her hands and began unleashing arrow after arrow. "Who in the hell are they?"

I peered through a window. Twin white flames streaked overhead, a set of orange streaks pacing them. They arced to the ground and landed fifty yards away. A woman with wings of orange fire stood next to a man with pinions of Brilliance. I instantly recognized both of them and my guts twisted into knots.

I'd only met the woman once, but I remembered the face all too well. "My god, that's Emily Glass."

"And fucking Cain." Shelton's hand tightened around his compact staff.

"No, that is not Emily," Vitania said. "That is her half-sister Olivia."

"Oh, thank god!" I sighed in relief. "Man, I thought Emily went over to the dark side."

"Just in case you hadn't noticed, you ain't in no position to fight your evil twin today." Shelton flicked his staff out to full length. "I hope the Siren and Fae are up to snuff."

The flames in Olivia's hair died down, leaving bright orange locks. She said something to Cain and the pair burst into laughter.

Cain stroked his black goatee. "I think we look good with a beard, brother."

I scoffed. "What are you, my twin from the mirror universe?"

Vitania interrupted his response. "I take it you are responsible for our visitors tonight?"

"I take it you are responsible?" Olivia repeated her words in a mocking tone. "Duh, old lady. And we totally tricked you too."

"It was cute watching Shelton and Elyssa uncover our fakes," Cain said. His voice sounded just like mine, except a whole lot more condescending. His eyes lingered on Elyssa, a hint of longing in them.

What the hell? I wondered if my feelings for Elyssa had transferred into him when Baal split us apart.

Vitania pursed her lips and regarded them for a moment. "What was the point of your exercise, children? Your demons are vanquished, and you gloat over nothing."

Cain's eyes locked onto me. "You don't look well, brother. Did Elyssa wear you out in bed?"

"You jealous, Cain?" I steeled myself, trying to draw on my demon strength, only to find that Kalesh was nothing but a tiny speck in the back corner of my mind. *What's wrong with you?*

No response. My demon side was scared to death of Cain.

Olivia giggled. "That little girl wears him out in bed?" She smacked her ass and winked. "He couldn't handle a real woman."

I tried to come up with a witty response, but ended up staring blankly at Olivia. I didn't know a thing about this woman. Vitania and Lumia hadn't mentioned Emily having a sister.

Vitania tapped her foot on the ground, an impatient mother waiting for a response from children. "Again, I ask, what is the point of your exercise? Fighting me is futile."

The answer came to me out of the blue. "I'll tell you why they're here," I said. "Cain is Baal's right hand in Eden now. They don't want us getting help from Vitania or Lumia, so they're here to put a stop to it."

Cain clapped his hands. "I knew I got my smarts from somewhere, brother."

"You're not my brother, you sick jackass." My knees wanted to buckle but I somehow remained standing. "You'll be happy to know that Vitania and Lumia refused to fight with us. They don't give a rat's ass who's in charge."

"Sounds right." Olivia sneered. "They didn't lift a finger to help poor Emily after she left here. They don't care about anything or anyone but themselves."

Cain grinned and stroked his beard again. "Smart. Very smart." He stared at our group for a moment. "Let's just say that if we come back tomorrow and you're still here, we'll set loose hellfire demons on the little town over there. If you try to stop us, we'll pick another random city on this little shithole island."

"You wouldn't dare!" Elyssa said. "Not even Baal wants the noms to know about the supernatural."

"Don't worry. We're pretty good at covering it up." Olivia smirked and raised an eyebrow. "Well, what are you waiting for? Get the fuck out of here!"

"You will leave." Vitania's eyes flashed green. "My guests will be on their way momentarily."

"I'd prefer to wait," Olivia said.

Vitania began to sing.

Olivia covered her ears. Cain scowled and did the same. But I knew from experience that covering your ears did nothing to keep out the song. The pair started screaming and prancing around as if they'd fallen in a bed of fire ants. Their wings blazed to life and they jetted into the air, vanishing into the darkening sky.

"What song was that?" Shelton asked.

"A song you do not want to experience," Vitania said. Her lips peeled back from her teeth in a snarl. "I had not planned to help you very much, but those impetuous children changed my mind."

My hopes lifted. "You'll fight with us?"

She shook her head. "No, but I will find out what Dactia plans for the Sirens and request an audience. Though I have been gone from my people for a long while, they will still listen to their mother."

Even with her newfound helpfulness, I couldn't get my hopes up. I didn't know much about Olivia, but if her powers were anything like Emily's then she wielded great power over demons. With Cain as her partner in crime, our future promised to be bloody and filled with hellfire.

CHAPTER 11

F inding Emily Glass was more important than ever with her bat-shit crazy sister in the picture.

But I was worried big time after seeing Cain. My fake brother seemed to have picked up flying with no problem at all. Despite hours of practice, that was one skill I still hadn't learned. The best I could manage was the flying equivalent of the doggie-paddle—slow and silly looking. If he'd mastered that, I worried about how strong he might be in other areas.

"Why didn't you mention Emily had a sister earlier?" I asked Vitania. "She wasn't in the reports I read on the Demonicus Incident."

"She is not to be trifled with," Vitania said. "The girl bore tremendous hate in her heart when I first met her a decade ago. It has probably festered since then."

Shelton scratched his chin. "Mind explaining how's she's Emily's half-sister?"

Lumia exchanged a look with Vitania. The Siren seemed content to let the Fae answer. "Emily's mother, Victoria, has a twin sister named Lydia.

Lydia tricked Emily's father, Patrick, into bedding her. She hid the resulting pregnancy and gave up the child after birth."

"Holy shit." Shelton grimaced. "That's messed up!"

Lumia sighed. "Olivia was abused by foster parents. When her powers manifested, she found comfort in demons. She called herself the Infernal Blade, the weapon of the Netherlord."

"Netherlord?" Elyssa quirked an eyebrow. "Is that another name for Baal?"

"It is the old name for the lord of Hell in ancient times," Vitania said. "It's possible Baal took the name as a message to the other overlords."

"Tell me more about Olivia." Not only was I intrigued, but I wanted to know everything about this dangerous woman. "How did you meet her?"

"Stories can wait for another time." Vitania clasped her hands in front of her. "There are more urgent things to take care of and only six days left before your truce with Xanos ends. Believe me when I say there will be no peace talks. Whatever she truly plans will be devastating."

Shelton scoffed. "Geez, no need to beat it into our skulls."

Vitania switched subjects. "Lumia and I will speak with Pyra and Glacia. After we have secured support from them, we will go to Aquilis and gain an audience with Dactia. When we are ready, we will contact you."

I leaned against Elyssa for support. "We'll pick up Emily's trail and see where it leads. Sounds like Fjoeruss might have some breadcrumbs to follow—provided we can find him."

Vitania traced a pattern in the air and a portal opened. A massive oak tree stood on the other side.

"You remembered!" Lumia rubbed the other woman's arm. "I wondered where you would open the portal."

"It was a good day." Vitania smiled as if remembering something. "How could I forget?"

I was a bit curious about their inside conversation, but Elyssa began marching us to the portal. Adam leaned on Shelton for support and they made for the gateway ahead of us.

Lumia stepped in front of them and caressed Adam's cheek. "You are an intelligent and gentle soul. I see now how even the gods still find themselves drawn to mortals."

Adam gulped. "Gods?"

Her four-foot frame grew until she stood only slightly shorter than Adam. While Shelton watched in wide-eyed amazement, Lumia gave Adam a kiss I'm sure he wouldn't soon forget.

Elyssa sighed. "Since the invention of the kiss, there have been five kisses that have been rated the most passionate, the most pure. This one left them all behind."

I chuckled. "Hey, I thought our kisses did that."

She nipped my ear. "We can always try to beat this one."

Adam sagged when Lumia left him. "Wow, I don't know what to say."

"Well deserved, mortal." Vitania patted his head as if he were a puppy. "Lumia rarely grants favor to mortals, especially not men."

"But, aren't you a couple?" Shelton said.

Vitania smiled fondly. "After centuries together, we are far more than that." She made a shooing motion with her hands. "Now, go, children."

The portal winked away the moment we were through. We stood in a thick forest, mountains all around us. I took out Nookli and pulled up the map. "We're in the Blue Ridge Mountains."

"Nice spot," Elyssa said. "But not exactly close to Decatur." She took a picture and sent a text to the Templars at the omniarch near the mansion. A moment later, a portal opened in front of us.

The Templars in the omniarch room looked a bit concerned when Elyssa practically carried me past them. It was all I could do to stay awake as she guided me across the last twenty yards to the mansion. The last thing I remembered was flopping down on the bed.

SIX MORE DAYS UNTIL DOOMSDAY.

I rolled out of the fart sack early the next morning feeling pretty good, considering how much I'd strained myself the day before. Shelton had pancakes, bacon, and eggs heaped on the table by the time I got to the kitchen.

He looked at me and scratched his chin. "Growing a beard?"

I rubbed my scruff. "Hell no. Cain's got enough douche factor for the both of us."

"How's the magical mojo?" Shelton looked a little worried. "Feeling better?"

I summoned an orb of Brilliance in my right hand and sensed no pain or abnormal pressures in my head. "I think I'm back to normal. I guess years of pushing myself to the limit finally paid off."

Shelton bit off a piece of bacon and nodded. "Sure be handy if you could open portals, but not if it's gonna put you out of commission."

Elyssa stepped into the kitchen, raven hair hanging damp around her shoulders. She buttered a piece of bread and sat down next to me. "We've got a problem."

"You mean besides Xanos, Baal, and insane siblings?" Shelton said.

Elyssa took a bite of her bread and nodded. "Exactly."

I put a stack of pancakes on my plate. "What problem are you referring to?"

"We don't know how to find Fjoeruss." She tapped on her arcphone and projected a holographic list of companies. "These seven companies were owned indirectly by Gray Fusion, one of Fjoeruss's holding companies. But they were all sold off and Gray Fusion no longer exists. It appears he made some major changes during the decade we were gone."

"Hardly surprising." Shelton munched on more bacon. "Does he have anything in the Atlanta area?"

"He took me to China the one time he kidnapped me." I poured a cup of OJ. "He's got companies everywhere."

"Well, even if we can't find him, we can look up Emily's family members." Elyssa flicked over to another screen and typed in *Patrick Glass*. The image flickered and returned an answer: *MIA. Operation unlisted.*

Shelton frowned. "What the hell does that mean?"

"It means he went missing during a black ops mission." Elyssa scowled. "Only his handler would know the real operation details."

I pointed to a number at the top of the file. "That's the date right?"

"Yes. Nearly eight years ago." Elyssa shook her head. "Two strikes. Let's hope the last query isn't a swing and a miss too." She typed in *George Walker*. The database repeated the same answer. *MIA. Operation unlisted.*

"Gee, let me guess." Shelton slapped a hand on the table. "He went missing on the same mission."

"The dates match," Elyssa said. "Strike three."

"We're not out yet." I pinched the bridge of my nose as if that would help me think better. I tried to picture the office Fjoeruss had taken me to during my first visit, but while a general image formed, it wasn't enough to guarantee a portal would open.

Adam stumbled into the kitchen, his thick hair sticking up every which way, and dark circles beneath his eyes. "Is this what a zombie feels like?" He slumped into a chair. "I feel like I got hit by a truck and then it backed up and ran me over again."

"You look like it too." Shelton poured his friend a cup of coffee and pushed it over to him. "Drink up, man. This'll get you feeling right as rain in no time."

Adam gulped the coffee and sighed in relief. He noticed the database query projecting from Elyssa's phone. "What's that about?"

"Trying to find someone, anyone connected to Emily Glass." Elyssa snatched an apple from the fruit dish and chomped on it like an angry animal.

Adam made a thoughtful grunt. "I thought Fjoeruss was our first stop."

"He would be, but he sold off his businesses." Elyssa flicked to the screen with the company names.

Adam glanced at the names and nodded. "Company names aren't really important. What matters is that Fjoeruss owns physical property that can't easily be sold off to noms."

I snapped my fingers. "Yeah, the company he took me to in China had an Obsidian Arch beneath it. He wouldn't sell off property like that."

Adam nodded. "Back during my hacker days, I used to track down Overworld companies that posed as nom corporations so I could buy things that weren't strictly legal." He took another sip of coffee. "Most of them were pretty small, dealing in black market spells and such. But then I stumbled onto one of Fjoeruss's conglomerates. At the time, I didn't know who it belonged to, and I didn't care. I wasn't about to poke my nose into that business."

"Good thinking," Shelton said. "You probably would've lost more than your nose."

"No doubt." Adam stared into his coffee. "They owned a building in

Atlanta. I'd be willing to bet it's another structure he wouldn't just sell off."

Elyssa bit the inside of her lip. "Let's say he still owns it. How are we supposed to find it?"

"By using our eyes, of course." Adam made binoculars with his hands. "We just fly around the city and look for a building with heavy wards on it."

"Fjoeruss ain't no amateur," Shelton said. "Any Arcane worth a damn knows how to camouflage their wards and he's an old-school Seraphim who knows what he's doing. The point to having wards is to not advertise they're there. We'd have to fly close to every building and scan them. It'd take days."

"Normally that would be true. But we have a secret weapon." Adam looked at me. "Our very own half-Daemos, half-Seraphim."

It took a moment for me to realize what he meant. "Oh, yeah. I can see buildings with aether concentrations around them." Magical energy, aether, flowed through leylines in the ground and drifted in the air all around us. Except in extremely high concentrations like those found in Seraphina, aether was invisible. As a Daemos, I could see people's auras and their soul essence. Something about the way that ability interacted with my Seraphim powers allowed me to see aether.

I shifted my focus to demon vision. Ghostly halos faded into view around my friends. Little cloudlets of white, purple, and gray aether drifted through the air all around us. If I channeled magical power, I'd suck up the free aether like a vacuum cleaner.

Shelton seemed to know I was testing my ability and pointed to the pantry. "I put a ward on there to stop people from stealing my cookies. Do you see it?"

"No wonder I can never find the cookies," Adam grumbled. "I put a bag of Fig Newtons in there last week and they vanished."

Elyssa tutted. "Hiding other people's cookies from them, Shelton? That's low even for you."

I glanced around the pantry door and spotted a faint knot of Cyrinthian code. "I see it."

"Excellent," Adam said. "If you can see that, then spotting wards from a distance shouldn't be a problem."

"I thought you guys had spells that could see wards," Elyssa said.

"Yes, but they have to be used in very close proximity," Adam said. "Justin's demon sight allows him to see from a distance. I have a pair of magnifying spectacles that should allow him to decipher wards from several hundred yards away."

"Maybe so, but where in the hell do we start looking?" Shelton said. "There are thousands of company buildings in Atlanta."

Elyssa grunted. "Downtown, Midtown, or Buckhead, of course. There are major leylines running beneath those parts of the city, not to mention the tallest, fanciest buildings in town."

I swallowed a mouthful of pancakes. "Then let's get on it. We don't have time to waste." I polished off my eggs and bacon then went up to my room to shower and get ready.

Shelton, Adam, and Elyssa were already waiting at the bottom of the stairs when I came out.

I gave them a stern look. "Did everyone go potty before we leave? I don't want our mission interrupted because somebody has to go tinkle."

Adam saluted. "Bladder is empty, sir."

"What is this, a long car ride with my parents?" Shelton scoffed. "Be right back."

"Don't forget to wash your hands," Elyssa called after him.

"Lift the toilet seat," Adam said.

Shelton stuck out his tongue. "Don't tell me what to do!"

When he got back, we went to the omniarch room and portaled to the underground garage at the Ranch. Elyssa texted a status update to her father since he was in a meeting, and we took one of the black sedans parked near the ramp. Elyssa hopped in the driver's seat and I took shotgun. Adam and Shelton got cozy in the back. We drove up the ramp and out of the barn, then Elyssa activated the camouflage and took the car into the air.

There wasn't a cloud in the bright blue sky and very little haze, despite the clogged traffic below us. That was both good and bad. Visibility was great for the task at hand, but it also meant that if our camouflage failed, thousands of people would see a flying car. Thankfully, the power sources in Templar cars had improved in our absence.

Shelton grunted. "This car was made by Arc Corp, also known as Tiberius Industries. Are the Templars really buying from that wannabe dictator?"

"Xander donated them." Elyssa met his gaze in the rear-view mirror. "He knows enough to stay in our good graces."

Shelton scoffed. "He's barking up the wrong tree if he thinks bribing Thomas Borathen is gonna get him anywhere."

Elyssa headed for Midtown since it was closest to us. I shifted to demon sight and held a pair of spectacles to my eyes for a closer look. Dozens of wards surrounded a purple Victorian-style house in a residential neighborhood. Without the spectacles, they would've looked like webs of glowing lines. With the spectacles, I could zoom in far enough to make out individual lines of code. These particular wards were designed to keep vampires away.

More wards glowed around a beige brick building a few blocks down. I zoomed in with the spectacles and examined the symbols. They were just simple alarm wards, probably set by an Arcane who didn't want to be bothered with a nom alarm company.

I spotted dozens of warded houses and commercial buildings in the neighborhoods below. Most were alarm wards, but many seemed set to capture or repel specific kinds of supers. "I never realized so many Arcanes lived in these parts." I blinked out of demon vision.

"It was safer out here than in the Grotto and other pocket cities," Elyssa said. "At least until Razor began hunting supers."

Shelton huffed. "Yeah, the whole Overworld went to shit while we were away."

With so many warded buildings to examine, this could take days. And time was something we didn't have.

CHAPTER 12

I face-palmed. "My god, this is going to take forever!"

"Don't be so dramatic," Elyssa said.

"I wouldn't worry about scanning small buildings." Adam gave my shoulder a comforting pat. "Fjoeruss probably owns a high-rise." He pointed to the tall buildings on the horizon. "Do you see anything there?"

I shifted focus back to demon vision and peered through the spectacles. Glowing webs of magic surrounded three of the tallest buildings. I zoomed in, but we were still too far away for even the spectacles to make sense of the code. "To answer your question, I see a lot more than expected." I shifted my view toward downtown, but the bright sunlight made it impossible to see if there were any wards on the buildings there.

"How many buildings are warded?" Shelton said.

I told him what I saw. "That doesn't count dozens of little buildings in between. I'm beginning to think there must be an Arcane running an alarm business in town."

"Back in our day that was illegal," Shelton said. "But the supers will play when the Templars are away."

Elyssa groaned. "There's not a shred of order anymore. It's going to take years just to get everything back under control."

"Provided Xanos or Baal don't kill us," Adam said.

Elyssa swooped toward the high-rise buildings I mentioned and flew around them. Two of the buildings were condominiums, mostly protected by alarm wards and illusions designed to hide the balconies. We didn't fly close enough to see through the illusions and moved on to the corporate office building. What had looked like wards there were maintenance charms that kept the windows and building clean.

I described what I saw.

Adam grunted. "Arcanes must be racking up some serious dough."

"Just when I thought we'd be on easy street with Justin's demon sight." Shelton blew out a breath. "Now every Tom, Dick, and Harry's running illegal magic services. Next thing you know we'll see ads about wizard detectives in the yellow pages."

"Anything else?" Elyssa asked.

I shook my head and she headed south to downtown. When we closed to within a mile, I spotted more warded buildings than I could count. The long groan that ground out of my throat was more than enough to let everyone know this wasn't going to be a walk in the park.

It took an hour to scan the buildings at the edge of downtown. Elyssa parked the car on a helipad to let the aether batteries recharge while I used the spectacles to scope out more skyscrapers. It was time for lunch before I was even halfway done, so we went to a nearby restaurant for some hot eats and cool treats.

"There are way too many warded buildings." I munched on a French fry and stared out the window at the snarled downtown traffic. "Down-town is going to take days to clear."

"Maybe we're doing this the wrong way," Adam said. "So far, all you've found were basic Arcane wards, right?"

"Cleaning wards, alarm wards, repulsion wards, and even some bug zapper wards." I sighed. "Fjoeruss's building is another needle in another haystack."

Adam fiddled with his phone and scrunched his lips. "Maybe not." He turned the screen so I could see it. Layers upon layers of glowing symbols scrolled down the screen. They were so dense, I had trouble making heads or tails of them.

"What in the hell is that?" I said.

"This is the code Mzodi used to enchant a gem." Adam set down his phone. "It's complex beyond belief. That's why it took so long for me and Shelton to hack gems."

"Talk about headaches." Shelton massaged his forehead. "Even the door gems were a pain in the ass."

"What's your point?" I said.

Adam stirred his ketchup with a French fry. "My point is Arcane wards are like stick figures drawn in crayon compared to Seraphim wards. I think we can just perform a cursory scan of the buildings until we find one with code so complex it sticks out from the others."

"And if you're wrong?" Shelton said.

Adam shrugged. "If I'm wrong, we just go back to doing it the hard way."

"So the search might take hours instead of days." Elyssa nodded. "I think it's worth the risk."

"Then let's get back to it." I dropped some cash on the table to cover the bill, and we went back outside to the car.

Elyssa found a vacant alley, activated camouflage, and took us up, up, and away. She consulted a map and started in the southeast quadrant near Grady Memorial Hospital. Then she followed the grid pattern of the roads below. I shifted to demon vision and scanned each side of the road with the spectacles.

Once again, I found more warded buildings than I could count, but none of them were complex enough to be Seraphim wards. We finished downtown in three hours without finding a thing.

Elyssa stared down at the city and blew out a breath. "I hope we didn't miss anything."

Adam pointed toward high-rises on the near horizon. "Buckhead is next."

Shelton hadn't said much for the past hour, seemingly content to browse the internet on his phone. I couldn't blame him. This felt hopeless. What if Fjoeruss didn't have anything worth keeping in Atlanta? What if he'd packed up shop and moved on?

"Bingo!" Shelton slapped the back of my seat and made everyone except Elyssa jump.

"What is wrong with you?" I turned in my seat. "Are you playing bingo on your phone?"

He held his phone so I could see it. "I think I narrowed down the search."

I took the phone and read aloud an article titled: *Pilots Report Strange Sightings in Buckhead*. "Jerry Baskins flies into Peachtree DeKalb Airport on a regular basis. He's not one to believe in aliens or the supernatural, but he'll be the first one to claim seeing strange objects in the skies of Buckhead."

"Can you summarize?" Elyssa said.

"Allow me." Shelton took back his phone. "Several pilots reported seeing an impossibly tall skyscraper in Buckhead two years ago during a major lightning storm while they were waiting for clearance to land at a small airport northeast of Buckhead. They said it was so tall it went into the clouds. But then it vanished." Shelton wiggled his fingers. "Just like magic."

Adam peered at the Buckhead skyline a few miles ahead. "I don't see anything indicative of camouflage."

I shifted to demon vision and held up the spectacles, but didn't see anything except a bit of haze. "Nothing." I turned to Elyssa. Her eyes flicked back and forth across the horizon. "See anything?"

"No."

Shelton scooted to the middle of the back seat and leaned between the front seats. I turned so I could see him. His eyes twitched back and forth, giving him a slightly crazy look. Adam's looked even more insane, almost rolling in his head. It was so odd that it gave me pause.

I turned back around and forced my eyes to look straight ahead.

Elyssa snorted. "Your eyes are going crazy, Justin. Something wrong?"

"Are they flicking back and forth?" I asked.

"Yeah."

Adam snapped his fingers. "An avoidance ward, and a powerful one at that."

"You gotta be kidding me." Shelton's face screwed up in concentration. "I can usually beat an avoidance ward by forcing myself to find it. But that ain't working."

"It's probably a cocktail of various wards, all woven by a master of trickery." Adam flattened his lips into a look of grudging respect. "Powerful enough to hide an impossibly tall building on a cloudless day."

"But it's not camouflage?" I said.

"It might use camouflage as well, but I'll bet the avoidance ward is to prevent planes and birds from flying into the building." Adam bit the inside of his lip. "Do you see wards on many of the high-rises, Justin?"

I scanned with the spectacles and began counting. "Fifteen so far."

"Mhm." Adam pushed a finger up his nose. "Now tell me, are there any tall buildings without wards?"

I pointed them out. "That really tall one with all the dark windows, and a couple of those hotels."

"That's it, guaranteed." Shelton indicated the first one. "Fly us over the roof."

Elyssa headed toward it. It seemed like I'd just blinked my eyes and suddenly we were on the other side of the building and headed away from it. Elyssa flinched as if realizing the same thing. She spun the car around and hovered in place. "I don't remember passing the building."

"Yep, that's the one." Adam looked above it, but his eyes started twitching again. "This is industrial strength protection. I don't know if there's a way for us to see through the ward or not."

"I've got a better idea," Adam said. He leaned between the seats and tapped on the car's touchscreen console. "Since we can't beat the ward, let's see if it affects the car."

"You're programming in an auto-drive route by hand?" Shelton snorted. "Just make sure we don't crash into the building."

"Maybe we could just go into the lobby and ask for Fjoeruss," Elyssa said.

Adam stopped what he was doing. "Um, maybe you're right. Repro-gramming the auto-drive could take a while."

"Keep it simple, stupid." Shelton pulled Adam back by his shirt. "Let's not overthink things."

Elyssa landed in an alley and turned off the camouflage. It took us ten minutes to drive three blocks back to the building, but of course there was nowhere to park on the street.

"I'll stay with the car," Adam said. "I'll program in the route just in case this doesn't work."

"I don't think that'll be a problem." Shelton pointed to a group of men in gray suits exiting the front door. Each one wore their gray hair slicked back. But only one of them resembled Fjoeruss.

"Are those gray men?" Elyssa stopped the car and stared at them. "Their skin isn't gray."

Judging from the dead looks in their gray eyes, I knew without a doubt what they were. "Park here," I said.

The gray men were some of the most lifelike golems I'd seen. Infernus were even more lifelike, but they weren't exactly golems by the standard definition. The gray man that looked like Fjoeruss stopped outside the car and waited, its dead eyes staring at us.

I got out and stepped up to it. "I need to see Fjoeruss. It's vitally important."

My friends got out of the car even though it was illegally parked.

A couple of normal pedestrians gave us dirty looks, as if we thought we were something special just leaving our car parked in the middle of the side road.

One of the gray men climbed into the driver's seat. Elyssa tapped her arcphone to activate the car, and the golem drove it away. Then the first gray man turned and walked toward the building, flanked by his companions.

The secretary in the front lobby didn't bat an eyelash as we walked past with our escorts, and the security guards didn't even bother to scan us with their paddle scanners. We got into an elevator and the doors closed behind us. According to the buttons, the elevator was fifty stories tall. But the elevator shot upward without anyone touching a button.

We traveled so fast that the floor number above the elevator door could barely keep up. The moment we passed fifty, the walls shimmered and turned into windows, giving us a spectacular view of the city. By the time the elevator slowed, we were at least a hundred stories higher than the closest building. I could practically see the curve of the horizon.

"Ought to bring some flat-earthers up here," Shelton mumbled.

Adam snorted. "That would be funny."

The doors slid open to reveal an empty office that looked very similar to the one I'd visited so long ago. The golems stepped out and we followed. Without a word, the golems went back into the elevator and the doors closed.

I walked over to the window and took in the view. It was like being on top of the world.

Adam whistled. "My god. I can't imagine the wards that keep this place hidden. They must draw a tremendous amount of power." He slapped his forehead. "You know what? We could've found this place by tracking powers surges in the leylines."

"Would've taken just as long," Shelton said. "Guaranteed."

"I disagree." Adam tapped on his phone. "By modifying this power amplification spell, I could search for extreme variances in aether levels. That would—"

The elevator opened and a man in a dark gray suit stepped out. Fjoeruss looked every bit as stony-faced as I remembered him from the last time. If anything, he looked a bit irritated. I wished I could be sure it was the real Fjoeruss, because the first time we'd met, he carried on a big charade by posing as a golem named Lornicus while using a gray man to play the part as Fjoeruss.

I'd fallen for it, hook, line, and sinker, only figuring it out much later. But since I didn't have any easy way to confirm his identity without tearing off an arm or something, I decided to hope for the best.

"Fjoeruss, I presume?" I gave him a suspicious look. "Or are you a golem?"

"It's really me, Mr. Slade." Fjoeruss's gaze drifted across the room. "It took you longer than expected to return to Eden. I had given up on ever seeing you again."

"Did you really care, Grandad?" While in Seraphina, I'd learned that Fjoeruss might be my great-great grandfather. Between him and Baal, holiday gatherings were going to be real interesting.

He raised an eyebrow. "I see you learned about your heritage while you were there."

"And that you might even be the first Seraphim ever." I shrugged. "It's not such a big deal in the grand scheme of things, but with my birthday coming up, I was kind of hoping you could come to the party at Chuck. E. Cheese."

Fjoeruss didn't crack a smile. "I'm glad you found your way back, Mr. Slade. Is there something I can help you with?"

I knew damned well that he knew about Xanos and probably about Baal. But he wasn't one to give away information for free. He wanted me to be the one to confirm that I knew that he knew about the secret war raging for the realms.

Whatever. I refused to play his game. "We're looking for Emily Glass. Last I heard, she was in your employ."

Fjoeruss raised an eyebrow. "You're remarkably well informed for someone who's been absent a decade."

"We tracked down Vitania and Lumia," I said. "It's vital we find Emily."

"It seems you're on another mission to save the world, Mr. Slade." Fjoeruss clasped his hands behind his back. "I'm not so keen to help you this time."

And just like that, it felt like the bad old days all over again.

CHAPTER 13

"You don't care if Xanos controls Eden?" I said. "You really think it'll be business as usual?"

Fjoeruss's poker face didn't give away much, but the twitch in his right eye was enough to tell me that I'd just surprised the hell out of him.

"Hold on—you don't know about Xanos?" I could hardly believe it. "I could have charged you a buck oh five for that information."

"Xanos is in the Abyss," Fjoeruss said. "She's no threat."

"Wow." I took a moment to appreciate his ignorance. "You are way behind on this one, bro. Xanos has been free for the past decade. I accidentally freed her during a battle against Daelissa's forces. I thought you knew."

"I recall you unleashed an Abyssal demon, but not one of the Apocryphan." Fjoeruss's forehead pinched. "What proof do you have?"

"Well," I said, "I've got her driver's license in my pocket and pictures of her stealing candy from babies."

His gaze hardened. "No games, Mr. Slade."

"Fine." I took out my arcphone. "This should be all the proof you need." I played him video recorded during Xanos's visit to the Templar compound. "She took over that old lady's body, but if you listen carefully, you can hear her many voices."

Fjoeruss watched intently for the entire duration. Then he put a hand to his chin and stared out of the window for a long time before speaking again. "So, an Apocryphan controls Razor. I've always kept a close eye on the anti-supernatural agencies, but none of them were a threat until now. Razor's technology is formidable, and now I know why. The designs come from the mind of a demigod."

"And the part about Baal?" I said. "He wants to smash all the realms back into one Earth."

"That would explain other things." He didn't look back. "Such as why relics of Juranthemon have suddenly gone missing from collections. Two years ago, one of my secret vaults was breached. Millions of dollars in valuables was untouched, but two dangerous relics were taken."

"The theory is that if enough Relics of Jura are put in close proximity, they'll recombine to form Juranthemon and pull the realms back together." I wasn't at all reassured to learn that even Fjoeruss's relics weren't safe. "Will you help us find Emily?"

Elyssa narrowed her eyes. "Or would you prefer to deal with Xanos or Baal?"

"I could deal with Xanos." Fjoeruss tapped a finger on his chin. "An Apocryphan would be very useful."

"Useful?" In all my dealings with Fjoeruss, there was one thing I still hadn't figured out. Why was an ancient Seraphim content to be a poser businessman? He had incredible powers, but he seemed every bit as detached as Underborn, always willing to do whatever kept him in business. "What's your endgame, Fjoeruss?" I waved a hand toward the blue skies outside. "What makes you want to get out of bed every morning?"

He turned and a smile crept across his face. "That's the first intelligent question you've asked since arriving here, Mr. Slade. As a reward, I'll answer."

Shelton and Adam exchanged a confused look. I tried not to look as surprised as I felt.

"I'm all ears," I said.

The Seraphim pointed out into the blue. "There is more—so much more than this world and its realms. There is an entire universe and multiverse out there and right here. Somewhere in all this vastness exist the old gods. I seek their knowledge. I want to know what lies beyond my reach. I want to experience something new. But physical and technological limitations are the banes to my aspirations."

"Holy shit." Shelton whistled. "You just want to understand the universe like everyone else."

"Not even Science Academy has the technology to breach interdimensional barriers," Adam said. "They also can't make spaceships that travel fast enough to make long-distance space travel feasible."

"I am responsible for much of the tech at Science Academy," Fjoeruss said. "Who do you think paid for research and development?"

"So that explains your business models." I clapped my hands together. "Now that you know about Xanos, you wonder if she might have answers."

"An Apocryphan might know more about the universe, but would she help or enslave me?" Fjoeruss turned from the window. "And while Razor's technology is impressive, perhaps Xanos does not have all the answers either, or she would have already conquered this realm."

"We might not have the answers you want, but we're your best chance to keep an apocalypse from wiping out your empire," I said. "Because if Xanos doesn't do it you can bet that Baal will."

"I have pushed the limits of what is possible for centuries." Fjoeruss almost sounded a little sad. "I have orchestrated world-changing events and prevented others from happening. But this might be the endgame, Mr. Slade." Fjoeruss looked out the window again. "I'm not sure what you hope to accomplish by finding Emily Glass."

"I'd like to exchange information, Fjoeruss." I dropped onto a white leather divan and tried to act like I knew what I was doing. "I think I've already earned information pertaining to Emily."

Fjoeruss nodded. "The Demonicus Incident infuriated the demon over-lord, Domathus. He put a price on Miss Glass's head. I helped fake her death with the stipulation she return to work for me, rooting out demon agents within my companies."

"Why would someone infiltrate your companies with demons?" I asked.

Fjoeruss took a seat behind his desk. "Grays also went missing."

"You mean your gray men golems?" I asked.

He nodded. "I later discovered someone stole them as part of something called the Infernus Project. Someone wanted to find a way for demons to inhabit golems."

Shelton whistled. "How long ago was that?"

"Over ten years ago." Fjoeruss pursed his lips. "Only a few years ago, I discovered working prototypes posing as employees."

"We encountered infernus in Seraphina," I said. "Victus Edison developed them for Baal."

The Seraphim nodded. "Miss Glass was in my employ for over two years. She also worked with the Custodians in her spare time. By the time she completed her contract with me, we had purged over four hundred demonic agents from my companies."

"Were they all involved in the Infernus Project?" Adam asked.

"No." Fjoeruss idly tapped a finger on his desk. "It seems someone else took an interest in my research into interdimensional and space travel.

Most of the demons didn't know who they worked for. Miss Glass was only able to pry names from a few of them."

I hazarded a guess. "Baal?"

He nodded. "One of my theories is that so long as Earth is divided into realms, we are cut off from interdimensional travel. The quantum tunnels connecting the realms are tangled with those that would lead to other dimensions."

Adam's thumbs tapped furiously on his phone. "That goes hand in hand with articles I've read on the Einstein Rosen bridge theory. Because of quantum entanglement among the realms, formations of wormholes to other dimensions are impossible."

Fjoeruss raised an eyebrow. "It seems you're better versed on the subject than most."

Adam beamed. "I love this stuff."

"Project Rift was intended to make a device that would open portals between dimensions." Fjoeruss projected an image from his arcphone and zoomed in. "But the facility blew up in a freak accident several months ago and I don't know if it's worth reviving."

Elyssa and I stared at the image, mouths hanging open. A large white ring segmented by black bands hung in the center of a vast warehouse. It was identical to what we'd seen in Thunder Rock.

"I don't think it was an accident," I said. "Because we saw that exact device in Thunder Rock."

"Xanos stole your device," Elyssa said. "And she's using it to open portals to other realms."

Fjoeruss's jaw clenched and his eyes flashed white. "I am beset on all sides by those who would conquer the world."

I did my best not to sigh impatiently and returned to the matter at hand. "Do you know where Emily Glass is?"

He clasped his hands in front of him. "She and Mr. Rock planned to disappear since certain demonic agents discovered she was still alive." Fjoeruss paused as if considering something. "I thought it wise to keep track of her in case I needed her services again. Mr. Rock was particularly fond of my cars, so I gave him one. They used it to travel the world for a time, but then it remained in one place without moving for weeks."

Just when I'd started to hope he knew their whereabouts, my heart dropped. "You lost them."

"They were in Dubai in a hotel room paid two months in advance." Fjoeruss shook his head. "The car was there. All their clothing and suitcases were in the room, unpacked and in drawers. But Miss Glass and Mr. Rock were gone."

"Do you think they figured out you were tracking them?" Elyssa said.

"Perhaps, but why leave all your belongings?" Fjoeruss shook his head again. "Only a faint, lingering odor remained. And there were burn marks on the carpet."

"Odor?" I said. "What odor?"

"Brimstone."

"Shit!" Shelton slapped the back of a chair. "Demon assassins finally got them."

"I'm not certain." Fjoeruss removed an arctablet from the drawer in his desk and swiped on the screen. He found what he was looking for and projected the video recording of a fancy hotel suite complete with foyer, large bedroom, and a bathroom with hot tub and huge shower.

The video lingered on faint black marks on the carpet. Burn marks marred the walls. The camera panned around the room, stopped, and swung back to something lying on the bed. A hand reached out and picked up a rainbow-hued flower that looked as if it had been cut from a bush. A faint glow emanated from the petals.

"Is that a bioluminescent flower?" Adam said.

"It's a clue," Fjoeruss said. "A flower that doesn't exist in Eden and certainly not in Haedaemos."

Relief began to displace the panic building in me. "So they somehow escaped to another realm?"

"That's my theory. Miss Glass didn't tell me much about what happened during the two weeks before she came to work for me, but she was a much different person than the one who came to me for help." Fjoeruss turned off the video. "I suspect she may have discovered a portal device."

I knew exactly what it was. *Emily Glass can open portals to other realms!* But which realm had she gone to? It took a lot of willpower not to mention Emily's powers. I believed in sharing information for the good of everyone, but Fjoeruss simply didn't work that way.

"I feel like we've been through this before, Fjoeruss." I studied his expression, but there were no cracks in his demeanor to betray his thoughts. "Unless you want to see everything you've worked for destroyed, you should help us."

"There is little question I must do something," Fjoeruss said.

Shelton grunted. "A whole lot of something, or everything we fought for is going away."

"The Overworld has been in turmoil since you left for Seraphina," Fjoeruss said. "Victus Edison brought the entire system crashing down and it has yet to recover. How do you plan to fight a war with no infrastructure?"

Fjoeruss was evaluating his options. Baal and Xanos might be unsavory options, but Team Justin was the underdog by a long shot. I sensed a whole lot of calculations going on in the Seraphim's shrewd mind. Whatever I said next might make or break an important alliance.

"When you fought with us in the Second Seraphim War, you did your part and went right back to business as usual." I waved a hand around at the office. "Nothing really changed for you. But if you choose Xanos or

Baal, you won't be working *with* them, you'll be working *for* them. They will use you and discard you because they don't care about anything except themselves."

"I can see you've somehow retained your naïve optimism." Fjoeruss pursed his lips. "Did nothing jade you in the past ten years?"

"Oh, plenty of awful stuff happened." I looked at Elyssa, Shelton, and Adam. "But I have the best friends in the universe. They've dragged me back from the cliffs of despair more times than I can count. We never gave up even when the odds weren't in our favor." I turned my gaze on Fjoeruss. "You can bet that we won't give up on Eden whether you're on our side or not."

"Unbridled optimism." The Seraphim still didn't look convinced. "I will think about it and get back to you."

"You have a solid infrastructure," Elyssa said. "Your companies span the world, and I'd be willing to bet you've got an army of grays at your disposal. If we had you to help us rebuild the Overworld and reclaim our cities from Razor, then we might have a fighting chance."

Fjoeruss tilted his head slightly and stared at her for a moment. "Razor holds seventy-two percent of Overworld cities. Eighty percent of the Overworld population is in Queens Gate. Xanos has effectively contained you and your army. How do you propose to overcome such a massive disadvantage?"

"We agreed to a one-week ceasefire with Xanos so she can supposedly consider an alliance against Baal," Elyssa said. "We know better than to believe her."

I nodded. "We're strong enough to hold her off in Queens Gate, but don't have the resources to take back other cities. Even so, we've been poking and prodding her defenses, trying to figure out what she's up to."

"The truce is to buy her time so she can complete an objective without your interference," Fjoeruss said. "She hopes to hit a power spike by the end of the truce so she can wipe you out once and for all."

"That's what we think," Elyssa said. "But if we were to bring in new allies, we could foil her plans."

"What other allies?" Fjoeruss said. "Did you bring the Brightling army from Seraphina?"

"We reunited the Brightlings and Darklings and created a new empire," I said. "So, yes, we do have a Seraphim army, but it's been whittled down over the last decade by constant battles with Baal and his dragon army."

Fjoeruss's eye twitched again. "You reunited the factions?"

I tried not to smile at the surprise in his voice. "We accomplished a lot in Seraphina until Baal came around and ruined everything." I held out my hands in a welcoming gesture. "So what do you say? Are you on the team?"

Fjoeruss turned and stared out the window. "I'm sorry, but I won't help you."

CHAPTER 14

My happy balloon popped and my hopes plummeted. Gaining Fjoeruss as an ally was absolutely critical.

Elyssa wasn't ready to give up just yet. "What if I told you we've also begun negotiations with the Sirens and the Fae?"

Fjoeruss turned back around. "You found the Fae?"

"You wouldn't believe who all we've found." I shrugged. "But I guess none of that matters, right?"

His lips pressed into a flat line. "Perhaps I should visit Queens Gate and evaluate the situation before making a decision."

My hopes lifted ever so slightly. "That would be smart."

"Let me give you the symbols for the gatekeeper." Elyssa held up her arcphone. "They can open a portal for you whenever you're ready. I'll also tell Commander Borathen to expect you."

Fjoeruss slipped an arcphone from his pocket and bumped it against Elyssa's to transfer the symbols. "Very well, then." He walked around his desk and sat down. "I'm sorry I couldn't help you find Miss Glass."

"Every bread crumb helps," I said. "Did you question hotel staff or find any other clues?"

"I'll transfer everything I have." Fjoeruss held out the arctablet with the video to Elyssa. "I haven't devoted many resources to the investigation since there was little to be gained from locating Miss Glass."

"There's a whole lot more at stake than you can imagine," I said. I hated giving away more free information, but it might light a fire under his ass to start helping us. "Emily is apparently a lot more powerful than anyone realized. She has the ability to open portals into other realms without an arch."

Fjoeruss stared blankly at me for a moment. "Impossible. Miss Glass has unique abilities, but nothing to suggest rift magic."

"That's probably how she vanished from the hotel room." I held out my hands helplessly. "But we have no idea where she went and no way to follow her."

"I don't think you understand what this means," Fjoeruss said. "Even I cannot open a portal to another realm. Only the ancient gods were capable of that. There is perhaps only one person who is capable of such a feat, and that would be Vitania of the Sirens."

Shelton opened his mouth, but Adam elbowed him before he could blurt out anything.

Fjoeruss's eyes narrowed. "I sense there's a great deal you're not telling me."

"That's for damned sure." I tapped my temple. "What I've got up here is enough to blow your mind." It felt pretty damned good having the edge for once.

"Perhaps we can come to an arrangement," Fjoeruss said. "My help for more information."

I shook my head. "Once you think about everything, you'll realize that you've got no choice but to help us." I hoped I wasn't overplaying my hand, but Fjoeruss really had nowhere else to go if he wanted to keep the status quo. "If you have other information that's useful, then we can consider a trade."

"I was wrong, Mr. Slade." Fjoeruss clasped his hands in front of him. "Perhaps you're no longer that naïve boy I remember."

"I might be optimistic, but I'm not stupid." I turned to Elyssa. "Did you transfer all the Emily Glass files?"

She waggled her phone. "It's all here now."

"Then we'll be going." I nodded at Fjoeruss. "See you soon."

"Good day, Mr. Slade."

The elevator doors parted, and a gray held them open until we got in. We descended and emerged in a parking garage. Our car waited in a slot reserved for the company CEO, Fjorn Gray. Apparently, that was the moniker he presented to the normal world.

Everyone climbed inside the car. While Elyssa drove us out of the garage, Adam's phone began to chime.

"Phone call?" Shelton said.

Adam shook his head. He popped off the cover for the dome light and plucked a small silver device the size and shape of a watch battery from inside. "Hang on." A moment later, he found another device beneath the passenger seat. He rolled down the window and flicked them outside. "Fjoeruss bugged the car."

Shelton huffed. "Figures. Is that everything?"

"One more." Adam leaned between the front seats and peeled a black dot from a nook in the dashboard. "One magic tracker and two science-based ones."

"Covering all his bases as usual," Shelton said.

Adam frowned. "There's a tracker too, but I think it's on the under-carriage."

I nodded. "We'll remove it when we get to the Ranch."

Elyssa found an empty alley and activated the camouflage before taking to the skies.

"If nobody else is gonna say it, then I will," Shelton said. "There's no way for us to track down Emily Glass if she's in another realm. We just hit a dead end."

"Not exactly." Adam scrolled through a long list of files on his phone. "Cinder and I tested hundreds of theories when we were trying to find a way to open a portal from Seraphina to Eden. Most of them didn't pay off, but we stumbled into some interesting phenomenon along the way."

"Like what?" Shelton said. "The only thing I remember was fumbling blindly in the dark and praying we hit pay dirt."

"Fun times." Adam blew out a breath. "Man, I've got way too many files filed under arch research. I've got to clean this out sometime."

I turned sideways in my seat so I could look back. "What are you looking for?"

"Ah, here it is." Adam projected a holographic video. A face that looked identical to Fjoeruss's stared back at us. It wasn't the ancient Seraphim, but Cinder, one of his gray men who'd mysteriously gained sentience.

Most gray men were automatons, controlled remotely by Fjoeruss. Somehow Cinder had broken free and become a free-thinking being all on his own. We'd never questioned how or why that had happened, but something from our conversation with Fjoeruss sparked an interesting idea.

"I know this is off subject, but I might know how Cinder got free will."

Adam looked through the hologram at me, eyebrow raised. "That's a subject I discussed at great length with Cinder. He was obsessed with finding out how he came to be and why."

"Can't blame him," Shelton said. "He's the only sentient gray man in the world."

It seemed like ages ago that I'd been a prisoner of Maximus, the wannabe vampire overlord, but I still remembered the scene like it was yesterday. "When Maximus took me prisoner, there was a pile of gray men and golem body parts in the room with me. What if those golems were part of the Infernus Project?"

Adam frowned. "You think that's what Dash Armstrong was working on?"

Shelton chuckled. "That name still makes me laugh."

"We never did find out what Dash was doing with all those gray men," I said. "According to the timeline Fjoeruss gave us, that would be right around the same time his golems went missing."

"Wow. Maybe there is a connection," Adam said. "If they were trying to put souls inside golems, it's possible they gave Cinder that extra little spark needed to give him free will."

"Cinder would be thrilled to know," Elyssa said.

"To know what?" Adam shook his head. "We don't have any facts, just supposition without supporting evidence."

I was a little surprised by his lack of enthusiasm. "Yeah, but it's a start, right?"

"Cinder hasn't talked about his origin for a long time," Adam said. "I think bringing it up now without solid proof would just be tearing open old wounds."

I frowned. "I didn't realize he was that sensitive about it."

"He was an accident, and he knows it," Shelton said. "Everyone wants to feel like they have a purpose, but it's hard when you think you weren't even supposed to be created in the first place."

Elyssa shook her head. "You're looking at it the wrong way. I think people who were accidentally conceived are the ones the universe most wanted to be here."

Adam grunted. "Never thought of it that way. None of us would be here if Cinder hadn't saved us on more than one occasion."

"He got us out of that mess in Utopia," Shelton said.

I nodded. "He saved me from Maximus. If not for him, my story would've ended right then and there. Daelissa might even control the world."

"You see?" Elyssa smiled. "The universe knew we needed Cinder so much that it made sure he existed."

I squeezed her hand. "Maybe we should take the time to let Cinder know how much we need him."

"He's a national treasure," Shelton said.

"Perhaps this is another time Cinder has the answers we need." Adam tapped on the paused video and let it play.

Cinder spoke. "Portal replication, attempt one thousand, four hundred and twenty-three." He stood at the prow of one of the Mzodi flying ships just off the massive gray storm wall of Voltis.

"I'm ready," said an all-too-familiar voice. The camera panned to show Bliss, an infernus created with a soul shard from Nightliss. She stood in front of a giant gem mounted at the prow of the ship. Bliss had sacrificed her life to save Cinder from Vokan, a loss he still mourned.

"Commence," Cinder said.

Bliss channeled streams of Murk and Brilliance into a beam of gray Stasis and directed it through the massive gem. Issana, another Nightliss infernus clone, stepped up to Bliss's side and wove Murk and Brilliance back into the Stasis. The beam shimmered into nearly transparent Clarity.

Clarity was one of the four elements of power in Seraphim magic, but it wasn't physical like Brilliance, Murk, and Stasis. When directed at a living being, it showed them their true nature—a moment of brutally honest insight. Sometimes the truth was too much to bear. Daelissa found that out the hard way.

It came as no surprise to me that Clarity didn't open a portal. But Cinder zoomed in the camera on something odd. Clarity seemed to reveal tiny translucent fissures in the storm clouds. It was like looking through a web of cracks in a damaged window.

"Interesting," Cinder said. The recording jostled as he moved closer. "I wonder what these are."

Adam froze the image and spoke. "Cinder had previously opened several portals in this exact spot already. What he later figured out is that Clarity doesn't open portals, but it reveals scars and cracks left behind in the quantum veil after a portal has opened and closed."

"Whoa, you mean every portal permanently scars the fabric of reality?" Shelton said.

"Not permanently," Adam replied. "They eventually heal, but we don't know how long it takes for complete recovery."

"Do we need to go to Atlantis and get that gem?" I asked.

Adam shook his head. "Cinder also found out that you don't need to channel through a gem to see the scars. All you need is Clarity."

Elyssa pursed her lips. "Even if we go to Dubai and find the scars where Emily opened a portal, what good does that do us?"

"Cinder and I came up with another theory," Adam said. "A scar is essentially a crack in the quantum veil. What if there's a way to pry it back open?"

"Ain't no way," Shelton said. "Trying to open a portal knocked you and Justin on your asses. Why would prying open an old portal be any easier?"

"Because the veil is much weaker when it's cracked," Adam said. "Don't get me wrong, it would still take a great deal of power, but we might be able to pull it off."

I was a little wary of trying to open another portal because I still felt a little weak in the knees from the attempt in Iceland. This week was bound to be full of challenges and I couldn't afford to be exhausted when the proverbial shit hit the fan.

But there was another option.

"Is there any way to measure the kind of power we'll need to open a rift scar?" I said.

"Not without experimenting," Adam said.

Elyssa shook her head. "We can't risk another attempt. Justin won't be able to fight if he drains himself again."

"What I really need are a few Seraphim." Most of the refugees from Seraphina were in Utopia, but Voltis had to be in alignment with Eden for us to use the portal ship to reach them. Nightliss could help, but I didn't know who else we could count on.

Elyssa veered the car around a flock of birds and glanced over at me. "What does that mean?"

"I can link with other Seraphim to increase my power output." I shrugged. "Maybe that'll give me enough power to pry open a scar."

"That's an excellent idea," Adam said. "I'd forgotten you could do that."

"It's been a while," I admitted. "And I don't know how many Seraphim are actually in Eden right now."

"Not many," Elyssa said. "Most of them went to Utopia to help with the relocation effort."

"Well, you got Nightliss," Shelton said. "But your mom and Ivy are in the Glimmer."

"I'd definitely need more than one." Considering it took everything I had just to open a tiny hole, I wasn't sure even four Seraphim would be enough.

"What about Issana?" Elyssa said.

Adam shrugged. "She isn't very powerful, but every little bit helps."

"Two questions," Shelton said. "Where do we find a scar and how are we supposed to pry it open once we find one?"

"Should be plenty of scars in the omniarch room near the Mansion," Adam said.

Shelton frowned. "Yeah, but they don't go to other realms."

"Shouldn't matter." Adam looked back down at his phone. "Justin needs to wedge Murk into the crack and then pry it open."

"Like a crowbar?" Shelton snorted. "I don't think it works that way."

"Think of it like a speculum." Adam held his fingers flat with his thumb pressed to his index finger. Then he made a show of prying them open. "The Murk will force an opening and we just slip through the hole in between."

Elyssa's mouth dropped open. "Did you really just use a freaking speculum as an analogy?"

"What in the hell is a speculum?" Shelton said. "Some kind of magical device?"

Elyssa scoffed. "Imagine a cold, metal device shoved up your ass so they can pry it open to look inside."

"Oh, Jesus!" Shelton clenched his butt cheeks so hard, he straightened in his seat. "What kind of medieval torture device are you talking about?"

Adam sighed. "Nom gynecologists use it to inspect female anatomy. It might be unpleasant to think about, but it's an apt analogy."

I took out my arcphone. "Nookli, show me a speculum."

It replied in a robotic female voice. "Justin, there are three Indian restaurants nearby. Shall I make a reservation?"

"Sometimes I think my phone just likes to mess with me." I repeated my request. The pictures that appeared on my phone showed a device that made me clench my ass too. Still, I had to admit that forming Murk into something similar might just do the trick.

"I ain't even gonna say what I'm thinking," Shelton said.

Elyssa grinned. "Best idea you ever had."

I just hoped Adam's plan worked. If it didn't, we had no way of finding Emily Glass.

CHAPTER 15

N ightliss wasn't at the Ranch.

According to the omniarch gatekeeper on duty, she'd returned to the mansion earlier in the day. So we portaled back to the omniarch room and headed toward the underground house.

A long line of people snaked through the corridor outside. I stopped at the first person I saw, a man in a business suit. "Why are you waiting in a line?"

His forehead pinched. "To enlist. Isn't that why you're here?"

"To enlist?" Shelton looked just as confused as the rest of us.

The businessman slid a nom cell phone from his suit pocket and showed us a text. *Overworld recruits needed! Text YES and send a picture of a private location to join the Overworld. A portal will be provided for transportation.*

"You've got to be kidding me." Elyssa snatched the phone and stared at it. "My father didn't authorize a nom draft."

"Son of a bitch. I'll bet I know who did." Shelton bared his teeth. "Xander Tiberius."

"I was so excited," the businessman said. "It's not every day you get a chance to become supernatural."

"Now I'm really freaking confused." Elyssa stalked down the line and turned into the gauntlet room on the left. Dozens of little cubicles with curtains across their entrances were lined up along the middle of the room. A man in a white lab coat escorted the next person in line to one of the cubicles and closed the curtain behind them.

A petite woman in mom jeans and a pink shirt stepped out of the nearest cubicle, staring at her hands in astonishment. A woman in a lab coat spoke with her for a moment before directing her to another group of people waiting near the exit to the room.

Elyssa's eyes locked on the woman and met her before she joined the group. "What's going on here?"

"Oh, isn't it exciting?" The woman clasped her hands together as if offering a joyful prayer. "I feel so much stronger already."

Elyssa narrowed her eyes. "What did they do to you?"

"Well, they injected me with this glowing blue liquid." She hugged herself and giggled. "Within twenty-four hours, I'm supposed to become super strong and fast so I can join the Overworld army."

"You look like a housewife," Shelton said. "And you want to join the freaking army?"

Pain flashed across the woman's face and she looked down. She took a shuddering breath and met our eyes. "I lost my family when one of Victus Edison's evil creatures got loose in London. Custodians saved me and helped me through orientation. From what I understand, there's a big war coming, and I want to help any way I can."

Elyssa shook her head. "It's not that easy." She threw up her hands. "Who in the hell authorized this?"

A bald man in black robes emerged from one of the cubicles. His gaze wandered around and locked onto us. I recognized him as quickly as he recognized us. "That's Fitwit."

"I knew Xander was behind this," Shelton said. "Always trying to stir up more trouble."

Elyssa strode over to Fitwit. The man held his ground and watched us approach. "What kind of madness is this?" she said. "You can't bring untrained noms into a war."

"They won't be untrained when we're finished with them." Fitwit rubbed the side of his face with a hand marred with burn scars. "Besides, we need every body we can get."

"What are you giving them?" I already suspected the answer but wanted to hear it from him.

"A super serum," Fitwit said. "It's safe and effective."

I stared him down. "Is it the vampire serum Maximus developed?"

He shrugged. "I don't know. It's something Victus cooked up. Overlord Tiberius had it tested and replicated."

"Well, until we know exactly what it is, I'm putting a stop to all this." Elyssa threw up her hands. "I can't believe the Templars didn't stop you."

Fitwit gave her a smug grin. "They tried to earlier, but Xander Tiberius is still the Arcanus Primus and he has jurisdiction over the administration of potions to volunteers. This area is also considered part of Arcane University, and he has supreme authority over all matters Arcane."

Shelton blinked. "He what?"

Adam looked up from his phone. "The law is in one of the obscure sections of the Overworld Conclave, I'm afraid. The Arcanus Primus has the authority to command the administration of potions and serums to anyone who requests them, even if the requestor means to end their life."

"That's the euthanasia clause," Elyssa said. "It wasn't meant to be used like this."

Fitwit shrugged. "It's a technicality, but it works." He waved a hand at the mass of people waiting their turns. "Before long, we'll have a small army of brand-new supers. When the next battle starts, you'll be happy we do."

"They ain't nothing but cannon fodder." Shelton poked the other man in the chest. "You'd better damn well make sure they get good training." He jabbed a finger towards the woman in mom jeans. "Because if you're responsible for little Sally homemaker getting vaporized by Razor, then I'll do my damnedest to make sure you're next."

Fitwit trembled and his face turned red. "Threaten me all you want, but you have no authority here." He turned and went back into one of the cubicles.

Elyssa's fists clenched and released. Then she barged into one of the cubicles and returned with a vial of blue liquid. She handed it to Adam. "Can you find out what's in this?"

"Sure." He pocketed it. "But don't we have bigger fish to fry?"

Elyssa took a deep breath and exhaled slowly. "Yes. Yes, we do."

"Just what we need," Shelton grumbled. "Another power grab by Xander. You can bet he's up to something that isn't good for the rest of us."

I dug in my pockets and found my com badge, a small chunk of metal shaped like an ankh. I tapped on it with a finger. "Nightliss, where are you?"

Her reply came a moment later, but it was garbled and full of static. The badge didn't have much range, which meant she was probably above-ground somewhere at the university. We went back to the omniarch room and had to wait in line as a steady stream of noms arrived to enlist in Xander's army.

"This is ridiculous," Shelton said. "Can't you pull rank, Elyssa?"

She shrugged. "I try to save that for emergencies."

"This *is* a freaking emergency." Shelton huffed. "We've got six days until Xanos unveils a nasty little surprise and wipes us out."

"Or she might sign a treaty." Elyssa shook her head. "I can't just abuse my position as the commander's daughter, Shelton."

"I admire your ethics," Adam said, "but I really think the situation justifies it."

I agreed with Shelton and Adam but appreciated Elyssa's hesitation. So I decided to be the one to abuse my power. I walked over to the pair of Templar gatekeepers and offered them a friendly smile. "Hey, we've got important business and need to skip in line. Can you open a portal—"

The first Templar, a middle-aged man with long, greasy hair, and a five o'clock shadow, narrowed his eyes at me. "No."

The lanky Templar to his right glared at us. "We've got a backlog of thirty more noms. The gatekeepers who were here a minute ago might be fine with breaking the rules, but we aren't."

Elyssa's eyes flashed. "That's no way to talk to a commander. What are your names?"

"We report to Commander Jefferson Ames, not you," the first Templar replied. "While you were away, someone had to keep law and order."

"Yeah? Well, it sure as hell wasn't you," Shelton said. "The whole Overworld went to shit while we were away."

I repressed the urge to pick up both of them by their throats. "If you don't open a portal for me, then I'll remove you and do it myself."

"Sure, fine." The lanky Templar held up his hands. "Physically threatening people isn't lawful, but we all know you'll just bully us out of here, won't you?"

"I'm not bullying you!" The temperature in my face rose several degrees.

"But we've got until the end of the week to locate someone and it's an emergency!"

The greasy-haired guy shrugged. "Well, all you had to do was say that instead of acting like some spoiled brat who's better than everyone else."

"Where to?" the other guy said.

My jaw went slack. I wasn't sure if I was in the wrong here or if they were. Maybe I hadn't clearly articulated why I needed to break in line. Maybe I had come across like an entitled brat.

"Arcane University," Shelton said.

The lanky Templar did the honors and opened a gateway to the main entrance of Arcane University. He bowed and motioned us through in the most mocking way possible.

Shelton gripped his staff, obviously wanting to whack the guy on the head with it but restrained his primal urges. After the portal closed behind us, Elyssa growled with the frustration of a thousand caged lions.

"I wanted to strangle both of them!" She clenched both fists. "The Templars who joined the force while we were away are just garbage."

"Unfortunately, Victus decimated the remaining Templar forces after we left," Adam said. "Then he created a force of so-called peacekeepers as his enforcers when he overthrew the Overworld government. Most of those peacekeepers transitioned to being Templars after Ivy defeated Victus."

"Jefferson Ames was Victus's head enforcer," Shelton said. "Somehow, he became the Templar commander of Eden after Victus died the first time."

"The Templars under his command are untrained thugs," Elyssa said. "I'm surprised my father hasn't disbanded them."

"I don't think he can," Adam said. "They were lawfully chartered while we were in exile and Ames became the supreme commander here in Eden. Technically, he has the same powers as your father."

"Ugh. I hate that you're right." Elyssa set her hands on her hips. "And the Templar Synod doesn't exist anymore, so there's no governing body with the authority to disband them."

"Well, it sucks, but we've got a mission." I tapped my com badge. "Nightliss, do you copy?"

"Oh, it's you, Justin." She laughed. "I couldn't understand you earlier."

"Where are you? We could really use your help."

"I'm in Cinder's lab," she said.

"We'll be right there." I decided against requesting another portal even though walking from one point to another in the university was akin to navigating a maze in the dark with one leg tied behind your back. It had been a long time since I'd walked these hallways, but I'd rather go through the hassle than deal with those asshole gatekeepers again.

Burns and claw marks still marred the main doors of Arcane University, scars from a battle between Xander's goons and Galfandor, the former headmaster of the university. Unfortunately, Xander had won and crowned himself Overworld Overlord. Our treaty might have demoted him to Arcanus Primus, but our recent encounter with Fitwit and the Eden Templars proved Xander still had plenty of power to abuse.

I pushed through the wooden doors and consulted my phone for a map.

"Shelton!" A young man with bright blond hair ran over to us.

"Well, well, well, if it ain't Maxwell Tiberius." Shelton clapped the youngest son of Xander Tiberius on the shoulder. "I thought you were in the Glimmer with the others."

"Conrad, Ambria, and I just got back a few hours ago." Max shook his head. "Still no luck waking the Glimmer folk, and Ambria thought it was more important for us to help repair and clean up the university." He shrugged. "She loves bossing people around."

Shelton grinned. "Volunteer work is good for the soul, kid."

I looked around for other familiar faces. "Are my mom and Ivy still over there?"

"Yes," Max said. "I'm afraid they won't be leaving anytime soon."

I'd expected as much. "Do you know how to get to Cinder's lab?"

"Sure do!" Max spun on his heel and motioned us to follow. "Right this way."

We followed him through twisting hallways, up a set of stairs, down another, and through a tunnel that spun around us until we reached another hallway of classrooms.

"Maxwell Tiberius." A young woman with a stern expression stepped in front of Max. "Why aren't you working upstairs?" Ambria Rax suddenly noticed the rest of us. "You're trying to get out of work so you can play with Shelton, aren't you?"

Shelton snorted. "Yeah, we were gonna go throw a baseball. Want to come?"

"There's no time for fun and games." She bowed towards Elyssa. "Good to see you again, Madam Commander. Perhaps you can talk sense to Max and Shelton."

Elyssa winced. "For the last time, Ambria, please stop calling me that."

Ambria raked her glare across the rest of the group. "Where, exactly, are you all rushing off to?"

"Cinder's lab," Max said.

"Important business," Shelton added. "Maybe you ought to get back to emptying trash cans, Ambria."

"Nonsense." She brushed off her hands. "I'd like to see what's so important."

"Then let's go." Max headed off again.

We followed him down the hall, took four left turns, and somehow didn't end up right back where we'd come from. At last, we reached a familiar set of stairs. An old man with a long beard and pointy wizard hat waved when he saw us.

"Ah, Max and Ambria. It's good to see you." He nodded at the rest of us. "You must be Justin Slade, Harry Shelton, Elyssa Borathen, and Adam Nosti, yes?"

"Uh, have we met?" Shelton said.

"Regrettably, no." The old man shook his head. "I'm Galfandor. I owe you a debt of gratitude for freeing me from Xander's prison."

"Oh, yeah." Max slapped his forehead. "I forgot you hadn't met yet. Xander released all his political prisoners not long after we beat Razor."

"Max and Ambria, what are you doing here?" Conrad Edison stepped out of a nearby doorway. "I thought I heard your voices."

"Shelton and the others are going to Cinder's lab," Max said. "So I thought I'd help them find it."

"Welp, the gang's all here," Shelton said. "Maybe we should just throw a party."

I turned back to the old man. "Conrad told me a lot about you, but it's good to finally meet the man who helped him survive Victus."

"Oh, I didn't really do much," Galfandor said. "Conrad and his friends managed quite well on their own."

"That's for sure," Ambria said.

"I was just down in Cinder's lab," Galfandor said. "Since Xander won't restore my position as headmaster, I'm afraid I have little else to do except gossip. Your golem friend is quite interesting."

Shelton laughed. "He's odd if that's what you mean."

"I think that describes most of us," Adam said.

"So who's leading the university?" I asked.

Galfandor sighed. "I'm afraid Xander has put his own people in charge. As long as he's in power, there will be no learning, only indoctrination."

It seemed our fragile alliance was in danger of being torn apart from the inside.

CHAPTER 16

S helton huffed. "Xander turns everything he touches into shit. I can't believe we've got to endure him for two more years."

"It's quite unfortunate, but there's little to be done so long as greater threats hover over our heads." Galfandor began to turn away. "It was nice to finally meet you all."

"Same here," I said. I had to agree with Shelton. Everything under Xander was so much worse than it needed to be. But unless we broke the treaty and deposed him, there wasn't much we could do.

Max resumed guiding us down the stairs and into a long stone passageway I remembered all too well. It was here that I'd fought Mr. Bigglesworth, a Flark who'd once been Ivy's bodyguard, and rescued Paul MacLean, a professor and former Illuminatus.

Never a dull moment at Arcane University!

We took the third door on the right and entered a room cluttered with contraptions. I recognized many of them from Serena's Gloom fortress and wondered how in the hell Cinder got them here.

Cinder wore his usual somber ensemble of gray slacks and a gray shirt.

His skin, once gray like his golem brethren, now looked perfectly natural. Only his silver hair and gray eyes remained the same.

"Hey buddy!" Shelton called out when we were halfway across the room.

Cinder looked up from a project on his workbench. "Hello, everyone. It is good to see you."

Nightliss stepped out from behind a tall tower and beamed a smile that warmed me down to the bones. "Hello, my friends."

Max sighed. "She's so pretty."

Shelton chuckled and patted him on the back. "A little out of your age range, kiddo."

Adam snorted. "Pot, meet kettle. Bella's centuries older than Shelton."

Shelton scoffed. "Hey, I like older women."

"You like being a hypocrite," Ambria said.

"Yeah, well you like hurting people's feelings," Shelton shot back.

Conrad seemed blissfully unaware of the argument and continued walking to the others. I suspected he was so used to Ambria giving everyone a hard time that he automatically filtered it out.

Adam got straight to the point. "We made some epic discoveries in Iceland."

Cinder's eyebrows rose. He was getting much better at expressions. "I assume this is in regard to Lulu's advice that you seek out the first siren."

Shelton nodded. "Exactly."

Lulu was a giant purple earth dragon who hung out with Altash, an equally huge, red earth dragon. During the final evacuation of Seraphina, Lulu had come to us with a message: Find the first Siren in the land of ice and snow because she might know about Baal's origins and have the key to defeating him. Vitania hadn't helped much in that regard, but she'd gotten us a step closer to finding Emily.

Having Emily's ability to open rifts between realms would give us a massive advantage. I prayed she was still alive.

Adam told the story about our brief adventure in Iceland and then played the video he'd shown us earlier.

"Clarity can reveal portal scars?" Nightliss seemed amazed. "Perhaps this is a way it shows the truth about reality itself."

"That's a good way of putting it," Shelton said.

"And you think we can utilize Clarity to find a portal scar left behind by Emily Glass in Dubai?" Cinder said.

I nodded. "So we can reopen it."

Cinder tilted his head slightly. "But you don't have the power to open a portal."

"No," I said, "but I might be able to reopen one if I form Murk into a speculum."

"A what?" Ambria said.

Shelton cleared his throat uneasily. "Uh, let's not get into particulars."

Cinder answered in his dry, technical manner. "A device used by nom gynecologists to pry open the vaginal cavity for examination."

"Eww!" Ambria cringed.

Nightliss's mouth dropped open. "Barbaric!"

I veered the conversation back on topic so I didn't have to think about prying open women's hoo-hahs with cold metal. "If Nightliss links with me, we might have enough energy to pry open a scar and see where Emily went."

"Why is Emily so important?" Ambria said. "Your time would be better spent recruiting more allies."

"Were you listening?" Shelton said. "Emily can open rifts to other realms. With her on our side, we could travel to any realm any time and find allies way faster than waiting for Voltis to align in Eden."

Ambria quirked her lips to the side. "Yes, I suppose that is a good reason." She tutted. "It seems once again a woman will save the world."

Shelton groaned. "I don't care who saves the world, just so long as they do it."

"Why do people care about gender so much?" Cinder tapped a finger on his chin. "The reasoning behind some human behaviors eludes me."

"Yeah, well some people don't reason," Shelton said.

Adam rapped his knuckles on Cinder's workbench. "Could we return to the matter at hand? I'd like to test our theory as quickly as possible."

"Certainly." Cinder pointed to a small square space marked off by yellow tape. "Perhaps we can start there."

"Is that the designated portal zone?" Shelton said.

"It is." Cinder indicated a tall jade statue of Poseidon given to him by an artist in Atlantis. Whoever carved it had given the god of the seas a boner nearly a foot long and testicles the size of baseballs. "I move around the items in this room quite often, but I left this here so people could use an image to reach it."

Shelton glanced down at the generously proportioned privates. "Yeah, I'll bet everyone remembers this schlong."

Ambria sighed. "It's art, Shelton. Not that you could appreciate it."

I clapped my hands. "Hey, let's keep the topic on point, okay?"

Adam snickered. "Just the tip?"

Shelton guffawed. "Let's go balls deep, people."

"Good lord." I face-palmed. "The end of the world is at hand and you're making dick jokes."

"Wow, you guys really shafted the conversation." Max howled with laughter.

Ambria giggled. "That was actually a good one, Max."

Conrad grinned. "I wish I knew some penis jokes, but I've got nothing."

"Kid, I've got plenty." Shelton reached his hand out as if to ruffle Conrad's hair, but seemed to think better of it and clapped him on the shoulder instead. "Man, you don't know how deprived you've been until you've got a solid repertoire of inappropriate jokes at your disposal."

I knew how Conrad felt. I tried to scrape up a penis joke of my own but came up empty.

"I don't understand why male genitalia is considered humorous." Cinder put a hand to his chin and really seemed to think about it.

I finally came up with something witty. "I'm going to grab this conversation by the balls and drag it back on target."

Shelton grimaced. "Man, that's weak."

Adam shook his head. "Justin, man, I know you can do better than that."

"They're right." Elyssa shook her head sadly. "You're not even trying are you?"

I threw up my hands and walked to the portal zone. "When I come up with something better, I'll let you know."

Their banter continued, but I ignored it and summoned Murk in my left hand and Brilliance in my right. I wove the strands into a sphere of Stasis. Then I channeled Murk in my left eye, and Brilliance in my right, and speared them through the gray sphere. A translucent beam speared out of the other side, rippling the air like a heat wave.

It passed right through the portal zone and hit Poseidon in the stomach. A face with one giant eye stared back at me. A maw of sharp teeth clenched tight, and a horrific wail filled the air.

"Jesus Christ on a pogo stick, that statue is possessed!" Shelton shouted.

The monster inside the statue roared again. Apparently, demons didn't like Clarity. But whatever truths it revealed to the demon weren't enough to kill it. They just seemed to make it mad.

The statue rocked back and forth. Jade cracked and fell away, revealing dark brown, bristly fur beneath. A humanoid creature burst out and that was when I realized the statue wasn't possessed—there had been an actual monster inside of it.

"That's no demon," Elyssa said.

The creature stood on two legs that ended in sharp hooves. Thick brown hair covered every inch except for its exceptionally large privates. It had a single large eye and a doglike muzzle filled with sharp teeth.

"What in the hell is that thing?" Shelton said.

The monster attacked before anyone answered. It came at me first since I was the closest. It swiped with sharp claws. I held up an arm to block it. Pain shot through my arm. I heard a snap and flipped through the air. I crashed into something with a loud clang and slumped on the floor. My jaw felt dislocated and my arm felt broken.

I tried to talk, but my mouth wouldn't respond.

I'd landed behind a metal contraption somewhere in the lab. I couldn't see my friends, but I heard their screams and shouts.

Consciousness drifted away. I used my good hand to squeeze the broken bone. The pain jolted me awake. The bone hadn't broken through the skin, but my hand hung at a gruesome angle. I tried to stand, but was too dazed.

Where the hell is my super healing when I need it?

I held my arm just below the break and shifted the bones back into place. The pain was blinding, but I couldn't have screamed even if I wanted to because of all the blood in my mouth. I tried to shift into partial demon form, but my inner demon shrank away from me, as if trying to hide in the darkest recesses of my mind.

Endorphins finally flushed me with relief, giving me enough clarity of mind to focus on my demon half. I used all my willpower to yank him out of his cage and felt demonic power surging through my body. Muscles coiled around my damaged arm, pulling the bones back into place. I spat blood from my mouth and felt encouraged when it didn't fill up again

I didn't have time for everything to knit back into place, so I summoned all my demonic strength and climbed to my feet. I'd only partially manifested demon form, but it was enough to make my pants and shoes painfully tight. I stormed back out and saw Nightliss holding the monster at bay with an ultraviolet dome of Murk.

Conrad stood behind her, azure energy crackling at his fingertips. Max and Ambria flanked him, wands drawn.

The monster pounded against the dome, sending cracks racing along its surface. The entire room reeked of brimstone, every bit as strong as what I'd smelled in our fight against the demons sent by Cain and Olivia.

Elyssa nearly collided with me when I rounded the corner. "My god, Justin! Are you okay?"

"Not great," I mumbled. Moving my mouth was agonizing. I poked the cheek with my tongue and felt it go through a deep wound and outside. I heaved. "Oh, shit. That thing sliced me up good."

"Your skin isn't healing." Elyssa's eyes filled with worry. "Something orange is oozing out of the cuts."

I gagged on bile. Forced it back down.

"I can barely contain it," Nightliss said. "I need help."

Baring my teeth against the pain, I limped over and put a hand on

Nightliss's back. I summoned Murk and channeled it into her, increasing her power output. The cracks in her shield healed, but every blow from the monster produced fresh ones.

"How do we get rid of it?" Shelton said. "I threw everything I had at it, and barely singed its fur."

"My light arrows only seemed to make it madder," Elyssa said. "So Nightliss shielded it to hold it at bay."

"We can handle it," Ambria said. "Max has his banana peel bombs ready. While it's slipping, Conrad and I will attack."

Shelton threw up his hands. "I'm willing to try anything at this point."

I didn't have any answers and I sure as hell wasn't ready to go toe-to-toe with that thing again even with my demon powers. But then the creature brayed like a mad donkey and rammed its shoulder into the shield. Nightliss cried out and the Murk barrier shattered like glass.

Conrad threw up a shield in time to protect himself and his friends from the shards. The beast brayed. Flaming orange goop sprayed from its mouth and covered Conrad's shield. Black smoke filled the air.

"Holy hell that thing makes a stink!" Shelton thrust out his staff. Red lightning crackled against the beast. Its fur caught fire and the monster brayed in pain. Bolt after bolt of energy exploded against its hide, but did little else to damage it.

My demon spirit tried to run away like a frightened child. I summoned all my willpower and dragged it kicking and screaming right back. I forced it to grant me more demonic strength. I grew nearly as tall as the beast. Horns sprouted from my forehead. My legs and feet swelled until my pants and shoes ripped and burst. A prehensile tail with a sharp tip grew from the base of my spine and whipped the air.

The monster brayed again and came right at me. I roared back and charged him. The room shook from the impact and my bones ached. I grappled with the beast, but despite all my strength, his was just slightly more.

"Use your training, Justin!" Elyssa shouted.

I'd trained long and hard to learn her ninja skills, but they hadn't become second nature to me yet.

The monster spoke in a guttural tongue. I didn't know exactly what he'd said, but I recognized it as the demon language.

"Yeah, you stink too," I growled. And then I went limp.

The monster was pushing against me so hard that the sudden absence of pushback sent him stumbling forward. I tucked my tail and rolled backward, using my leg to catapult the beast overhead. He smashed into the wall with an incredible racket.

"I've got an idea," Adam said from somewhere to the side.

I didn't have time to ask him what it was before the monster regained its feet. This time it ignored me and went straight for Cinder. I blurred on an intercept course and smashed into the monster with a shoulder. It was like hitting a brick wall, but I managed to knock the creature off course just enough to miss my golem friend.

I heard Adam shouting at someone. "It's an emergency! Give us a damned portal!"

Shelton screamed obscenities. The monster reared back its head and brayed with the rage of a thousand donkeys, then made another attempt for Cinder.

"Justin, get ready!" Adam said.

"Ready for—" breath exploded out of me as the beast plowed over me. It lunged for Cinder, but my tail coiled around a leg and tripped it.

I rolled over to get up and saw an open portal. I didn't know where it went, but I knew it had to be part of Adam's plan. I hoped it worked, because I was all out of ideas.

CHAPTER 17

efore the beast could regain its feet, I kicked it with all my might. It slid across the floor and into the portal.

Adam shouted, "Go after it, Justin!"

So I did.

I leapt through the portal and landed in an arch control room. Dozens of black arches lined the room. Most of them had numbers that coordinated with similar arches in other control rooms across the world. But the one with the portal in it was an omniarch.

Two Templars stared at the monster with raw fear. They were obviously Xander's people. Real Templars would have drawn swords and surrounded it. Because any Templar worth their salt had already faced plenty of monsters and stared death in the face.

But these guys were just like the ones we'd met earlier. They talked a big game, but when trouble came knocking, they were the first ones to shit their britches and run.

Luckily for them, they were about to be saved by an angel.

Nightliss leapt through the portal behind me. She braced her feet and slid to a stop. Beams of ultraviolet Murk shot from her fists and coiled around the monster, lifting him off the floor so he couldn't run. Adam stumbled through the portal and closed it with a wave of his hand.

"Justin, duck!" he shouted. The beast roared. Adam concentrated on the omniarch and a portal opened to absolute blackness. "Now!"

Nightliss swung the bound monster by its ultraviolet bonds and released it. It flew through the portal. At the last instant its hands gripped the sides. I blurred forward, braced on my left foot, and focused all my momentum into my right, delivering a kick that knocked the monster loose and sent it flying into darkness. A roar from within chilled me all the way to the core. It wasn't our monster that roared. It was something much, much worse.

The Beast in the Void.

Something even blacker than darkness surged toward the creature. The monster's brays of agony went silent an instant later. And then the portal winked off.

Nightliss slumped against the arch. Adam wiped sweat off his forehead, breathing heavily and shaking.

"I think I peed my pants." Adam looked down at his crotch. "Or maybe I'm just sweating all over."

My demon side saw its chance and slipped away, back to hiding in the back of my mind. I was too exhausted to try to fight it. My body shrank back to normal proportions. My clothes didn't. At least my underwear wasn't squeezing my balls like a vice anymore.

With the adrenaline fading, the pain in my shredded cheek grew nearly unbearable once again. *Why isn't it healing?* My demonic healing usually only needed a few minutes with a wound, but this one wasn't responding.

"What was that thing?" one of the Templars said.

Adam snarled and grabbed the closest Templar by his uniform. "The next time you question an emergency, I'll feed you to the Beast, you idiots!"

The other Templar gaped at me. "Your face. It looks like raw meat."

I didn't even want to imagine how I looked. The circle around the portal was still sealed, but I couldn't open another portal to the lab since the statue was now gone. I needed an updated image.

My com badge chimed. "Justin, are you okay?"

Elyssa's voice filled me with relief. "I'm fine. Can you send a picture so we can get back down there?"

"It's on the way."

My phone dinged a moment later with a picture of the wall where the statue had been. I fixed the image in my mind and opened a portal.

"Wait, we've got questions, the Templars said.

Adam thrust out his hand. "Talk to the hand, assholes."

Nightliss put his arm over her shoulder and helped the shaky Arcane through the portal. I closed it the moment we were through.

Nightliss helped Adam to a seat. "I've never fought such raw physical strength," she said. "That creature was like nothing I've encountered before."

Elyssa rushed to my side and began inspecting my face. "We need a healer."

"I already requested one," Cinder said. "They're on the way."

I tried to ignore the pain, but it seemed to worsen with every passing second. For some reason, my supernatural healing wasn't doing the trick. The stench of brimstone was so strong, even I was getting sick of it.

"If nobody else is gonna say it, then I will." Shelton collapsed his staff to compact form and slid it in its holster. "That thing was a demon."

"From where?" Nightliss said. "There was no summoning pattern. It was hiding inside the statue."

"Cinder, who gave you that blasted statue?" Shelton said.

The golem tilted his head as if thinking about it. It was a well-practiced mannerism totally unnecessary to him recalling anything, and I had to admit he was getting pretty good at acting human. "A group of refugees from Seraphina said they built it to show appreciation for my part in saving them."

"Well, that doesn't sound suspicious at all," Ambria said.

Shelton nodded. "Took the words right out of my mouth."

"Do you remember the specific people who gave it to you?" Elyssa asked.

"I remember them very well," Cinder said. "They told me their names several times. Bandia, Anya, Alfo, and Leod. It seemed quite odd that they laughed every time they said their names."

"Did they always give their names in that order?" Adam said.

Cinder pursed his lips. "Yes, they did."

"First initials of each name." Adam blew out a breath. "That bastard planted a demon bomb."

It took me a second to realize what he meant. "Their first initials spell Baal."

"Yeah, his people gave Cinder a Trojan horse," Shelton said. "We gotta make sure no one else received one of those things."

Ambria huffed. "Clever bastard."

"I'll put the Templars on alert." She dialed her father's assistant and gave her the details.

Conrad frowned. "How long have you had that statue?"

"Nearly a month," Cinder said.

"What was the point of it?" Conrad looked down at the burn marks in the stone floor where the orange gunk was drying into stony gray lumps. "Did he mean to spring the trap so it could kill as many people as possible? Or was it there for some other purpose?"

"First of all, do we agree it's a demon?" Shelton said.

Conrad nodded. "It was no ordinary demon, but it was a demon."

"I agree," Ambria said. "And it certainly wasn't an infernus. Conjured demon flesh isn't impervious to damage."

"Yeah, even armored scorps take damage," Shelton said.

Cinder tapped a finger on his chin. "I concur. The beast was infernal."

"That stuff it spewed out was like the hellfire we saw in Iceland," Adam said. "Are there such things as physical demons who don't need to be summoned?"

"Who needs help?" A familiar voice called from the other side of the room. Meghan Andretti appeared from the maze of contraptions in the middle of the room. "Why does it smell like brimstone in here?" Meghan came to an abrupt halt when she saw us. "Oh. Hi, Adam."

Adam's mouth dropped open. "What are you doing here?"

She stiffened. "Orders." Her sharp blue eyes found me. "What in the world happened to you?" Meghan ignored everyone else and grabbed me by the arm. She directed me to a nearby table. "Lie down."

I followed her orders.

She leaned over and began examining the wounds. Meghan flicked her wand and my cheek went numb. Her wand wove another pattern and I felt something tugging at my flesh. She held up her wand. A tendril of blue energy coiled around a gray lump. "What is this?"

"We don't know," Cinder said from somewhere to the side.

"Well, whatever it is, it's inhibiting Justin's healing." The blue tendril dropped the gray lump and Meghan went back to work.

Elyssa appeared at Meghan's side a moment later, a small mirror in her hands. "I thought you might want to watch." She angled it so I could see what was happening.

Meghan worked the blue energy through the wounds, prying loose the dried gray lumps. It was gruesome and fascinating, especially since I could see my teeth through the gashes. One wound was completely coated. She tried to loosen the gray stuff to no avail. Her wand flicked through another pattern and a red energy blade appeared at the tip. She used it to carve away the flesh.

Someone made a retching sound.

"Holy hot damn I did not need to see that," Shelton said.

When she cleaned the last of the residue from my wounds, I looked like something out of a horror show. Bloodied teeth showed through ribbons of torn, blackened flesh.

"Am I infected?" My numbed cheek and mouth slurred my words.

"I don't think so." Meghan used another spell to stitch the skin together. "It appears the substance was inhibiting your healing, because now your skin is knitting together on its own."

"Thank god." Elyssa put down the mirror and held my hand. "What is that stuff anyway?"

"Dollars to dog nuts it's got something to do with hellfire," Shelton said.

"Hellfire?" Ambria's wide-eyed face appeared behind Elyssa.

I sat up. Aside from a little dizziness, I felt much better.

Shelton sighed. "Yeah. We found out about hellfire the hard way in Iceland."

"So you went to the land of ice and snow in search of the first Siren?" Conrad said.

"And we found her," Shelton said. "Along with the first Fae. Then we had a family reunion with Justin's daddy brother, Cain."

"Daddy brother?" Ambria gave him a blank stare.

"Yeah, because Baal used Justin's dad to create his twin brother." Shelton waved his hand as if shooing away a pesky fly. "Then we found out Emily Glass has an evil twin half-sister."

"What a bloody mess," Max said.

"They summoned hellfire demons, and boy were those things nasty." Shelton blew out a breath. "Vitania couldn't even put out their flames with the ocean so she opened a portal right underneath them and sent them to another realm."

"Man, I wish I'd been there to see that." Max slumped. "All we did was sit around and do nothing in the Glimmer."

Ambria scoffed. "If you're that eager to die, Max, then I'm certain we can find another demon to entertain you."

"Vitania cut the head off one demon with a portal, and it dried into a substance very similar to this." Adam poked the stone-like material with his wand. "It's almost like lava."

"Don't you mean magma?" Max said.

Adam shook his head. "Lava is molten stone aboveground. Magma is the same, but underground."

Shelton snorted. "Know-it-all."

"I'm happy someone does," Conrad said. "Because I feel confused most of the time."

Shelton clapped him on the back. "Amen to that."

Meghan used her wand to weave a skin-colored cast around my broken arm. "It's already healing, but this will ensure it's not crooked."

"Thanks," I said.

"If you experience any other side-effects or sudden onset of illness, let me know." Meghan packed her white doctor's bag and began to turn away.

Adam opened his mouth as if to say something, then closed it, but he watched her until she disappeared in the maze of contraptions.

"I am sorry your relationship with Meghan was terminated," Cinder said. He offered two precise pats on Adam's back. "But at least she is still alive."

Adam shrugged. "I dunno. She might as well be dead to me."

"Oh, you dated her?" Ambria gave him a sad look. "She seems a bit cold."

Max chuckled.

Ambria raised an eyebrow. "What's so funny?"

"Just that most people seem cold compared to that hot temper of yours."

"Max Tiberius!" Ambria slapped his shoulder but couldn't stop a smile from reaching her lips. Her eyes flared with a hint of craziness. "You'll never have to worry about me being cold."

For once, Conrad looked a little scared of his girlfriend. Elyssa gave me the crazy eyes one might imagine from an overly attached girlfriend and then burst into laughter. I wanted to laugh, but my cheek was still too tender.

"Hey, didn't we come down here to do something besides fight a demon?" Max said.

Shelton snapped his fingers. "Oh, yeah. We still need to check for a portal scar."

I flexed the hand on the broken arm. It hurt, but the cast held everything in place. "I'll give it a go, but I'm not fighting another demon."

"Sure be nice if we could drop demons into portals on command like Vitania," Adam said.

Shelton snorted. "Then let's find Emily so we have the option."

I went back to the portal zone. Some of the yellow tape was missing or burned, but it was still hard to miss with all the jade fragments littering the area. I wove Stasis with my hands and then channeled Murk and Brilliance into it to create a wide beam of Clarity. Faint white cracks crisscrossed in the air before me, hidden wounds in the quantum fabric.

"So we just gotta pry open one scar, right?" Shelton said.

I shrugged. "Only one way to find out."

"How are you gonna pry open a scar while you're using Clarity to reveal it?" Shelton said.

"Uh, I didn't think that far ahead." I looked at Nightliss. "Can you try to pry open a crack with Murk?"

She stood next to me. "I will try." The petite angel's green eyes narrowed in concentration and she wove a slender thread of ultraviolet energy.

Adam examined the web of cracks. "Fascinating." He tried to poke one with his wand, but it was as insubstantial as the air around it.

Nightliss's Murk thread also passed right through it. Her forehead creased. The energy thread poked and prodded several more cracks. "There is nothing solid for me to pry into."

Cinder walked next to Adam and inspected the cracks from all angles. "They are two dimensional. They have length and width but can't be seen from the side."

Adam stepped to the side and looked at them. "Wow, yeah."

"So how do you pry open something that ain't solid?" Shelton said.

Conrad and his friends crowded around the cracks.

"Hey, don't get in the Clarity beam unless you want a really rude awakening," I warned.

Ambria raised an eyebrow. "Whatever do you mean?"

"It reveals the unvarnished nasty truth about yourself," Shelton said. "Complete insight."

"Well, if you can make sense of it," Elyssa said. "For me it was like floating in a calm lake."

"I imagine it was particularly awful for Shelton," Ambria said.

Shelton snorted. "I ain't stupid enough to experience it."

Conrad wove an azure thread into a crack but encountered the same problem Nightliss had. "It's not solid. We can see the scars, but we can't manipulate them."

I groaned. "So damned close."

Shelton slumped. "But no banana."

CHAPTER 18

It was so frustrating to be able to see the scars but not be able to do anything with them. They were ghosts to us, insubstantial as smoke.

Adam grunted and narrowed his eyes. "I have a theory."

Sweat trickled into my eyes from the strain of channeling Clarity for so long. "Please tell me it's good one."

"As good as any," he said. "The cracks don't actually exist in physical form on our plane. They only exist on a quantum level, sort of caught between two different planes." He sandwiched his hands together and held them a fraction of an inch apart. "They exist between this place and the quantum tunnels."

"Ah yes," Cinder nodded. "The cracks vibrate at a different frequency from our own. We would have to bring our world and the quantum veil into alignment."

More sweat dripped down my forehead. "I can't keep channeling Clarity forever. Any ideas?"

Adam turned to Nightliss. "The cracks exist because on some level, they're vibrating close to our frequency. We need to slow that down. Try channeling Stasis instead."

Nightliss wove a thread of Brilliance with the Murk, turning it into Stasis. The tip encountered the crack but passed through it. "I don't think it's working."

"I need you to completely cover a crack in Stasis for a moment," Adam said.

She nodded and wove the Stasis into a cloud of fog around a vertical crack in the center. As we watched with bated breath, the crack crystalized like frosted glass. Adam poked at it with his wand. It tapped against something solid.

Shelton whooped. "Holy smokes, the boy genius did it again."

"Now do I pry it open?" Nightliss asked.

Adam nodded. "Give it a shot."

Nightliss tied off the Stasis weave and fired a sliver of Murk at the crack. It speared through it. Adam stepped to the side. "Hey, I don't see it on the other side. It must have entered the quantum tunnel."

The angel fired Murk from all ten fingers and channeled it inside the crack. Then she moved her hands apart, as if prying open elevator doors. Nightliss gritted her teeth and made a cute growling sound.

"She's so adorable," Ambria said.

A thunderclap boomed through the lab, sending Adam, Shelton, and Max jumping back. Ambria shrieked. Elyssa grimaced and covered her ears. With the cracking sound of two giant icebergs colliding, the air ripped open to reveal a very familiar room on the other side.

The gatekeeper Templars in the Mansion omniarch room gaped in fear and astonishment from the other side, swords held clumsily in front of them.

"It worked!" Shelton whooped again and high-fived Max, Adam, and Ambria in turn.

Nightliss cried out and released the Murk. The crack shut again, thankfully without the thunderous boom. My knees wobbled with fatigue, so I released the Clarity and leaned against Elyssa for support. My healing jaw ached again as the pain relief spell wore off.

"Wow, how did you do it by yourself?" Adam took Nightliss's hands in his and inspected them. "Your hands are freezing."

She nodded. "They are usually like that after channeling Murk for an extended time."

Adam rubbed them briskly. "Does this help?"

She laughed. "Yes, it does."

"She's so powerful." Ambria sighed. "I wish I could be as strong as Nightliss and Elyssa."

"Girl, I've seen you fight," Elyssa said. "You are strong."

Ambria beamed. "You really think so?"

"I wonder if I could pry open one," Conrad said. "Do you think the cracks would be visible with just Stasis?"

I shrugged. "Maybe."

"It's worth a try," Adam said. "If we can replicate this, then we'll have a powerful new tool."

"I need to catch my breath," I said.

Nightliss took a deep breath. "I'll try." She wove another blanket of Stasis over the portal zone, but this time, no cracks crystallized.

"Odd," Cinder said. "Justin, can you add Clarity again?"

I took a deep breath. "Yeah, but only for a moment." I wove Clarity again and intersected Nightliss's Stasis weave. The cracks reappeared and began to crystalize in the Stasis.

Conrad speared into the crack with azure energy. He gritted his teeth and funneled a wedge of energy into the crack. With another thunderous boom, a portal opened. The Templars on the other side shouted in dismay. Conrad released the power and the portal snapped shut.

"Yes, you did it!" Max clapped his hands.

"I had no doubt he could," Ambria said.

I released Clarity and dropped onto a nearby bench.

"The kid's got what it takes," Shelton said.

"The cracks don't crystallize without Clarity first revealing them." Cinder tapped a finger on his chin. "Perhaps there's another aspect to Clarity we don't understand."

Adam nodded. "Agreed. Maybe it links our world with the quantum plane and allows Stasis to freeze the vibrations so we can physically access them."

"A sound theory." Cinder stroked his chin. "The next question is whether or not a normal Arcane could also open the cracks."

"I ain't even gonna try," Shelton said. "But I'd be willing to bet Conrad can open portals from scratch. With that fancy primal fount of his, he's got the power of Grayskull."

"The power of what?" Ambria said.

"Hmm." I pursed my lips. "You might be right."

Conrad looked from Shelton to me. "How do you open a portal from scratch?"

"With Cyrinthian runes, of course." Adam took out his phone and projected Vitania's list of realms.

Conrad studied them for a moment. "Do I need a wand to trace the patterns?"

"If you're a noob." Shelton shrugged. "It's like spell coding, except you gotta fix the power words in your mind and then will a portal to open."

"It's nothing you didn't do a thousand times at school," Adam said. "But the trick is having enough power to actually open the rift."

"And if you don't," I said, "well, let's just say you'll feel like you got run over by a steamroller."

"I don't know if it's a good idea," Elyssa said. "We don't want to risk burning out Conrad."

"It won't burn him out," Shelton said. "It'll just knock him on his ass like it did Adam."

"And me," I reminded him.

"I barely opened a pinhole," Adam said. "Justin managed a window."

"So let's give it a shot," Shelton said. "It'd be real damned handy."

"Why don't we see if he can open a portal within Eden first?" I suggested. "Vitania said that requires less energy."

Conrad looked a bit hesitant. "Explain the process precisely, please."

"It's simple," Shelton said. "You just charge the power words in your mind, close the circuit and will a portal to open in a certain size and shape. Now, to open one from one point to another in Eden, you have to be able to imagine it perfectly—just like opening an omniarch portal."

"It's not the spell part that's hard," Adam said, "it's the power required to open the portal."

"Got it," Conrad said. "Do I need to imagine a location perfectly to open a portal in another realm?"

Shelton shook his head. "Vitania says you'll just open a portal to a random place—wherever that quantum tunnel happens to lead at the time."

"Imagine each realm is covered in an intricate web of invisible quantum tunnels." Adam held his hands apart as if to illustrate a globe. "You can use them to travel from point-to-point within a realm, or outside a realm."

"Fascinating," Cinder said. "I wonder if there are artificial means that could reproduce this."

"That's what the arches were for," Shelton said. "Vitania said the Sirens intentionally made them more complicated than they needed to be. But that's also why they need to be right over a leylines since they draw so much power."

"Perhaps we could replicate their operation somehow." Cinder pursed his lips. "I will conduct experimental trials."

Conrad moved his lips as if silently reciting something. Then he said the words aloud. "Eden, xhi budi tuan zot." He closed his eyes and repeated the power words several more times. Took a deep breath. Opened his eyes. "I'm ready."

"Stand way back." Shelton put out his arms and backed Max and Ambria up along with him. Amazingly, Ambria didn't resist.

Conrad narrowed his eyes and stared at a spot in the air. Azure blue energy crackled across his hands—aether drawn from the primal fount. The energy darkened and his eyes began to glow. His hair lifted on end. "Eden, xhi budi tuan zot!" He thrust his hands forward and a torrent of power burst into the air. It flattened out and a portal ripped open. It spread wide enough to narrowly admit one person. Conrad cried out and even more power flooded from his hands. The portal grew another foot in all directions.

"Conrad, that's enough!" Ambria said.

Shelton's and Adam's mouths hung open, their faces lit from the massive power display.

I peered at the portal and saw a small room on the other side. But I was afraid to actually step through with the power flooding from Conrad's hands into the portal. Cinder, the only one of us who remained calm, took a potted plant from his work bench and held it into the stream of energy.

The thin stem bent slightly as if in a slight breeze, but the plant seemed to suffer no harm.

Conrad twisted his hands in a pattern and tied off the portal weave. He slumped but a huge grin spread across his face. "This is going to hurt in the morning."

Shelton, his mouth still hanging open, walked over to the portal and looked through. "How long will this thing stay open?"

Conrad shrugged. "I don't know. I poured as much excess energy into it as I could."

"Maybe we should test it," Adam said.

Cinder tossed the plant through the portal. The ceramic pot shattered on the stone floor in the room on the other side. "It appears to work."

"I'm going in," Shelton said. He stepped toward the portal. Just as he stepped into it, the portal winked off. Shelton yelped and began hopping on one foot. The tip of his boot was gone and blood trickled from a neat hole in his sock. "That damned thing nearly took off my toe!"

"Jesus, Shelton!" Adam helped steady him. "What kind of idiot move was that? We didn't know how long the portal would remain open. It could have cut you in half when it closed."

"I timed it from creation to termination," Cinder said. "It last seventy-three seconds from when it first opened, and thirty-nine from the time Conrad tied it off."

Ambria sighed. "Let me see that toe."

"Why?" Shelton said.

"Because we learned first aid in school." She took out her wand. "Now, sit."

Shelton hooped over to a stool and sat down. Ambria flicked her wand and Shelton sighed in relief. "Man, I forgot all those first aid spells a long time ago."

Conrad's grin faded and sadness seemed to pool in his eyes. "We learned them from an excellent teacher."

Conrad's real mother, Delectra, had disguised herself as a defensive magic teacher. She and her son had grown close before he discovered her true identity. But they didn't have a chance to develop more of a relationship before she'd died protecting Conrad from Victus.

Cinder didn't seem to pick up on the emotional cues. "Do you remember how to replicate that exactly, Conrad?"

Eyes still downcast, the young man nodded. "But I stretched past my limits. I'll have magic sickness tomorrow."

"Ugh." I gave his shoulder a sympathetic squeeze. "I feel your pain."

Ambria opened a small leather pouch on her belt and took out a doughy green block. "That's why I carry this with me." She walked over to him and held it toward him. "Open your mouth like a big boy."

Conrad's face flushed red, but he opened his mouth and Ambria popped it in.

She smiled. "What would you do without me?"

I grinned and met Elyssa's lovely violet gaze. She gave me a knowing wink. Without her, I would've died a dozen times over, and vice versa. We were a good team in more ways than one.

"I wonder if Conrad can open portals to other realms," Shelton said. "Guess we'd have to wait for him to recover to find out."

Adam blew out a breath. "Vitania opened portals big enough to drive a herd of elephants through and she didn't even break a sweat. I don't understand where she gets all that power."

"Ain't no telling," Shelton said. "But it ain't the same place ours comes from."

"I've seen the place where all the powers in the universe flow from the primal fount." I wasn't sure if it was actually a place, or just a simplified illustration sent to me in a waking dream. "Seraphim powers flow from one river. I imagine the Sirens have one of their own."

"I've seen this place too, Justin." Conrad chewed on the green gum Ambria had given him. "It's like a diagram of the universal power flow. The primal fount is just raw power. That means I can potentially shape it into any kind of magic I want, provided I learn how."

"That makes sense," Adam said. "I wonder how it's converted to different kinds of magic in the first place."

"There's another side to it though," Conrad said. "I only glimpsed it once, but there's an opposing source of magic, and it was the color of the hell-fire magic that demon used."

"Son of a bitch." Shelton groaned. "You're telling me those demons are tapping into a primal fount of their own?"

"I know what it's called," I said. Vitania had told us as much when she described the hellfire demons. "The opposite of the primal fount is the infernal fount in Hell."

"Wait a bloody minute," Max said. "Is that like Heaven and Hell?"

"There was a whole lot Vitania didn't explain," Shelton said. "All that talk of old gods and so forth didn't make much sense to me. Hell, I never even heard of the Apocryphan until relatively recently."

"I feel uninformed," Cinder said. "It would seem you have some stories to tell me."

"Yeah, we do." Shelton launched into a profanity-laced and heavily embellished recount of our latest adventure, but his summary was at least accurate and precise. "So Vitania went to Aquilis to see if Queen Dactia will help. Lumia went to have a chat with her daughters, Glacia and Pyra about joining the alliance. And we gotta go to Dubai and try to reopen the scar left behind by Emily Glass so we can get her on our side."

"I believe I can help the most by trying to replicate the portal technology by artificial means," Cinder said. "I believe an Mzodi gem charmer could be of great use."

"Uh, didn't we leave them all on Utopia?" Adam said.

"Not all of them," Elyssa said. "Two Mzodi ships are still here because Eden went out of alignment with Voltis and stranded them. I think their ships are sitting in the waters off the coast of Bermuda until the next alignment."

"I will find them," Cinder said.

Elyssa nodded. "Talk to my father to make sure you receive priority omniarch use, okay?"

I checked the time on my phone. It was getting late and those of us who could open scars were exhausted. "Let's get a good night's rest and meet up at the mansion first thing in the morning." I rubbed my hands together. "Tomorrow, we're going after Emily Glass."

CHAPTER 19

Five days until the truce ends.

Everyone was bright-eyed and bushy-tailed when we met after breakfast the next morning. Well, all of us except for me and Conrad. Nightliss didn't seem the least bit affected by her channeling the day before, but I felt it in my bones. Holding onto a complex weave like Clarity was no mean feat.

Conrad chewed on more of the nausea-reducing gum, but the green cast to his face told me aether poisoning was squirming in his guts like an eel. Ambria held his hand and rubbed it, as if that would fix everything. Then again, judging from the smile on his face, maybe it did.

Everyone wore backpacks loaded with supplies and brooms strapped to the sides. We didn't know what to expect when we went through the reopened portal, so it was best to be prepared for anything.

I'd wanted Nightingale armor for everyone, but the Templars still had none to spare. They also hadn't had time to repair the damage done to our last sets of armor. I hoped our magical and survival skills were enough to protect us from whatever dangers waited for us in the unknown.

In addition to the long line of nom recruits, there were dozens of white tents set up at the far end of the corridor. Most of the Borathen Templars and many of those in the Eden army who'd opted to remain in Queens Gate had taken up quarters in the old prisons in the Burrows, leaving little room for anything else. Xander's nom army had compounded the limited space problem and was now setting up in the corridor itself.

"Those idiots." Elyssa set her hands on her hips and glared at the camp. "We need to move them aboveground. There's no room for them here."

"As if we don't have enough problems as it is." I blew out a breath and tried to squash swelling despair. "It's almost as if Xander is trying to make things harder on us."

"Flooding our ranks with incompetent noms does feel like sabotage." Elyssa's eyes narrowed. "Either Xander is very clever, or very stupid."

"I wouldn't trust him farther than I can throw an elephant," Max said. "He doesn't care about anything except power and maybe Devon and Rhys."

"Speak of the devils." Shelton nodded toward the entrance to the omniarch room where a pair of sneering twin boys stood next to the idiot Templars we'd met yesterday. Their group faced down a pair of Borathen Templars who now guarded the entrance.

They seemed to sense us coming and spun to face our group, smirks at the ready. Long platinum locks hung around narrow jaws and high cheekbones. They definitely looked like serial killers—the kind who kept victims in a pit and made them put on lotion.

"Little brother, what a wonderful surprise." Devon ignored the rest of us. "Off on another adventure?"

"Hardly," Max said. "We're going to buy food in bulk to support all these noms Father keeps bringing in."

"Finally, a good use for your time." Rhys turned a smug smile on Elyssa.

"Look, we've got our people handling security down here. I don't see a reason for your father to interfere in our affairs."

Elyssa returned his smug grin with one of her own. "The omniarch in this room is a critical war resource. As such, it falls under Templar jurisdiction, per the Overworld Conclave. That supersedes the right of the Arcanus Primus even within Arcane University."

"Our recruiting efforts are critical to the war effort and supersede your authority," Devon replied. "Kindly tell your guards to remove themselves."

The Borathen Templars didn't so much as flinch at the venom in his tone.

"I'm afraid you're wrong," Elyssa said.

Devon grunted. "I disagree and invoke the conclave arbitration clause."

"Which is only applicable during times of peace." Elyssa tutted. "Sorry, boys, but the treaty with Xander explicitly states a wartime emergency." She made a shooing motion. "Now kindly remove yourselves."

Rhys's pale face turned red. "Then I request a log of all travel made through this and other omniarches as evidence that you are not using it for emergencies, but for personal use that interferes with our recruitment efforts."

"I think you'll find that falls within our right," Devon said in a cold voice.

"Gladly," Elyssa said. "Please fill out, in triplicate, forms OC-792A, OC-792C, and ARC-1099."

The twins clenched their fists and looked ready to blow their fuses. Devon sneered at Elyssa. "We will have them to you shortly." He and his brother stalked away from the omniarch, the Eden Templars skulking along behind them.

Elyssa's lips pressed together. "Xander is definitely up to something."

She turned to the Borathen Templars. "Whatever you do, don't let Eden Templars man this post. Do you understand?"

"Yes, sir." The pair saluted, fists to their chests.

Elyssa brushed her hands together. "I think we're ready to go, then."

"Commander Borathen, there is a backlog on the portal," the first Templar said. "Do you wish to use your priority pass?"

"Yes, please." Elyssa looked back to make sure Devon and Rhys weren't lurking about, and then showed the Templar a picture of the hotel room in Dubai. "That's our destination."

"At once." The first Templar sealed the silver circle around the omniarch and stared at the picture. A vertical line split the air and widened into a portal to the hotel room. I went through first, followed by the others. I nearly tripped over my own feet when I saw two open suitcases sitting on the bench against the wall.

"Someone's staying in this room," I hissed. But the portal closed before we could reverse course back through it.

Shelton rolled his eyes and called out, "Room service!"

No one answered.

"What if someone had been here, Shelton?" Elyssa threw up her hands. "Were we supposed to knock them out?"

"Meh, whatever works." Shelton grabbed a bottled water from the fridge and took a sip. "They have any complimentary peanuts in here?"

Elyssa huffed and walked to the door. She clicked the deadbolt and flicked the lock bar in place. Then she picked up some literature from a table and looked out the window at a monstrous skyscraper. "That's the Burj Khalifa, the tallest building in the world."

Shelton scoffed. "Tallest nom building. Fjoeruss's building is at least twice as tall."

"We'll sightsee later," I said. "Let's get to work before the occupants come back."

I channeled translucent beam of Clarity and scanned the bedroom, the den, and the kitchen. I accidentally nicked Shelton when I swept it into the closet. He shouted in alarm and went stiff as a board. I winced and jerked the beam away from him.

"Holy shit." Shelton held onto a dresser for support and dropped onto the couch. "What happened?"

"You got caught in Clarity." Adam leaned over and looked into his eyes. "What did you see?"

Shelton seemed too shaken to answer.

"Hold on." Ambria gripped my arm. "Point the Clarity at the floor in the foyer again."

I moved it back to the area near the door. Faint lines appeared in the carpet. We walked over and inspected it. The carpet looked fine, but the faint lines of an intricate pattern were visible.

"That's a demon diagram," Conrad said. "It must have etched into the floor beneath the carpet."

As with the portal scars, it seemed Clarity could pick up the remnants of other powerful magic as well. I whistled. "So a demon was here at some point."

"Maybe that's why they left," Ambria said.

"I think you're right." It was an interesting clue, but not the one we really needed to find. What if Emily and Tyler hadn't left through a portal in the room? What if they'd run into the hallway or somewhere else first? But the instant I swept the Clarity beam into the bathroom, I discovered what we were looking for.

"Found it!" The beam highlighted a long vertical scar just inside the bathroom door. I continued to channel the beam and walked inside to scan the interior but found nothing else.

"Did you scan the entire suite?" Elyssa said. "We don't want to miss anything."

"Yeah, no other scars." I moved out of Nightliss's way. "This is the one."

The bathroom was nearly half as large as the house I'd grown up in. A shower with dozens of nozzles and showerheads occupied nearly half the room and looked big enough to hold six people. A jet tub with enough room to accommodate the people from the shower ran along the length of a window overlooking the cityscape.

Adam whistled. "Emily and Tyler sure know how to live it up."

"Dude's a billionaire." Shelton's voice sounded weak. "He could stay here a year if he wanted."

Nightliss channeled Stasis around the portal scar until it crystallized. Then she quickly switched to Murk and wedged it inside. Gritting her teeth, forehead pinched in concentration, she thrust her hands apart. Thunder boomed. The windows cracked and buckled. The wall-length mirror shattered. The glass shower doors exploded into shards. The entire room shook beneath our feet.

Adam covered his head with his hands. "Holy crap!"

"Open!" Nightliss cried and pushed her hands farther apart. The portal opened wide enough for us to fit through.

I stopped channeling Clarity and Nightliss tied off the weave holding open the portal. Blue ocean waves crashed onto white, sugary sand. Dozens of bioluminescent rainbow flowers like the one Fjoeruss showed us grew all along the shore.

"Looks safe enough," Elyssa said. "Everyone through before hotel security shows up."

Everyone dashed for the portal. Nightliss went through right before me. I plowed into her and Elyssa stumbled into me. I barely noticed the rest of the group pushing through because I was too stunned by what I saw.

Beyond the sugary sands of the beach, a creature tore the leaves from the top of a tropical tree. It was something I'd fantasized about seeing ever since I was a kid, but without a time machine, figured it was impossible.

"Am I dreaming or is that a freaking dinosaur?" Shelton said.

"It's a freaking dinosaur!" I clapped my hands and danced in place. "Can you believe it?"

"Wow!" Adam giggled like a kid. "That's a brontosaurus!"

Even Conrad looked impressed. "I can hardly believe it."

Ambria swatted a large mosquito away from her face. "Good lord! That bug was big enough to bite off a finger!"

Elyssa sighed. "After fighting giant dragons, you're impressed with a dinosaur?"

"They're supposed to be extinct." I took a deep breath to contain my excitement. "And yet here they are!"

"It's hot as a dinosaur's tit out here." Shelton took off his hat and fanned his face.

The humidity felt thick enough to drink, but it wasn't much worse than what I'd experienced during summers in Atlanta. The ocean breeze helped a little, but not much. It was certainly a prime climate for dinosaurs to thrive.

Adam recorded video with his arcphone. "I can't wait to show this to everyone back home."

"Look, there's a whole herd of leaf-eaters." Shelton pointed further down the beach where dozens of massive heads poked out of the jungle canopy.

Elyssa removed a tiny silver marble from her fanny pack and tossed it into the air. The ASE—all-seeing-eye—flew away and began transmitting panoramic video back to Elyssa's arcphone. She projected a hologram so we could all watch. The ASE swept over miles of jungle and reached a grassy plain where dozens of smaller dinosaurs grazed.

"T-rex!" Max shouted.

Thankfully, it was in the video and not racing out of the jungle to eat us.

With the initial excitement dying down, I started to think about our objective again. "Do you think Tyler and Emily are still here?"

Elyssa didn't take her eyes off the video. "I don't know. A realm full of dinosaurs doesn't seem like the ideal place to find refuge."

"Wait, stop the ASE," Adam said.

Elyssa tapped on her screen and the video stopped over another vast section of jungle. The panoramic video displayed everything in a radius around the ASE, but the fishbowl effect warped the edges.

Adam pointed to something glinting in the sun right at the edge of the video. "What's that?"

"Good question." Elyssa directed the ASE in that direction until it crossed from the edge of the hologram and resolved into something too smooth and perfectly curved to be anything but artificial.

"It's a dome," Adam said.

"It looks like glass, but it's gotta be something else," Shelton said.

The glare from reflected sunlight made it hard to see anything except the silhouettes of structures inside. The ASE raced over rivers and jungle until it reached the massive dome. The buildings inside were of many shapes and sizes, but not a one of them had angles. They were all smoothly curved like the dome around them.

Max's eyebrows rose. "Do you think there are humans here?"

183

"I see movement." Adam pointed to a building near the edge of the dome. "Zoom in."

Tiny figures in the distance abruptly swelled to fill the screen. They were bipedal and walked upright, but that was where the comparison to humans ended. Some had two arms, others had four. Most had tails, but some had none. Their skin colors ranged from shades of brown, to gray, and green, but they all had one thing in common—scales. Because these people weren't mammals—they were reptiles.

Most of them didn't wear clothing of any kind. Only a few wore what seemed to be scaled vests made of glassy material.

"This is amazeballs!" Max put his hands to his cheeks. "A realm where reptiles are the dominant species."

Shelton blew out a breath. "And pretty damned advanced."

"Reptile people?" Ambria shook her head. "I never would have imagined."

Adam pointed to two of the reptile people with the vests. "If I had to guess, I'd say that's armor. And the only reptiles wearing it are of the Godzilla variety."

Shelton chuckled. "Yeah, they do look kind of like mini-Godzillas."

The ones they spoke of were dark green with small heads perched on bulky bodies. They towered above the others and had long, thick alligator tails. Smaller reptiles made up the bulk of the population. Some resembled geckos, others had eyes on stalks that seemed able to look in all directions.

"I don't think this is a reptile civilization," Adam said. "All I see are lizards."

"I think you're right," Elyssa said. "I don't see snakes or turtles—just lizards."

Adam nodded. "With forward-facing eyes."

"Maybe we could talk to them," Ambria said. "They'd certainly remember seeing any humans pass through here."

"Not a good idea," Elyssa said. "We don't know how they'd react to our presence." She tapped her phone screen and the image panned around the dome city.

"Yeah, I don't think Emily and Tyler would risk travelling through the jungle around here," I said. "You've got dinosaurs and giant mosquitoes to contend with."

Elyssa nodded. "Besides, that city is miles away, and I doubt Emily and Tyler had an ASE to locate it for them."

"True." Adam picked up a seashell and tossed it into the water. "Vitania said Emily had a list but it was older without the same details ours had. I doubt she knew much about this realm before jumping to it."

Elyssa pursed her lips. "They were being pursued by demons, so they chose the first realm they saw and portaled here."

Adam held a hand over his phone screen to shield it from the sun. "The first thing they saw were the dinosaurs."

Max snapped his fingers. "Without extra clothes or food, they probably decided to leave as quickly as possible."

"Precisely," Adam said. "As soon as she was able, Emily probably made another portal and they left."

"So the scar would be nearby," Shelton said.

Elyssa flicked her gaze to me. "Give the area a scan?"

I was still pretty tired from scanning the hotel room, but had some juice left. "Sure." I went through the rigmarole of weaving Clarity and swept it through the air around us. Everyone made sure to stay well away from the beam, especially Shelton. Just behind us was the scar from the portal we'd just used, but I didn't see a second one nearby.

Sweat stung my eyes and trickled down my back. Between the humidity and the strain of channeling, I felt like I was about to overheat, so I released the weave and took a deep breath. "I don't see anything."

Adam blew out a breath. "Damn. That means they could've made a portal anywhere."

"You look exhausted," Nightliss said.

I groaned. "I feel it in my bones."

"You both look tired," Ambria said. "Perhaps the strain of opening a portal exhausted Emily too."

"I think you're right," Conrad said. "They might have arrived here and had to rest a while."

Elyssa turned in a circle. "There's not much nearby except jungle and beach." She pointed to a rocky cove a few hundred yards down the beach. Large boulders formed a natural wall, protecting it from the waves and the jungle. "If I needed a safe resting spot for a few hours, I'd probably take shelter there."

I fanned my face with a hand. "Let's check it out."

The thick sand made walking tedious, so we moved to the damp sand where the waves lapped the shore.

Adam looked up and around, recording video with his phone and taking notes. "I've noted only one small moon which would account for the weak tidal pattern." He picked up another seashell and examined it as we walked. "Sea life might be similar to Eden's judging from the size and shape of shells I've found."

Shelton nudged his friend in the ribs. "You don't stop, do you?"

"It's fascinating," Adam said. "If Earth hadn't been split into realms, none of this might exist. Evolution took a different path here, leading to a lizard civilization."

"Yeah. Remember when we were hunting for Eden and we found that world with the snake man?"

Adam nodded. "I'd love to hunt down that realm and explore it too."

Ambria grimaced. "What if the snake people are poisonous?"

"Well, what if they're nice?" Max countered. "Just because they're snakes doesn't make them mean."

Elyssa jogged ahead of us and reached the cove first. I assumed it was because she didn't want to hear Ambria and Max bickering like they usually did. She vanished behind the rocks and quickly reappeared, waving her arms wildly.

Something was horribly wrong.

CHAPTER 20

E lyssa put a finger to her mouth. I turned around and shushed the others. "Quiet! Red alert."

We waited for Elyssa to return before taking another step. She gathered us into a huddle. "There's something huge inside that cove," she said. "All I saw were scales and piles of bones."

"Oh, god." Ambria put a hand to her mouth. "Human bones?"

Elyssa shook her head. "I'm not sure. I recalled the ASE so it could take a look, but it'll take it a minute to get here."

Shelton's eyes went wide and locked onto something. "Christ Almighty. Look at that thing!"

A massive green head appeared from the edge of the boulders. A forked tongue slithered from the mouth and beady red eyes looked our way. A huge webbed foot emerged, followed by a thick trunk.

Adam recorded it with his phone. "It resembles a monitor lizard, but with webbed feet for swimming."

The lizard navigated around the boulders and began running down the beach at us. It was bigger than a city bus and a whole lot faster.

"What now?" Shelton gripped his staff.

Conrad stepped up beside me. "I think it's safe to say Emily and Tyler didn't take refuge in those rocks."

"I think you're right." Elyssa took out her light bow and snapped it out to full length. She put her fingers in the middle. A beam of energy formed the bowstring and a nocked arrow. She pulled back and fired. The energy arrow struck the lizard in the snout and stuck there. It hissed and rubbed its muzzle in the sand.

Elyssa nocked another arrow. It modulated from bright red to ice blue at her mental commands. She sent it streaking into the lizard's nose and followed it up with four more. Frost crackled along its muzzle. It buried its nose in the sand again, but that did nothing to dissipate the freezing energy. It plunged into the ocean and swam away from shore.

"Frost arrows." Shelton grinned. "Good thinking."

Elyssa watched the ripples left by the fleeing lizard for a moment before compacting her bow and holstering it. "I still want to look at the cove. It's possible Emily and Tyler went in when the lizard wasn't there."

"And got eaten?" Max shuddered. "How awful!"

Conrad heaved and turned away from us. He went down on his knees.

"I didn't mean to make you sick," Max said.

Ambria rushed to Conrad's side and gave him a piece of green gum. "It's the magic sickness, dummy."

Max grimace. "Oh, I forgot."

Conrad climbed to his feet after his dry heaves produced nothing. His face was paler than the sand, but he swallowed hard and began walking.

The odor of rotting fish grew stronger the closer we got to the cove. I followed Elyssa around the boulders and up a slight rise. A half-eaten fish head as big as my body lay near the water's edge. Fish bones littered the sandy shore. Driftwood and dry seaweed formed a nest full of eggs.

"They definitely would've seen that," Shelton said. "Ain't no way they didn't turn right around and run for it."

But Elyssa kept walking along the irregular wall of boulders. Only a few feet in, she turned left and vanished. I rounded the corner behind her and saw a narrow space between the rocks just big enough for a human to walk through. I navigated the crevice and emerged into a small space enclosed by stone.

"Look what I found." Elyssa held up a scrap of foil. "A peanut packet from the hotel."

"And a water bottle." Ambria picked up the empty container. "They were here. I just knew Elyssa was right."

The space was only about thirty feet long and half as wide, but it was definitely safe enough for anyone avoiding giant lizards.

"Everyone hug the wall behind me," I said. Once they did, I took a deep breath to rally my strength and scanned the area with Clarity. A diagonal slash appeared near the center of the clearing.

Shelton whooped. "Yes!"

Nightliss smiled. "I don't know how you do it, Elyssa."

Elyssa shrugged. "I always wanted to be a Templar inquisitor. Investigating leads and hunting down culprits was way more exciting to me than combat and enforcement."

I grinned. "Guess I lucked out when you ran into me on your first big investigation."

"Seems like a lifetime ago." Elyssa sighed. "Nightliss, can you do the honors?"

The petite angel stepped up beside me and hosed down the crack with

Stasis. She grunted and strained to pry open the crack. Thunder boomed as the scar ripped open.

"Hurry through," Nightliss said. "I can't tie it open for long."

I released the Clarity weave and tried to run through, but my knees felt like jelly. Elyssa slung my arm over her shoulder and wrapped another one around my waist. She dragged me through the portal and into the next realm.

The ground on the other side was purple and jiggled beneath our feet. The only vegetation was clusters of waist-high weeds. Small hills—bumps actually—no more than a few feet tall, gave the landscape an even odder appearance.

Adam helped Nightliss through the portal and the rest of the gang filed after them. The portal remained open another twenty seconds before collapsing shut.

"What in the hell kind of place is this?" Shelton said. He knelt and rubbed his fingers on the ground. "The ground feels like rubber."

Max turned in a circle. "No trees or grass. Just weeds."

"Purple weeds, purple bumps, purple everything." Shelton shook his head. "Something's off about this place."

"I'd like to know what made them choose it," Ambria said. "Surely they had time to pick their next destination."

"Yeah, but Vitania said the list Emily has doesn't have any descriptions." I shrugged. "They probably didn't have enough information to know what it was like."

Elyssa rubbed my back. "Can you stand up okay?"

"I prefer to sit." I sat down on a small bump and was surprised by how springy it was. "Man, this place is weird. The ground is cushioned."

Shelton grunted. "Yeah, I'm kinda freaked out."

Max bent down and tried to pick up what looked like a purple stone, but it wouldn't budge. He got on his knees and looked at it sideways. "This might sound strange, but I think this rock is actually part of the ground."

Adam inspected another rock. "I think you're right. There are no seams."

Conrad looked up and around. "At least the sky is blue, and the sun is yellow."

"That's about the only normal thing about this place," Shelton said.

Ambria slid a water bottle from the side of her backpack and took a long drink.

"Go easy on the water," Elyssa said. "I don't see any fresh water sources nearby and we'll probably need to stay here the night so Justin and Nightliss can recover."

"How am I supposed to cook bacon for breakfast?" Shelton said. "I don't see any wood in in this stupid place."

"Hey, what's that?" Ambria pointed to a fuzzy red cloud drifting in the sky.

Adam produced spectacles from his backpack and peered through them. "It's not a normal cloud. Almost looks like dandelion fluff."

"Probably some kind of plant life," Max said.

Shelton looked around. "Yeah, but I don't see anything like it growing around here."

Elyssa checked her arcphone. "It's past lunchtime in our native time zone, and I'm starving. Let's eat and talk about next moves."

"That's an excellent plan!" Max rubbed his belly. "I'm starving."

"You and me both, kid." Shelton sat on the ground next to him and started unpacking a bundle of Colombian arepas and empanadas. "Man, I love Bella's cooking. I packed plenty of pancake mix, a few pounds of bacon, and anything else that fit in the preservation compartment."

Elyssa unwrapped hunk of dried meat and sliced off a piece. "If I'd known Shelton was bringing the entire pantry, I wouldn't have bothered packing anything."

Shelton sprinkled salt on an arepa and bit into it with gusto. "I just wish I still had my magic satchel. I could literally fit an entire pig's worth of bacon in that thing."

"These were the best backpacks I could find in Queens Gate," Adam said. "A lot of good companies vanished while we were gone."

Max shook his head sadly. "Victus purged hundreds of people, sometimes even entire families. That killed off a lot of family businesses and the economy still hasn't recovered."

"I guess you were just a little thing back then," Shelton said.

Max nodded. "I was five or six. Old enough to remember some things. Victus didn't rule for very long, but he did a lot of damage in a short amount of time."

"Ivy still doesn't remember the events leading up to her defeating Victus," I said. "I'd like to know how it went down."

"There's almost nothing written about it," Max said. "Victus and Delectra faked their deaths, and Ivy disappeared right after that. There was a power vacuum that my father tried to fill, but he wasn't powerful enough to hold on. Then the people who took over tried to take credit for everything Ivy had done."

I tore off a hunk of dried meat and chewed it. "Victus and Cephus played us like idiots. After I thought Nightliss died in the Crystoid Incident, all I wanted was revenge."

"We had to go to Seraphina," Elyssa said. "We couldn't let Cephus launch another crystoid attack or something worse. We had no way of knowing that he and Victus were plotting together."

"I'm not even gonna lie," Adam said. "I'm kind of jealous of Victus's ability to plot and scheme. I'd put him right up there with Baal."

Elyssa nodded. "I wish I could disagree, but he fooled all of us."

"My father was sick in the head." Conrad stabbed a knife into a hunk of cheese. "He twisted a good woman into a monster. Used demons to turn me into a vessel for his soul. He genetically designed and bred an army of mutants to help him take power. But every time he got what he wanted someone was there to knock him off his throne." A wry smile crossed his lips. "So in the end, all his hard work was for absolutely nothing."

Ambria rubbed his back. "You're a better person in every way, Conrad."

He shook his head. "No. My father was ten times smarter. He just didn't have a single friend in the world." Conrad took her hand and kissed it. "It's amazing what odds you can overcome when you have something to fight for."

"Amen!" Shelton held up his water bottle. "Screw Baal, screw Xanos, and screw all the other assholes while we're at it."

I held up my water bottle. "Here's to friends, true love, and tacos."

The others held up their bottles in a toast. "Friends, true love, and tacos!"

Shelton face-palmed. "I knew I forgot to pack one of the major food groups."

Max pointed skyward. "Uh, is my vision going wonky or is that cloud coming toward us?"

I shielded my eyes and looked up. The cloud was not only lower, but it seemed to be on a direct course for us. "Your eyes are fine."

Elyssa jammed her dried meat into her backpack and whipped out her light bow. "Prep a defensive shield. I don't like the way this looks."

Ambria produced her wand. "I'm ready, Madam Commander."

Shelton snapped his staff out to full length. "I ain't afraid of no cloud."

Adam tapped on his arcphone. "I have a shield spell ready."

I wished I could do something, but my demon half was still hiding from me and my Seraphim half was tired as hell from channeling so much Clarity. Nightliss didn't seem in much better shape than me and Conrad looked ready to barf at any moment. Thankfully, we had my fearless ninja girlfriend and three strong Arcanes for backup.

The cloud angled lower and lower until it was about fifty feet off the ground and only a few hundred yards away. The closer it came, the less it looked like a cloud and the more it resembled a flying sea urchin. Countless red spikes quivered and undulated along its irregular length. It went from spherical to oblong in the space of a minute, then stretched wider the next, almost as if it had no defined shape.

Shelton held his wand up to his throat and spoke in a magically amplified voice. "If you understand me, stop where you are."

Ambria raised an eyebrow. "Talking to clouds, Shelton?"

He shrugged. "After everything I've seen, I figure it's worth a shot if it means not fighting whatever that thing is."

The cloud, however, didn't stop. If anything, it picked up speed.

Elyssa nocked a flaming arrow and loosed it skyward. It plunged into the cloud. The needle-like protrusions exploded in all directions. And what lay beneath was horrifying.

CHAPTER 21

The spikes hid a bulbous red mass, a floating blob with a round orifice on the bottom. Rows of flat tooth-like protrusions ground against each other. Anything that went inside that mouth would be reduced to paste in minutes.

Flaming needles fell to earth. But those that hadn't been hit by the arrow took flight. Their wings were so narrow that when closed, looked like spikes. The winged creatures had four legs covered in spiky hair. They had no eyes or mouths that I could see along their stubby bodies but that made them no less terrifying.

Their size at a distance had been deceptive. Their bodies were nearly as large as a human head and their wings spanned several feet. The floating blob was larger than an adult elephant.

"Jesus H. Jones!" Shelton shouted. "Open fire!"

Elyssa fired arrow after arrow at the insects. Ambria and Max targeted them with their wands, taking down two or three at a time. But that barely put a dent in their numbers. Shelton unleashed a wide beam of energy, incinerating a group of them, but the swarm spread apart and circled around them.

"It's adapting to our attacks!" Elyssa took down another flier and ducked beneath the grasping legs of another.

Ambria shrieked. The hairy spikes from one of the bugs stabbed into her shoulder, but she was too heavy for it to lift off the ground. Conrad roared. Blue energy exploded from his hands and the bug splattered, sending red goo everywhere. Conrad stumbled to his knees and heaved.

He pounded the ground with a fist. "No! I will not be sick!"

Adam tapped his phone and an energy shield formed around us. Electricity crackled, zapping the nearest bugs. The creatures backed off, hovering all around the dome until they blocked out the light and left us in the dark.

"Ambria, are you okay?" Conrad climbed unsteadily to his feet and examined her shoulder. One of the bug legs dangled from her flesh, the spike still embedded too deep for it to fall out. Red goop coated her hair and torso. The spike measured about twelve inches long and was as big around as my index finger. Ambria's blood glistened on cruel barbs.

Tears rolled down Ambria's cheeks. Her face contorted with pain. "Get it out!"

Nightliss began to channel but Elyssa held up a hand to stop her. "No. We need you and Justin to conserve all your energy. There's no way we can stay the night in this hellhole."

"Amen." Shelton ground his teeth. "How in the hell could Emily and Tyler survive this shit storm?"

"I hope they didn't get eaten." Max cast light with the glowing tip of his wand. "That cloud monster wouldn't even leave a skeleton behind if it ate you."

Elyssa slipped a potion bottle from her backpack and dripped the contents over Ambria's shoulder. "This should numb the pain for now."

Ambria's taut grimace slackened as the numbing agent kicked in. Elyssa produced a dagger and sawed off the spike close to the leg so about six inches protruded from the puckered wound. Elyssa inspected the other spikes on the legs. "They're barbed." She winced. "I'm sorry, but this is going to hurt, Ambria."

The girl clenched her teeth and nodded. Elyssa examined the front of Ambria's shoulder where the tip of the spike protruded. "There's not enough sticking out for me to grab." She walked around to the back. "Someone hold her steady."

Max braced Ambria's left shoulder and Shelton held onto her right, his hand a few inches from the wound.

"Hang on." Shelton grabbed a piece of Elyssa's dried beef from her backpack and held it to Ambria's mouth. "Brace your teeth on this."

Ambria opened wide and Shelton slid it in so she could clamp down with her molars. Then he braced her shoulder and nodded.

Elyssa counted down. "Three, two, one." Using the flat of her dagger, she punched the spike through the gory hole. Ambria screamed as several inches burst from the front of her shoulder. Her knees gave way, but Shelton and Max held her up. Grimacing, Elyssa stepped in front of Ambria and yanked the spike the rest of the way through.

Blood streamed from the wound. Elyssa poured water on it and dried it with black cloth she took from her medic pack. It soaked up everything, leaving behind the torn flesh. Elyssa applied another patch of black cloth to cover the front wound then repeated the process for the back.

"Glad I brought a Templar field medic kit." Elyssa slid it into her backpack. "I just hope those spikes aren't poisoned."

Ambria collapsed against Shelton. He patted her head. "Hey, you're one tough gal. Adam would've passed out."

Conrad tried to speak, but only managed to dry heave again.

Adam looked at his phone screen. "Not to cause undue worry, but we're trapped in here, and the minute this shield drops, we're all getting spiked."

Elyssa wiped the blood from her hands with a black cloth while she looked up and around at the dark swarm overhead. "How long do we have before the shield drops?"

"About an hour," Adam said. "The phone's battery will run dry by then."

Shelton looked at me and Nightliss. "Any chance you'll have enough juice to open the scar back to lizard world by then?"

I shrugged. "Maybe."

Nightliss winced. "I might be able to open the scar, but I won't be able to hold it open long enough for all of us to get through."

"Then it's a no-go," I said. "Either we all make it, or none of us do."

"I might have an idea," Max said.

Shelton helped Ambria take a seat on the ground, then turned to his student. "Whatcha got?"

"Those insects don't have mouths," Max said. "That means they don't eat." He pointed through a narrow gap in the bugs at the undulating blimp creature. "But that thing does."

"I don't see the point," Elyssa said.

Max pointed up again. "It means that these bugs might be part of a hive mind. They collect food and feed it to the brain."

Shelton snapped his fingers. "And if we blast the brain, the bugs ain't a problem!"

Adam worked his jaw back and forth. "How do we destroy the brain before the bugs kill us? I can't exactly open a hole in the shield that we can fire though."

"I've got an idea." Shelton rapidly flicked the screen on his phone and grunted when he found what he wanted. "Get ready to drop your shield."

"Say what?" Adam grabbed Shelton's arcphone and looked at it. "Dude, you haven't used this spell since you kicked Arturo's ass. You sure it's up to snuff?"

"I guarantee it," Shelton said."

"Hey, wait, what spell?" I said.

"Drop your shield in three, two, one, now!" Shelton tapped the screen on his phone. Adam's shield blinked off and for a split instant, nothing but a few yards of open air remained between us and the hum of wings. The bug drones dove at us.

And smacked into a honeycombed shield—the very same geodesic shield Shelton used to win my mother the throne to the Brightling Empire. "Yes, it worked!" Shelton pumped a fist.

"Uh, you just said that like you're surprised," Adam said.

Shelton shrugged. "Well, you never know, right?"

The drones smacked repeatedly into the panels. Unlike Adam's bug zapper shield, this one didn't harm them. It was like listening to a flock of birds crash into a windshield.

Elyssa stepped up to a section of shield with a clear view of the floating brain. "We'll probably get just one shot before that thing blocks us with its drones."

"So we have to it hit hard." Adam punched his palm. "The problem is, it's too far away for a spell to hit it with maximum power."

Shelton nodded. "It's about thirty yards away. Even my strongest spell will only hit at about seventy percent strength from this distance."

The bugs continued to slam into the shield over and over again, raising a racket that hurt my ears.

"What about the light bow?" I shouted over the noise. "The longer you hold an arrow, the stronger it gets."

"But only to a certain point," Elyssa said. "It'll charge to max in five seconds, but I don't think that would be enough to significantly hurt the brain."

Adam pursed his lips. "Hey, maybe we can add a little something of our own to the arrow."

"You mean overcharge it?" Shelton said.

"Exactly." Adam tapped the bow. "When you pull back on the energy string, it forms a cohesive energy bolt based on the will of the wielder. It contains that energy by using metamorphic shield arcnology that I don't quite understand."

"Yeah, even the current Atlanteans don't understand half the ancient weapons they have," Shelton said. "So how do we overcharge an arrow if we don't understand the tech behind it?"

"We don't have to understand it; we just have to overcharge the energy string right when Elyssa nocks the arrow." Adam mimicked grasping the string. "Since the string charges the arrow for up to five seconds, we should be able to overcharge it by transmitting power through the string."

Shelton grunted. "It might work. If it doesn't, then what?"

"I don't have to fire the arrow," Elyssa said. "I can slowly release the string and it'll dissipate."

"All right." Shelton snapped his staff to full length. "Then let's see if it works."

Elyssa readied the bow. Adam and Shelton charged their staffs until the energy hum grew nearly as loud as the bodies crashing into the shield.

"Go," Adam said.

Elyssa nocked an arrow. Shelton and Adam touched their staffs to the energy string. Power pulsed along it and into the arrow. The arrow began to swell. Electrical currents crackled and spat sparks.

One hit my arm. I shouted and leapt back. "Holy shit. It's like being smacked with a branding iron!"

"Everyone back away!" Elyssa said, but there wasn't much room in the shield. "This arrow is about to explode!"

Shelton dropped his staff and grabbed his phone. "Get your aim ready!"

Elyssa gritted her teeth and pointed it toward the brain. The arrow shimmered and crackled violently. Sparks bounced off Elyssa's skin, sizzling and filling the shield with the odor of burnt flesh. Tears of pain welled in her eyes. "Drop it now!"

"Here it comes." Shelton tapped the phone. Nothing happened. "What the hell?"

"It's burns like a mother fucker!" Elyssa's arms trembled. "I don't think this arrow will dissipate if I don't fire it."

"The explosion will incinerate us!" Adam said. "Open the damned panel, Shelton!"

"It's not working!" he shouted back. "We'll have to drop the entire shield."

"My phone needs to charge before I can reactivate my shield," Adam said. "If you drop this shield, we're gonna be wide open."

Max took out his wand. "Then drop the entire shield. I'll keep us safe until Elyssa can fire."

"Son of a ball-licking bastard!" Shelton gave Max a long look. "Good luck, kid."

Max flicked his wand through a pattern and power glowed at the tip. "I'm ready."

Shelton tapped his phone screen and the shield vanished.

Three things happened in quick succession.

Elyssa released the arrow. The drones swarmed toward us. And Max, bless his bright little mind, unleashed a firestorm from his wand.

The first wave of bug drones went down in a blaze.

Max waved his wand in a circle, forming a barrier of fire in the air above us that barely held off the drones. Elyssa's gaze was locked on the target. Her crackling arrow soared high and arced down. Drones buzzed away from us in a desperate attempt to intercept the energy missile, but they were too slow.

The arrow buried itself right on top of the brain. An instant later, it exploded in a ball of blue and golden energy. Flesh bubbled and smoked. The brain shrieked. Drones flocked away from us and toward it but there was nothing they could do. The brain drifted lower and into a field of weeds.

The weeds twitched and stretched as if they had life of their own. They ensnared the brain and dragged it lower. The drones attacked the weeds, but were snatched from the air. The ground opened up and swallowed them whole. The surviving drones flew back and forth erratically, as if the brain was losing control of them.

"Oh, sweet baby Jesus." Shelton looked down at the ground and the nearby patches of weeds. "Those are freaking tentacles and the ground is a fucking monster!"

"We're in even more danger than I realized." Adam froze in place. "Whatever you do, don't touch those weeds."

Elyssa dropped her bow and fell to her knees. Tears streamed from her eyes. She tried to open her satchel, but her burned hands refused her commands.

"Babe!" I scrambled to her pack and opened the med kit. A dozen potions were strapped inside.

"Blue one," she said through clenched teeth.

I popped the cork and dribbled it over her hands. The cracked, blackened skin began to peel away. Elyssa screamed behind gritted teeth. A bug drone zipped out of nowhere and slammed into my chest. I tumbled backwards and rolled about five feet, coming to rest on my back.

"Ow!" I struggled to get up but something wrapped around my torso and bound me to the ground.

"It's got Justin!" Shelton shouted.

I felt the rubbery ground opening beneath me. I turned my head as far as I could and saw a pit of darkness. Burbling liquid echoed from the pit. It reeked like acidic puke. I had little doubt it would dissolve me in minutes.

Max appeared at my side. He slashed with his wand and the tentacle went slack. Unfortunately, there was no ground to catch me and I fell screaming into the pit.

CHAPTER 22

Hands gripped my ankles. My head bounced against the fleshy sides of the pit.

"It's closing up!" Shelton shouted.

"Got him!" Adam yelled back as another pair of hands grabbed my other ankle.

My back squeaked against the side of the pit and daylight filled my vision again. Adam and Shelton dragged me back to the small area of safety before helping me to my feet.

Elyssa lay on her side, eyes closed. Ambria huddled next to her, eyes filled with pain. Meanwhile, the floating brain was embroiled in an all-out war for survival against the ground. The fleshy earth quivered beneath us, sending chills up my spine.

Max zapped a couple more bugs that flew too close.

"This place is a freaking nightmare." I shivered, suddenly cold. "I'd rather be trapped on lizard world than be eaten by the ground I'm standing on."

"But you and Nightliss are exhausted." Shelton shook his head. "We've got no way to leave."

Nightliss rubbed my arm. "I won't be able to hold open the scar long enough for everyone to go through, but maybe it's for the best."

"No." My lips felt rubbery and my vision blurred. "No one left behind." I tried to collect my wits, but my brain wanted no part of it.

"We have to rest." I could barely keep my eyes open. "We need rest."

Shelton's forehead pinched. "How the hell are we supposed to survive without Elyssa's help?"

I felt almost drunk from exhaustion. And that was when I realized something awful. "Tentacles are poisoned."

Shelton's panicked face was the last thing I saw before the darkness took me.

I WOKE UP, which was something of a surprise. I honestly thought I was going to die from whatever that ground tentacle put in me. Instead, I felt well rested and bursting with energy.

"He's finally awake!" Shelton got in my face and gripped my shoulders. "We need to freaking go now!" He jerked me to my feet.

I wiped the sleep crud from my eyes and flinched when the world snapped into focus. The blubbery purple ground had receded about thirty yards in all directions, leaving hard-packed dirt. The edges where the flesh met the dirt were blackened and scarred. A small shield covered our party.

Nightliss was awake. Elyssa and Ambria lay against each other, eyes fluttering feverishly. Adam, Shelton, and Max looked dead on their feet. Purple goop stained their clothes, and Shelton sported a cut over his right eye. Conrad was curled in the fetal position behind Ambria.

Hundreds of bug drones swarmed in the sky overhead, red, yellow, and green, attacking rival brains and each other. Winged bodies littered the ground, and the ground was trying to make meals of at least two more brain clouds. But the ground apparently wasn't the apex predator in this land. Ostriches over ten feet tall attacked the ground tentacles with razor-sharp claws and beaks, trying to take their share of the fallen cloud brain.

The entire area was a warzone and a tiny shield was the only thing keeping us from becoming the next feast.

"Please tell me you can open the damned scar!" Shelton lightly slapped my cheek. "Justin? You in there?"

I nodded. "Yeah, I'm good to go." I glanced at Nightliss. "Are you?"

"Yes." She flexed her hands.

Thankfully, we hadn't moved far from the scar we'd come through. I channeled Clarity and scanned. The diagonal scar appeared about a foot outside the safety of our shield. I glimpsed something and aimed the Clarity beam up and a little to the right. A crooked horizontal scar appeared only a little behind the one we'd used to come to this world.

"Maybe we shouldn't go back to lizard world," I said. "Maybe we should push onward." I released the Clarity weave to conserve my energy.

Shelton wiped sweat off his forehead. "Dude, just get us the hell out of here!"

"Please!" Max held a wand with trembling fingers. "I'm so tired."

"My phone is almost dead," Adam said. "We had to rotate shield duty all night."

Max looked down at his slumbering friend. "Conrad fought off a huge attack when the shield went out. He blasted everything and then passed out."

"The shield went down twice more, and we almost died." Shelton leaned heavily on his staff. "Just get us through."

I turned to Nightliss. "Let's do this fast."

She nodded. "I'm ready."

"We've got to drop the shield to open the scar." I grabbed Shelton's shoulder. "Be ready to move." I turned to Nightliss. "Hit the scar with Stasis as fast as possible so I can stop channeling Clarity. Then I'll grab the others and shield us while you open the portal, okay?"

She squeezed my hand. "Whatever happens, it's been good going on an adventure again."

I flashed a grin. "Never a shortage of those, am I right?"

Nightliss kissed my cheek. "Not with you, my friend."

Nightliss and I slung on our backpacks. Shelton and the others followed suit. I wove Clarity and highlighted the crooked horizontal scar. "Drop the shield now!"

Shelton dropped it.

Thankfully, the monsters were too busy killing each other to realize a veritable snack-pack had just opened right next to them.

Nightliss solidified the scar with a beam of Stasis and pried into it with Murk. I released the Clarity weave and snatched Elyssa and Ambria off the ground. Max and Adam gathered the remaining backpacks. Shelton slung Conrad over his shoulder.

Excited squawks told me the killer birds realized we were out in the open. Two of them raced toward us, their sharp claws throwing up dirt where Conrad had blasted away the ground flesh.

Thankfully, I was full of piss and vinegar this morning. I set Elyssa on the ground and turned to fight. A bolt of Brilliance sizzled from my fingers. I slashed it at the attackers. Their little bird heads flew off and the bodies ran in circles like giant chickens with their heads cut off. This attracted the attention of an orange cloud brain. Drones dove from the sky and began digging their spikes into birds.

Other drones attacked, eager to win the fresh meat.

Thunder rumbled and a shockwave washed across the land. Drones fell from the skies and scattered like dust in the wind.

"It's open!" Nightliss ripped open the scar.

A snowy wasteland waited on the other side. Unfortunately, beggars couldn't be choosers, especially not in this horrific realm. I grabbed Elyssa again and leapt through with her and Ambria tucked under my arms. Shelton came through next with Conrad, and the rest of the party leapt through. The portal shut an instant later.

The moment I landed, I realized that the white stuff all over the ground wasn't snow. It was ash. The air reeked of smoke and there was nothing but blackened ground and ash as far as the eye could see.

"Son of a biscuit-eating ass melon." Shelton took off his cowboy hat and wiped his sweaty forehead. "It's just one nightmare after another, isn't it? I hope Emily and her godlike powers are worth it."

Adam sneezed. "This place is awful, but it already looks like paradise compared to the last realm."

"Agreed." Max looked at the ground, as if trying to decide whether he wanted to sit in the calf-high ashes.

Shelton blew out a breath and looked around. He cleared a space with his boot and set Conrad down with a backpack as a pillow.

Adam bent over and picked up a handful of ash. It puffed like fine powder. "There's nothing solid at all in these ashes. Whatever burned through here was hot enough to reduce everything to dust."

Shelton leaned back his head and sniffed. "I smell fire, but I don't see smoke."

"The ashes are cold," Adam said. "The fire must have happened within the past few days or so."

"Well, at least we didn't land in the middle of a forest fire," Max said.

I hated to put Ambria and Elyssa down in the ashes but there wasn't much else I could do with them. They both trembled feverishly, and their faces were sickly pale. We had to get them medical help as soon as possible. I channeled a wall of Murk and cleared a wide space, then set down Ambria and Elyssa. Taking them back to Eden wasn't an option. Nightliss and I were the only two who could open portals and none of us were in any shape to face the carnivorous world or the lizard realm again.

"Fire must have happened longer ago than we thought." Shelton knelt and touched a tiny green shoot poking through the blackened dirt.

Adam shrugged. "So maybe it happened weeks ago. I'm not a botanist. I don't know how long it takes for plants to regrow."

I put a hand on Nightliss's shoulder. "How are you feeling?"

"Good." She flexed her bicep. "Strong."

"I'm going to check and see if there's a scar nearby." I blew out a breath. "Let's hope Emily and Tyler didn't go far from here."

A distant rumbling perked my ears. I knew for damned sure that whatever it was wasn't good for our health. So far, this trip had been nothing but disaster after disaster. I swept the beam of Clarity in a circle around us but didn't find anything.

"Hey look at this." Adam dusted off something shiny and metallic. He held up a blackened arcphone. "Emily or Tyler must have lost this when they got here."

"That thing's protected by a beaver box case." Shelton took it and wiped the blackened front with the sleeve of his leather duster. He cleared away enough to reveal the actual phone screen underneath the protector. "It might still work."

"Let me see it." Adam took back the phone and pried at the edges. The case snapped open and an undamaged phone fell out. "Wow, these cases are something else." He tapped on the screen and the phone flickered on.

"That's the GPS app," Shelton said. He peered at the screen. "Looks like they were recording where they went so they could find their way back to the same spot if they got lost."

There was a time index at the bottom of the map with a slider to reverse back through it. It had evidently stopped recording after sitting in the same place for five minutes.

Shelton sighed. "The last time index is from over a year and a half ago. What if they went through a hundred portals since then?"

"We've got to find Emily," I said.

Shelton threw up his hands. "Look, we're three realms into what could be a wild goose chase, and no way to get back to Eden except by going back the way we came."

"Emily would be our shortcut home," Max said. "Maybe she's on the next world."

"Except they could have gone in any direction from here." Shelton held out his arms. "Are we really gonna hunt every square mile of this damned realm?"

The rumbling I'd heard earlier grew slightly louder and I felt a slight vibration beneath my feet. "Not to sound the alarm bell, but does anyone else hear rumbling?"

Nightliss nodded. "I heard it a moment ago."

"Great." Shelton took off his hat and ran a hand through his short hair. "We've got no way out of here except going back to carnivorous world."

Adam seemed preoccupied with the phone he'd found. "This is weird." He changed the map to three-dimensional view. "Watch the dot." He tapped the slider and it played back the last few minutes before it was lost. The dot representing the location of the phone zipped back and forth, as if whoever held it was trying to dodge something. Then the dot abruptly shot up into the air for nearly a hundred feet before stopping.

The dot hovered for several minutes before plummeting back to the ground. Adam stopped the playback. "The phone sat there until it turned off."

"Any pictures or video recordings?" Max asked.

Adam shook his head. "How did the phone end up in the air?"

"Flying brooms?" I said.

"Judging by how fast they left their hotel room, I doubt they had much but the clothes on their backs," Shelton said.

I unstrapped my broom and looked up and around at the sky. *No sign of killer clouds*. It looked safe enough to fly. "I'll be right back."

Shelton dropped to the ground. "I'm taking a nap. I can barely keep my eyes open."

I flew up until I was as high as Emily's phone had been, according to the GPS recording. I didn't see anything of note, just scorched earth and rolling hills. I dropped lower. "You guys rest up. I'm going to see where that rumbling noise is coming from."

Shelton was already snoring.

Adam shielded his eyes and looked up at me. "Be careful."

Max lay down and curled up next to Conrad.

"Shall I come with you?" Nightliss asked.

I shook my head. "We're the only two in fighting condition right now. Keep an eye on things. I'll be back."

Her green eyes tightened. "Be careful."

"You don't have to tell me twice." I cupped a hand to an ear and gauged the direction of the rumbling, then climbed into the air and flew at top speed. I passed over a hilly landscape covered in fine, gray ash. Gusting wind choked the air with dust and ash, so I climbed higher to get above it.

Dark clouds gathered on the horizon. Lightning flashed and sheets of rain fell. "Oh, it's a stupid thunderstorm." I felt relieved to know the source was mundane. *Or is it?* Maybe the rain was acidic or filled with carnivorous worms, or something just as awful as the last realm. "Don't trust anything."

I flew closer to the storm, frightened about what new terror I might discover. It slowly dawned on me that the rumbling wasn't part of the thunderstorm, but a constant sound underlying everything else. The air grew chilly. The smoky odor faded, replaced by the fresh scent of rain. I crossed over a range of tall, rocky hills and stopped at the edge of a cliff overlooking a valley.

The sky was so thick with rain I could barely make out the landscape below. Loose rocks on the cliff vibrated. Clumps of damp ash shifted and bounced. I peered through spectacles for a better look at the rain.

No worms. No monsters hiding in the rain. It looked normal. The only alarming thing about it was the constant earthquake. And that was when I saw the source. It was at the far end of the valley, maybe five miles away, but clearly visible with the spectacles. In the distance between here and there, the ground literally squirmed.

It wasn't from worms or snakes, but plants. New buds sprouted from the ashes, bushes, weeds, and trees growing faster than vegetation in a time-lapse video. Saplings exploded from the earth, reaching skyward, trunks expanding and roots fighting for real estate with the other plant life.

The vegetation was growing so fast, it literally caused the ground to shake.

I used the vantage point to scope out the surrounding horizon. The rainclouds covered the entire eastern horizon as far as I could see. There was nothing but clear skies north, south, and west. Something on a cliff to the south glinted in the hazy sunlight. I wondered if it might be another clue left by Emily and Tyler.

Except I was miles away from the others and the portal scar. It didn't seem likely Emily and Tyler would have hiked all the way here, especially across all the hills and valleys. More than likely, they would have decided to try their luck with another portal.

But where?

I had no idea. And unless we wanted to be stuck in this new realm, we might have no choice but to backtrack through all the horrors of the past two realms.

CHAPTER 23

The thought of going back to the last realm filled me with dread. "No way in hell are we going back to that last world. There's got to be a way to find where they went."

I peered toward the glinting object through the spectacles. The shiny chrome exterior resembled a rocket ship from a fifties sci-fi movie. That meant intelligent life of some sort lived here—maybe people, maybe giant carnivorous slugs. There was absolutely no telling.

With the storm still miles away, it seemed safe enough to investigate, so I urged the broom to top speed toward the object. When I got closer, it became evident that it wasn't a rocket, but a building about fifty feet tall and maybe thirty feet in diameter. Seams in the rounded cone on top indicated it was designed to open like a missile silo.

I spotted what looked like an entrance and landed next to it. Two metal doors sat in the recess, a tiny crack where they didn't quite meet in the middle. I pried into the crack with Murk and the doors slid into the walls with little resistance. I leaned my broom against the outside of the building and sent an orb of light inside.

I half-expected monsters to rush out, or maybe even a flock of startled bats. But the only noise was the distant rumble from the hyper-growth forest and the storm. I poked my head inside the door and looked around. Metal coils and pipes ran along the walls. They met at a thick golden rod in the middle of the room. The rod reached up into the ceiling where it intersected a web of bare wires.

A low hum sounded, and white lights flickered on, lighting up the interior. A monstrous, hairy creature appeared out of nowhere, spread its paws wide, and roared.

If I hadn't seen even worse creatures in the last world, I might have shat my pants right then and there. Instead, I flung up a shield and readied myself to fight. But the beast didn't move. Instead, it growled, roared, rumbled, and hacked like it was trying to cough up a fur ball. Apparently, it was talking. It also bore an uncanny resemblance to a mythical creature from Eden—bigfoot.

"Who are you?" I said.

It stopped talking and a series of symbols appeared in the air in front of it. That was when I realized the truth. The monster was a hologram.

I released the shield and eased closer to the beast. I waved a hand through its hairy leg. It shimmered as my digits passed through it. "Well, that's a relief." I took a step back and examined the symbols. They resembled Cyrinthian, but with subtle differences that foiled my attempts to translate them.

I swiped a finger across one of the symbols.

The bigfoot beast growled and gagged on its awful language. It turned and faced the contraption in the middle of the room, hands gesturing. Apparently, this was the nickel tour and I didn't have a clue what he was saying.

I passed my finger through the second symbol in the list and hoped for the best.

The hologram reset with a flicker and switched to a new video. Bigfoot spoke in slow, measured tones, which is to say that he sounded like someone was choking a bear and spanking a cat at the same time. The hairy beast vanished, replaced with an overhead view of the rocket building. Green arrows illustrated sunlight beaming into the metal exterior of the silo. An empty meter shaped like a thermometer shaded green from top to bottom—probably illustrating how the sun charged it. It appeared the metal exterior itself absorbed solar energy. That explained how the building still had power.

The conical roof split open like a budding flower and the golden rod extended. The view panned away, showing the building and a cloudy sky. Electrical currents shot into the clouds, charging them with a bluish glow—the very same glow I'd noticed in the distant rain. The perspective glided further back, showing dozens of the same buildings all across the land, firing into clouds.

Rain fell from the holographic clouds and the video zoomed in on the ground. Glowing water seeped into the earth and found a seed. The seed burst open and a new plant pushed up through the ground, soon forming a green stalk that resembled wheat. The video zoomed back and showed an entire field of the crop sprouting to full growth in minutes.

The video ended.

That explained the hyper-growth forest, but not much else. What happened to the people? How did everything burn to the ground? I tapped the third item in the holographic list and hoped it had more answers. A small compartment next to the golden rod slid open to reveal a bundle of wires. I swiped the last item in the control list. Another maintenance compartment opened. I inspected the rest of the room but found nothing else of interest.

I wondered if the supercharged clouds had ravaged the entire realm, or if they were contained to a certain geographic area. The video had offered only a tantalizing glimpse into a bigger mystery. For all I knew,

JOHN CORWIN

flying a few miles in one direction might lead me straight to a thriving city. Or it might lead me nowhere.

For now, it was more important to get back to my people. Unless the storm clouds changed course, they'd be right over our camp within the hour.

I stepped outside, hopped on my broom, and flew to the top of the silo. From there I scouted through the spectacles. I spotted several more silos, some in the valley below, and others across the plains around me. But in the northern part of the valley, I saw something else. Something that told me a story of science gone awry.

A few metallic structures rose above the valley floor, footprints of a city now covered in ash. Outlines of covered structures were visible beneath soot and grime. The town had once sprawled for miles. Now nothing remained but its bones.

The storm had already reached the eastern side of the dead city. Rain washed away the ashes. Weeds and other vegetation squirmed through the soil, wrapping around the eroded structures.

I really wanted to watch longer but getting back to the others was more important. I spun the broom west and headed out.

I spotted another collection of metal frames about a mile to the north. More of them clustered in the southwest. I suspected they'd once been farms. A butte in the far west rose from the plains, a block of rough rock hundreds of feet tall with sheer cliffs. Something glinted on the top.

I peered through the spectacles for a better view. There were intact structures at the top. They'd probably survived for the same reason the silo had—they sat on solid rock. Algae and moss might grow there, but nothing that could deal the same destruction as trees and bushes exploding from the ground.

We didn't have long before the storm reached our camp, and as of yet, we had no clue where the next scar was. For now, it seemed best to find a safe place and shelter from the storm. Once it passed, we could go back out and search.

I arrived back at camp a few minutes later. Shelton, Adam, and Max were sacked out. Elyssa watched me with glassy eyes. She managed a weak smile, but the dark circles under her eyes and the sickly pale cast to her skin told me she was in bad shape.

Black bandages completely covered her hands, and she shivered even when I wrapped my arms around her to keep her warm. "Baby, are you okay?" I asked.

Elyssa nodded. "I'm fine. Out of numbing potion."

"She's badly burnt, Justin." Ambria looked even worse than Elyssa. Black bruises covered her injured arm and her right eye was swollen.

I winced. "Jesus, are you feeling okay?"

"I don't know what else to do, Justin." Nightliss knelt next to me. "They are in very bad shape."

"Damn it, we need to find the next scar." I turned in a circle as if it might miraculously appear to me. I dropped to a knee next to Elyssa. "We have to move camp. There's a big storm coming, and we don't want to be here when it hits."

"A storm?" Elyssa frowned. "A little rain can't be worse than the last realm."

I shook my head. "No, it's a lot worse, believe me." I looked over at the slumbering Conrad. "Has he woken up at all?"

"No," Ambria said. "He completely overextended himself last night to keep us alive."

I blew a raspberry. "This is gonna make things difficult, but we've got no choice." I patted Elyssa's backpack. "Any chance you packed a flying carpet?"

She shook her head. "No space."

"Okay, then we've got to tie Conrad to a broom and tow it."

Ambria tried to get up but I stopped her. "Are you kidding me? The way you look, I'll be surprised if we don't have to tie you to a broom too."

Her shoulders stiffened and she winced in pain. "I think I can manage."

With Nightliss's help, we bound Conrad to his broom with strands of Murk. I set his broom on levitate and left him hovering in place. The rumbling of the storm and the hyper-growth forest grew louder. The fringe of dark clouds looked less than two miles away. It had gained speed once it left the valley.

I shook Shelton and the others awake.

Max sneezed violently and struggled to stand. His face was covered in soot. Another time I might have laughed, but the time for jokes was past. I didn't know what would happen when that supercharged rain hit. It might burn us alive or electrocute us. And if that didn't happen, the hyper-growth vegetation might do to us what it had done to that city in the valley.

"What the hell, man?" Shelton coughed up soot. "Why didn't you let us sleep?"

"Now that everyone is awake, I'll explain." I pointed to the storm. "The people of this world built machines that supercharge the rain clouds. The rain causes all plant life to sprout from seed to full growth in minutes. I saw a city that was completely destroyed by the plants and if we don't get out of the path of the storm, the same thing might happen to us."

Shelton suddenly looked wide awake. He looked north and south along the seemingly endless storm system. "Where the hell are we supposed to go?"

Adam dusted off his sooty fingers and tapped on his phone screen. "Justin, did you see the plants growing?"

"Yes." I grabbed his wrist. "Put away the phone, get packed, and get on your broom, now."

He flinched, seemingly surprised at my tone, then did as I requested. Elyssa struggled to her feet and straddled her broom, but her bandaged hands made it impossible for her to grasp the broom handle. I set her broom to levitate.

"I'll tether you to my broom." I motioned Max over. "I'm tethering Conrad to your broom, okay?"

He nodded somberly and brought his broom over. I channeled Murk and tied off several weaves from Max's broom to Conrad's.

Ambria struggled onto her broom but seemed able to control it. Max reached over and buckled her in. He smiled. "Be safe."

A tear trickled down her cheek. "Thank you, Max."

"It's been one damned survival horror after another ever since we left Eden." Shelton dusted off his wide-brimmed hat and slapped it back on his head. "Let's get a move on."

I buckled Elyssa down and kissed her cheek. "I love you."

She tried to touch my cheek but seemed to remember that her hands were bandaged and dropped her arms. "I love you too."

I tethered her broom to mine with Murk. "We're going to be okay."

Elyssa nodded, but wouldn't meet my gaze. "Yeah."

She looked as depressed as I felt. We'd thrown our bodies out into the unknown, thinking we could handle anything, and man, had we been wrong. We might be chasing a ghost. Hell, Emily and Tyler might have died where we found that arcphone. Their bodies might be among the ashes we slept in. Maybe that was why there hadn't been another scar. I managed to smile, but Elyssa wasn't looking.

Thunder rumbled in the near distance. We were running out of time.

I lifted off slowly so I wouldn't jostle Elyssa too much. The seatbelt would hold her down, but she couldn't steady her torso with her hands if I yanked her off-balance.

We flew west, a bedraggled convoy that had seen too much and barely survived to tell the tale. I turned around every so often to check on Elyssa, but she slumped in her seat, eyes heavy with fatigue. I wished I could hug her and tell her everything would be all right, but at this point, nothing was even remotely all right.

Everyone else seemed lost in their own thoughts and worries. Adam stared at his phone, mumbling to himself. Shelton kept casting worried looks at Conrad and Ambria. Max looked ready to doze off at any minute. Nightliss and I were the only ones firing on all cylinders today.

We reached the butte twenty minutes later. The shiny metal buildings on top clustered in hexagonal patterns, each connected to the other by square tunnels of the same metal. A large domed building, a nexus sat in the middle of the pattern. A tunnel ran from the first hexagonal cluster to a large rectangular building. A tunnel on the other side joined with an identical cluster of buildings. The pattern repeated from one end of the butte to the other.

I saw none of the silo buildings, or any other structures that strayed from the cluster designs. It looked as if someone could enter the first building and walk through miles of tunnel to end up in the very last building on the opposite side of the plateau. I wondered if this place had been built as a safe haven from the storm.

I drifted in for a landing in front of the closest square building. It had a recess in the front like the silo. Metals doors in the recess slid open when I approached.

"Whoa." Shelton drew his wand. "What kind of people live here?"

I held up a hand. "Wait here."

"Hang on, now—"

I turned on him. "Wait here." I jabbed a finger at the ground. I turned to Nightliss. "Will you watch my back?"

She nodded. "Of course."

Shelton muttered something, but I ignored him and went inside.

A fine layer of dust covered the floor of a wide room. Bare counters and shelves to our left hinted at what might have once been a kitchen. A hallway led us to smaller rooms and a sliding door in the back that opened into another tunnel. It presumably led to the next block house in the hexagon.

"Looks like this was a house," I said. "But the people packed up and left."

Nightliss nodded. "I think it's safe to shelter here."

"Yeah, it seems so." I reached out and touched the shiny metal wall. It was smooth and slick but didn't feel like metal. "What is this stuff?"

Nightliss touched it and shook her head. "I don't know. But if it gives us shelter, then I don't care."

I managed a smile. "Yeah, you're right."

Once again, we'd have to spend the night in a strange world. I just hoped this one didn't kill us.

CHAPTER 24

We went back outside. Miraculously, no one had wandered off from the group. Max pulled Conrad's levitating broom inside and I helped unload his friend. The floor was hard, but we used clothes from Conrad's backpack to cushion his head.

I gathered Elyssa's and Ambria's backpacks and began to unpack food so they could eat. Crimson liquid oozed from the contents of Elyssa's pack. I pulled out everything, separating the wet from the dry along with foil packs that held critical nutritional supplements. All but one had burst, probably during the fight in the last realm. Crusted and coagulating blood covered Elyssa's spare clothes.

Holding one of the foil packs, I went over to her and set it down in front of her. "Did you know all your blood packs are broken?"

Elyssa shook her head. "I didn't think to check."

"You sound awful." I held out my wrist. "You need blood."

She gave me a pained look. "You know how I get when I drink from you."

"Yes, but it doesn't matter." I put my wrist to her mouth. "Drink, babe." I nodded at her bandaged hands. "You need blood to heal."

Elyssa licked her lips. Dhampyrs didn't need as much blood as vampires, but if she went too long without, bloodlust would drive her crazy. Fangs slid from beneath her perfect lips and without another moment of hesitation, she sank them into my flesh.

The weight lifted from my body, replaced by euphoria. Elyssa moaned with pleasure and tried to grab my arm, but her bandaged hands denied her. Her fangs pressed harder. The cloud of euphoria I rode began to sink, weighed down with sudden exhaustion. The violet glow in her eyes deepened to crimson fire. That was when I knew she'd had her fill.

I tried to pull away, but she wrapped her bandaged arms around mine, holding on with desperate strength. I grabbed her hair and tried to pull her back, but she only moaned and drank deeper. So I did the one thing that usually worked.

I thumped her nose. Hard.

Elyssa jerked back, eyes filled with tears of pain. "Ouch!" The glow in her eyes began to fade and she blinked, as if waking from a trance.

"You back?" I said.

She bared her blood-stained teeth. "You knew I'd lose control!"

"Yeah, so I gave you a nose thump. It usually works."

She rubbed a bandaged hand against her nose. "It hurts!"

"Feeling any better?" I said.

Elyssa managed a smile. "Better, except for my nose."

I smiled sheepishly. "Sorry."

"This is so cool!" Adam stood in front of a window that hadn't been there a moment before. He touched the wall and the window shifted back into metal. "This stuff is a miracle of modern science."

Shelton lay on his back, hat covering his eyes. "Can you go enjoy science somewhere else? I'm tired."

"I'm going to explore." Adam turned to me. "Is that okay?"

"I will go with you." Nightliss hooked her arm through his. "Just in case."

"Yeah, that's a good idea," I said. "We don't know if any of the locals are still around."

"I wonder what they look liked," Adam said.

In my haste to get everyone out of harm's way, I'd omitted that detail from my story. "They look like bigfoot."

Shelton sat up and his hat slid into his lap. "We're on bigfoot world?"

"It seems so." I went to the wall and touched it where Adam had. The window appeared, a front-row seat to the oncoming storm. "And they're way more advanced than humans."

"Or they were," Adam said. "It seems hubris might have brought them down."

Shelton leaned against his backpack and perched his hat over his eyes. "Well, wake me up if you find any. I've got questions."

I took inventory of our med kit. Most of the potions were gone, and only a few scraps of the special black bandages remained. The night on bug world had taken a heavy toll on our supplies.

Ambria huddled up next to Conrad, lying on her good shoulder. The other one was bandaged up and hopefully healing. Conrad didn't even stir when she pressed against him. I fashioned a pillow out of my spare clothes and made Elyssa comfortable, then went outside to watch the storm.

Darkness swept across the ash-choked plains and rain fell at our original camp. Gray sheets of water lowered visibility significantly, but the spectacles offered glimpses of activity a mile east of our original camp.

226

Massive trees exploded upward, throwing plumes of soil into the air. Foliage thrashed and twined its way between the trees, soon filling the gaps with green. Patches of the wheat-like plant grew in places, possibly the only remnants of the original crops the rains were meant to enhance.

Greenery spread across the dead landscape, like the high-speed rendering of a terraforming project. As fascinating as it was to watch, once the darkness spread to the base of the butte, I hurried back inside to watch from safety.

Wind howled and rain hammered against the building. Apparently, the miracle metal didn't insulate against loud sounds. Blue and green algae sprouted on the rocks outside. Scrub bushes and cacti sprang from crevices, forming prickly clumps. Within twenty minutes, new life sprang up, creating an ecosystem from ash.

I tapped on the wall on the opposite side of the room to make another window and watched the storm recede into the distance. I was a little concerned about going outside in the damp, so I opened the doors and peered outside at the damp earth. Glowing water gathered in puddles a few feet from the door.

I hadn't seen another living creature on this world. Not a bird, a worm, or an insect. There was probably a reason for that, and I suspected it had something to do with the water. I wasn't about to go outside and touch the stuff. For all I knew it might make me grow ten feet tall or cause me to explode.

Our point of arrival on this world looked nothing like it had before. A thick hardwood forest replaced the wasteland of ash. It'd be a miracle if we could even find the portal scar in all that greenery.

I wondered if Emily and Tyler had died down there. Without brooms, there was no way they could've made it up here. I wondered if the forest had been there when they'd arrived or if it had burned down long ago. Anything could have happened over the past year and a half.

Adam burst into the room, Nightliss close behind. "Dude, you're gonna want to see this."

Shelton grunted and moved his hat. "Find a bigfoot?"

"The next best thing." Adam nudged Shelton's boot with a foot. "Come see."

Max blinked bleary eyes. "Did you say, bigfoot?"

"Yep." I reached down a hand and helped Max to his feet. "Let's go see what he found."

We followed Adam to a door, walked through a tunnel to the next house, and went through two more tunnels and houses before arriving in a large, round room.

Adam waved a hand around the room. "This was some kind of entertainment center." Unlike the house, it still had furniture—wooden tables about two feet higher than normal, huge chairs, and couches.

"What is this stuff?" Shelton pinched a chair and left an imprint in it. "Feels like dough."

I sat down in one. The material molded to my butt and back. It was nearly as comfortable as the cloud chairs on Seraphina. The couches seemed to be made of the same stuff. "Maybe we should sleep in here." I counted four couches. "This is way better than sleeping on the floor."

Max plopped down on a couch and moaned. "This is paradise."

"All this is cool, but where's the damned bigfoot?" Shelton said.

Adam walked behind the couches to a long bar situated on the side of the room. A few plastic containers and bottles were strewn around it, but there was nothing left of the former contents. He tapped his finger against the bar. A holographic menu appeared. Adam touched the first one and a dignified, but hairy face appeared and began hawking up what passed for language in these parts.

"Holy shit!" Shelton knocked his hat off so it hung by the stampede string. "That is one ugly mother."

From a distance, one might mistake these people as giant apes. But they had smaller noses, higher foreheads, and mouths that more closely resembled humans than chimps. If anything, they looked like a human-chimp hybrid.

The bigfoot stopped talking and a menu appeared. Shelton leaned in. "Is that Cyrinthian?"

"It's a Cyrinthian dialect of some kind," Adam said. "But it's just different enough that my translator can't decipher it."

Nightliss's forehead scrunched. "It looks familiar, but I can't read it."

I touched the first item in the menu and the hologram went black. Red words flashed on the screen and then it went back to the menu. "I guess it's broken."

This might be the equivalent of a television," Adam said. "But it's not picking up any live broadcasts." He fiddled with his phone. "I'm scanning in all the symbols I find and running them through the translator. If there's some common link with Cyrinthian, maybe I can make sense of it."

"Wonder if this means the bigfoots got wiped out," Shelton said.

Adam's lips pressed together. "It doesn't look good."

My stomach rumbled. "I'm hungry. I'm going to help the others relocate here, and then get a bite to eat." I glanced over at Max who was already slumbering peacefully on one of the couches. Thanks to the generous size of the bigfoots, there was plenty of room for two human adults.

I left Adam and Shelton puzzling over the holographic television and went back to the other house with Nightliss.

"How are you feeling?" I asked.

She smiled. "I feel fine, but I'm concerned for the others."

I patted her shoulder. "You're always concerned."

Nightliss looked down. "Because we are always putting ourselves in danger." She sighed and patted my hand. "Perhaps one day we will find lasting peace."

I scoffed. "We won't find it. We'll have to force-feed it down everyone's throats."

We roused Elyssa and Ambria and packed their stuff into their backpacks. I cradled Conrad like a baby and carried him to the entertainment room. I laid Conrad on a couch and Ambria immediately snuggled next to him. Elyssa's face had regained some color thanks to my blood, and she seemed in better spirits.

I told her what Adam found and got her situated on a couch. "Do you want anything to eat?"

She shook her head and leaned back against the conforming material. "I'm fine now." She put a bandaged hand to my cheek. "Thanks for taking care of me."

I gently touched her hand and wished it wasn't covered. "I'll always be there for you."

"Well, you did go to another world, overthrow the government, and bring back their best healer just to save my life."

I chuckled. "Yeah, that wasn't how I planned it."

"It never is, is it?"

A sigh escaped me. "Nope."

She leaned back and closed her eyes. I kissed her forehead and left her to rest.

After eating, I left the rec room and went on the hunt for the one thing we hadn't found yet—a bathroom. The block houses had bedrooms and a family room, but no kitchens or bathrooms. The rec room looked as if it had once been a hub for eating and entertainment for two of the hexagonal housing clusters. That led me to believe the bathrooms might be communal as well.

The only building we hadn't explored so far was the dome that sat in the center of each cluster, so I set course for one of those. After back-tracking through the tunnel to the original housing cluster, I found a door in one of the side rooms. It slid open and the lights flickered on in the tunnel beyond. I stopped and listened for any threatening sounds, but it was just as quiet as the rest of the domiciles had been.

I continued to the other end. The door at the end slid open and I stepped inside. I stopped walking to give the lights a moment to flicker on. It was a good thing I had, because a circular pit gaped less than three feet away. There were six more just like it, each one twenty feet in diameter and at least ten feet deep. Aside from benches and couches with the doughy cushions, everything was made of the ubiquitous shiny metal.

"Looks like I found the bathhouse." I wondered if the design of this place was indicative of bigfoot communities in general, or if this had been built for a civilization's last stand against environmental disaster.

I stepped up to a cylindrical pedestal situated next to the closest tub and tapped the top of it to see what would happen. A single long slit opened about two inches below the lip of the tub and water poured out of it. I jumped back, not wanting to get splashed. The water didn't glow like the rainwater, but that didn't mean anything. If this water came from an underground river or lake, it could be contaminated.

Even if I trusted the water not to kill me, a bath wasn't at the top of my mind right now. I walked past a partition to my right and found a row of open rooms. I stepped into the first one. The metal flooring dipped into a bowl near the back wall. Giant foot-shaped indentations on either side gave me a good idea as to what they were.

Apparently, the bigfoots are squatters.

There was no way I could straddle that toilet bowl, not unless I shifted into full demon form. I'd never pooped while in demon form and really didn't feel like trying. Considering how much of a pansy my demon half had been lately, I probably couldn't do it even if I wanted to. I put a foot in one of the indents. It was about six inches wider and eight inches longer than my shoe. I might be bigger than a bigfoot kid, but probably not by much.

"Oh yeah!" Why was I trying to use an adult stall when there might smaller ones for kids? After a brief search I found two children stalls on the other end of the room. I was able to straddle and squat comfortably over the bowl. Once I finished my messy business, I ran my hand along the wall to figure out to flush. I should have expected what happened next, but it hadn't even occurred to me.

Water squirted right between my ass cheeks. I yelped and jumped up. Water swirled around the bowl and a drain opened, leaving behind a perfectly clean toilet.

I wasn't concerned about having a dripping wet ass, but I was freaking out because if the water was contaminated, this might be the last poop I ever took.

CHAPTER 25

I used my dirty shirt to dry off and examined my limbs for any sign they might start glowing or growing. I hurried out of the bath-house, through the tunnel, and back to the entertainment room. Nothing much had changed since I'd been gone.

Nightliss was munching on food, and everyone else except Adam and Shelton were asleep. The latter two were still fiddling with the holographic TV. I went over to them and told them about my bathroom experience.

"Damn, I didn't even know this place had a bathroom," Shelton said. "I took a piss in the corner earlier."

I wrinkled my nose. "In here?"

"Nah, in one of the connecting houses."

"I did too," Adam said. "But I've got other business to take care of, if you know what I mean."

"Yeah, I do." I pointed at my rear end. "What if my ass is contaminated now?"

Shelton snorted. "It sure is, and that's without glowing rainwater."

Adam guffawed. "Man, you backed right into that one, Justin."

"Ha, ha." I slashed a hand through the air. "Dude, this is serious. We need to know if the water is dangerous."

Adam sobered. "Fine. I've got some spells for that. I'll scan it before I drop the kids at the pool."

Shelton chuckled. "You know things are better when the poop jokes are funny again."

I sighed. "Yeah. But we're a long way from home, and our food supplies weren't meant to last for more than a week. We need to find the next portal scar or go home."

Adam nodded. "Agreed." His stomach rumbled. "Oops, I'd better go." He jogged away at bathroom emergency speed.

I nodded at the holographic menu. "Any luck with that?"

"Yep." Shelton showed me his arcphone screen. Five of the alien symbols were paired with Cyrinthian symbols at the top left. Foreign words and combinations scrolled past in the middle of the screen. "We went through all the menus and scanned in all the words and symbols. It's not a lot, but it's enough to start a comparison. We also found a long list that seems to be some kind of channel or entertainment show index and scanned that in. It's processing them now, looking for identical Cyrinthian words."

"Sounds like a good start." I ran a hand along the metal countertop. "I'd love to know what this stuff is. I mean, I didn't hold back in the bathroom, and it hardly took any water to flush that bowl sparkly clean."

Shelton grimaced. "Too much info, dude."

I scoffed. "For you? Yeah, right."

I went back over to Elyssa and sat next to her on the couch, stroking her hair and feeling her forehead for fever. She mumbled in her sleep but didn't wake up. That wasn't a great sign, considering her ninja reflexes usually woke her at the first sign of danger. I chalked it up to her recovery and prayed she'd heal soon. A skilled healer would have her on her feet in no time, but we didn't have that luxury.

I wish we'd brought Meghan with us!

Adam returned about thirty minutes later and claimed he hadn't spent all that time relieving himself. "I scanned the water in the baths and the toilets," he said. "Then I scanned a puddle of glowing water outside the front door."

"What did you find?" Shelton said.

"I can't identify the kind of energy stored in the rainwater, but I can tell you it's not present in the bath or toilet water." Adam pushed a finger up the bridge of his nose. "The water inside the facilities seems safe to touch and drink."

"Thank god for that." Shelton looked at his grubby hands. "I'm gonna take a bath." He started walking, stopped, and turned around. "The bath-room is communal?"

Adam nodded. "Yeah, it's wide open in there."

"Then warn the others not to come." He winked. "Unless they want to see what they're missing."

I barked a laugh. "Because every woman wants a hairy ass that glows in the dark."

Adam burst into laughter. "I know that's right."

"There's another building cluster through that door." I pointed to the other exit. "You can use that one if you want your privacy."

"Eh, I'll take my chances." Shelton turned and left.

"I really like how the toilet washed and then blow-dried my butt." Adam sighed. "So much better than toilet paper."

"It dried your butt?" I apparently hadn't waited long enough for it to finish. Now my underwear was damp.

"Yep." Adam checked his phone then tucked it into a pocket. "The floor just outside the bath pools will also blow dry you if you touch the pedestals with a wet hand. It's very intuitive."

"Amazing. I wish I could meet a bigfoot and find out more about them and this awesome tech they have."

Adam sighed. "Man, I'm bushed." He went to an empty couch and lay down. "Good night, day, or whatever it is here." He rolled on his side and covered his head with a jacket.

I was feeling pretty grubby, so I went the opposite way Shelton had and sauntered on over to the bathhouse in the neighboring cluster. I tapped the pedestal next to the first tub and warm water poured in from a slit around the inside. Once I confirmed it wasn't glowing, I climbed in and sat on the bench. My feet dangled off it like I was a kid, and my head barely reached the top of the tub.

I feared the water would fill all the way to the top and force me to stand on the bench, but something seemed to detect that I was smaller than the average bear and it stopped once it reached my neck.

My skin tingled, and all the grit and grime lifted from my body, forming a dirty film on the top of the water. I ducked my head underwater and massaged my hair until it felt squeaky clean. It wasn't quite as magical as the mist showers in Seraphina, but it made my sore body feel good as new. I dunked my dirty clothes in the water, and it seemed to clean them just as well as it had my body.

"Oh, this looks wonderful!"

I yelped and just about jumped straight up and out of the pool.

Nightliss looked down at me from the edge of the pool. "I'm sorry, I didn't mean to frighten you."

I shoved my washed clothes underwater to cover my tidbits. "Sorry, I thought I was alone."

Nightliss disrobed without a hint of embarrassment and jumped into the water with a small splash. Her head burst from under the water, a happy smile on her face. "Oh, I can feel it cleaning me!"

"Yeah." I managed a smile. "It's magical."

"Yes, it is." She went underwater and vigorously rubbed her hair.

I took the chance to climb out of the bath and covered my bum with my wet shirt. I tapped the top of the pedestal. Warm air blew up from the floor. I was thankful for the speed dry because it allowed me to get into a change of pants without exposing myself for long.

"Oh, I forgot you're shy about nudity." Nightliss perched on the bench, the water up to her chin. "I should not have come in here until you were done."

I tried to act casual. "Nah, it's fine. Sorry I'm such a prude."

She smiled. "You are who you are, Justin, and that is why you are my friend."

I gave her a lame thumbs-up. "Enjoy the bath!" Then I left. Truth be told, I was more concerned about what Elyssa would think of me naked in the same bath with Nightliss than anything else. That just made me wish Elyssa was well enough to get naked with me and have some fun in the water.

The main room was silent aside from gentle snores emanating from beneath the jacket over Adam's face and a faint chiming. Shelton hadn't returned, so I knew the chiming wasn't him fiddling with his phone. I suspected it might be Adam's phone, but symbols flashing in the holographic display at the bar suggested otherwise.

The holographic symbols flickered off. I walked over and tapped the bar to activate the hologram, but it only displayed the list Shelton had told me about earlier. I turned to leave, but the symbols blinked back on and began to chime again.

One set of symbols was red, the other green. I didn't know what they meant, but green generally meant yes and go while red meant the opposite—at least in Eden. They might be reversed in this realm. And what if touching them activated something bad?

Praying that I wasn't making a huge mistake, I touched the green symbols. A three-dimensional bigfoot about two feet tall appeared on the bar. He stood before a dark wall with little else around him. With shaggy white hair and striking blue eyes, he looked like a snow yeti.

I figured I'd just activated another recorded video, but the bigfoot cried out, eyes wide with horror and his arm flew up, finger pointing at me. Other guttural voices sounded somewhere off-camera.

My mouth dropped open. "Holy crap, you're alive!"

The bigfoot stared at me, his nose wrinkled with disgust. He began to speak, and it seemed he was addressing me.

I waved him off. "I don't understand what you're saying."

The image flickered and static filled the screen until I could barely see the bigfoot.

The bigfoot looked to the side and spoke, probably to someone nearby, then put up its hands in a universal helpless gesture. It looked at me and started to talk, but white noise filled the image and it blinked off.

A moment later, the hologram chimed again. I answered it and the yeti dude reappeared. He thumped a fist to his chest and started talking and gesturing as if trying to convey something. Once again, static and interference made it nearly impossible to understand him. The signal cleared up again after a few seconds, so I took out my arcphone and started recording.

"Nookli, can you translate any of this from Cyrinthian?"

"Monitoring and translating, Justin," Nookli replied.

The bigfoot kept talking and after a few minutes, I realized it was saying the same thing over and over again, each time a little slower. Apparently, the signal was weak out here.

I gave him the helpless hands gesture and shook my head. Then static filled the image and it blinked off.

"Did any of that make sense?" I asked my phone.

"Insufficient data to translate," Nookli replied.

"Oh, well." I waited a few minutes, but the bigfoot didn't call back. Then I began to get a little paranoid. What if they were sending people to find us? For all we knew, armed bigfoots might storm in here in the middle of the night.

"What's bugging you?" Shelton stepped in the door from the other cluster. "You look like you just ate a lemon."

I told him what happened and showed him the recording. "We might be in danger."

"Hot damn." Shelton whistled. "I guess they didn't kill themselves off."

"Do we know for certain this entire facility is abandoned?"

He shook his head. "I mean, it looked abandoned from the air, but maybe it ain't. Bigfoots could live in the clusters on the far side and we'd never know."

I sat on a barstool. "How did they know to call this exact room?"

Shelton put a hand to his chin. "The lights and power are automatic. Maybe activating the power triggered an alarm somewhere."

"Possibly." I surveyed the slumbering forms on the couches. "Now we have to worry about someone barging in on us in the middle of the night."

"I won't let that happen." Shelton produced his wand. "I'll put alarm wards on the main entrance and the tunnel doors from both ways. We'll know if anyone comes."

"Yeah, but we'll be trapped in here."

"We can always go out another door," Shelton said. "But I'll put a shield ward on the doors to give us a little extra time."

I nodded. "Yeah, do that. Elyssa, Conrad, and Ambria need to rest, and we've got nowhere else to go."

"That's for damned sure." Shelton blew out a breath. "I'll be back soon. Maybe you should catch some shuteye too."

"Agreed." I felt much better knowing Shelton would take care of security. I wasn't tired, but I curled up next to Elyssa on the couch. She trembled and muttered something in her sleep. I kissed her forehead and traced the curve of her lips with my finger. She was so beautiful, so fierce. I couldn't stop thinking about the energy from the light bow cooking her flesh. About the scarring on her hands.

I hope you're okay.

Her dhampyr abilities gave her accelerated healing, but it wasn't quite as good as mine. I just hoped she wouldn't be left with any permanent damage.

Nightliss returned from the bathhouse a little later and stopped by us. "How is she, Justin?"

"Recovering, hopefully."

She gently touched Elyssa's bandaged arms and closed her eyes. "I wish I was more skilled at healing. Flava could probably make her whole with little effort."

"True, but Flava is probably in Utopia by now." I sighed. "Not much we can do but hope for the best." Flava was the Darkling healer who'd brought Elyssa back from the brink of death after Daelissa nearly killed her.

Nightliss's eyes grew sad. "I fear we have reached the end of our search for Emily."

"Maybe." I shook my head. "I hope they didn't die where we found that phone."

"We have to consider the possibility that they did." Nightliss knelt next to the couch. "Justin, we may need to return tomorrow before this world kills us too."

"It's three hops to get back to Eden," I said. "The question is, do we have the endurance to make that run?"

"It might be safe to stay a night in the lizard realm," Nightliss said. "The rocks where we found the scar provided ample cover."

"Maybe." I shuddered at the thought of backtracking through the carnivorous realm. "We might have more immediate problems to consider." I sat up and showed her the video of my conversation with the bigfoot. "Shelton is warding the entrances in case uninvited guests show up."

Her eyes grew even more troubled. "Perhaps one of us should guard the entrance."

"Who?" I said. "You and I need our sleep. Shelton is running on fumes from staying up all night protecting us in the last realm. The same goes for everyone else."

"Sleep will not do us much good if we are taken in the middle of the night by the bigfoot people."

"Shelton's wards will wake us up the instant anyone breaks them." I touched her hand. "Let's trust the wards and try to get some sleep. That way we'll stand a chance if we have to backtrack to Eden."

Nightliss's forehead pinched, but she nodded after a brief hesitation. "I will try to sleep." She kissed my cheek and lay down on the other end of Adam's couch.

I turned onto my back and stared up at the ceiling. *What if the wards don't wake us up? What if there's another way in that we don't know about?* I wished I'd never answered that damned call. It was my fault the bigfoots knew strange beings had invaded their realm. And there was no telling what they'd do.

CHAPTER 26

Two miracles happened that night.

One, I slept like a rock, and two, the alarm wards didn't go off. *Four days to go.*

I woke up early and rummaged in my backpack for a breakfast bar. Everyone else was sound asleep, so I went to the bathroom to relieve myself. I'd just entered the room when I saw movement out of the corner of my eye. I hit a rolling dive and came up on my knees, ready to engage the intruder.

Conrad jumped back, hands held up in surrender. "Justin?"

"Holy crap, dude." I put a hand on my heart. "You scared the crap out of me."

"I woke up an hour ago." He smiled apologetically. "It took me some time to find the bathroom. This place is a maze."

"Yeah, it might seem so since you've been asleep since we got here." I looked him up and down. "How are you feeling?"

"Much improved, thank you." He put a hand to his belly. "I'm famished, though. I couldn't find my backpack and didn't want to take food from anyone else."

"Oh, it might have gotten left in the first house." I held up a finger. "Give me a minute." I went into a stall and relieved myself, then motioned him to follow me. "What's the last thing you remember?"

He walked beside me, tapping a finger on his chin. "There was a major onslaught of cloud creatures, and the flesh ground beneath us began to grow tentacles. I was afraid the ground would eat us, so I incinerated the flesh beneath us so nothing could grow. Then I made a dome of energy and used it to blast away the cloud brains. After that, everything is fuzzy."

"Wow. That explains why you slept an entire day and night." I patted his back. "Great job keeping us safe. I'm sorry I couldn't help."

Conrad smiled. "It's understandable, given the circumstances."

I realized he probably didn't know a thing about this world, so I filled him in while we walked through the tunnels back to the first house.

He looked up at the high ceilings. "Goodness, these bigfoots must be huge."

"At least ten feet tall, I think." I shrugged. "Maybe even taller."

We found his backpack in the corner of the first room, forgotten in our rush to get everyone to the common room.

"So everything is made of this metal?" Conrad touched a wall. "It doesn't feel cold like metal. It feels slick like glass or plastic."

"Yeah, we have no idea what it's made of." I touched the outer wall and it shimmered to transparency. The sun shone on a completely different landscape than the one we'd left outside a few hours ago. Thick jungle choked the plains. Palm trees the size of giant redwoods rose far above the canopy. In some places, patches of the wheat-like crop interrupted the rainforest.

"This was nothing but smoking ash yesterday." I whistled. "Hard to believe."

Conrad put a hand to the wall. "Is it safe to go outside?"

I nodded. "Looks dry enough." I approached the front doors. They parted ways. The water puddles had evaporated, so I ventured out onto the plateau.

Conrad knelt next to a scrub bush. "This looks like it hasn't had water for days." The browning leaves crackled at his touch.

"It wasn't even here yesterday." I looked around at the other bushes. Brown and black spots mottled their leaves. A giant palm tree in the near distance toppled over. A plume of gray dust rose where it fell.

Creaks and groans echoed from below the plateau. We walked to the edge and looked down. What few bushes and trees jutted from the rocky cliffs looked rotten and decaying. The greenery below looked slightly less green than it had moments ago.

Conrad watched with concern. "Everything is dying."

Over the space of the next few minutes, the rain forest lost its healthy hue, turning brown and then gray. Trees collapsed in clouds of ash. Smoke rose from some trees, even though there was no hint of fire to be seen. It was as if everything was incinerated from the inside out.

"The energy rain you told me about—it must accelerate the life cycle of the plants continuously. They don't stop aging and die in a matter of hours."

"But what's burning them?" I said. "There's no fire."

"Maybe the energy leftover from the rain. Once the plants begin to rot and dry, it causes them to burn from the inside."

"God help anyone who gets that rain on them," I said. "If it affects bugs and animals the same way it affects vegetation, that would explain why there's nothing else living out here."

"The plants grow, drop seeds and pollinate, then die in hours," Conrad said. "When the rains come again, it all starts over, but this time there are thousands more seeds and plants."

The top of the plateau offered perfect visibility all the way to the bend in the horizon where the sky was already turning cloudy. "My god, is it already going to rain again?"

"So many plants dying all at once must release a tremendous amount of water into the atmosphere," Conrad said. "It probably creates a nearly endless cycle."

At the rate the forest was decaying, it would all be gone in under an hour. "We've got to get back to our starting point in this realm and find the portal scar Emily and Tyler left behind."

"If they escaped," Conrad said. "Justin, it's possible they didn't survive."

I shook my head. "No. They made it through the carnivorous realm. A hyper-growth rainforest wouldn't kill them."

"I hope they survived. But they could have gone in any direction." Conrad shook his head. "There's no telling where the next scar might be."

"I'll scan every square inch if I have to." Sunlight glinted off something in the west. It was too high to be a building, so I plucked the spectacles from my pocket and held them to my eyes. A small, round object came into focus, flying a hundred feet over the rainforest. It didn't look large enough to carry bigfoot passengers, but that didn't mean it wasn't dangerous. It could be an armed drone.

"I think we're running out of time." I gave Conrad the spectacles. "We can't stay here much longer."

"Should we take the brooms out and intercept it?" Conrad said. "If it fires on us, we'll know their intentions."

I nodded. "Good idea." I went back to the rec room, grabbed the brooms, and almost rushed out, but common sense prevailed. Rushing headlong into the unknown without letting anyone know was just plain dumb. What if we were shot down and killed? No one else would even know where we were or what had happened. Max was the closest, so I shook him awake.

"Huh?" He opened bleary eyes.

"Get up and stretch. I need to know you're awake."

Max sat up, suddenly alert. "What's wrong?"

I told him about the incoming object and mine and Conrad's plan. "Get everyone up and ready to move in case we have to leave in a hurry."

"I'm on it!" Max grabbed my wrist. "Please don't die. We can't go home without you."

That was another good point I hadn't considered. "I'll be extra careful then." I squeezed his shoulder. "Now get to it." I dashed through the exit and tunnels until I reached the outside again. The flying object was only about a mile out by now.

Conrad hopped on his broom. "I've got a shield weave ready."

"Me too." I summoned Murk, ready to channel a barrier in an instant. "Let's do this."

We climbed at a steep angle until we were right in the object's path and flew straight at it. Heart racing, muscles tense, I steeled myself for the worst. This thing might have advanced weaponry. It might be able to disintegrate us before we even knew what happened.

"Let's not take any chances." I formed a shield in front of me. "We have no idea what this thing is capable of."

Conrad nodded. "Better to be safe than dead." He thrust out his hand, casting blue energy ahead of him.

The drone stopped and hovered in place when we closed to within a hundred feet. We stopped, braced for whatever might happen next. A turret atop the drone rotated toward us. I readied a blast of Brilliance and hoped this thing wasn't magic resistant.

The barrel flashed. Instead of lasers, it projected a hologram—a list of foreign words. I vaguely recognized the first word as the strange Cyrinthian dialect used here, but many of the following symbols didn't even remotely resemble the first—all except the fourth one down.

The fourth word in the list, translated from Cyrinthian said, *Kortol Ling*.

I grunted. "It's a list of languages."

Conrad stared at the list. "I've never heard of the Kortol language, but it seems to use Cyrinthian symbols."

Speaking in Cyrinthian, I said, "Can you understand me?"

More words appeared, this time in Cyrinthian—or at least a dialect much closer than the language the bigfoots used. I understood at least eighty percent of the words, but some of them looked like nonsense combinations.

Cyrinthian was a complex language with hundreds of characters and combinations that went completely unused in the spoken language. Arcanes used some symbols for spells, and the Mzodi gem enchanters used even more complex combinations for their work.

I translated into English and skipped the words I didn't know. "What is the reason...danger...death."

"That doesn't sound good," Conrad said.

I shook my head. "Maybe it's a warning." I spoke in Cyrinthian to the drone. "We arrived here by accident. We mean no harm."

The message vanished and another of the yeti bigfoots appeared. It spoke in Cyrinthian, but its guttural inflections made it hard to follow. "What are you? Where from? How speak Kortol?"

He probably wasn't talking like that, but I couldn't understand every word out of his mouth. I didn't know how much the bigfoots knew about the realms, but it was obvious they hadn't seen humans before. I spoke slowly in Cyrinthian and hoped he understood. "We are humans —beings from another realm—another dimension. We are trying to find someone who came here before us. Did you have contact with others who looked like us?"

His bushy eyebrows sprang up. "Others like you?" He shook his head. "No. You are first we see like you. You are not from another planet?"

"No," I replied. "Another dimension." Realms weren't quite the same as dimensions, but it was close enough. "What is the name of your world?"

He turned and spoke to someone off camera. Nodded. "I speak with scientist. She explains dimensions. She has many questions and requests that you follow drone to us."

I exchanged a look with Conrad then turned back to the hologram. "We don't have time for that. We have to find the people who came here before us."

"You are in forbidden zone," the bigfoot said. "The Sasquo conducted unauthorized experiments. They destroyed many cities and environment. Thousands died from the rain. You must leave zone immediately."

"We can't," I said. "If we can't find our people, then we will return home."

The translator turned and spoke in his native tongue to whoever was off-screen. He nodded a few times and turned back to us. "You cannot stay. We will send people to bring you to us if you do not come."

"Now it's getting nasty," Conrad said.

Since I had no intention of going to them, I decided that the best thing to do was stall for time. So I smiled, nodded, and agreed. "Okay. We will come to you. But I need to gather my people."

The translator narrowed his big brown eyes. He turned and spoke to the others, then turned back to me. "The drone will follow you. You have thirty minutes to gather your people."

That wasn't a lot of time. But with the rainclouds already gathering on the horizon, we probably had less than a couple of hours before the deadly rains swept through here again.

I spoke to Conrad in English. "Let's get the others."

"We're not actually going, are we?"

"No." I spun my broom around and headed for the housing facility. "We're going back down to the original portal scar and taking one last look around. If we don't find anything, then we're backtracking to Eden. We've got no other choice."

"Maybe we could ask these people for their help," he said.

"Bad idea." I angled for the plateau below. "They've never seen humans before. We'll probably be locked up and studied like lab rats."

Conrad grimaced. "Good point."

We landed in front of the main door, the drone following close behind. It was too large to fit through the door, so I turned to our holographic translator. "We'll be back soon."

"You have twenty-seven minutes left," he said.

I went inside without comment. Once the door closed, I jogged through the house and tunnels to get back to the common room. Everyone was up and about, all backpacks packed and ready to go. Nightliss was peeling off Elyssa's bandages. Judging from the winces of pain, it didn't feel too good.

"Houston, we have a problem," I announced.

"Yeah, really?" Shelton scoffed. "Since when don't we have a problem?"

"The good news is we figured out how to talk to the bigfoots. The bad news is they gave us thirty minutes to follow a drone somewhere so they can ask us questions and study us for science."

Max grimaced. "What are we going to do?"

"We're gonna make like bananas and split." I told them what I'd told Conrad. "We're going back to the original portal scar for one last look around. If we don't find another scar, then we're backtracking to Eden." I looked around at the others. "Agreed?"

No one objected, so I dashed over to Elyssa and Nightliss. The skin beneath Elyssa's bandages was pink and raw. It looked like melted wax in places, scars left from fire.

"My hands aren't healing right." Elyssa seemed to be fighting back tears. "I don't understand."

I gently touched her shoulder. "Baby, maybe you should keep on the bandages."

"No." Her violet eyes flashed. "I need my hands. I won't be useless again."

"You'll be in pain just trying to hold onto anything," I said. "Maybe we can redo the bandages so you can use your hands."

Nightliss held up the bloodied remains. "We have no more bandages, Justin."

"Dammit." My fists clenched. "If only we'd had Nightingale armor, this wouldn't have happened."

"We knew the risks," Elyssa said firmly. "I'll deal with the consequences."

I turned to the others. "Does anyone have gloves?"

A chorus of negatives replied.

Conrad sat next to Ambria and kissed her cheek. The color had returned to her face, but she winced when she moved. Without a healer, it would take her shoulder a long time to heal, but at least she could ride a broom.

We were banged up, physically and mentally. We'd encountered the unknown and it had kicked our collective asses. From the downcast looks and troubled gazes, it was plain to see that everyone thought we'd failed the mission. I hated to admit it, but they were right. All the optimism and vigor was gone, and it had only taken two days to lose it.

Granted, those days involved escaping giant lizards and nearly being eaten by flying brains and a carnivorous realm. We'd survived the deadly rain and hyper-growth forests of this realm only to slam into a dead end. I didn't hold out much hope that we'd find a scar left by Emily. If anything, I suspected she'd met her end on this world.

It was enough to make a grown man cry.

CHAPTER 27

I stiffened my upper lip and prepared myself mentally for the dangerous journey home. I had to do everything in my power to make sure we got back to Eden alive.

"Hey, Justin." Adam tapped me on the shoulder and jolted me from my pity party.

"What's up?" I asked.

"How did you communicate with the bigfoots?"

"Oh, well it turns out there's another group or nation—I'm not clear which it is—that speaks a dialect closer to Cyrinthian than theirs." I shrugged. "So we were able to mostly understand each other."

Adam gave me a hopeful look. "I guess we won't be sticking around to play question and answer though, huh?"

"Not a chance." I watched Nightliss remove Elyssa's other bandages. "If we don't get out of here, then we'll probably end up on a dissection table at worst, or permanent guests at best."

"You're probably right." He bit his lower lip. "I'd love to know what happened to this world."

"And I'd love to raise an army of bigfoots to help us fight the war." I sighed. "But we've got bigger fish to fry."

Max walked up behind Adam while we spoke. "We're not going to find Emily, are we?"

I wasn't sure what to say, because I hated to just give up, but we didn't even know if Emily survived. "I don't think so."

Adam blew a raspberry. "I can't imagine how terrifying their last hours were. Giant lizards, man-eating brains, and then this insane place. I'll bet the forest shot up from the ground right under their feet and killed them."

Nightliss stopped what she was doing. "Do not give up. There is always a chance."

Elyssa slumped and looked down. "I don't want to give up, but I think Max is right."

Shelton walked over. "We ready to move out?"

Elyssa tried to flex her hands. Tears of pain pooled in her eyes. "As ready as I'll ever be."

We got our stuff and went outside. The drone waited about twenty feet from the door, Cyrinthian numbers ticked off a countdown to zero. We still had eleven minutes until our time ran out.

The image flickered and the bigfoot translator replaced the numbers. "You are ready?"

"Almost." I pointed toward the decaying jungle. "We dropped important equipment down there and need to retrieve it."

"Too dangerous," he said. "Follow the drone."

"How far away are you?" I asked.

"Several hours. The storm in the east is not the only system. Another forms in the southwest and drifts to the north. You must escape the zone before the two systems trap you."

"Why not destroy the towers that fuel the storms?" I said. "Wouldn't the area recover?"

He shook his head. "The cloud seeders are no longer active. The plants now convert solar light into seeding energy that is soaked up by the clouds when the plants die."

Someone off-camera spoke to him in their native language. He nodded and looked back at us. "Come now."

"You got it." I climbed on my broom and watched Elyssa to make sure she could handle this.

She got on her broom easily enough, but her hands didn't quite want to squeeze the broom handle. Teeth gritting in determination, she somehow made her damaged muscles do her bidding. Ambria wasn't much better off. Face screwed up in pain, she gripped her broom with her good arm.

I pointed up and circled my finger in the air. Then we took off—in the opposite direction of the drone. The dying rainforest crackled and smoked beneath us, giant trees exploding into hot ash, entire sections of greenery crumbling in seconds. The odor of burning wood stung my nose even though I never saw a hint of fire.

I glanced over my shoulder. "Adam, what are the exact coordinates?"

He checked the phone we'd found. "I've got the GPS on. Follow me." Adam took the lead and we turned to follow.

The drone caught up and paced me. The concerned face of my yeti translator appeared. "Turn around."

I shook my head. "Sorry, but we're going home. We might return to talk about another matter that threatens all the realms if you promise not to treat us like lab rats."

He looked confused, probably because the idiom escaped him. "A threat to realms? What do you mean?"

"Two very powerful beings want to control all the realms." I didn't have time to explain everything, so I didn't even try. "Look, we can't stay because if we do, then those powerful beings will destroy everything you love."

His forehead etched with concern. "Please stay."

"Sorry, can't."

"We're here." Adam hovered in place above a grove of massive palms that toppled one by one and exploding into ash. The air shimmered with heat. Humidity turned the surroundings into a stifling sauna.

"Uh, how are we gonna get down there when it's so damned hot?" Shelton said.

I didn't have an answer. "I would use Murk to cool it down, but Nightliss and I will need all our strength to get us back home again."

Shelton covered his nose with the top of his T-shirt. "Man, I don't know how much longer I can take this." Sweat dripped down his face.

Our yeti translator continued speaking in imploring tones, trying to get us to follow the drone.

I stared at the last tree as it fell and turned to ash. Somewhere down there in all that heat and ash was the portal scar. When we'd arrived yesterday, the ash had already cooled. It might take hours before it was cool enough for us to brave. The yetis would be on us well before that happened.

Like the trees, all our plans had turned to dust.

And that was when it hit me.

The trees.

An idea kicked me in the forebrain. One so simple I couldn't believe it hadn't occurred to me before. I spun to Adam. "Show me the last few minutes the GPS recorded on the phone."

"Sure." Adam projected the screen and played back the final moments. The dot representing the phone shot a hundred feet in the air and hung there for a moment before plummeting back to the ground.

"Get me to the exact spot where that dot was in the air," I said.

Adam's eyes widened. "Holy crap, I didn't even think of that."

"Think of what?" Shelton said.

"The phone got stuck in a tree and fell," Adam said. He set the GPS to guide us to the exact altitude the phone reached. "It was here."

I wove Murk and Brilliance into Stasis, then channeled two more threads back into the Stasis to make Clarity. The yeti translator started shouting in his native tongue. Other voices joined his. Apparently, they hadn't seen magic before.

I shined the beam of Clarity straight ahead. Found nothing. I swept it down. Still nothing. I moved it up. A diagonal slash appeared in the air only a few feet from me.

"I'll be a bigfoot's uncle," Shelton said. "Emily and Tyler must have gotten stuck in a tree when it grew underneath them. So she created a portal at the top."

"But they would have gotten wet," Adam said. "How did they survive the rain?"

"That's a good question," I said. "Let's just find out where they went."

Nightliss hovered next to me and crystallized the scar with Stasis. Then she pried it open with Murk. The sonic blast cleared ash from the ground below and sent it billowing in all directions.

The bigfoots continued shouting, but I couldn't tell if they were excited or pissed.

I held up a hand. "I'll go first." I flew through and hovered a few feet over a giant tree. Birds chirped, insects hummed, and a gentle breeze met my face. This place had a friendly vibe to it, which meant it would definitely try to kill us. "Everyone through!" I shouted through the portal.

The drone zipped through first, spinning in circles as if trying to record everything. Everyone else filed through with Nightliss bringing up the rear. The portal collapsed a moment later, and the drone stopped moving. It hovered in place and then lowered itself to the ground for a controlled landing.

"Guess it's programmed to land when it loses signal," Adam said. "I wonder if we should take it."

"I ain't got space to lug that thing around," Shelton said. "It's nearly five feet in diameter!"

"First things first," I said. "Is anything here going to kill us in the next ten minutes?"

Shelton looked around. "Looks kind of normal to me. Almost like Eden."

I took out my phone, but it didn't have a signal. "It's not Eden." I pointed to the giant oak trees. "Never seen anything that big in our realm."

"At least it looks safe." Elyssa winced and loosened the grip on her broom. "But let's not take any chances."

"Amen," Shelton said.

We landed in a grassy meadow beneath the shade of the giant oak. I bent down and touched it to make sure it wouldn't try to eat us. Thankfully, it continued to behave like normal grass.

Adam grunted as he hefted the drone by the edge. "This thing is heavier than it looks. I wonder how it flies." He eased it back down, apparently giving up his dream of taking it.

I didn't feel like wasting any more time here than was necessary.

"Everyone back up so I can look for a scar." Once they were out of the way, I swept Clarity around, but found nothing.

"Not again," Shelton said. "Man, Emily sure didn't make this easy."

"Maybe she stayed this time," Nightliss said. "It seems to be the first realm without immediate danger."

"Maybe." I scanned the area using all my enhanced senses. The air smelled fresh and clean. A red squirrel eyed us curiously from a tree as it stuffed an acorn in his mouth pouch. Aside from birds and insects, I heard nothing that pricked the hairs on my neck. I climbed back on my broom. "I'm going up for a look around."

"I'll come with you," Shelton said.

Max got back on his broom. "Me too!"

"I'll stay here," Conrad said. He helped Ambria into the shade of a tree. "Perhaps we should make a camp."

I nodded. "Yeah, do that. But don't get too comfortable." I still didn't trust this place. For all we knew, it was ruled by carnivorous mushrooms.

Max, Shelton, and I gained altitude until we had a good view of the surroundings. There wasn't much to see except forest and snow-capped mountains in the distance. A stream burbled below, and a pair of large birds circled above a clearing about a mile away.

"Are those hawks?" Shelton said.

Max looked through a pair of spectacles. "No. They look like giant magpies."

I took a closer look through my spectacles. The birds were black with white chests and yellow beaks. I'd never seen anything like them before, which meant they'd definitely try to kill us.

One of the birds stopped circling and glided our way. Its companion did the same. It was hard to judge their real size through the spectacles, but they were definitely bigger than us. "Holy crap. We're on giant bird world." I clenched a fist. "We can't let these things find the others."

Shelton used Max's spectacles to scope them out. "Hot damn. Those are some big-ass birds."

"We've got to fight them before they get here." I clenched the broom handle.

"But they're birds," Max said. "What makes you think they want to eat us?"

"We ain't much bigger than worms to them," Shelton said. "Unless you want to get eaten and pooped out on someone's clean car, you'd better get ready to fight."

Max gulped and drew his wand. "I'm ready."

"You reckon giant birds carried Tyler and Emily off?" Shelton said. "Maybe baby-birded them to their young?"

I gagged. "Jesus, Shelton. Why'd you have to give me that visual?"

Max's forehead scrunched. "Baby-birded?"

"Yeah." Shelton grimaced. "The momma or daddy bird chews up the food and barfs it back into the mouths of their young."

It was Max's turn to gag. "I don't want to be baby-birded!"

The birds were nearly upon us, avians the size of small dragons. They warbled back and forth in harsh, almost digital tones I might have mistaken for car alarms back in Eden. They split apart about fifty yards away and circled us, buzzing excitedly. They met on the other side of us and landed in one of the giant hardwoods.

We spun our brooms to face them.

"They didn't attack," Max said.

"Not yet." I held Brilliance in my palm. "Maybe they're waiting on backup."

"Waiting," said a strange voice. "Waiting on backup."

Shelton flinched. "Holy shit, it's talking!"

The other bird opened its beak. "Holy shit. Holy shit."

Max laughed. "They're like parrots!"

I cupped my hands to my mouth and shouted, "Do you understand me?"

The birds cocked their heads and started buzzing, whirring, and warbling.

"Yeah, I don't think so," Shelton said.

The birds leapt into the air and flew past us, raising quite a racket. They circled us once then flew back to where we'd originally seen them.

"Well, that was anticlimactic." Shelton holstered his staff. "I guess they don't eat humans."

Max wiped his forehead. "Thank goodness. I didn't want to kill birds. It just doesn't seem right, you know?"

I released the destructive energy from my hands. "Yeah. It's a relief not to have to fight." I watched the birds for a moment. "But I still don't trust them."

One of the birds veered back toward us and I tensed again. Once again, it didn't come straight at us, but flew in a circle. "Come," it said. "Come."

Shelton's mouth dropped open. "Is that bird actually talking to us?"

"Yes," the bird said. "Come."

"Wowie!" Max looked back and forth from me to the bird. "They're really talking!"

I frowned. "Max, go back to camp and tell them where we're going. Then I want you to fly back out here but stay a safe distance away unless I give you the signal that it's all safe."

"I'm on it!" Max spun his broom around, stopped, turned back to me. "What's the all-safe signal?"

"Thumbs up means you can come in. Thumbs down, go back and warn the others."

He gave me a thumbs up. "I gotcha."

Shelton and I exchanged glances, then followed the big bird. Before long, the trees ended at the rocky shores of a lake. Dark water ran for miles in all directions. The bird continued across the lake where it met a craggy black mountainside. Something caught my eye—trees that had grown together too perfectly to be natural. They were even larger than the other trees, with trunks at least thirty feet in diameter.

The front of the center tree had been hollowed into a rectangle—a doorway. The bird landed in front of the trees and looked at me for a moment before flapping away to join its friend in the sky above.

Shelton gave me an uneasy look. "Maybe we gotta worry about witches with gingerbread houses instead of the birds."

I landed about thirty yards out from the trees. "Cover me."

Shelton landed and whipped out his staff. "I got your back."

I looked back and saw Max hovering above the lake. Then I turned around and faced the doorway in the center tree. A shadow stirred within. "Who's there?"

A young man stepped into the light. I recognized the handsome face almost immediately. I'd only met him once, and that had been enough. "Tyler Rock?" I said.

He blinked. "Justin Slade?"

"It's Justin Slade?" A petite woman with long brown hair pushed past Tyler. "What in the bloody hell are you doing here?"

At long last, we had found Emily Glass.

CHAPTER 28

Shelton whistled. "Jiminy Cricket on a fishing pole. Is that Emily Glass?"

I went weak with relief. "You won't believe what we've been through to find you." I held up a thumb to give Max the all-clear signal.

Emily followed the angle of my arm and spotted Max. "How many people are with you?"

"Several." I almost launched into a narrative, but something about her behavior seemed off. She seemed disappointed that we were here. "Is something wrong?"

Tyler looked at Emily and she looked up at him. Tyler spoke. "We came here to hide because there was nowhere to run in Eden."

"Who were you running from?" I said.

"Baal. Xanos." Tyler shrugged. "Other overlords. Once word got out about Emily's abilities, everyone wanted her either working for them, or dead."

"Holy smokes." Shelton took off his hat and ran a hand through his hair. "Is it because you can open portals to other realms?"

Emily pursed her lips. "How did you find me?"

"Uh, well, we found a way to track where you opened portals." I made a flicking motion with my hand as if casting a spell. "Then we reopened the portals and followed you through three different realms."

"You can track portals that I've opened?" Emily's eyebrows rose. "Explain, please."

I blew out a breath. "Well, we tracked down Vitania and Lumia in Iceland. They told us you went to work for Fjoeruss so we went to him next. He said you were last seen in a hotel in Dubai. So we went there. I channeled Clarity to highlight the portal scar and then Nightliss—"

Emily scowled. "Nightliss died in the Crystoid Incident."

"Yeah, we thought so too," I said. "Turns out Victus Edison kidnapped her and made an infernus copy. His son, Conrad, rescued her and my sister, Ivy."

"Wow, this is really confusing." Tyler looked at Shelton. "Who are you, by the way?"

"Harry Shelton." He tipped the front of his hat. "And it's all true. Nightliss never died and she's here with us."

Tears sparkled in Emily's eyes. "I would dearly love to see her. We only met a couple of times, but I always liked her."

I smiled. "Yeah. She's a pure soul."

Max landed next to me. "All good?"

"Max, this is Emily Glass and Tyler Rock." I waved a hand at the couple.

"Pleased to meet you," Max said.

"British." Emily raised an eyebrow. "I don't suppose you brought any Earl Grey with you?"

"Ambria might have some," Max said. "I forgot to bring my tea."

Emily's smile brightened and she seemed to relax a bit. "Perfect."

"Max, can you go get the others?" I tried to contain my excitement. "Tell them we found Emily."

Max saluted. "I'm on it!" He hopped on his broom and took off.

Emily's shoulders loosened. "Well, this is quite a surprise, I must admit. And also a bit disconcerting. If you could track me down, that means others might be able to as well."

"Have you been living here all this time?" I said.

Tyler nodded. "For over a year."

"Let's save the stories for everyone," Emily said. "I get tired of repeating myself."

I chuckled. "I know exactly how you feel."

Shelton looked up at the magpies. "What's with the birds?"

Emily raised an eyebrow. "Another subject that can wait until your friends arrive."

I'd met Emily during the Crystoid Incident, nearly a decade ago by Eden time. She didn't look much older on the outside, but her eyes had lost their youthful shine. These eyes guarded a soul that had seen a lot in the past ten years, most of it bad, if I had to guess.

Tyler, on the other hand, reminded me a lot of my dad. He wore a wolfish grin and seemed carefree on the surface, but judging from his tense shoulders and wary gaze, he was ready to spring into action at a moment's notice.

The rest of our group arrived twenty minutes later.

Nightliss's eyes brightened when she saw Emily. "It is so good to see you again."

"Is it really you?" Emily walked up to angel and peered into her eyes. "When I heard you died, it devastated me."

"It is really me," Nightliss said.

Emily watched her carefully. "What happened the first time we met?"

"I tried to give you the Templar blessing, but your body rejected it."

The other woman's gaze softened. "It is you."

Nightliss took Emily's hands. "I know you have been through trying times, but you can trust us."

Tyler also seemed to relax. "I'm sorry for the lukewarm response, but we've been fooled by infernus before. It nearly cost us our lives."

"I can usually glimpse people's auras, but more advanced infernus can project false images." Emily sighed. "It's awful when you can't trust anyone."

Elyssa nodded at Emily. "It's good to see you again."

"The pleasure is all mine." Emily's forehead pinched. "What's wrong with your hands?"

Elyssa winced. "I was injured during a fight on the carnivorous world."

Tyler grimaced. "The one where the ground tries to eat you?"

Elyssa nodded.

"Let me introduce everyone." I started on my right. "You met Shelton. That's Adam, our resident genius, Conrad Edison, Ambria Rax, Max Tiberius, and you know the rest of us."

"Conrad Edison." Emily's head tilted ever so slightly. "Aren't you Victus Edison's son?"

"Yes, but he's dead now," Conrad replied in a calm voice.

"Maybe we should sit down somewhere and exchange stories?" I said.

266

Emily nodded. "Please, come inside."

We followed her through the door and into a hollow trunk the size of a small house. The ceiling and floor were smooth and ringed as if someone neatly sliced out the core. The floor had more rings than I could even begin to count. A staircase on the far wall led up through a hole in the ceiling and down through another hole in the trunk.

A small kitchen, complete with modern appliances and hood, occupied one half. A nicely furnished den with television and other amenities took up the other half. Emily pointed to a sectional couch. It hugged the curve of the wall for about twenty feet, more than enough seating space for all of us.

I gave Elyssa the corner section so she could lean against the armrest. Emily and Tyler dropped onto a smaller couch opposite us.

No one spoke for a moment, so I took the initiative and launched into my well-practiced storyteller mode. I told the couple about our involvement in the Crystoid Incident and how it led to Cephus and Seraphina. How Victus betrayed us and trapped us there. How we united ancient enemies to save the realm but lost to Baal and his dragon army in the end. I brought them up to date on current events in Eden and our clashes with Razor Echelon and finished with our journey to the present.

"Your father is dead?" Tyler asked when I reached the end of the tale.

"Not dead," I said. "His body was taken over by the demon seed that became Cain. I thought Emily and her demon banishing abilities might help me restore him to his body."

Emily frowned. "I've never heard of anything like that. I don't know if I can help or not."

My hopes dimmed, but I tried not to let it show. "All I ask is that you try."

Tyler pressed his lips together. "So you met that bitch, Olivia."

"Uh, yeah." I watched Emily's expressions carefully, uncertain how she felt about her half-sister.

"Both of our evil siblings serve Baal now," Emily said. "How wonderful."

Shelton grunted. "When do we get to hear your story? And what's the deal with the giant birds?"

Emily managed a wry smile. "After the Demonicus Incident, Domathus put a price on my head." She explained how Fjoeruss had helped fake her death, how she'd met Vitania and Lumia, and discovered the origins of her powers.

I could barely believe the last part. "Whoa, hang on a minute. Vitania didn't say a thing about this to us." I shook my head like a wet dog as if that would clear the cobwebs. "Your grandmother—"

Emily nodded. "Is Eve."

"Dude, we met her." Adam took out his arcphone and projected a video.

A woman hovering on the other side of a portal said, "You are not the Fallen."

Adam paused the video. "This is your grandmother?"

Emily's forehead pinched. She tilted her head slightly. Nodded. "Her eyes are a different color and her face is a little different, but it's definitely her."

"Different face?" Max looked confused. "She can change her appearance?"

Adam scoffed. "You heard Emily's story. Eve is the mother of humanity. Changing her facial appearance is probably child's play."

"She looked rather plain when she lost her powers," Emily said almost smugly.

Elyssa shook her head slowly. "Have you developed other powers since all that happened?"

"I've practiced and grown stronger," Emily said, "but I can't create worlds or humans."

Tyler chuckled. "Well, not unless I plant my seed in her belly."

Emily rolled her eyes and gave him a look. "You are too much sometimes."

He grinned and squeezed her hand. "You can never get too much of something this good."

"You said you stole the powers from a lycan," Adam said. "Can you do the same for Arcanes and vampires?"

"You still haven't explained the birds," Shelton said before Emily could answer.

Emily glared at him. "You're certainly persistent."

"And annoying," Adam added.

"He'll never shut up until he gets what he wants," Ambria said in a weak voice.

Shelton nodded. "Yup."

A genuine smile graced Emily's face and a tear twinkled in her eye. "You're all family, aren't you?"

Shelton cleared his throat uneasily. "Uh, yeah. But don't go getting sentimental about it."

"Max and Ambria were the only real family I had," Conrad said. "Then I met Justin, Shelton, Elyssa, and Adam, and I felt a similar connection. Some of them wear gruff exteriors and act like they don't care, but they'll always stick by your side no matter the danger."

Ambria's eyes sparkled with tears. "Yes, this is our extended family, Emily. Even grumpy old Shelton."

Shelton scowled. "Hey, I ain't old."

Tyler laughed. "Damn, it feels good to be around people again."

Emily nodded. "Yes, it does."

"You people are about to give me cavities with all the sweet stuff." Shelton tried to hide a grin and failed. "So—the birds?"

Ambria tried to face-palm but hissed in pain when her shoulder denied the request.

Emily smiled and nodded. "This realm is Avianas. The various avian factions call it by different names, but most translate to Nest."

"How original," Shelton said. "So the birds are intelligent?"

"The evolved species are sentient. But like the apes in Eden, there are less-evolved birds." Emily leaned against Tyler. "They speak like normal birds, with whistles, tweets, warbles, and so forth. Human ears have no way to hear the entire range. The magpies are probably the smartest and they're the ones who figured out how to translate between their language and English."

I whistled. "Wow, that's incredible."

"Their intelligence is the only reason they've survived war for so long," Tyler said. "You should see the giant eagles and hawks. Now those are some scary looking birds."

"The magpies are at war with eagles and hawks?" Adam frowned. "That's not an even match at all."

"We stay out of the way," Emily said.

"So all you do is hide?" Ambria looked disappointed. "That seems like a waste for someone of your abilities."

"For a time we did," Emily said. "But in the years while the Eden army was trapped in Seraphina, we undertook another mission. Someone was stealing relics of Juranthemon. Somehow, Underborn found out about my abilities and recruited me to help spread the relics around the realms to keep them out of the hands of the mysterious collector."

"The Fallen were doing that too," Conrad said.

"After we settled in here, we continued our mission," Emily said.

Max tilted his head. "You never did tell us how you got here."

Ambria scoffed. "Because Shelton wanted to know about birds."

"Like me," Emily said, "Olivia can open rifts from one place to another within a realm so long as she can clearly envision it."

"Like an omniarch," Adam said.

"Exactly." Emily leaned forward, elbows on knees. "That made my mission to hide Juranthemon relics quite difficult since Olivia was collecting them for Baal. As you can imagine, we encountered each other frequently, and fought over relics."

Tyler scowled. "Olivia nearly killed us with hellfire demons the first time we ran into her."

Emily nodded. "One night, Olivia showed up at a restaurant while we were eating. We escaped in a flying car Fjoeruss had given us. Then she showed up outside our condo hours later. We packed our suitcases and drove the car through a rift to Europe. I had us and our car scanned for trackers, but everything was clean."

"Then she showed up at our hotel," Tyler said. "Right when things were getting nice and hot in the bedroom too."

Ambria's face paled and her mouth dropped open.

Shelton and Adam burst into laughter.

Emily gave Tyler a momentary side-glare before continuing with her story. "We took the car through five rifts, from South Africa to Iceland, to Buenos Aries, Argentina, so forth and so on until we stopped in Dubai. Olivia and a dozen demons kicked down the door four hours later."

"We didn't even have time to get properly clothed," Tyler said.

"We grabbed what we could and ran into the bathroom," Emily said. "I'd memorized the symbols to another realm just in case Olivia found us again. Unfortunately, the list Vitania gave me didn't tell me anything about the realms, so I'd memorized a few at random. I never expected to encounter a Tyrannosaurus Rex two minutes after we leapt through the rift."

"I had one leg in my pants when that happened," Tyler said. "It was hilarious and terrifying at the same time."

"We ran down the beach and into some rocks where another giant lizard tried to eat us." Emily shuddered. "Luckily, I fended it off and we found a safe place to rest. The next morning, I opened another rift. I stepped barefooted onto that disgusting flesh world and immediately knew something was horribly wrong with that place."

"I had on pants at least." Tyler's nose wrinkled. "A swarm of big, hopping bugs came at us before we even had a chance to get comfortable. Then the ground opened up and ate half of them."

"I opened another rift." Emily sighed. "We stepped through and into a storm."

"The rain lit everything in electric blue." Tyler rubbed the top of his arm. "Getting wet was like bathing in electric acid."

"We barely took two steps when the ground shook and a tree grew right underneath us." Emily's hand tightened on Tyler's leg. "It was all we could do to hold on."

Tyler looked downcast. "And I lost my arcphone."

Ambria frowned. "You were almost killed by glowing rain, and that was your biggest concern?"

Tyler grinned. "Priorities."

Emily continued. "I'd memorized the symbols to six realms. Three of them tried to kill us the moment we arrived."

"Why didn't the glowing rain hurt you?" I asked. "And how did you heal Tyler?"

"The lycan aura healed me." Emily tapped a finger against her chest. "I opened a rift and brought him here before the rain killed him. His demon spirit boosts his human body's ability to heal, but it still took a week of rest."

"Emily hunted for food in wolf form and we camped out underneath a tree until I was strong enough to walk." Tyler smiled fondly at her. "Then we made friends with the magpies, built ourselves this home, and the rest is history."

"It's amazing you survived with nothing but your magic and wits," Elyssa said. "The realms are far more dangerous than I suspected."

"I've seen far worse," Emily said. "Some worlds would kill a human in an instant."

Now seemed a good time to deliver my save the world pitch. "We came a long way to find you because we desperately need your help." I held open my hands imploringly. "Emily, will you come back to Eden and help us defeat Razor and Baal?"

Emily didn't even hesitate to answer. "No."

CHAPTER 29

S helton slapped his leg. "Son of a nut-licking squirrel. You didn't even think about it!"

"Just no?" I said. "Why not?"

"Baal has hundreds of minions searching the realms for relics of Juran-themon. He's already collected most of the major pieces." Emily shook her head. "If Baal gets just a few more objects, then nothing we do will stop the realms from recombining."

"He's also ravaging realms with his dragon army," Elyssa said. "We have to stop him on all fronts, not just one."

"Saila was at the center of the Sundering," Emily said. "That's why the most powerful relics are parts of her. Underborn believes Baal has almost completed her and is missing only the right foot, the heart, the eye, and dagger."

"Is it like piecing together a jigsaw puzzle?" Shelton said.

"It's exactly like that." Emily bit her lower lip. "No one knows exactly what will happen if Baal completes her, but we've already observed some side effects."

"It's like the other relics want to be close to her," Tyler said. "Blink stones, hairbrushes, cups, and other junk caught in the initial blast of the Sundering started vanishing all by themselves."

"Because all the pieces of Saila in one place are like a magical magnet," Emily said.

"What about the lost room?" Conrad said.

"It hasn't been affected," Emily said. "Underborn still has it."

I waved off her objections. "Everything you've done has bought us precious time. But if Baal is really so close to completing Saila, then we need to find out where he's keeping the pieces and steal them."

"I already know where he's keeping them." Emily leaned back and crossed her arms. "He has them in the physical domain of Haedaemos—Hell."

Shelton whistled. "You can physically go to Hell?"

"I hear it's a great vacation spot," Tyler said.

"I'm confused." Adam rubbed his eyes. "How can Hell be physical?"

"When the Earth was sundered into realms, only two places remained untouched—Mount Olympus and Hell."

"We knew about Atlantis, but how did Hell escape being blown to bits?"

"During my brief stint as a goddess, I learned a few things." Emily pressed her lips together. "Hell is where the infernal fount resides in our physical plane and Mount Olympus is the location of the primal fount."

Conrad's eyes flared. "I didn't think the primal fount had a physical location."

"That is where it intersects our dimension." Emily clicked her tongue as if trying to think of the words to describe a concept difficult to comprehend. "The founts are both spiritual and physical and exist across all dimensions at once. Each instance vibrates at a slightly different

275

frequency so touching one fount is not the same as touching them all across the multiverse."

Adam snapped his fingers. "They form a quantum matrix, the positive and negative poles of the universal battery, so to speak."

Emily's eyebrows rose. "Have you done time as a god?"

Shelton snorted. "Nerd god, maybe."

Adam blushed. "No, but it meshes with a theory I've been developing as we learn more about the realms and multiverse." He projected a holographic globe from his arcphone. A blue dot highlighted an area near Bermuda. "That's the location of Atlantis in Eden."

"Shouldn't it be right over Kratos?" Shelton said. "That's where Voltis aligns in Eden."

"Remember, the Voltis storm wall is the outer perimeter of Atlantis," Adam said. "And technically, Olympus is the exact center, not the city of Atlantis. That's why the dot is miles away from Kratos."

"Uh, yeah." Shelton backhanded the air. "So what's the deal then?"

"From here, it's quite simple. The infernal fount is the antipode to the primal fount." A red dot blinked into existence on the other side of the globe. Adam rotated it to show the location. "It looks like Hell is somewhere beneath Lake MacKay in Australia."

"Now that I believe." Shelton laughed. "It's no wonder everything in Australia is out to kill you."

"You're saying that Hell literally exists underground somewhere around there?" I said.

Adam nodded. "But there might be something equivalent to Voltis that we'd need to traverse to reach it."

"Oh, joy." Shelton clapped his hands. "Another adventure through Voltis."

"This is fascinating stuff, really is," I said. "*But*, it doesn't help us against Razor, and it doesn't stop Baal's dragon army."

"I won't return to Eden," Emily said. "I can't afford to spend time fighting Razor while Baal collects the last few artifacts."

"What if I said we don't have to return to Eden right away?" I waved a hand at the room. "There are hundreds of realms, some of which have potential allies. With your powers, we could quickly travel the realms and transport entire armies back to Eden."

Emily pursed her lips. "You realize it's not that simple, right? You can't just show up in a realm and convince whatever beings live there to come fight for you."

"I already have hundreds of allies in other realms, I just don't have a way to reach them." I stood and held out my hand. "Join us, Emily. We have cookies."

Tyler rubbed his hands. "Cookies? I'm in."

Emily looked uncertain. "But it'll still take me away from my primary mission."

Tyler put a hand on her shoulder. "Babe, we haven't kept up with Baal at all. In the past few months, we were too late to keep his minions from grabbing three major relics." He shrugged. "Maybe it's time we tried something different."

Elyssa winced and held a burned hand awkwardly in front of her. "We're losing the war on all fronts, Emily. You're our game-changer."

"I can touch the primal fount if that counts for anything," Conrad said. "Perhaps you could teach me to wield the power."

Emily flicked her gaze to him. "You can tap directly into the fount?"

"My grandfather, Moses showed me how," he said.

"A descendant of Moses, the first Arcane?" Emily put a hand to her forehead as if trying to remember something. "I thought I glimpsed something different about you."

I steered the conversation back on track. "Will you help us, Emily?"

Emily blew out a long breath.

A loud explosion rocked the tree. The front door exploded into splinters. A creature from my worst nightmares burst into the room—a humanoid with the head and tentacles of giant octopus.

"Sister dearest!" The sing-song voice sounded awfully familiar. "I've finally found you."

"What the hell is that thing?" Shelton shouted.

Tyler bared his teeth "Octalon."

"An old pal, I hope?" Shelton said.

Tyler shook his head. "No. An old enemy."

Emily stared down the beast and scowled. "Out of my house, demon." She slashed a hand and a portal in the ground swallowed the creature. Emily turned to us. "Up the stairs, now! We're getting out of here."

Nightliss wove a thick Murk shield over the doorway. I reinforced the wooden walls, and then we ran upstairs after the others. Everyone clustered in a large bedroom.

Emily peered through a window. "That bitch." She slapped the wall with a hand. "How did she find me again?"

"Is Cain with her?" I felt my demon half shrinking away inside me at the mere thought.

Emily nodded. "Yes."

"Oh, fudge." Sweat broke out on my forehead. "What now?"

"We leave." Emily took out a brown seashell and rubbed it. Water misted from inside the shell, forming a list of realms in the air, just like the one Vitania had given me.

Tyler sighed. "Fugitives again. Always on the run."

"Why run?" Elyssa said. "Let's stand and fight."

Fear shone in Emily's eyes. "I can't beat Olivia. Baal trained her personally."

"You can't even hold your bow," I told Elyssa.

"Fucking Olivia," Tyler said. "Looks like she's graduated from hellfire demons to summoning deep ones."

"She's a royal terror," Shelton agreed.

I took out the seashell Vitania had given me. "Use this instead of yours. It's more up to date. Maybe we can avoid the deadlier realms."

Conrad shook his head. "Why are we running? Justin, you and Nightliss are at full strength, and now we have Emily. Surely the four of us are a match for Olivia."

Shelton scoffed. "Hey, what am I, chopped liver?"

"I can help too," Adam said.

Elyssa removed her bow from the holster, face locked in a grimace of pain. "Me too."

Ambria stood next to Elyssa. "I can't very well let our commander fight injured without me to protect her."

Max stared with wide eyes out the window. "Uh, some huge portals just opened outside, and I see orange flames."

I turned to Emily. "Maybe we should stand and fight."

Worry shone in her eyes. She looked about as confident as I felt. "I guess so." Forehead furrowed in concentration, stared at the wall next to the window. At first, I thought she was trying not to crap her pants, but then a portal sliced open. Judging from the grass and trees, it was a portal outside.

Emily waved us through. "Go."

We ran through and emerged in the woods a few hundred yards to the north of the house. Twin portals gaped open to the south, gateways to the bowels of Hell. And from the bowels game two demonic turds—big, flaming turds just like the ones we'd faced in Iceland.

Olivia hovered a few feet off the ground, orange flames trailing from her hair and feet. Cain hovered next to her on wings of red flame.

"It's not fair," I said. "How come the bad guys can fly?"

"Well, maybe we can't fly on our own, but we got brooms." Shelton climbed on his and readied his staff. "Let's go kick some demonic ass."

Conrad took Ambria aside. "Please wait here."

She shook her head. "I won't watch helplessly from the sidelines!"

I turned to Elyssa, but the violet glow in her eyes told me all I needed to know. "I can't talk you into staying back, can I?"

Face locked with pain, she shook her head. "I'm with you all the way."

"I can at least help a little." Ambria flicked her wand and tapped it to Elyssa's hands.

Elyssa's face went slack with relief. "What was that?"

Ambria tapped the wand to her shoulder and sighed. "It's a numbing spell. Unfortunately, it halts the healing process while it's active."

"I'll take it." Elyssa flexed her hands. "I can't feel them at all."

"Yeah, that's another downside," Max said. "Make sure you don't injure yourself worse without knowing it."

I climbed on my broom and turned to Emily. "Maybe someone can loan you a broom."

Emily shook her head. "I don't need one." She held out her hands. Azure and golden light crackled along her skin. She rose into the air.

"You're using the primal fount," Conrad said.

She nodded and looked at him. "From what I know, there are only two kinds of people who can draw on the primal or infernal founts. Gods and their offspring."

Conrad frowned. "The ancient earth dragon, Altash, gave Moses the ability to touch the primal fount. Moses wasn't a god."

"Then perhaps Altash is more than he seems." Emily flexed her hands. "Are we ready?"

I nodded. "Let's do it."

"Hey, I don't have a broom," Tyler said.

"Take mine." Adam handed it to him. "I'll be better off fighting from the ground."

"Sweet!" Tyler hopped on and spun it in a circle. "I love these things."

Emily smiled at him fondly. "Okay, now we're ready."

I chopped my hand forward and we sped out of the trees, Emily pacing us without difficulty. *She's a lot more powerful than she lets on.* I didn't understand why she feared Olivia.

The hellfire demons saw us coming. Great flaming maws dropped open, thunderous roars split the air. Olivia and Cain spun to face us. Orange flames glowed in my fake twin's eyes and licked from the ends of his spiked hair.

Olivia cackled like a madwoman. "Not running this time, sister?"

Emily bared her teeth. "Not today, bitch."

The demons raced toward us, flaming humanoids three stories tall, one with the head of a bull, the other that of a boar. Thirty-foot tusks with razor edges gleamed in the boar demon's mouth. The bull demon's horns looked every bit as sharp as its companion's.

I'd been too weak to fight the hellfire demons in Iceland, but now I was ready to see what I could do. I flew straight at the bull demon and unleashed a torrent of Brilliance in its face. Destructive energy carved a line in the demon's rocky flesh, but did nothing to hurt him. Nightliss flew in from the other side and coated the demon's legs in Murk.

Legs locked in place but unable to slow its forward momentum, the beast toppled forward with a great roar. It smashed into the ground. Shockwaves rippled through the grass. Treetops shook and flocks of smaller birds exploded into the air.

Olivia and Emily waged a battle of wills for the fate of the other demon. Emily opened portal after portal to drop the boar demon into, but Olivia snapped them shut just in time. Shelton and Conrad circled the boar, firing spells and energy into its face to keep it disoriented.

The bull demon bellowed. The Murk binding its legs cracked and shattered. Nightliss tried to bind them again, but the beast blocked her attack with a giant clawed hand. Murk encased it. Rather than try to break it, the beast used it as a giant sledgehammer and swung it at Nightliss.

She dodged away at the last instant.

None of our attacks seemed to hurt the damned thing in the slightest. *Maybe I should fight fire with fire.* I was, after all, part Daemos. The last time I'd summoned a demon to fight, it turned out to be a really bad idea and set Xanos free in the world. But maybe I could summon a powerful demon not from the Abyss.

I circled away from the demon and turned my vision inward through the window in my soul. My demon half was in there, but hiding. *You talk a big game, but Baal sure turned you into a pansy.* I didn't even want to see that part of myself. My consciousness drifted into Haedaemos and sensed dozens of nearby entities. Some were doglike—ideal for hell-hounds. Others were too weak or tiny to be of much good.

I searched until I found the biggest, nastiest demon I could. It wasn't a hellfire demon, but it burned with insatiable hunger. It had feasted on the souls of mortals and demons alike. I focused on the ground below. Black tar bubbled in the grass. A long leg struggled free, followed by ten more. An abdomen broke free of the birthing pool. Screaming human faces pressed against the insides of the abdomen, stretching it like plastic.

The presence of the giant crawler weighed down on me, but it wasn't nearly as bad as controlling Xanos all those years ago. The monster shrieked with hunger and pounced on the nearest demon.

The bull caught the crawler in mid-air and tore it open with a mighty swipe of its claws. Green ichor sprayed across the field and the crawler went silent. Bellowing in victory, the bull threw the remains and me and Nightliss. I strafed to the side just in time.

Nightliss gave me a worried look and I knew exactly how she felt.

I'd just brought forth the biggest, meanest crawler I'd ever summoned, and the hellfire demon killed it in a heartbeat.

I had nothing in my arsenal that could defeat this thing.

CHAPTER 30

"You've got to be kidding me!" Shelton shouted. "Did that thing just kill a crawler?"

"Ordinary demons are garbage versus hellfire demons," Tyler shouted. "Don't even bother with them."

"Anything else I should know?" I said.

"Yeah," Tyler said. "They spit fire if they get too close."

Cain bellowed with laughter as he watched Emily and Olivia play ring around the demon. The only upside was that my doppelganger hadn't come for me yet. His eyes met mine, as if he sensed me watching him and he smirked. His lips moved, but I couldn't hear him over the roar of the bull demon.

"There's got to be something I can do against these damned things!" I flew in a wide circle around the demon. It swiped at me, claws trailing orange flames. I'd fought goliaths—golems twice as tall as this thing—and won. But that was because I could destroy their weapons and power sources.

Normal demons took on physical shells that I could kill with my magic. But hellfire demons were made of much tougher material. Emily had once defeated Olivia because the strain of controlling multiple physical demons overwhelmed her. But that had been over a decade ago and Olivia had grown in strength since then.

Emily might be the Great Banisher, but her sister was the Great Summoner.

I flew away from the demon and paced Tyler. "A hellfire demon is here in the flesh, right?"

"Yep." He quirked an eyebrow. "Why?"

"Do they have hearts, organs, or any vulnerabilities?"

"I have no idea," he said. "I only heard rumors about them when I lived in Haedaemos."

"If they're physical then they're like any other living being." I spun around and watched as Nightliss danced her broom around the bull demon, doing her best to keep it occupied.

"The other demon, Octalon, is another kind of hellion," Tyler said. "He's a deep one."

"Like Cthulhu? I said.

"You've heard of them?"

"Are you kidding me?" I grimaced. "I thought he was a myth!"

"Most myths have true origins." Tyler shrugged. "Sorry."

"We have more immediate worries." I clenched a fist. "But I think I have an idea."

Tyler nodded. "If you need me, just scream."

I dove toward the bull demon, weaving Murk and Brilliance into a ball of Stasis. The demon roared and swiped a massive claw at me. I fired a beam of Stasis at the beast's wrist, but it was hard focusing on the moving target. The bull bellowed in pain and yanked back its arm.

"You didn't like that, did you, big boy?" While he nursed his wrist, I dove and nailed his ankles with Stasis. "I don't care how big you are, you can't walk without feet!"

Nightliss caught on. With a fierce shout, she dove and blasted the other ankle with Stasis. The bull stumbled. One leg snapped off at the ankle. A roar of pure rage rippled through the air. But even as the monster crawled on hands and knees, new ankles and feet began to grow from the stumps.

"Son of a bitch." We'd crippled it but only temporarily. We had to hit it while it was down. "Get the arms!" I shouted.

Nightliss dodged around the monster's flashing claws and hit the bull in the left shoulder. I nailed the right shoulder. The rocky flesh turned cold and gray and its arms snapped off. The burning flesh around the stumps flowed like lava, slowly growing new limbs. Now we had time for the finishing touch—or so I hoped.

"The head!" I blasted the head from one side and Nightliss hit it from the other.

"Die, foul beast!" she cried.

The flames in the head hissed and flickered out. The head turned to a gray lump of stone. But the fire in the rest of the body didn't die. The arms and feet began to grow back. The gray boulder that had once been the head rolled away as a new one began to form.

I was about ready to give up, but Nightliss growled in anger. "Let's kill the whole body at once!"

"Justin, watch out!" Tyler shouted.

I saw an orange streak from the corner of my eye and glanced Cain on an intercept course. He bared his teeth in a feral grin. "Hey, are you molesting my favorite demon?"

I swung around to face him, but even as I did, he began to spawn. His skin shaded dark red, black horns spiraled up from his forehead, and his muscles swelled until his arms were bigger than my thighs. His flaming wings grew three sizes larger. His black unitard stretched to accommodate his new size, outlining every massive muscle.

"Why can't I have a cool uniform?" I muttered.

The beast! My demon spirit cried out in fear and hid before I could say a word.

"Well, this isn't good." I fired a beam of Stasis at Cain.

He smirked and dodged. My chances of hitting him from this distance were slim, but chances of hitting the downed demon were pretty damned good. It'd take Cain another thirty seconds to get here and he was just trying to divert mine and Nightliss's attention long enough so he could defend his nasty pet.

"Kill the demon!" I shouted.

Nightliss blasted the torso from the head down. I worked up from the opposite direction spraying Stasis like a giant fire extinguisher. Even for two of us, the huge demon had a lot of real estate to cover.

"Stop!" Cain shouted, dropping his nonchalant façade.

But Nightliss and I extinguished the demon's fire and still had two seconds to spare before my fake brother was on us. He slammed into me so hard, my bones cracked.

He grunted and vanished, leaving me to plummet to earth. Something gripped my shirt and slowed my descent. Fabric bit my armpits, but I didn't fall. I looked up and met Elyssa's gaze.

"You looked like you needed help," she said.

"Don't I always?" I looked around but didn't see Cain. "Where'd he go?"

"Into the woods." Elyssa's broom couldn't maintain altitude with two of us, so she dropped lower.

Ultraviolet flashes and explosions sounded from the woods. Demonic roars and Nightliss's shouts echoed. I hit the ground running.

I need you! My demon half didn't answer. *Look, if you don't help me, then I'll die and you'll die with me. Are you scared because of what Baal did to us, or are you scared to fight your doppelganger?*

The answer came as a whimper. *I thought I was the ultimate destroyer, but I am nothing. Baal took everything from me.*

Yeah, because Baal is the god damned king of demons. He took my father from me and the only way to get him back is to defeat Cain without killing him.

Impossible, my demon replied.

Do you still want me to call you Kalesh?

Kalesh is dead. I am nothing now.

He was being worse than a dramatic goth teenager at high school prom. *If you don't let me manifest into demon form, Cain will win. That means Baal wins again. But if we beat Cain, then we take something valuable from Baal. It's better to try and die than to live like cowards!*

I could literally feel that part of me pondering it. Inasmuch as Kalesh was part and parcel of me, there were parts of my demon spirit I didn't control. Dad once told me that aspect changed dramatically with age and experience. Apparently, Kalesh and I had a long way to go.

We would make Baal angry and sad like me. Kalesh sounded guardedly happy.

I decided to appeal to his hurt ego. *We would get revenge. Baal would be so pissed.*

But you do not want to kill Cain.

All we have to do is beat him up and knock him out. Then we can remove Cain and put my dad back in his body. That would make Baal even angrier than if we killed Cain.

Yes. Because killing Cain kills Dad. That would make Baal a little happy. I want Baal angry and sad like me! Cain must live so we can spit in Baal's eye.

So, we're doing this?

Kalesh mentally bared his teeth. *Yes. We are.*

Something red streaked from the trees. Cain thrust his fists forward and fired a blast of red-tinged Brilliance at me. I threw up a reflective shield of Murk. It bounced the attack back at Cain. He veered out of the way and fired again. I swiveled the shield, but his attack struck the ground near my feet.

Grass and dirt exploded. The blast threw me back ten feet. I rolled to the side to avoid another blast. But he was coming in so fast, I couldn't move fast enough. I dove behind one of the massive trees to buy a few more seconds.

Cain curved straight up and fired down at the tree. The blast split the huge trunk. Smoke filled the air and the tree began to topple. Wood creaked and groaned. One half of the trunk fell toward me. The other half rested against a neighboring tree.

"How the hell is he so strong?" I ran further into the forest. "That bastard can fly almost as fast as a broom and still unleash all that power like it's nothing!"

He taps the infernal fount, Kalesh said.

"Baal must have given him the ability." That meant we were on totally uneven terms. Unfortunately, I had no choice but to fight. *Kalesh, it's morphing time.*

Let us fight to the death and devour the souls of the conquered.

"Well, that's a bit melodramatic, but I'll take it." I shed all my clothes except the stretchy athletic underwear underneath. Then I unleashed the chains.

Muscles snaked around my arms and legs. My body expanded and grew. Horns spiraled from my forehead and a long tail with a spike unfurled from my backside. Claws pushed out my toenails and fingernails and my skin turned dark blue.

I reared back my head and roared, "Daddy's home and he's got the belt!"

Cain glided overhead, glowing like a beacon in the dusky sky. Apparently, he lost sight of me after blasting the tree. Orange and golden flashes lit up the sky where Emily and Olivia fought. The bull demon was nothing but a cold lump of rock in the field. I didn't see where Nightliss or Elyssa had gone, but I prayed they were okay.

I couldn't fly like Cain, but with my demon claws, I could climb like a squirrel on steroids. I sank my grip into the nearest tree and raced up it. Cain must have seen the branches vibrating at the last minute, because his head swiveled right at me as I leapt from the top. He reacted a split-second too late. I latched onto his beefy leg and sank my claws in as deep as they could go.

"Fuck!" he screamed. It must have been enough to shatter his concentration, because his flames went out and we dropped like rocks. My back smashed through branches. Somehow, I maintained my hold on Cain even as he flailed to grab something to stop the fall.

This is my chance. I can get Dad back!

Ignoring the pain and the primal fear of falling, I channeled a sledgehammer of Murk and slammed it against Cain's head. A horn snapped off, eliciting another cry of pain. So I hit him again and again and again. I smashed against a branch big enough to resist my fall. It flipped me forward and then I lost my hold on Cain.

We must have hit every branch on the way down until there was nothing else to catch us for the final thirty feet. Cain bounced off the roots an instant before I crashed on top of him.

He groaned, so I popped him in the head again. His demon form melted away, leaving a bloody and bruised copy of me. Cain had shaved the sides of his head, leaving a wide, thick patch of long hair on the top. *His barber must have dozed off halfway through.*

We have him! Kalesh growled. *We should devour his spirit.*

I shook my head. "No. Eating a spirit that powerful will only poison us again. We need Emily to banish the spirit and bring back Dad."

Kalesh remained quiet a moment, then surprised me. *You are right.*

Maybe we were growing a little closer.

Maybe we devour just a little spirit.

Or maybe not.

I slung Cain over a shoulder and ran out into the field. My long demon legs ate up the distance. I spotted Nightliss battling the second demon. She couldn't channel enough Stasis to outpace the demon's regeneration. Emily and Olivia danced in the night sky, hurling fireballs at each other as if they had all the energy in the world.

Flashes of azure energy zipped across the field a hundred yards away. Conrad, Max, and the others fought Octalon. Somehow the demon octopus-headed demon had returned. I soon realized he wasn't alone. A massive shark demon and eight-headed serpent demon were right by his side.

"Where in the hell did they come from?" I said.

I didn't have my broom anymore, but I had to help Nightliss with the other hellfire demon. To do that, I'd have to put down Cain. His supernatural healing would heal him quickly. So putting him down was about as good as letting him go.

"Shit." I kept running toward Nightliss, unwilling to drop my prize. I could probably blanket him in Stasis without killing him, but I didn't have the same precise control that Fjoeruss did. If I accidentally killed the body, I'd never get my dad back.

I closed to within twenty yards of the demon. Even with my greater height, it towered over me like a human to a Chihuahua. Nightliss had frozen one of its feet, but she couldn't muster the energy to take off the other one.

"Nightliss, I'm here!" I encased Cain from head to toe in Murk, leaving only a breathing hole for his face, and set him on the ground.

She flew her broom toward me. "I'm so tired, Justin."

"Just a little more," I said. I blasted the boar demon's other foot with Stasis.

The boar heaved like a sick dog. Flames and lava erupted from its mouth. Nightliss yanked her broom to the side, but a flaming lump of brimstone struck the bristles and erupted in flames. She leapt from her ride and stumbled on the ground.

I blurred to the side and unleashed more Stasis on the foot. It snapped off and the boar crashed onto its knees. It heaved another stream of hellfire, but I strafed out of the way. I swept the beam of Stasis up its leg, holding it there long enough for it to completely engulf it.

The boar suddenly seemed to reconsider its life choices. Instead of attacking, it turned tail and fled, hopping on stumps and clawing its way back to the Hell portal. I tried to chase after it, but even crippled, its strides were too long for me to match.

I shook a fist. "Come back, you big coward!"

But it scrambled through the portal and back to safety.

"Justin!" Nightliss raced toward the cube of Murk holding Cain.

Red cracks formed in the surface. Cain roared, veins popping in his neck and forehead. His prison shattered into a million pieces. Nightliss flung strands of Murk at Cain, snared his ankles. He went down. Before I could get to him, fireballs slammed the earth. Burnt grass and dirt showered around me.

Olivia and Emily fought overhead and their crossfire was as dangerous to us as it was to them. Cain broke free of Nightliss's restraints. Red fire glowed around him and he leapt into the air.

Without a broom, I couldn't catch him. Cain was going to escape.

CHAPTER 31

He will not escape my wrath! Kalesh took control before I could stop him. Giant bat-like wings grew from my back. My leg muscles coiled and launched me into the air. Wings spread and flapped furiously, driven by my demon spirit. I usually fought back my demon half when he vied for control, but this time I let him go at it. I channeled Murk and lassoed Cain's ankle with a strand.

My god, we're actually sharing control! It was a huge first for me and Kalesh. But now was no time to celebrate.

Cain manifested back into demon form but kept his fire wings instead of growing bat wings. I yanked hard on the Murk and reeled him in, a big red fish. He bared pointy teeth and yanked right back, drawing me toward him. Kalesh thrust with our wings and we surged upward, claws outstretched.

But my evil twin had a surprise. He flung out his hand and a torrent of crimson-laced Brilliance nearly melted off my face. My reflexes kicked in. I channeled a shield of Murk from my skin. It protected me from first-degree burns, but the impact threw me backward. Apparently,

Cain hadn't thought through his attack very well, because the Murk tether yanked him down with me.

A bolt of azure energy speared past me and nailed Cain in the ribs. Conrad zipped in on his broom, firing a barrage of attacks. Cain shouted, face twisting in pain. He spun around and jetted toward the open portal, dragging me along in his wake.

"Fuck!" Olivia screamed in frustration. "Why won't you just die?" She thrust her fists forward. A beam of energy large enough to consume a city bus narrowly missed Emily and blasted a giant tree to splinters.

Emily rolled gracefully to the side, firing a volley of energy back at her sister. "How did you track me?"

Oliva bared her teeth. "You'll figure it out soon enough. This isn't even the real fight, you moron."

"Justin!" Conrad was trying to catch up to me, but Cain was a hell of a lot faster than I'd realized. He didn't seem to care that he was taking me on a joyride with him.

Conrad cupped his hands over his mouth. "Let go, Justin! Don't let him take you inside!"

I saw Olivia streaking toward us, Emily close behind. She would reach the portal at almost the same time as Cain. And that was when I understood his plan. If I went through with him and Olivia, I'd be done for. Baal had let me go before because he wanted me to fight Xanos. So maybe he'd let me go again. But maybe he'd think I was too much trouble and put me down.

I had no idea what lay on the other side of the portal. A shimmering curtain of orange energy obstructed the view. If the demons came from that portal, then it probably went straight to Hell. While it sounded like a cool place to mark on my map of places I'd visited, this was not the time for tourism.

Do not give up! Kalesh said.

We had about thirty seconds, give or take, before we hit the portal. I could do an awful lot in that time instead of letting myself be dragged along for the ride. *Let's see if we can't slow him down.* I flared my wings as wide as possible and slowed Cain by a third. Hand-over-hand, I pulled myself closer.

A tall, bearded man stepped from the portal, a smirk on his face and I nearly lost my grip. The man was an infernus, one of Baal's vessels. A squad of monstrous demons flanked him.

"Holy shit. He brought the freaking demon cavalry with him!" If I didn't let go right now, I'd be in range of all those nasties. "Shit!" A part of me was so furious it didn't want to let go. It didn't care about anything except dragging Cain kicking and screaming back with me.

Oddly enough, it was Kalesh who forced my hand. *Today is not the day.* He let go.

Cain spun around and stopped, fired a strand of red-streaked Murk. It coiled around my wrist. Cain laughed. "Too late, brother. Too late."

"Too late for what, bitch?" Before he could react, I flared my wings and yanked the tether as hard as I could. I grabbed his leg and sank my claws deep into his thigh.

He cried out in pain but somehow managed to laugh. "You're just bait, idiot."

"Bait for what?" I looked back and saw Emily flying not after Olivia, but on an intercept path to save me. It wasn't me Baal wanted at all. He wanted to remove a thorn in his side—the woman who fought to keep the relics out of his control. Once he had her, he could find the last few that kept him from completing Saila.

Despite my claws in his leg, Cain flew toward Baal. I channeled Murk and Brilliance from my eyes and crossed them. I probably looked like an idiot, but it was the only way to weave the beams into Stasis without the use of my hand. Despite double vision, I sliced through the Murk tether binding my wrist.

Using Cain's leg as an anchor, I swung up my foot and nailed him right in the ass just as I let go. I folded my wings and dove for the ground. Orange fireballs streaked past me.

"Get him, Cain!" Olivia screamed.

I saw Baal racing across the field to intercept me, his demons lurching behind him. I spread my wings and angled away. Heat exploded against my back. The ground rushed to meet me. I plowed into the dirt and skidded until my horns cracked into something hard. Woozy and disoriented, I pulled my head out of the ground and discovered a gray boulder with a piece of broken horn jutting from it.

"Ow." I staggered to my feet and spun around.

Olivia dove right at me, Emily close behind. Conrad approached from another angle on his broom. Cain veered around and aimed for me while Baal and his minions raced across the field beneath him.

I waved off Emily. "Turn around! It's you they want, not me!" I waved my arms at Conrad. "Go back to the others!"

My only choice was to run back toward the giant tree house. Olivia and Cain might be faster, but I could put some distance between me and Baal's hell squad. And then the ground dropped out from beneath me. I fell about twenty feet and landed in the field right next to Elyssa. I saw Olivia and Cain a few hundred yards in the distance.

Elyssa looked just as surprised as I felt. "What happened?"

Emily and Conrad spun around and came toward us. Shelton, Adam, Max, and Ambria emerged from the forest.

"What in the hell happened?" Shelton said.

Tyler glided in on a broom and landed. He flashed a grin. "Did you see the looks on their faces?"

I belatedly realized what happened. "Emily opened a portal beneath me and dropped me here."

He chuckled. "Yep."

Emily and Conrad sped toward us, Olivia and Cain in hot pursuit. Baal and his demons weren't far behind.

"What's the plan?" Shelton said. "I thought we had those two on the ropes, but now they've got backup."

Nightliss leaned against Adam. "I'm too tired to fight more demons. We need to reach safety."

Emily swooped in for a graceful landing. Brow furrowed, she stared at the ground a few feet away. Instead of a portal, an inky black pool of tar spread across the ground. "Everyone in!"

"In?" Shelton grimaced in disgust. "Why the hell would I jump into that?"

"Do it now!" Emily shouted. Sweat poured down her forehead. "It's the only safe place I can think of."

"Shelton, just do it." Adam took Nightliss by the hand and the pair hopped into the pitch. It swallowed them slowly, like oil. "I instantly regret my decision!" Adam shouted before vanishing into the murky depths.

"Fuck it." Shelton caressed his broom and jumped in.

Elyssa and I went next. Icy cold bit through flesh and into bone. Even in my demon form, it hurt so much I wanted to cry. I sank in up to my armpits. I couldn't move. Couldn't breathe. It felt like I was going to die. Darkness consumed me. I plummeted through an inky void. Hands and claws seemed to grasp at me from all sides.

And then I stumbled forward, tripped on a pile of rocks, and fell down.

Stars dusted the night sky. Hues of violet and pink streaked the heavens, casting light on rocky, barren soil. Oddly enough, it was bright enough to see all around me, but black shadows stood like giant cutouts against the horizon. This place looked a lot like somewhere I'd been before.

Shelton and the others huddled nearby, gazing warily at the alien scenery.

"Something feels really wrong about this place," Shelton said. "What realm is this?"

"I think it's Nowhere," I said. "The place where Baal spoke to me. If that's the case, I don't know what Emily is thinking."

Ambria, Max, and the others appeared feet-first through the tar portal, rotating slowly as their bodies adjusted to the change in orientation. At the last moment, they stumbled to the ground, brains unable to process the shift from falling through the ground to moving forward from a vertical portal.

Emily came through last and closed the portal with a sweep of her hand. She blew out a long breath. "They won't dare follow us here."

"Is this Nowhere?" I said.

Emily raised an eyebrow. "You've been there?"

"Yeah, it's where Baal planted the demon seed in my soul." I shivered. "We're not safe here at all."

"That's not where we are." Emily leaned heavily on Tyler. "I'm exhausted. I've got to rest."

"I don't even remotely understand how you went balls to the wall for so long," Shelton said. "How does your body handle the strain?"

"Years of practice and pushing my limits." Emily drooped. "I couldn't afford not to push myself, not with Olivia doing the same."

Tyler eased her into a sitting position against a boulder. "So, babe. Where are we, exactly?"

Emily smiled. "You're going to love this."

Some of the confidence drained from his grin. "Oh, shit. What have you done?"

Her smiled widened. "There's one place that even Baal won't venture. He might not even know how to get here." She shrugged. "And I doubt he'll send Olivia and Cain in here alone."

Shelton gulped. "I don't even want to know where we are now. If Baal's afraid, then I'm gonna shit myself when I find out."

Adam looked around with a critical eye. "I smell brimstone, but I know this can't be Hell. So if I had to guess—"

"I'd appreciate giving the big reveal," Emily said. She waved a hand at the environs. "Everyone, welcome to your new favorite vacation spot, the Abyss." And then she snuggled up against Tyler and went to sleep.

Shelton leapt up and opened his mouth. Then he clamped a hand over his mouth, eyes wide with fear. He moved his hand and whispered. "We're going to die."

I was almost too tired to worry about it but, considering the Apocryphan and tons of other awful creatures lived here, I decided worrying might be better than sleep in this case.

"We can't stay here long," Adam said. "Remember the time dilation in Utopia? Well, it was caused by its proximity to the Abyss. Even one minute might be a whole week in the outside world."

"Damn, she finally did it." Tyler stroked Emily's hair and smiled like a proud parent. "She finally surprised the hell out of me."

"You've got to wake her up," Shelton said. "We can't stay here."

"Emily's been here before," Tyler said. "She didn't mention anything about time dilation."

"Yeah, well how long was she here?" Shelton said.

Tyler shrugged. "An hour, I think."

Adam frowned and looked around. "It's possible that space-time behaves differently inside the Abyss than outside of it, but I have no data to support that." He turned to me. "Does Vitania's list have any information?"

I tore my eyes off the unsettling sky. "I hope so." I took out the brown shell and rubbed the top. Water misted from within and formed the list. I scrolled down until I found the Abyss. I touched the name to expand the description. Calling it a description was an understatement. It was more like an essay.

Naturally, Adam finished reading before I had a chance to even digest the first part, so he explained the situation to everyone else. "The outer fringe of the Abyss is subject to extreme time dilation due to the immense gravitational forces used to keep the prisoners from escaping." He flicked through the rest of the text. "The core acts as the eye of the storm, meaning we're safe from time dilation. Gravity increases exponentially the further you go into the fringe. Most of us would be crushed before we got anywhere close."

"How in the hell is the core not subject to time dilation?" Shelton said. "It doesn't make any sense."

Adam scrolled through more text. "There's an entire section on how they built the Abyss, and it's pretty ugly. Vitania and other Sirens sacrificed several realms to create a pocket singularity that served as the prison walls. Then they plugged the entrance with the infernal fount." He blew out a breath. "I can't even fathom how it was possible. Apparently, several hundred Sirens perished in the attempt, not to mention the thousands of sentient lives snuffed out when they trashed the realms to make a miniature black hole."

"I guess they felt imprisoning the Apocryphan was worth the sacrifice," Elyssa said.

"I'm just happy we're safe for now." Ambria sat down against a rock and pulled Conrad next to her with her good arm. "I'm exhausted."

I inspected Elyssa's hands. Blood seeped from the burn wounds, and the flesh looked irritated and raw. "Babe, you've got to rest."

Elyssa winced when she looked at them. "I don't feel any pain."

Ambria gave her a sad look. "You will soon, I'm afraid."

Nightliss took Elyssa's hands and channeled ultraviolet mist over them. "This should sooth the wounds once the numbing magic wears off. I wish my healing abilities were better."

Elyssa smiled. "I'm thankful for anything at this point."

"You guys get some rest." I paced restlessly at the ring of jagged rocks surrounding our camp. "I'm going to look around."

Shelton grabbed his broom. "Me too."

"May I come?" Max said.

Adam looked up from the dense text. "I'm coming too."

Conrad started to get up.

"No, you're staying here." Ambria wrapped her arm around his. "If they all die, we'll need someone to help the injured."

Conrad looked back and forth between us and Ambria.

"It ain't worth it." Shelton grinned. "Just do what she says."

Ambria smirked. "For once, you're right."

Conrad sighed and sank back against the rock. "I've heard so much about this place. I just wish I could see it."

Ambria began to tear up. "Well, if you really feel it's that important."

"No, it's fine." Conrad wiped her tears away. "I'll stay."

Shelton slow clapped. "Masterful performance."

Ambria stuck out her tongue at him.

"I could learn a thing or two from her," Elyssa said. She pecked a kiss on my cheek. "Please don't antagonize the Apocryphan, okay?"

I winked. "I'll do my best."

And then we were off to explore a place of legend.

CHAPTER 32

Shelton, Adam, Max, and I hopped on our brooms and climbed into the air for a better view. An orange glow lit the skyline to my right. The compass app on my arcphone spun uselessly, so I decided if the sun was that way, then it had to be east.

Adam pointed north where jagged mountains stood like black cutouts against the starry sky. "That's part of the wall guarding the fringe. If you go over those mountains, gravity increases until you can't move another step."

A distant explosion echoed from somewhere to the east.

Shelton perked up. "Let's not go in the direction that came from."

But Adam pointed east. "I think I know what's causing that glow."

"The sun?" Max said hopefully.

"There's no daylight here," Adam said. "You've got starlight and some-where over there should be the proverbial door to the prison."

It was my turn to perk up. "The infernal fount?"

He nodded. "Yep."

"It's probably a terrible idea, but I want to see it." I glanced at the others.

Adam nodded. "It's the worst idea ever, but I can't leave here without taking a look." He grinned. "It's the next best thing to getting a tour of Hell."

"Great." I pressed my hands together. "Let's go Instagram the infernal fount so everyone thinks we're cool."

Max frowned. "Instagram?"

Shelton rolled his eyes. "Stupid nom stuff." He turned his broom east. "Let's do it."

We flew low above the rocky landscape, keeping an eye out for bad guys, but there were no signs of life except for intermittent explosions in the direction of the fount.

Rocky formations rose to form canyons and hills a few miles from the camp. Gossamer webs glistened in a canyon to the north. Despite being friends with a giant spider, even Max didn't want to explore that area.

"That must be where Araxos lives," Adam said in a loud whisper. "She's the non-humanoid Apocryphan."

Shelton shuddered. "Ain't no way I'm going near a spider god."

White light shone from a side canyon ahead. Unless we diverted to go closer to the webbed canyon, there was no good way to avoid it. We hugged ground cover as best we could and flew on. Even knowing there might be an Apocryphan lurking nearby, we slowed to admire rows of glowing crystals casting yellow light through the canyon.

Grass and shrubs grew along the walls and floor of the canyon. Further in, the walls spread apart. Nestled within was a garden of trees, branches heavy with fruits, flowers, and more greenery.

"How in the hell?" Shelton said in a quiet voice.

Adam shrugged.

I waved them on. "Keep going."

The cliffs flattened into rocky plains again, but scrub brush and tall grasses grew here. Water burbled to the south, and craggy trees jutted from the sandy soil. Another explosion lit the eastern horizon, causing everyone to flinch in unison.

There wasn't much cover between us and a distant rise, so we stayed as low as possible and sped onward, using the thick patches of grass and copses of trees to obscure us from view in case anyone stood there.

We reached the rise and glided up the slope to the top. Once we were a few feet from the top, we hopped off our brooms and walked the rest of the way. I peeked over the edge. Two purple-skinned giants sat on boulders, staring at a pool of orange lava with dead eyes.

The first looked as if he'd been chiseled from stone, but not polished into final form. He was broad-shouldered and barrel-chested. A bald, oval head perched atop a thick neck. His eyes were so deeply inset into his skull they looked like empty black pits. His arms were thick as trees and nearly as wide as his legs. His feet were almost too small for his body, each one tipped with comically tiny toes.

The other was the opposite, all the rough edges polished into smooth curves. Narrow shoulders and broad hips gave her a decidedly pear shape. Her eyes were huge, garnet irises sparkling like jewels. Catlike ears protruded from black hair. She was as beautiful as her companion was ugly.

The male raised a fist. A globe of crackling green energy large enough to incinerate a jumbo jet exploded against the lava to no effect. His arm dropped and he continued staring at the fount. He looked like someone who was completely dead inside. And I couldn't blame him for feeling that way, trapped in this place for thousands of years.

Shelton's mouth dropped open. The four of us exchanged frightened glances but didn't utter a word. Adam held up his phone and recorded a video of the pair.

The female's nostrils flared. She flicked her gaze our way. In a flash, she topped the rise and towered over us. Green energy crackled at her fingertips.

Someone blasted a nervous fart and the rest of us scrambled to our feet. Before we could make a break for it, the female's shoulders slumped. "When will the torment end?" She said in Cyrinthian. She released the power. "I tire of your master and his ceaseless games."

I managed to find my voice. "Baal?"

"What is it, Couriondral?" The other giant stomped up the hill after her.

"More of the false-bodied demons." She turned her back on us and walked back down. "I will give Baal no further entertainment."

The male clenched a fist but turned back for his boulder.

"Well, that was anticlimactic," Shelton said. "Let's get the hell out of here."

I nodded. "Get on your brooms. But if they're not going to kill us, maybe I can at least talk to them."

"Are you out of your fucking mind?" Shelton grabbed my shoulders. "If they don't kill you, Elyssa will."

"Dude, we have a chance to ask the Apocryphan questions." I stepped out of his grasp. "Maybe they know Xanos's weaknesses or something."

"Valid point, but still stupidly dangerous," Adam said. "I'm in."

"Uh, me too?" Max said in a questioning tone.

"Nah." Shelton guided Max to the brooms. "Get on your broom, kid. I'm not getting you killed too."

"The rest of you stay here." I picked up my broom just in case. "I'll be right back."

I took a deep breath then marched over the rise and down the hill toward the source of all infernal power. The infernal fount was a lot smaller than I thought it would be—maybe twenty yards in diameter. The lava didn't bubble up so much as it bubbled down. Then it occurred to me that we were on the backside of the fount. The true surface was on the other side in Hell.

Even so, I couldn't help but feel awed and excited even as another part of me wanted to run screaming in the opposite direction. *What in the hell am I doing?* These beings could destroy me with barely a thought. But they might know valuable information about Xanos. It was imperative I learn anything I could about her.

Couriondral glowered at me. "Leave now or I will blast your physical form to ash."

I gulped. "I only wish to ask a few questions."

"We will not tell you where the relics are hidden," she said. "Not unless your master frees us."

Holy crap, there are relics of Jura in here? I now knew three useful things, the first being that Baal had a way to send his infernus into the Abyss. The second had just been revealed to me, but the third was even better —Baal presumably had a way to bring his infernus back out of the Abyss if he wanted to get the relics.

I wondered if Baal was sending in his own vessels, or other demons. If the Apocryphan blasted the other infernus, that would free the demon spirit inside—or so I presumed. That left them free to leave the same way they entered. Whatever method Baal had for accessing the Abyss, the Apocryphan obviously hadn't figured it out yet.

I shook my head, showing disinterest in the relics. "I need information about Xanos."

The pair narrowed their eyes and shared a questioning look.

"We banished her to the fringe long ago," the male said. "She killed Kathazal and would have led us all to our doom had we not seen through her trickery."

The king of the Apocryphan is dead?

I tried not to look as shocked as I felt. I adopted a slightly more formal tone since I doubted Baal or his minions would talk like me. "Xanos can sway hearts to do her bidding. How did you resist?" If we could break her hold on the mortals in Razor, that would be huge.

"Imprisonment left Kathazal's mind weak." Couriondral looked at her companion. "Even Posthanied could not right our father's mind."

Posthanied clenched his fists. "Weak minds are easily seduced. Xanos drove Kathazal mad unbeknownst to us. He would have killed us all had we not defeated him. When we discovered Xanos's treachery, we banished our evil sister to the fringe where she will rot for eternity."

"So there's no way to break her hold on the weak-minded?" I said.

"She speaks with the all-voice," Couriondral said. "One of the many will find its way into your mind. Unless you are strong of will, you will see her way as the only way."

I frowned. "Is that how she tricked you all into a war that led to the Sundering?"

Anger glowed in their eyes, but their shoulders slumped, and the light dimmed to shame.

"Cease your torment, demon." Couriondral looked at the ground. "We are beaten, our egos ground to dust long ago."

"Why endure such torture? Wouldn't death be better?" I said.

Her eyes flared. "What good would that do? Our souls would still be trapped here."

Posthanied bared his teeth. "Even worse, Baal might be able to take our souls."

Despite their crimes against the world, I felt bad for them. Not even death offered them escape. While they hadn't told me much about Xanos, I was able to infer tidbits. They had no idea Xanos had escaped, or that she even now was prosecuting a war to take over the realms. These once mighty beings had been thoroughly beaten down and humiliated. I entertained the most dangerous of thoughts—what if we could recruit the other Apocryphan? Would they be willing to fight Baal and Xanos in exchange for their freedom?

I didn't want to push them too hard because they might snap and incinerate me, so I asked one more question. "What would you do if you were freed?"

They glared at me.

"Perhaps it is time you return to your maker," Couriondral growled. She raised a fist.

I reflexively threw up a shield before I could stop myself. A bolt of intense green energy slammed into it. The shield exploded. I flew backward, arms flailing. Rough stones bit into my back. I rolled to a stop just feet from edge of the infernal fount.

It was like standing too close to a bonfire, the heat scorching my face. Couriondral didn't even seem to care that she hadn't killed me. Her dead eyes glazed over with boredom. I was nothing to her—an annoying fly she no longer cared about so long as I didn't buzz around her ears.

Baal and Xanos probably looked at me the same way. Sure, I'd had a hand in foiling their plans, but it cost hundreds of lives every single time. Even Emily with all her powers couldn't stand against these monsters. Maybe I was here for a reason. Maybe this was the place where I could claim my heritage and take the power that would help me defeat our enemies.

All I had to do was reach out and grasp it.

So I did. I crawled toward the infernal fount until it felt as if my skin would catch fire and burn. Oddly enough, it didn't even singe the hair on my arm. Grimacing in pain, I plunged my hand into the lake of fire.

Fire scorched me all the way down to my soul. I screamed. Kalesh's cries of pain joined my own. The world blinked away. Visions of my past swept by—a fight with Brad Nichols in high school. Running from hellhounds, Katie Johnson riding on my back. Wrestling gray men in the back of a garbage hauler truck. Massive battles between our forces and Daelissa's. Giant demons battling with an equally huge Abyssal demon —Xanos before I knew who she was.

The heat faded and cold air sent shivers down my flesh.

I gasped for breath and looked into the inhumanly large face of Posthanied. This close up, his skin looked rough as sandpaper, pitted and scarred as though he'd endured a meteor storm.

"You are not one of Baal's." His massive hand was wrapped around my torso. Thankfully, he didn't squeeze me to a pulp.

"He is Seraphim," Couriondral said. She stepped closer. "How did you get in here, little angel?"

Lying was probably the best option, but I couldn't think of anything terribly convincing beneath the weight of their stares. So I came up with something of a mix. "Xanos banished me here. She's now in the mortal realm and seeks to control it."

Posthanied unceremoniously dropped me and began slamming his giant fists against his bald head, roaring in rage with every blow. "This cannot be true!"

Red veins streaked my hand and slowly snaked up my arm, flushing my skin like sunburn. I sensed Kalesh balled up in pain, his blue form streaked with red. Touching the fount hadn't killed me, but it sure as hell hadn't given me godlike powers.

I climbed to my feet and backed away, but Posthanied didn't seem interested in picking me up again. "It's true. She tricked someone into summoning her and escaped."

"How cruel is the universe, that she goes free while the rest of us are left in eternal torment?" Posthanied reared back his head and roared at the sky. Twin beams of jade speared into space.

This seemed like my best chance to beat it. I found my broom lying a few feet away and grabbed it, hopped on, and sped up the hill.

"Wait!" Couriondral raced after me. "You will stay and answer our questions, Seraphim! There is no escaping us in this place."

I cleared the rise and saw the others near the bottom. Max flicked his wand at me. A ray of light struck me in the forehead. I shouted in alarm before realizing that I hadn't even felt it. A copy of me separated from my body and flew back in the opposite direction. Couriondral's voice rose from the other side of the hill.

"Flee all you want, angel. We will catch you!" Her pounding footsteps followed the copy.

I glided to a stop next to Max. "What was that?"

"It's a diversion spell." He waved his wand and the air around us shimmered. "It makes an illusion version of you that comes in handy when a giant demigod is chasing you."

"Smart kid." Shelton clapped Max on the back. "Nice veil by the way."

Max beamed, perfectly happy to be called a kid by his hero. "I thought hiding us would be smart in case the giants came after us."

"Why is your skin so red?" Adam said.

I wiped sweat off my forehead. "I kinda decided to touch the infernal fount."

"Holy shit burgers." Shelton poked my arm with a finger. The skin turned white and then red again. "Dude, you roasted yourself."

"Why would you do something so dumb?" Adam repeated Shelton's experiment.

"Ouch!" I snatched my arm away. "Because I'm tired of being pushed around by demigods." Chills ran up my skin, drawing goosebumps. "I told the Apocryphan that Xanos banished me here and that she's in Eden. They didn't take it very well."

Shelton's eyes flared. "Did you find out anything useful?"

I told them what little I'd learned. "The only remotely useful information is that Xanos controls weak minds with her all-voice. Unfortunately, there are a hell of a lot of dumbass mortals she can control."

"Tell me more about the infernal fount," Adam said. "What did it feel like?"

"Burning," I said. "And my life flashed before my eyes."

I still burn, Kalesh moaned. I sensed him curled up in the corner of my consciousness. I felt the heat simmering inside like radiation sickness. It was possible I was dying. But I couldn't let that distract me right now. I still had plenty of chances to die in the near future.

"You know what's weird?" Max said. "I thought the Apocryphan were spirits like demons. I didn't realize they had actual bodies."

Shelton grunted. "You know, now that you mention it, I thought the same thing."

"I kind of thought the same thing," Adam said. "Someone told me they could shift to any form, but maybe some of them have different powers than the others."

And that was when an idea jumped out of nowhere and punched me in the noggin. Snapping it into the puzzle suddenly made dozens of other pieces fall neatly into place.

"Oh crap." Shelton snapped his fingers in front of my face to snap me out of my daze. "What did you just realize?"

I gripped my broom. "I think I know why Xanos wanted a week for the truce."

CHAPTER 33

I explained my suspicions to the others as we flew back to camp.

"Holy crap, you're right!" Adam blew out a breath. "It makes perfect sense."

"That's brilliant!" Max said. "I never would have thought of it."

"What if we're too late?" Shelton shook his head. "The Abyss is a big place to search."

"I guess we'll find out." I glided into camp and hopped off my broom. Everyone except Conrad was asleep, but Elyssa blinked awake the moment I landed. "Wake up, everyone!" I clapped my hands and jarred the others from their sleep. Emily didn't even stir.

Tyler yawned. "Whoa, you're back. How long have I been out?"

"Not that long," I said. "Maybe an hour."

Alarm creased Elyssa's brow. "Oh god. What happened? Who's coming to kill us?"

"No one, but we might have a chance to stop something terrible." I told them everything, drawing furious looks from Elyssa and wide-mouthed awe from Conrad and Tyler. Ambria just looked confused.

"You're damned lucky you escaped!" Elyssa pointed a finger at me and winced. "Justin, that was reckless and stupid. Emily's too tired to even wake up, so we're stuck here. Having the Apocryphan hunting us down would be a nightmare."

Nightliss looked concerned. "Justin, are you unwell? Your skin looks awful."

"I'm fine." My insides felt too warm, like I'd just eaten too much spicy Indian food and it wasn't sitting well.

"So what's the big thing you figured out?" Tyler said.

I smiled at Elyssa. She glowered back. I cleared my throat uneasily. "Babe, remember that portal ring at Thunder Rock?"

Her eyes narrowed. "Yes, why?"

"Remember that glimpse we had of the other side? What did it look like?"

Her forehead pinched into a V. "Uh, rocky. Barren." She blinked and looked around. "A lot like this place."

I snapped my fingers. "Bingo!"

"Xanos was trying to open a portal to the Abyss?" Conrad said. "Does she plan to free the other Apocryphan to fight with her?"

"They loathe Xanos for everything she did to them," I said. "They wouldn't fight for her in a million years."

"Then why open a portal to the Abyss?" Nightliss said.

"Max made a comment that got me thinking." I held a hand above my head. "The Apocryphan are giants—ten feet tall at least."

"Explains why Xanos took the form of a normal human," Ambria said. "Otherwise her followers would know she's a super."

"Xanos could look like the Flying Spaghetti Monster and her followers wouldn't care," I said. "Her all-voice grants her plus one hundred charisma. People who don't like to think for themselves are easy prey for her."

Ambria frowned. "So she didn't morph into human form to hide her true self?"

"No. She didn't morph into human form at all. She's in human form because her soul possessed the body."

Elyssa grasped the point first. "When you summoned Xanos, you only pulled through her soul, not her body."

"So her body is still in the Abyss," Conrad added.

"Yep." I folded my arms over my chest. "I couldn't understand why Xanos hadn't used her powers to overwhelm us during the battle of Queens Gate or why she didn't blast us to ash when she visited the Ranch. After witnessing Posthanied's power, it became abundantly clear to me that Xanos should have been able to destroy us single-handedly."

"She doesn't have all her powers," Elyssa said. "Not until she's back in her real body."

I snapped my fingers. "Exactly. Xanos needs to recover her physical body from the Abyss and that portal device is how she plans to do it."

"It was almost working when we saw it," Elyssa said. "So she came to us knowing we'd try to strike a truce. She bought herself a week to finish the device."

"My god." Conrad got up and dusted off his pants. "We've got to find the body before it's too late."

"Odds are we're way late," Shelton said. "Portal generator might've started working days ago."

"We don't know for sure," I said. "And that's why we need to split into

JOHN CORWIN

two groups and search the border. Xanos was banished to the fringe, so I imagine her body will be somewhere out there."

"Technically, the fringe starts on the other side of the mountains." Adam pointed to the jagged silhouettes in the distance. "I doubt even she would cross them and enter the gravity well."

"So we have to search the mountains?" Tyler turned in a circle as if taking it all in. "How much real estate we talking about?"

Adam produced Vitania's seashell and summoned the list. He pulled up an image of the Abyss. From a distance, it looked like a black hole, surrounded by dense, black clouds and streaks of light. Zoomed in, the land was a tiny fraction of the place, a circular oasis. "According to this, the Abyss is fifty miles in diameter, give or take a mile or two."

"Area equals pie times radius squared." Ambria bit the inside of her lip. "That's nearly two thousand square miles."

"We're not worried about the area," Adam said. "Just the circumference."

"Which would be about a hundred and fifty-seven miles," Max said.

Shelton snorted. "And that's why you stay in school, kids."

Adam pointed to some text next to the image. "All that information is right here, but it warms my heart to know they can math with the best of us."

"A hundred and fifty-seven miles." Elyssa sighed. "I guess we should get started."

"Not you." Nightliss put a hand on her arm, turned to Ambria and shook her head. "And not you. You need to rest."

I expected Elyssa to protest, but she just nodded. "You're right. My hands aren't healing fast enough."

Conrad grabbed his broom and kissed Ambria on the forehead. "I'm going to help."

"Be careful." She caressed his cheek. "You don't know what horrors lie in wait out there."

"Ain't that the truth," Shelton said.

"We need to split into two groups," I said. "That's our best hope for searching the perimeter."

"How much food do we have left?" Max asked. "I'm hungry."

Ambria laughed. "As usual."

Shelton still had several pounds of cooked bacon, but the rest of us only had a couple of sandwiches left. We split up the food and rationed enough for two meals to each search party. We'd fly as one group to the mountains north of us, then Conrad, Shelton, and Max would go left, Nightliss, Adam, and I would go right. Tyler opted to remain behind in case he had to get the injured to safety.

It wasn't ideal, but we needed as many eyes as possible to find Xanos's body. We said our goodbyes and sped for the fringe.

After crossing rocky hills, we flew over a plain of scrub brush for a distance. Dark shadows scattered at our approach, like roaches exposed to light.

Shelton gulped. "What are those things?"

"Probably shades banished to the Abyss," Adam said. "Maybe the remnants of souls consumed by the Apocryphan."

Shelton shuddered. "That's not creepy at all."

"The Apocryphan must eat from the garden we passed on the way to the fount," Max said. "Maybe they eat souls for dessert."

"A hundred and fifty-seven miles of horrors." Shelton grimaced. "I ain't looking forward to this."

"Maybe there's an easier way to do this." Adam consulted the data on the Abyss as we flew toward the mountains. "By remaining near the fringe, Xanos increased her chances of being found when someone on the outside was searching for spirits to control. But she'd also know that her body would be left behind and wanted it to be somewhere safe."

I shook my head. "The first time I sensed Xanos, I was looking for a hellhound demon. How could I possibly find a spirit in the Abyss when I was searching Haedaemos for a hellhound demon?"

"As a Daemos, you're extra-sensitive," Adam said. "And maybe your powers allowed you to drill all the way through Haedaemos and into the Abyss without realizing it."

I shrugged. "Yeah, maybe."

Adam rotated the image of the Abyss, zooming in for close-ups of the mountains. "So far I've spotted three caves. There could be hundreds in the mountainsides and her body could be in any of those."

"What about the other spirits trapped inside the Abyss?" Shelton said. "Wouldn't she be worried one of them might take her body?"

Adam sucked in a breath between his teeth. "You're right. Which means she would've gone somewhere the other spirits couldn't."

"She went over the mountains?" Nightliss said.

"Yeah." Adam looked up at the approaching barrier and winced. "Xanos could have endured a little extra gravity, but she also knew she couldn't go too deep into the fringe since she needed to recover her body."

"So she would've gone just over the mountains where other spirits wouldn't go." Conrad looked up. "The best hiding spot would be at the very top of a mountain."

Shelton groaned. "How high are these things?"

"High enough that the oxygen will be thin." Adam looked at Vitania's data. "They range from twelve thousand to fourteen thousand feet in altitude."

"That's not too bad," Max said. "Mount Everest is twenty-nine thousand feet."

"Education to the rescue again," Shelton said.

Max beamed.

As we drew closer to the fringe, the craggy silhouettes resolved into steep cliffs. Even the most skilled rock climber would find it impossible to scale the perfectly smooth stone. The Apocryphan would have little issue climbing it, but we would've been screwed without brooms.

"Onward and upward." I pitched my broom at a steep angle and climbed, climbed, climbed so we'd be near the peak of the closest mountain by the time we reached it. The smooth cliff resumed a natural formation about a thousand feet up, complete with caves, crevices, and even a few hardy trees.

Shelton rubbed his eyes and looked down at the mountainside. "Am I seeing things, or is the ground moving?"

I followed his gaze and didn't see anything except coarse black stone. Shelton fired a blast from the end of his staff. Screeches and shrieks filled the air. The ground swarmed to life, parting to reveal gray stone hidden beneath multi-legged creatures with stony exoskeletons. A long, black tentacle squirmed from one of the caves and grabbed one of the creatures, smashing it until it cracked open like a crab, then dragged its remains into the darkness.

Shelton's face blanched. "Holy shit. And I thought the shades were creepy."

The rock monsters thinned out the further we climbed, leaving only bare stone for the last few hundred feet.

"Are those things demons?" Max said. "Or natives?"

"No idea," Adam said. "We want to avoid them either way."

The bowl-shaped Abyss spread out behind us, the infernal fount burning in the center. With the spectacles I could see Couriondral and Posthanied still sitting there, two demigods around a campfire. All they needed were marshmallows.

We reached the peak and stared out across the fringe. Inky clouds streaked with light swirled below. The mere thought of descending into them filled me with dread. Shelton flew a little further than the peak. His shoulders slumped and he bent over his broom with a groan.

"Oh, shit." Panting like a dog, he reversed course. Sweat trickled down his forehead and he looked white as a sheet. Shelton jabbed a finger at a crack in the peak. "Do not cross that line. That extra gravity is no joke."

Adam didn't seem to be paying attention, staring instead at lightning flashing on a distant peak. "Well, I would say this is where we need to split up, but I think I know where the body is."

I blinked. "Say what?"

He pointed to the lightning. "Either someone is using some heavy-duty magic, or there's an invisible thunderstorm over there."

I spied the suspicious event through the spectacles. Mountain peaks obscured the source of the light, but it was too repetitive to be lightning. It looked a lot like what Elyssa and I had witnessed at Thunder Rock. "They're opening another portal. We've got to get there as fast as possible!" I opened the broom's throttle to full and the others zipped after me.

We sped across the mountains, narrowing the distance between us and the light, but it felt as if we were flying in slow motion. The lightshow stopped a moment later, and I feared we'd just missed our opportunity. We sped around the last peak and reached a plateau between it and the next one.

Bodies in Razor uniforms were strewn across blackened earth. The surrounding rocks were scarred and scored as if struck with energy weapons or magic. This was definitely the right place, but I saw no sign of a giant purple body.

Adam glided down next to an unmoving Razor soldier and inspected her without getting off his broom. "I can't tell if she died from malfunctions in the portal generator or if something attacked her."

Max appeared from the other side of a large boulder "Hey, I found something!" He led us around to a narrow cave opening on the other side. I conjured a ball of light and sent it drifting inside. It looked barely large enough for a giant Apocryphan to fit through on hands and knees.

I figured it wasn't beneath Xanos to crawl inside and hide her body. I imagined her sitting inside, sending her spirit out into the void, a lure waiting for a Daemos to bite. I'd been the one to bite the lure and fish her spirit out of its not-so-eternal prison.

The tunnel stretched too far back for me to see inside. Since no tentacles or rock monsters had attacked it yet, it seemed safe to go on foot. "Everyone wait here."

"I'm going with you." Shelton flicked his staff out to full length. "You need at least one person to watch your back."

"Then I should go with him," Nightliss said.

"We can't just send our two most powerful people into an unknown cave," Shelton said. "One of you needs to stay outside."

I turned to Nightliss. "Watch our backs."

She sighed. "Be careful."

Shelton scoffed. "Ain't gotta tell me twice."

I tapped a foot cautiously against the ground. It didn't move or try to eat me, so I got off the broom and walked to the dark opening. While it might be small for an Apocryphan, it was tall enough for me and Shelton to walk through upright and side-by-side. I sent the light ball well ahead of us just in case.

The tunnel widened into a small cave about fifty feet in. A mountain of bones waited inside. Some resembled the craggy remains of rock monsters. Others might have once belonged to giant snakes. Someone had feasted on the monsters of the Abyss.

"Jesus!" Shelton shuddered. "The damned Apocryphan literally eat monsters for breakfast."

I tugged his sleeve and pointed toward the opposite wall. A woman marginally shorter than Couriondral leaned against the wall. Fiery red hair cascaded down lavender skin that was slightly darker than that of the other Apocryphan I'd met. A pert nose and rosebud lips made her cute rather than beautiful.

"Well, that figures." Shelton huffed. "She's a redhead."

Xanos sat cross-legged, back upright, eyes closed in meditation. A gentle white glow surrounded her, possibly a shield, or maybe even a preservation spell. The body of a demigod was ours for the taking.

CHAPTER 34

A towering shadow separated from the back of the cave and entered the light.

"Holy shit!" Shelton jumped back a foot.

I nearly tripped over my own feet as I scrambled backward.

The Apocryphan was square-jawed, thick, muscular, and bald like Posthanied. But his eyes were larger, forehead less pronounced. He stared at us with a neutral expression. "Xanos didn't send you," he said in Cyrinthian.

I retreated a few more steps toward the tunnel. "Who are you?"

He clenched sledgehammer fists, cracking every knuckle in sequence. "You're Baal's minions."

I held up my hands defensively. "No, we're humans."

"Humans?" He scoffed. "I doubt that."

"Did you kill those people outside?" I asked.

"I did." He took a giant step closer. "And I'll keep killing them until Xanos accepts my terms."

I immediately knew what he meant. "You're using her body as a bargaining chip for freedom."

"I am."

In other words, the only way to get Xanos's physical body was to go through this dude. Since Kathazal was dead, Araxos looked like a giant spider, and I knew where Couriondral and Posthanied were at this moment, that left only one person this could be. "You're Zon."

"Yes." His fists began to glow. "I don't know how you reached this place, demons, but you won't leave it alive."

I didn't have a lot of options left, so I did the only thing I could. I sucked in an ass-load of aether and unleashed all hell onto Xanos's body. A torrent of Brilliance washed over her. It should have left nothing but smoking bones, but it didn't even singe a hair on her head. The shield protecting her dimmed slightly but held.

Zon thrust his fists at us. Green energy blasted rocks to dust where we'd stood an instant before. Shelton and I weren't idiots. The moment my attack failed, we'd turned tail and run. Zon didn't shout in rage or growl. He just dropped to a knee, stuck his glowing fist inside the tunnel, and fired.

I channeled the thickest shield I could. His attack punched through it like it was paper. Shelton and I hugged the walls to avoid being barbequed.

"I smell my eyebrows burning!" Shelton shouted.

The blast stopped and we dashed outside.

"Run away!" I shouted. "Run away!" I leapt on my broom and sped for the cover of the next mountain peak a hundred yards away. The others saw my panic and fled along with me.

We reached the relative safety of boulders and hid. I peered around the edge and watched Zon crawl awkwardly out of the cave. He looked around calmly, not looking the least bit upset that we'd escaped. He rubbed a hand on his bald head and turned his gaze our way. I held my breath. The Apocryphan narrowed his eyes then turned the opposite way.

The infernal heat slow-cooking my insides grew even warmer. Sweat trickled down my forehead and my knees felt weak.

"Who in the hell is that?" Adam whispered.

"Zon." Shelton huffed. "He's using Xanos's body as a bargaining chip to escape this hellhole."

"How could he have possibly known her body was in there?" Max said.

"Who knows?" Shelton said. "Probably got bored and went looking for her one day."

"Perhaps we can sneak in and destroy the body," Nightliss said.

I shook my head. "Believe me, I tried. It's protected by a shield."

"What if we all hit it at once?" Conrad said. "Maybe that would be enough to break through."

Shelton scoffed. "Not with Zon waltzing around."

"We absolutely cannot let him complete that deal." I backed out of sight of the cave and turned to the others. "Somehow, we've got to get the body."

Adam tapped a finger on his chin. "I wonder how close he is to striking a deal with Xanos."

"Probably really damned close," Shelton said.

"The other Apocryphan hate her, and I doubt Zon is any different," I said. "First and foremost, she'll want to ensure that he doesn't come after her if she frees him. Second, she'll want to make sure he doesn't try to start his own competing kingdom."

Max grunted. "Maybe they'll never reach an agreement then."

"Perhaps we can use this to our advantage," Nightliss said. "We could also offer freedom to Zon."

"Uh, releasing another Apocryphan into the world will only make things worse," Shelton said.

"Perhaps an agreement can be reached," Nightliss said.

"How could we trust him to keep his word?" Max said.

"Yeah, but once Xanos gets her body back, she'll be unstoppable." Adam sighed. "There's got to be some way to steal it from Zon."

Blue lightning flashed on the other side of the cave. A glowing ring appeared just on the other side. "Xanos is opening another portal."

"I'm pretty sure that's what we saw a few minutes ago," Adam said. "My guess is that she's reached a decision."

I wiped sweat from my face. "We can't let her body survive."

"So, we attack?" Shelton said.

I looked at the others. "This is a suicide mission. I guarantee Zon won't let us survive."

"Don't matter." Shelton straightened his shoulders. "If we don't do this, Eden is doomed."

"I'm in," Max said.

Nightliss nodded. "Me too."

Conrad put a hand on Max's back. "I'm in, too."

Adam remained quiet, eyes distant. "There might be a brief window of opportunity to destroy the body."

Shelton pursed his lips. "I'm all ears."

"Zon might have to remove the shield around the body in order to move it." Adam watched the light show. "If so, we can swoop in and destroy it before he delivers it to Xanos."

"Sounds like our best bet." I tried not to let it show, but the building heat inside my chest was past the point of discomfort. It looked like Zon would kill me before the taint of the infernal fount did.

It burns, Kalesh moaned inside my head.

Zon walked around the cave and toward the opening portal.

"We'll need to be closer." Max flicked his wand and the air around us rippled. "I veiled us. Hopefully he can't see through it."

"Nice work." Shelton shifted in his saddle. "What next?"

"We get closer." I eased my broom forward. "I need to hear what they're saying." Sweat stung my eyes.

Shelton's forehead scrunched. "You okay, man?"

I nodded. "Just really warm." I thrust a hand forward. "Let's go."

We headed toward the cave, sticking close together so the veil would cover us. Zon's deep voice rose above the hum of the portal ring. "I will destroy the body if you don't let me through."

"And lose your only leverage?" Xanos's grandmotherly voice chided him. "Accept my offer and be free. But you must do it now or I will find another way."

"You ask too much," Zon said. "You ask me to fight for you, little sister, when all I want is to kill you. You ask me to seek no power in any of the realms of this world, when there is nothing else that brings me pleasure."

"I only ask that you fight one battle for me," Xanos said. "Then you are free to seek power on other worlds."

"Mother created us to control this world, not others."

"We are not bound to Eve's will, brother." I imagined Xanos reaching a hand toward him. "Take the soul oath and you will be freed this very hour from millennia of bondage."

Zon didn't reply for a long moment. "How do you propose we complete the oath when there is a barrier between us?"

"I will open a hole—just enough for our souls to complete the bond."

Another pause. "Then I agree."

We exchanged concerned looks.

"Can't we just steal the body while they're doing this?" Max said.

"Not with that shield around it," Shelton said. "I can guarantee that it wouldn't be easy to dispel either."

"Then we wait right outside the cave and blast the body when Zon brings it out," I said.

The others nodded.

I took Nightliss's hand. "You need to return to camp and tell the others what happened. Make sure they get somewhere safe, okay?"

Tears trickled down her cheeks. "Justin, I will not leave you to die."

"Even with all our firepower combined, we can't take down Zon." I wiped a tear from her cheek. "But the others need to know if we succeeded or failed."

She stiffened her shoulders. "Then I will just have to make sure we survive to tell the tale."

Shelton grinned. "It's a good day to live."

Adam's forehead pinched. "You mean a good day to die?"

Shelton scoffed. "Nah. It ain't ever a good day for that."

Xanos had been droning on the entire time we spoke, so I only caught the tail end of the oath she required from Zon.

"Max, position yourself and the veil about thirty feet that way." I pointed where I wanted him. He moved to the spot and vanished from view when he rotated to put the veil between him and me. There was barely a ripple in the air to even indicate it was there. Unless Zon could automatically see through veils, it would work well enough.

The soul oath must not have taken long to perform because giant feet stomped our way. I motioned the others into position and joined them behind Max's veil. Zon walked around the corner but he wasn't alone. A tight circle of Razor operatives surrounded a gray-haired woman.

"Zon isn't getting the body," I hissed. "Xanos is going in with him!"

"Oh shit." Shelton gripped his staff. "What now?"

I saw no choice. "We've got to kill Xanos's human body." I flung a hand forward. "Go, now!"

We sped toward them, the veil obscuring our approach. At the last instant, Zon twitched and looked at us, comprehension dawning in his eyes. He fired a blast of green energy. We scattered out of the way.

Xanos looked up at us, eyes flaring with surprise. I channeled every ounce of power I had and double-fist blasted her. Conrad hurled a beam of azure energy alongside mine. Zon thrust a hand forward and our attacks splashed harmlessly off a shield. Face emotionless, he balled a fist, gathering a miniature green star atop it.

"No." Xanos barely came up to his waist, but her voice resonated. "Do not fire."

The Razor operatives lowered their weapons and the energy snuffed from Zon's hand. But the shield remained in place.

I felt helpless as a child. I wanted to scream in rage, but infernal heat choked me. Sweat drenched me and it was all I could do to remain standing.

"Justin Slade, I have underestimated you time and time again." Xanos tutted. "We still have a truce in effect. Do you mean to break it?"

"The truce was only to buy you time so you could get your body." I felt my body swaying and wondered if I'd embarrass myself by passing out in front of Xanos. "We can't let you do that."

"I would love to know how you figured this out, little man." She shook her head. "And how did you get into the Abyss?"

I didn't want to admit that we'd come here only to escape Baal. Or that we'd only figured out Xanos's plan a short while ago. I plastered on a confident grin and tried not to fall over. "We have our resources, Xanos." My mind raced furiously, looking for any opening.

There was no way to punch through Zon's shield or get past him and to the cave. But there was another option.

I looked back at the others. "Destroy the portal ring. I'll distract her."

"On it," Shelton said.

"I won't honor a truce based on deceit." I put some growl into my voice to show I meant business. "I won't let you have your body." With that, I blasted the cliff above the cave entrance. The rock face cracked, crumbled, and collapsed. Dust filled the air and the entrance vanished. Shelton and the others zipped away during the confusion.

Xanos laughed. "Do you really think a collapsed cave will stop me?" She said something to Zon. Still keeping the shield in place, he swept the rocky debris away with a flattened blade of energy, opening the tunnel again.

Desperation released my last shreds of self-preservation. I dove at them, spawning into demon form. I leapt from my broom, bat wings furled, fists forward and unleashed everything I had. I smacked into Zon's shield like a bug and slid down it. He watched me hit the ground without expression. Xanos smirked and walked into the cave.

I struggled to my feet.

So hot. Kalesh felt as feverish as I did.

An explosion over the rise gave me brief hope. Shelton and the others returned, triumphant looks on their faces.

"It's gone!" Nightliss said. "The portal is destroyed."

Zon's teeth bared, the first sign of emotion on his stony face. "How are we to leave with no portal, Xanos?"

But Xanos didn't reply. Light flashed from within the cave. The ground trembled and the hill collapsed.

I dared hope for good news. *Maybe she killed herself.*

Rock crumbled. Xanos rose from the rubble, skin sparkling like the night sky. The human body she'd inhabited lay motionless, discarded like trash at her feet. Xanos stretched her arms wide, reveling in full naked glory. "I am whole again!"

Shelton's mouth dropped open. "Jesus, her boobs are bigger than my head!"

"Really?" Adam groaned. "That's the first thing that pops into your mind?"

Xanos traced fingers along her skin and moaned in pleasure. "Yes, yes, yes!" She brushed the dust from her flaming hair. "I am finally home."

The full-faced helmets hid the expressions of the Razor soldiers, but their body language indicated they weren't the least bit concerned with their leader's transformation.

"The portal is gone, Xanos." Zon faced her. "We are trapped again, and the oath is broken."

Xanos caressed his chin with her hand. "No, dear brother. It is not." She slashed the air with a hand and a portal tore open. The crater of Thunder Rock appeared on the other side.

Zon didn't laugh or betray any joy. He just nodded. "Then the oath still holds." He looked at me. "Shall I kill them?"

She put a hand on his. "No. Let us go." Xanos turned to the portal then looked back at us. "I no longer need your help against Baal, little ones. Once the truce ends, we will see each other one last time."

"No!" I shook a trembling fist at her.

Xanos and her companions stepped through the portal and it closed behind them.

"Xanos!" I shouted into the sky. "Xanos!"

"Talk about a Khan moment." Adam ran a hand down his face and groaned. "We're screwed, aren't we?"

"Utterly and royally fucked," Shelton said.

Fighting one Apocryphan was impossible. Now we had two to deal with. The resistance was over.

CHAPTER 35

We returned to camp with the bad news.

Sweat poured down my face and it was all I could do to remain upright. Using so much magic seemed to have amped the effects of the infernal taint. It seemed my quest for more power would be the end of me.

It seemed to hit Kalesh even harder. I sensed my demon spirit curled up in the corner of my consciousness, moaning like a dying cat.

"Justin, what's wrong?" Wincing in pain, Elyssa dragged me off the broom the moment I reached camp.

"Careful with your hands." I shivered, suddenly cold even though my insides felt feverishly hot.

Elyssa looked at Shelton. "What happened to him?"

"It's the infernal fount." I leaned against her. "Killing me from the inside out."

Tyler bit his lower lip. "Did you find Xanos's body?"

"Oh, yeah." Shelton threw up his hands. "We found her big brother, Zon, too. He struck a deal with Xanos, and she got her body back."

"We couldn't stop them," Conrad said. "Zon overpowered all of us."

"It was awful." Max filled in the rest of the blanks about our failed mission. "How are we supposed to defeat Xanos now?"

Elyssa stroked my sweat-drenched hair. "We can worry about that later. We've got to get Justin help."

Conrad summoned a trickle of power and reached toward my arm. A brilliant static pop startled everyone. He sighed. "I thought maybe I could neutralize it with the primal fount."

"I don't think it works that way," Adam said.

Elyssa looked at Emily's slumbering form. "Tyler, can you wake her? We need to get Justin to a healer immediately."

My vision faded in and out. I felt weak as an over cooked noodle. I reached out a trembling hand and touched Elyssa's cheek. "I love you."

"Justin, I love you too!" She pressed her cool lips to mine.

"I can die happy now." I stopped resisting and let the world fade away.

A WISP of golden light shined in the void. It grew closer, resolving into a woman who looked terribly familiar. "Emily?"

She alighted in front of me and smiled. "Not quite." Her cool hands soothed my fever. "You carelessly toyed with a powerful force. It is a wonder you survived so long."

"I just need some aspirin," I said. "Then I'll be all good."

She smiled. "I muted your Seraphim side so it would not interfere with the healing process. When you awaken, do not be alarmed."

My fingers grasped a strand of her green hair. "Hey, aren't you—" Fire rushed through every fiber of my being. I shouted and the void vanished, replaced with streaks of light and blurred faces. I felt as if fire had hollowed out my insides. And something that was normally there had gone missing.

"Justin, it's us!" Elyssa's reached me through the chaos.

A tortured scream escaped my throat. "I am fire and flame, the sun of the burnt souls, the light of eternal torment!"

"What the hell is that supposed to mean?" someone behind me said.

It wasn't me speaking. It was Kalesh. "Pass through the crucible. Forge our spirits brighter!"

"Everyone back!" a woman shouted.

Heat surged through me. I felt as if my body melted and reformed, erupted and reformed again. I screamed. The world burned and I burned with it. Existence flickered to nothingness and back. Back and forth it went, faster and faster, a cacophony of screams one instant to absolute silence the next.

And then it stopped.

My skin grew cold as ice. The world collapsed into focus. I lay in a patch of blackened grass. My filthy feet were bare, my legs hairless. I touched my head and felt smooth skin. Even my pubes were gone. I blinked, looked around and found my friends standing fifty feet away.

Only the golden woman remained near, a gentle smile on her face.

Holy shit, I'm naked in front of everyone!

I crossed my legs and covered my privates with my hands. "What happened to my hair?"

Shelton ran over, his duster flapping in the wind. He took it off and wrapped it around my shoulders. "Only for you, brother. Only for you."

I hugged him, tears burning my eyes. "What the hell? I thought I died."

Elyssa stole me from Shelton and kissed my face. Her formerly scarred hands looked new again. "Baby, I thought we'd lost you." She peppered my face with kisses.

I felt more hands touching me, more arms wrapping around me. I felt as if I'd been pulled back from the afterlife, put in a new body, and set on my feet.

Everything passes. Everything becomes something new, Kalesh said. *We are new.*

I didn't know what he meant, and I didn't care.

I turned to the green-haired woman. "You're Eve."

"I am." She touched my forehead like a concerned mother. "Your Seraphim side will eventually emerge again once your body has adjusted to the shock."

"Did I die?" I asked.

Eve nodded. "For a short while. But your demon spirit refused to let you go. He said you did not give up on him and he would not give up on you."

Elyssa wiped tears from her face. "His demon side saved him?"

"You're a goddess," Shelton said. "Can't you bring people back to life?"

"I can birth new life, but once a soul has separated from the body and entered the afterlife, that person is not the same." Eve shared a sad look with Emily. "What you think of as death is merely another stage of life. Even newborns are constituted from that which was formerly not alive."

My stomach rumbled and I felt as if I could devour an entire cow.

Eve smiled. "Let's get you some food." She led us through the forest. Birds landed on her shoulders and sang in her ears. Deer and their fawn bounced next to her and rubbed their heads against her arms and hands. Eve moved with grace through nature, sparing attention to even the insects that buzzed in front of her.

A cottage appeared in a sunlit meadow. Green slate tiled the roof. A gray stone chimney rose along one side. Every inch looked as if it had been handcrafted by fairy tale dwarves. I still felt a bit foggy in the noggin. "Am I really awake or am I dreaming about Snow White?"

Eve took my hand and led me into the cottage. The inside was a lot bigger than the outside. A table heaped with all sorts of food greeted me. I barely remembered running to it, shoveling food into my mouth until I couldn't chew fast enough to keep up.

"Whoa, big boy." Elyssa slapped my hand away from a fish. "Swallow your food first."

Shelton chuckled. "Yeah, don't want him getting diarrhea." He sat down and started stuffing his face.

Emily took a seat next to me. "I'm glad I was able to get you here in time."

"How long was I out?" I asked.

"A few hours." Emily looked down. "Tyler had trouble waking me up."

Tyler sat down next to her, a wolfish grin on his face. "Yeah, she's a real sleepyhead."

After I finished eating, Elyssa brought me fresh clothes from my backpack. I changed and gave Shelton back his duster. He wrinkled his nose. "Needs disinfecting."

"My balls didn't sweat too much," I said with a grin.

Adam and Max burst into laughter.

"I'm so happy I gave men testicles and penises," Eve said. "It gives them something to laugh about."

Adam paled and stopped laughing. "I'm so sorry. I think penises are great!"

She mussed his hair like a child's. "I think it's adorable."

Max breathed a sigh of relief. "Thank god—uh—goddess."

"Would you mind answering a few questions about life, the universe, and everything?" Adam said. "It would really help me out."

"Dude, don't bug the goddess," Shelton said.

I walked over to Eve. "I can't thank you enough for patching me up. But I have another favor to ask."

"I already told Emily no." Eve swirled golden liquid in a glass goblet. "I interfered in the affairs of man and god before and only made things worse. I birthed the Apocryphan and they broke the world. I would take that back if I could and unmake them."

"Well, you can unmake them now," I said. "Zon and Xanos are about to wreck Eden unless we stop them." I waved a hand around at the others. "We're not gods, Eve. We can't fight the Apocryphan without your help."

"Even if your mortal bodies are killed, your souls will live on in the afterlife," Eve said. "You will transition to a new plane, a new existence."

Shelton gulped. "Is there bacon in the afterlife?"

She turned her golden eyes on him and raised an eyebrow.

Emily scoffed. "What she's not telling you is that the Apocryphan can feed on souls at the moment of death. If Xanos or Zon kill you and siphon your soul, your shade can't go to the afterlife and will be eternally tortured around the infernal fount."

"Jesus, Jehoshaphat, and Mary!" Shelton's wine glass slipped from his fingers and spilled on the table. "Xanos and Zon could eat our souls and that's that?"

"Yes," Eve said. "They are demigods, after all."

I scrunched my forehead. "Not full gods?"

She shook her head. "I took the genetic material of the old gods and birthed Kathazal. Then I mated with him and gave birth to the others."

Max grimaced. "Isn't that incest?"

She took a sip of golden nectar. "By human standards, perhaps. It does not work the same for gods."

"Where are the old gods?" I said.

"They left to explore other parts of the universe," Eve said. "Some few might have remained on Earth, but I haven't seen any of them since the Sundering."

I got down on my knees. "Please, Eve, I'm begging you. Help us."

She lifted me as easily as a cop lifts a jelly donut and set me on my feet. "Nothing you say can change my mind." Gold flashed in her eyes and steel filled her voice. "Do not ask again or I will remove you from my home."

I gulped.

Emily gave her a wry look. "Grandmother, Olivia has been tracking me no matter where I go. Do you know how?"

Eve's eyes went distant. "Interesting."

"Care to explain?" Emily said in her droll British accent.

"You both possessed my goddess aura for a time. It apparently left a connection between the three of us." Eve reached out a hand and rubbed her fingers together as if examining a thread. "It allows her to feel you when you are in the same realm. It draws her to you."

"Aha!" Tyler snapped his fingers. "That explains why she couldn't track you once we left Eden."

Emily pursed her lips. "Am I connected to you in the same way?"

"Yes, child." Eve put a hand to her own forehead. "The connection is already fading and will be gone in time."

"Can you get rid of it now?" Emily asked.

JOHN CORWIN

Eve made a scissoring motion with her index and middle finger near her forehead. Then she reached over and did the same near Emily. "I have snipped our connections to Olivia but retained ours."

Emily's gaze softened. "Why keep the connection between us?"

Eve smiled. "Because you're my favorite grandchild."

"I'm up for adoption," Shelton said.

Adam snorted.

"So how did Olivia find us on bird world?" Max said.

Eve cast her gaze around the room and stopped on me. I felt as if something brushed my very soul and removed a thorn. "There is a shard of spirit that is not your own." She brushed her fingers together. A puff of red vapor dissipated. "A powerful demon could track you across realms."

"Well, that explains things." Baal had left a little something lodged inside me when he split Cain from my soul. "Are we all free of trackers now?"

"I believe so." Eve sat down next to Conrad and observed him.

He regarded her warily. "Hello?"

"You have been touched by a god." Eve obviously didn't believe in beating around the bush.

Ambria watched the goddess, mouth hanging open in awe. "I just knew a woman was the creator."

"Males and females contributed to creation, child." Eve touched the girl's hand. "And those who came before us did not even have binary genders."

Conrad didn't look the least bit excited to have a goddess sitting next to him. If anything, he looked a bit wary. "What do you mean, touched by a god?"

"You touch the primal fount, child." Eve peered into his eyes as if looking for his soul. "Only gods and their children are able to do so.

340

Sometimes the gift can be granted by a god, but the vessel must be strong enough to bear it."

"I went into a sort of afterlife where Moses let me touch it," Conrad said.

"Ah, the first Arcane." Eve nodded. "You are related to him?"

"Yes, through my mother."

"Moses was the favorite of the dragon god, Altash." Eve took another sip of nectar. "Moses possessed uncommon strength, which makes me believe he was not entirely human."

Emily grunted. "So Altash is more than a dragon."

"Not entirely human?" I raised an eyebrow. "What else was he then?"

"I believe he had dragon blood in his veins." Eve took Conrad's hand and turned his arm to examine his wrist. "I sense the fire in you, child."

"Can he turn into a dragon?" Shelton said.

Eve scoffed. "Of course not."

I decided to get a few answers of my own. "What are the rules between the infernal and primal fount? Do only the bad guys use the infernal source?"

Eve laughed. "There is no such division as good and evil. A connection to either fount is usually determined by bloodline."

"How did they come to exist? Is one more powerful than the other?"

"Dude, I already explained that," Adam said. "They're like positive and negative battery poles. Neither one is stronger, but they're both necessary."

Eve's eyebrows arched. "You are smart for a human." She turned to me. "He is right. The sources are equal. The power and capacity to use them resides in the vessel."

I shook my head. "So Baal gave Cain access to the infernal fount?"

"Who is Cain?" Eve said.

Shelton scoffed. "Not the one you're thinking of."

"Don't bring up her sons," Ambria said. "It's probably painful for her."

Eve frowned. "You speak of Cain and Abel? They were among the earlier humans, but I barely knew them."

I steered the conversation back on track. "Cain is sort of a clone of me." I gave her the short version of how Baal planted a demon seed in my soul and used it to grow a copy, then banished my father's spirit to Haedaemos so he could plant the copy in his body.

For the first time, Eve looked troubled. "Baal should not be capable of such a thing. He is no god, merely a powerful spirit."

"Well, he figured out a way," I said. "And my copy can use the infernal fount."

"Baal must also touch it then," Eve said. "That would explain it." She put a hand to my forehead. "The fire has nearly burned out." She turned my hand palm up and traced a circle with her fingernail.

I shivered from her soothing touch. And then my hand felt as if it caught fire. A bright red spark leapt from my palm and vanished. The intense heat at my core faded to nothing.

Max oohed. "What was that?"

"Can Justin use the infernal fount now?" Conrad said.

Shelton scoffed. "I freaking hope so after nearly killing himself."

"Justin is related to Baal," Adam said. "Wouldn't that make him a natural?"

"No," Eve said. "The fount only grants power to those it accepts and kills those it denies. It rejected Justin. He is lucky to have survived."

It took everything not to cry like a baby. "I don't have the power?"

She shook her head. "I'm sorry."

"You've got to be kidding me," Shelton said.

Adam frowned. "How'd he survive?"

Eve ran her fingernail up my arm, eyes distant as if seeing something invisible to the naked eye. "Baal's demon seed merged with your soul and demon spirit. Though most of it left to form Cain, some of it became a part of you. It gave you the strength to survive the fount."

Adam grunted. "If Baal's not a god, how could he protect Justin from instant death?"

Eve gasped and her eyes widened as if she just glimpsed something. "That is because Baal is not simply a powerful spirit." Her gaze focused on me. "He was once a god."

CHAPTER 36

Shelton scoffed. "Well, I'm not surprised Baal was a god. The question is, which one?"

"He would have been of the infernal bloodlines." Eve tapped a finger on her chin. "There were many."

"I know exactly who he was." Emily leaned her elbows on the table. "Hades."

"Perhaps." Eve tapped a finger on her chin. "He was one of the few who openly remained on Earth and vanished after the Sundering."

"That must be why Olivia can use the infernal fount," Emily said.

Eve's forehead pinched into a V. "Your sister taps the infernal power? How could Baal give her the gift when my bloodline grants her the power of the primal fount?"

"Because she's mean and nasty," Ambria said.

Eve seemed too preoccupied to hear her. She got up and walked to Emily. "Stand, child."

Emily stood and faced her. Eve peered into the other woman's eyes for several seconds then reeled back with a horrified gasp. Her face flushed crimson and golden fire blazed in her eyes.

"What's wrong?" Emily said.

Eve bared her teeth and roared in such a thunderous voice the table shook, and frightened birds flew from the rafters. I scrambled out of my seat and well away from the outraged goddess.

When she grew silent, Shelton poked his head around a couch. "Is it safe to come out?"

Emily still stood next to Eve. Tyler was the only other one who hadn't fled the table. He popped a grape in his mouth, an amused look on his face. I felt a pang of sadness because he reminded me so much of Dad.

"Long ago, I cut myself off from most of my powers and fell in love with a mortal." Tears welled in Eve's eyes. "I thought he was the father of my children. " Her skin glowed brighter, fueled by rage. "Though the greater part of your soul touches the primal fount, a small part of it is drawn in the opposite direction. As a direct descendant of mine, your soul should be completely in synch with the primal fount."

"So if the mortal wasn't my grandfather, then who is?" Emily said.

Eve snarled. "A part of your soul comes from Baal."

"Holy smokes!" Adam clapped his hands like an excited schoolboy. "She can use both founts?"

Eve shook her head. "Too much of her belongs to the primal bloodline. The opposite must be true of Olivia, which is why she uses infernal power."

"Does that mean Emily and I are related?" I asked.

Tyler frowned. "Uh, Baal is technically my father too. So if he's Emily's grandfather—"

"Shut your mouth, Tyler Rock!" Emily slashed a hand through the air. "Baal is not physically related to either of us."

"True." Tyler pursed his lips. "Just parts of our souls are."

I tried one last time to pull Eve into our fight. "Will you confront Baal about his trickery?"

The anger drained from Eve's face. "What is done is done. I cannot change the past."

But he raped you! I almost said it out loud, but it was obvious Eve would have nothing to do with our war. "Why did you heal us, give us food and refuge if you don't want to interfere?"

"Because I am fond of my granddaughter." Eve took a deep breath. "Millions have died because of my interference. I decided long ago that while I am very good at creating, I am not so good at guiding it."

Considering her role in creating the Apocryphan, I couldn't argue. There was no use in trying to convince her. As usual, the fate of the world was up to us. I'd failed to give myself the power of the infernal fount. Only Emily stood a chance of beating Xanos. My Seraphim powers might not compare to that of a demigod's, but I was willing to be her sidekick if that's what it took to win.

We are stronger, Kalesh said. *We will win.*

I didn't know why he felt so optimistic. I felt like crying. I'd tried so hard, risked my life, and come back with nothing, not even a T-shirt. *I need more power!* "Eve, will you grant me access to the primal fount?"

The goddess didn't answer. Her gaze seemed lost in the breadbasket, but I imagined she was probably thinking about the past, wondering how Baal managed to impregnate her without her knowing. I imagined a part of him possessed a human and did it.

It just underscored how freaking dangerous Baal was. If he could trick a goddess, then fooling everyone else was child's play. Then again, it didn't look like it mattered much. Xanos was back in her body, and Zon had pledged to fight for her. Our resistance would be wiped from the face of Eden and then it would all boil down to the trickiest bastards in the universe—Baal and Xanos.

I had no idea who to bet on in that fight.

We couldn't overpower Xanos. We couldn't outsmart her. The only viable was to retreat to a safe realm and try to stay out of her way.

Elyssa rubbed my arm. "You're thinking about Xanos, aren't you?"

"We've only got three days until the truce is over." I shook my head. "What can we do in that short amount of time to prepare for Xanos?"

"Oh, you don't know." Elyssa grimaced. "You've been out for almost two days. We've got a little more than twenty-four hours before the truce ends."

I face-palmed. "Fuck my life."

"Even if we had a week, I don't think there's much we could do," Elyssa said.

"I need more power." I huffed. "Trying to fight Apocryphan with my Seraphim powers is like bringing a pellet gun to a nuclear war."

"I've given it a lot of thought." Elyssa watched Eve, eyes wary of the troubled goddess. "I think we need to step out of the way and let Baal and Xanos fight it out. Maybe by then we'll be strong enough to fight the victor."

I glanced at Emily. "Well, Emily can open portals and move thousands of people to other realms. But I don't know if she alone can evacuate everyone in Queens Gate in less than a day."

"Which means if we're going to do it, then it needs to be sooner rather than later." Elyssa rubbed my arm. "We need to go now."

"Maybe." I walked over to Eve and touched her shoulder.

She flinched from her reverie. "You asked if I could grant you primal powers."

347

I blinked. "Oh, you heard me?"

"Yes, but I was preoccupied."

"So, can you?"

Eve put a hand on my chest and looked into my eyes. "I cannot give you the power you seek. Your bloodline aligns you with the infernal fount, but it rejects you. You have no link to the primal fount, and there is nothing I can do to make it otherwise."

Her touch sent pleasant electrical tingles across my skin which I did my best to ignore. "Cain gets to fly around using the infernal fount and Seraphim powers. I'm stuck riding a broom."

"Perhaps you would be happier without powers." Eve raised an eyebrow and I suddenly felt weak as a baby.

Gravity pressed down on my shoulders. Aches and pains I'd never noticed crept into my joints and muscles. I hadn't felt like this since before my demonic powers came online.

"What did you do to me?" My limbs felt heavy as lead and I couldn't sense Kalesh. "What's wrong with me?"

Emily glared at Eve. "Did you strip him of his powers?"

"He complains too much." Eve flicked a finger and the missing parts of me suddenly snapped back into place.

Where were you? Kalesh sounded just as frightened as me.

I shivered in awe and fear of Eve's power. "You can make people power-less just like that? Why not strip the Apocryphan of their powers?"

"I would rather see them dead than powerless." Eve's lips pressed tight.

Emily gripped my arm and dragged me outside and far from the house. "Just leave it be, Justin. Eve does as Eve wills, and there's nothing you can do about it."

There were a lot of things I couldn't do anything about. I couldn't fight

Xanos, Zon, or Baal. I wasn't going to carry us to victory on the back of my powers. It meant we all had to band together and support Emily the best we could, because she was our only hope.

"Do you stand a chance against Xanos?" I said.

Emily pursed her lips. "Not without help."

"So there's no hope."

Emily shook her head. "There's always hope. We just have to outsmart her."

"Fat chance of that." I sat on the grass and sighed. "You know what's funny? I've heard all these stories about the Great Banisher saving the world, but we've only met once."

She sat next to me. "You're right. I only know you distantly as the hero of Eden. I never fought directly in the war against Daelissa and only met you that one time during the Crystoid Incident."

"Well, we've finally gotten our chance to fight side-by-side." I laughed. "And it looks pretty grim."

"Yep." She plucked a piece of grass and tossed it into the breeze. Then she stood, reached down a hand to me.

I took it and she pulled me to my feet as easily as Elyssa could. Still holding my hand, she shook it. "Justin, it's nice to meet you. I hope we can save the world together."

I felt a grin stretch my lips. "Emily, the pleasure is all mine. I'd love to save the world with you." I just wished I knew how.

The only being powerful enough to make a difference was Eve, and she was out. Not even our army could stand against Zon and Xanos. That narrowed down the options considerably. Nothing reasonable would help. That meant it was time to get desperate—like penniless meth addict desperate.

I took a breath and hoped Emily would hear me out. "This is going to sound crazy, but there's only one way we can beat the odds."

She listened, but the growing look of dismay on her face told me exactly what she thought of my idea. "Absolutely not." Emily shook her head emphatically. "Vitania would be furious, and there's no guarantee it wouldn't lead to even more destruction."

"But there's a way around that." I told her part two of my brilliant plan and that eased the tension a little.

"Perhaps it's doable." Emily folded her arms across her chest. "But I have another plan to consider first."

"I'm all ears."

Her plan even crazier than mine. I shook my head. "I think my plan is safer. It's at least worth trying before we do yours."

"Well, there's always the third option," Emily said. "We could evacuate our people from Eden."

"Yeah." I blew out a breath. "Baal drove us out of Seraphina and now Xanos might boot us out of Eden. We relocated all the Seraphim refugees to Utopia. They might take the rest of us too."

"It's certainly the least desirable plan," Emily said. "There's no guarantee Xanos and Baal would fight each other right away. And if Baal gets his hands on the last few relics, then there's nothing we can do. Utopia and every other realm will combine back into one, killing billions."

"Yep." I blew out a breath. "Let's discuss this with the others and see what they think."

Emily smirked. "That way we can share the blame when things go horribly wrong."

"Exactly!" I clapped her on the shoulder. "I like the way you think."

We went back inside and gathered the others in a circle. I let Emily explain her plan first, then I told them mine.

Eve's eyes narrowed when she heard my plan. "You would do far more harm than good."

I looked away, unwilling to confront her again. The ease with which she stole my powers had shaken me, and I wasn't about to risk her wrath.

Adam looked flabbergasted. "Justin, that's the worst idea you've ever had, and that's saying a lot."

"It's insane!" Shelton grinned. "But I love it. Dude, that would blow Xanos's mind!"

"Emily's plan is impossible," Max said. "I don't see how we could manage it."

"It does sound rather challenging," Ambria said. "Xanos will have her full powers back. She'll destroy you before you even get close."

"Ambria is right," Elyssa said. "Xanos and Zon will lead the charge because there's nothing we can do to stop them." She turned to Emily. "There's no way to execute your plan before we're all dead."

Emily sighed. "It sounded much better in my head."

"If Xanos were alone, we might have a chance." Elyssa's lips twisted to the side as she gave it more thought. "How hard is it to remove the powers of a demigod?"

"It's not easy if they know how to defend themselves," Emily said. "Xanos would have to be unconscious. Even then, it would be difficult."

Elyssa nodded. "So we agree Justin's plan might be the safer way to go?"

"I believe so," Emily said.

Others nodded in assent.

"You would risk unleashing chaos on the realms?" Eve stood. "Seeking the remaining Apocryphan as allies is madness!"

I really wanted to tell her what I thought about her opinion, but I wasn't about to risk pissing her off again.

Thankfully, Emily voiced the thoughts bouncing around in my head. "If you won't help us, Grandmother, then we have no choice but to find allies who are powerful enough to counter Xanos and Zon."

"Your interference will cost countless lives." Eve glared at her. "Leave my mistakes where they belong—in the Abyss."

"Then send Xanos and Zon back to the Abyss," Emily said. "Stop them from interfering with the realms and we won't have to do this."

"Xanos can escape again," Eve shot back. "She understands how to manipulate quantum tunnels."

"Then take her powers!"

Eve's face turned crimson. "I would rather she be dead!" Golden energy coalesced around her hand. "My daughter is the brightest star among her siblings. Her cleverness freed her, and she has proven herself worthy of the ideals I once hoped for in the Apocryphan." The goddess's hands clenched. "The others do not deserve their freedom."

Emily's face paled. Shock rippled across the other faces in the room.

"Are you actually hoping Xanos succeeds?" Emily said.

"She has earned her way back all on her own," Eve hissed. "If you cannot defeat her on your own, then you should support her."

I couldn't believe what I was hearing. Why in the hell would Eve want Xanos to rule?

Emily nodded as if she understood completely. "It all goes back to your original plan, doesn't it?" She scoffed. "Bort didn't work out. The Apocryphan made things worse. But Xanos, the black sheep of the family, escapes from the Abyss and now you think she can make everything perfect?" Emily shook her head. "You were wrong then, and you're wrong now, Grandmother."

Eve straightened, as if trying to regain her composure. "Then go on your foolish errand, but do not weep when it goes horribly wrong." She slashed a hand horizontally through the air and vanished into a portal.

The tension in the room vanished the moment the portal closed behind her.

Shelton chimed in first. "Uh, is it just me or is Eve fucking crazy?"

"She's erratic." Emily ran a hand down her face. "Despite her long existence, she still succumbs to emotion and whims."

My hands were still shaking. "I'm just glad she didn't do anything awful to us."

Elyssa took a deep breath and clapped her hands together. "Well, what's the plan?"

"We go to the Abyss and recruit any willing Apocryphan," Emily said.

"Do you think Eve will stop us?" Max asked.

"No." Emily sighed. "I never expected her to actually be proud of Xanos though."

"Xanos is her daughter," Nightliss said. "She created the Apocryphan in the hope they would perfect creation. Instead, they badly damaged it. Eve hopes Xanos will redeem her at long last."

"Probably." Emily shook her head. "But we've got to do what we've got to do."

Ambria looked worried. "I just hope Eve doesn't get in our way."

Shelton grunted. "Me and you both."

"So let's get down to brass tacks." I plucked a grape from the table and popped it in my mouth. "How do we form a soul bond with the Apocryphan and ensure they don't break their oath?"

"One of us extends our soul essence and binds it with the oath taker," Emily said. "They speak the oath and the bond is formed."

"And they can't break it?" Shelton said.

"They will damage their soul and lose their magic," Emily said. "A soul bond is the most powerful oath one can take. There's no way to dispel the bond except by completing the oath."

"Even if it never ends?" I said.

Emily nodded. "Even if it never ends."

I rubbed my hands together to combat trembling apprehension. This was far more likely to go horribly wrong than fantastically right. Emily would back me up, but even she might not be able to save me if it turned into a shit storm.

Because Couriondral, Posthanied, or Araxos might kill me before I even opened my mouth.

CHAPTER 37

I would ask the other Apocryphan to fight Xanos and Zon with us and agree to never seek power over the realms or harm any beings in them except for self-defense. In exchange, we'd free them from the Abyss.

I asked Elyssa to hammer out the full text on her arcphone since she was good at stuff like that. We didn't want to leave any loopholes in our agreement, or we'd end up right back at square one.

Part two of the plan was to evacuate Queens Gate. If the remaining Apocryphan agreed to help, then we wouldn't need our army. If they declined our offer, then there was nothing we could do to stop Xanos anyway, so evacuating was still our best option.

As usual, everything depended on us mustering one last dangerous gambit to overcome impossible odds.

Just another Monday at the office, folks.

We gathered outside Eve's cottage, backpacks refilled with food and not much else. Elyssa gripped my hand a little too tight. She and everyone but Tyler, Emily, and me were headed back to Queens Gate to start the evacuation and warn Thomas about the looming invasion.

Eve startled us all when she seemingly appeared from nowhere. "Safe journeys, children." She smiled pleasantly, but it didn't reach her eyes.

I imagined she was more than ready to be rid of us. After her earlier outburst, I was more than happy to get as far away from her as possible.

Emily slashed open a portal to the Queens Gate waystation without even breaking a sweat. I was a little jealous but also very happy to have something of a demigoddess on our side.

"It was very nice meeting you, Eve." Ambria curtseyed.

"A pleasure." Eve watched us expectantly, as if making sure none of us changed our minds and stuck around.

I nodded at the goddess. "Thank you for your hospitality." Then I stepped through the portal.

We filed through and into a nearly empty waystation. Since Xanos controlled most Overworld cities, there was no reason to use the Obsidian Arch. Portal-blocking statues prevented Xanos and Razor from opening portals anywhere in the waystation except for this tiny zone.

Emily closed the portal once everyone was through.

Elyssa gripped Emily's shoulder. "Bring Justin back to me."

The other woman put her hand over Elyssa's. "I will."

Elyssa turned and gave me a bone-crushing hug. She kissed me. "At the first sign of trouble, I want you to run."

"I will. Promise." I kissed her back. "See you soon."

"Be careful, man." Shelton clapped me on the back. "Don't trust those demigods any further than you can throw them."

I chuckled. "No chance of that."

We said the rest of our goodbyes and then Emily conjured a portal to the Abyss. I stared at the bubbling tar with apprehension. "Why does the gateway look like this?"

"Because it passed through the fringe." Emily sighed. "Believe, me, I don't like it any more than you do."

"Just lean back and enjoy the ride." Tyler turned his back the portal and fell backward into it. The inky mass slowly swallowed him.

I took a deep breath and followed him. As the pitch drew me into its chilling embrace, it was all I could do not to scream like a little boy. A moment later, I stumbled into the barren wasteland. Emily was so close behind, she ran into me.

Tyler picked up a rock and tossed it. "I sure hope you guys don't die, because I don't fancy being trapped in the Abyss forever."

Emily gave him a smoldering kiss. "At least you'll have that to remember me by."

Tyler nipped her ear. "That ought to hold me for a hundred years at least."

She laughed. "I was hoping for at least a thousand." Azure energy flecked with gold glowed around her body and she lifted from the ground.

"Why does your power sometimes look gold?" I said.

She shrugged. "Maybe because I'm growing stronger and more like Eve."

Tyler wrinkled his nose. "Yeah, just don't become too much like her. That girl is crazy."

I hopped on my broom, a little ashamed to be an angel that couldn't fly, and Emily and I flew toward the infernal fount. We landed when we reached the hill near the fount so I could make a stealthy approach. I didn't want to give the Apocryphan a clear shot in case they decided to blast me before asking questions. Emily remained a few feet behind to cover me in case things went horribly wrong.

I peered over the hill, expecting to see Posthanied and Couriondral. Instead, I counted three Apocryphan. Araxos, the giant spider, had joined them. But they weren't enjoying a family reunion or roasting marshmallows over the infernal fire. In fact, they weren't enjoying much of anything.

The Apocryphan we'd come to enlist in our cause would, without doubt, not join us. Not because they didn't want to, but because it was now impossible.

"Oh god." I dropped to my knees.

"What is it?" Emily sneaked up the rise and knelt next to me. Her eyes flared. "No!"

Couriondral and Posthanied sprawled near each other in a violet lake. Blood oozed from vicious wounds carved in their chests. As for Araxos, her head lay ten feet from her eight-legged body.

"This can't be real." I pounded a fist on the ground. "Xanos must have realized what we planned to do. She came back and murdered them!"

Emily leapt into the air and soared to the bodies. She hovered just above them, pressing her hands to Araxos and then Posthanied. She shook her head. When her hands touched Couriondral, a gasp escaped her lips. "She's alive, but barely."

I inspected the slash in the demi-god's chest. It didn't seem possible for anyone to survive such terrible wound. A heart the size of my head pounded furiously inside the gaping hole. Blackened veins stood out against her skin and the flesh around the wound almost seemed to be rotting away.

Emily shook her head. "I can't do anything for her. We've got to get her to a healer."

"Eve?" I said.

She nodded. "Eve's our only hope." She slashed open a portal. A surprised Tyler stood on the other side.

He leapt through and grimaced when he landed in blood. "What in the hell happened here?"

Emily closed the portal and opened a new one just outside Eve's cottage. A gentle bubble of energy lifted Couriondral from the ground and carried the giant woman into the bubbling portal. After another unpleasant transition, we all emerged in front of Eve's cottage.

The goddess sat on her porch, knitting what looked like spider silk and humming a strange melody. She didn't even seem to notice us until Emily called out to her.

"Eve, we need your help!"

The goddess's eyes flared then narrowed when she saw Couriondral. "What—what happened?" She stood up. "Did you do this?"

"No, of course I didn't!" Emily lowered the bubble holding the Apocryphan to the ground. "Can you save her?"

Tears pooled in Eve's eyes. She approached and knelt next to Couriondral. "Such a cruel wound."

Couriondral's eyes fluttered open. She saw Eve. "Mother, is it really you?"

Golden tears dripped from the goddess's eyes. "I am here, child." Eve put a hand to Couriondral's cheek. "You are free now."

"Can you heal her?" Eve knelt on the other side. "Can you?"

"Unmaker," Couriondral gasped.

Eve flinched. "Unmaker?" She traced a finger along the sickly black veins webbing the skin near the wound. "Yes, I see it now." She looked up at us. "Someone impaled her with Unmaker, the Sword of Jura. It is eating her from the inside out, and even I cannot stop it."

"No!" I doubled over, sick with despair. "Did Xanos do this?"

Couriondral's eyelids drooped. "Did not see." She shuddered, gasped for breath. "I heard a voice as we lay dying. She said our time had come to an end."

The knot in my stomach doubled. "Oh, shit."

Emily clenched her teeth and pressed her hands to Couriondral. "There must be something we can do!" She looked at Eve. "Can you get that magic poultice for me?"

"Child, it will do no good."

Emily's face constricted with worry. "Please, Grandmother?"

Eve sighed. "If it will make you feel better." She stepped away and went into the cottage.

Tyler scowled. "We're fucking screwed, aren't we?"

Emily's forehead furrowed in concentration. She gasped and reeled back. Then she gripped Tyler's arm. "I won't let it happen."

I was too furious to sit still. I stormed off into the trees and roared at the sky, Kalesh's demonic voice mingling with mine. Then I leaned my forehead against a tree and tried to calm myself. "I will not let it end this way." Calm determination replaced the rage. "I won't let Xanos bring the fight to us. We'll bring it to her."

By the time I returned to the others, Couriondral was dead. The skin around the wound continued to blacken and crumble. Soon, it seemed, there'd be nothing left but dust.

Eve held Couriondral's hand. She gingerly reached out and closed the demigod's eyes. "I am sorry I failed you, child. May your new journey begin with hope."

"What about the souls of Araxos and Posthanied?" Emily said. "Are they trapped in the Abyss?"

Eve stood and brushed off her knees. "I will go there and free them so they may have some peace in the afterlife."

"You could have freed them all this time." Disapproval laced Emily's words. "Made them swear by a soul bond to do no harm and given them a new life. But you chose to let them rot for eternity."

Eve smiled gently at Emily. "They were too dangerous to free, child."

"Why not remove their powers?" Eve said. "Then they would have been no trouble."

"Better they die quickly than to be stripped of power and left to rot." Eve shook her head sadly. "I am sorry." A rift to the barren lands of the Abyss opened. Eve stepped through and it closed behind her."

"How—how did she open a portal without the black stuff?" I said.

Emily didn't answer. She slashed open a portal.

Tyler paced in a forest on the other side of the gateway. He flinched in surprise. "Is she gone?"

Emily's face paled and tears pooled in her eyes. "Yes." She wiped her face angrily. "She's gone."

Tyler took her hand, caressed her cheek. "Babe, what's wrong?"

Emily dry heaved, took in a shuddering breath and backed away from the dead Apocryphan. She walked to the front door of the house and reached for the doorknob, but an invisible force pushed her hand away.

Emily stomped her foot on the ground. "Bitch!" She slashed a hand in the air and a portal opened to the Queens Gate waystation. Without a word, she dragged me and Tyler through after her and closed the rift.

Tyler's forehead creased with worry. "Emily, tell me what's wrong right now!"

She pushed him away, walked a few feet and screamed like a woman who just lost her best dress with pockets. A donkey in the stables brayed in answer, and the few people in the area hurriedly made themselves scarce before something went down.

"No way," Tyler said. "Do you really think—"

Emily turned her blazing eyes on us. "That lying bitch." She spat on the ground. "Eve killed them!"

CHAPTER 38

I couldn't even speak at first, my throat suddenly too dry. "Eve killed the Apocryphan?" I croaked.

"She never talked about the relics she hid for the Fallen," Emily said. "All I know is they're so dangerous, only a god could be trusted to protect them."

"And you think she has Unmaker?" I said. "You really think she killed her children just to keep us from freeing them?"

"I know she did." Golden flames flushed across her body and vanished. "But of course, she won't kill Xanos or Zon for us. Since they're already free, we have to do it ourselves."

"That's not even remotely logical!" I couldn't believe this. "Eve absolutely refused to interfere. Why would she change her mind and go to such an extreme to destroy our plans?"

"Stop trying to apply logic to Eve." Tyler blew out a breath. "She's erratic and probably more than half mad."

"He's right." Emily squeezed her eyes shut, sighed, and opened them again. "She's done so much good, even helped us over the years. I didn't want to see the awful truth no matter how many times Tyler pointed it out to me. Eve believed the Apocryphan in the Abyss were out of play. She didn't expect you to come up with such an insane plan to recruit them."

"Last thing I would've thought of," Tyler said dryly. "But maybe that's how you've survived so many conflicts."

"Yeah, maybe it is." I took deep breaths to ward off despair. "We're going to be okay." I felt like crying.

Tyler chuckled. "And you're overly optimistic."

I looked at Emily. "You tried to go into Eve's cottage to find that sword, didn't you?"

"Yes." Her lips curled into a snarl. "She knew I might suspect her, so she shielded the cottage and left to avoid confrontation."

Tyler scoffed. "That woman is fucked up."

"That sword would come in handy, but there's no way we're getting it from Eve." I straightened my shoulders and faced them. "I'm sick and tired of reacting to the enemy. If we just sit back and wait, Xanos is going to win. I think it's time we took the fight to her."

Emily blinked. "What in the bloody hell do you mean by that?"

"We don't have enough portal-blocking statues to keep Xanos from portaling into Queens Gate city. She could open a gateway to the university and the city at the same time and overwhelm us before we even knew what happened." I paced back and forth, assembling ideas in my head. "But we've got a demigod of our own. We initiate. Portal our army into Thunder Rock and blindside them."

"I'm not a demigod, Justin." A smirk lifted Emily's lips. "But I agree. If we're going down, let's fuck the bloody bastards right in the ass."

Tyler grinned. "Ooh, I like the sound of that."

I pulled up an image of the mansion on my arcphone. "Can you take us there, Emily?"

"Yep." She slashed open a portal and we stepped through.

The area teemed with Templars. Some paused their training when we appeared out of thin air.

One of them recognized me and saluted, hand over chest. "Commander Slade."

I saluted back. "As you were." I had to admit, it made me feel like a badass.

The roar of a crowd pulled my attention to the corridor outside. It was packed to the gills with refugees. Elyssa had somehow managed to get things moving even in the brief time Emily and I had been gone. Children huddled with parents. Arcanes, vampires, and other supers carried as many of their worldly possessions as they could, desperate to escape the looming attack.

I wondered how much of Xander's newly formed nom army was part of that line. His efforts to raise more bodies for the cause only made it more difficult to evacuate.

Emily looked around. "Quite an interesting place."

"Why is there a house underground?" Tyler said.

I started walking toward the mansion. "Shelton and I squatted in a mansion aboveground for a while. Then Daelissa attacked and burned it to the ground. Jeremiah Conroy—Moses—was killed during the attack. We built a replica underground since it was the safest place to be during the war."

"I've heard of it," Emily said. "I'd just forgotten about it."

We weaved between rows of training Templars and went through the open front door. I found Elyssa in the first place I checked—the war room. Thomas was already there along with the faction leaders.

"Aye, lad!" Colin McCloud held up a pint of beer when he saw me. "Just in time to fight a god, are ye?"

The giant slab of beef next to him nodded, yellow eyes glinting. Sabre, the leader of the felycans, rarely said anything. He was a man of action, not words.

Kassallandra's fiery eyes and gaze were muted for once. Her fair skin looked a shade paler, her expression less certain. "I cannot believe the Abyss failed to hold its prisoners." She met my gaze. "Even all our combined might is but a candle to the sun that is the Apocryphan."

Komad Rashad, the vampire leader, nodded in agreement. "We might as well assault them with pitchforks and torches."

"Good to see you, Justin." Captain Takei, leader of the Blue Cloaks stood next to Thomas, examining some sort of battle plan.

Elyssa threaded through the crowd, concerned eyes searching. She grabbed my hand and pulled me outside. Emily and Tyler followed.

"You're back already?" She looked back and forth between me and Emily. "Something's wrong."

I swallowed the knot in my throat.

Emily answered first. "Eve murdered Araxos, Posthanied, and Couriondral so we wouldn't free them."

Elyssa gasped. "What?"

"We don't know that for sure," I said.

Emily scoffed. "I'm certain of it. So we don't have new allies. We're on our own."

"Okay, then." Elyssa leaned against the wall, eyes distant. "We'll think of something."

"When does the truce expire?" I said.

"Midnight tonight," Elyssa said.

"Then we attack Thunder Rock," I said. "Xanos will never see it coming."

"Because Xanos will be here," Elyssa said slowly, as if speaking to an idiot child. "Destroying an undefended city."

"Then we attack five minutes early," I said. "At this point, it really doesn't matter."

"What, exactly, is the objective?" Elyssa said. "Are we trying to take Thunder Rock, or just destroy everything there?"

I nodded. "Yes."

"I agree with Justin," Emily said. "I'm not one for tactics, but if we take the war to Xanos, we'll buy time for evacuation."

"And if *you* die, we lose the ability to instantly move people to another realm." Elyssa folded her arms across her chest. "Then we'll have to ferry everyone to Kratos so the Mzodi can ship them to Atlantis."

"You really think it's a bad idea?" I said.

Elyssa sighed. "No. No matter which way you cut it, fighting two demigods is a lost cause."

Tyler winked. "We might have a secret weapon."

Emily glared at him. "Now is not the time for jokes." She ran a finger along her lips. "Zip it."

Tyler flinched as if she'd slapped him. He held up his hands in surrender. "Fine."

I cleared my throat. "Awkward."

Elyssa pushed off the wall. "I'll talk to the others about your idea, Justin." She kissed my cheek. "Maybe we can pull off another miracle." Then she went inside.

Emily grabbed Tyler's hand. "I'm starving." She slashed open a portal to a cobblestone alley. "Let's go eat."

"Where is that?" I said.

"My favorite fish and chips place." She pulled Tyler through after her. "We'll be back." The portal closed before I could say another word.

If our surprise attack was going to work, we needed every advantage at our disposal. Years of war tactics and counter-tactics had given me a few ideas that might even work against demigods.

I called Shelton and gave him a list of items we'd need.

"Man, the Templars got cleaned out while we were trapped in Seraphina." He blew out a breath. "But I'll call the Templar quartermaster and find out what they've got."

I didn't know if that would be enough, so I hunted around the mansion and found Conrad and pals drinking tea in the kitchen.

Conrad's eyes widened when he saw me. "Did the Apocryphan agree to help?"

I shook my head. "Long story short—Eve got there ahead of us and killed Araxos, Posthanied, and Couriondral with Unmaker, the Sword of Jura."

Ambria's eyes flared. "Eve killed them? She would never do such a thing!"

I shook my head. "Emily's the one who figured it out. If anyone knows Eve, it's her."

"Does that mean we try Emily's plan next?" Max asked.

"It means we need more tricks up our sleeves if we're gonna win." I sat down across from Conrad and Ambria. "Back during the war against Daelissa, they threw all sorts of devices against us. The Templars don't have much left, but maybe Arcane University does."

"Actually, I know a place where we can get anything." Conrad hopped up. "I suppose we'll have to walk since the omniarch is in use."

"You could just open a portal," Max said. "You already proved you could do it from one place to another inside the same realm."

"Yeah, but it's awfully tiring, Max." Conrad shook his head. "Let's do it the old-fashioned way."

"Where are we going?" I said.

"Moore Keep." Conrad finished his tea and headed for the door.

We grabbed our brooms and headed into the bathroom on the first floor of the mansion. Thankfully, it was vacant. I opened the secret exit across from the toilet and we jogged up the staircase and pushed open a trap door at the top. We flew over to the keeps—three houses named after bigwigs in the Overworld.

Moore Keep looked like a castle designed by someone on hallucinogenic mushrooms. A big square sat in front of two giant towers, each one with mini towers sprouting off them. We swooped down to the front door, hopped off our brooms, and went inside.

Conrad led us through a small museum filled with artifacts and hyper-realistic paintings of familiar landscapes. One of them looked exactly like the Glimmer. Another reminded me of the flesh-eating realm. Whoever made the paintings had obviously traveled the realms extensively.

We stopped in front of a painting of three circles. The edges of the circles touched to form a space in the middle. In that space was a tree. What was most impressive about the otherwise simple piece of artwork, was that it appeared to be floating right in front of my face. I reached out a hand and tried to touch it, but it was immaterial.

That was why it shocked the hell out of me when Conrad did the same thing and pulled a pendant bearing the tree and circles on it out of thin air. Max and Ambria hadn't even stopped to watch and continued down to another painting, this one of a stone door with the tree symbol in the middle.

I grunted. "Guess you've seen him do that a few times."

Conrad put the symbol on the door painting, and it seemed to jump off the canvas. He tugged on the handle. With a click, it opened into darkness. He apparently didn't sweat the pitch black beyond because he walked right in. Glowballs flickered on, lighting up a warehouse that seemed to stretch into eternity.

It just so happened that I'd been here before. "Holy crap, we're in Moore's Vault?"

For once, Conrad looked surprised. "You've been here?"

"Yeah!" I walked inside and looked around. "Don't mess with the snow globes. They affect the weather in real life."

Ambria laughed. "Max caused a freak snowstorm in London with one."

He groaned. "How was I supposed to know?"

Conrad walked to a nearby table where a thick tome of yellowed parchment rested. He flipped it open and traced a finger down a line. "This might take a little while."

I leaned over his shoulder and looked at the tome—an alphabetized inventory. The quilled ink was neat and legible, but dense.

"Good news," Conrad said. He tapped out a list on his arcphone. "Ezzek Moore has a separate area completely dedicated to war machines. Some of the items you want are on that list."

"Even soggers?" I said.

He nodded. "Even soggers."

"Do you really think these things will give us a chance?" Max asked, a hopeful look in his eyes.

I went into old-timer mode and give them a hope-inspiring anecdote. "Daelissa's first army nearly mowed us over. They had crystal armor and swords that could soak up everything we threw at them. Our metal swords shattered against theirs, and our physical attacks did nothing."

"How did you survive?" Ambria said.

"I didn't think we would." I sat on the edge of the table. "But when the Brightling army marched on the Ranch to finish us off, we improvised."

Max sat in a chair and leaned his elbows on the table. "And then what happened?"

"We used soggers to turn every field around the Ranch into a bog. In their arrogance, the Brightlings tried to march through it, but mired themselves in mud. Then we dropped a nom electrical wire into the water. It overloaded their armor and blew them to bits." I couldn't stop from smiling at the memory. "They retreated and we lived to fight another day."

"Water and electricity." Ambria grunted. "Who'd have thought that could defeat the mighty Brightling army?"

"Not me." I slid off the table. "Xanos thinks she's too powerful to stop now. She's overconfident, and that will be her downfall, just like it was Daelissa's. So let's go get our tricks and see if we can outsmart a demigod."

We hopped on our brooms and flew to the war section. It took a while to get past the long shelves housing other artifacts. A huge black arch sat in the empty space between the them and the section dedicated to war machines. A quick test proved it to be an omniarch.

"I guess that's how he got the big items in here," Ambria said.

I nodded. "He thought of almost everything."

We flew past it and reached the war section. I was not disappointed by what we found. Jeremiah Conroy might be dead, but he was still looking out for us.

I just hoped it was enough to win the day.

CHAPTER 39

W e used the omniarch to open a portal back to the war room in the Mansion. Elyssa and Thomas were still with the faction leaders mapping out the attack on Thunder Rock.

None of them looked terribly surprised to see me hop out of a portal in the middle of their meeting.

Elyssa's eyes narrowed. "What have you been up to?"

I grinned. "Improvising." I waved them through the portal. "Our arsenal is about to get a lot more interesting."

Everyone crowded through the gateway and into Moore's Vault. I took them through a quick tour of the war section and let them reach their own conclusions.

McCloud clapped me on the back. "Lad, you might have saved a lot of lives today."

"Indeed." Komad Rashad pursed his lips. "I still don't know how we deal with Xanos, but fighting her troops will be much easier."

I slapped a big hunk of machinery and indicated the six others just like it. "This is what's going to save our asses from Xanos herself."

Even Thomas almost smiled. "Are there enough aether pendants to go around?"

I kicked a nearby crate. "Thousands."

"Whoo, yeah!" McCloud threw a fist in the air. "Let's give that Apocryphan the beating of her life!"

Within minutes, Templars were pouring through the portal, tagging the contraptions we'd need and distributing components to the army. For the first time in a long while, I felt like we could actually pull this off.

Max waved us over to more crates. "Look what I found!" He pulled out a black and white medallion and put it in the center of his chest where it adhered.

McCloud peered closer at it. "What does it do, lad?"

"This." Max pressed the sides of the medallion. Black threads wrapped around him, weaving honeycombed armor from head to toe. It looked nearly identical to Nightingale armor, but a lot more stylish. Max ran a finger down the side of the mask. It melted away, revealing his grinning face. "It's called aphotic armor. It molds to any shape."

"May I?" McCloud held out a hand. Max handed him a medallion. He put it on his chest and activated it. "Oh, I bloody love it!" He rubbed his hands together like a kid at Christmas. Then he morphed into wolf form. The armor adjusted instantly. "It's the next best thing to beer!"

"Impressive." Thomas inspected Max's armor. "But how protective is it?"

"Well, here's the manual." Max handed him a brochure named *Aphotic Armor and You! How to survive the next big war.*

Thomas thumbed through the glossy colored pages. "If this information is true, it's slightly more damage resistant than Nightingale armor."

Komad pursed his lips. "Yes, but how many do we have?"

373

Max turned the crate to show the numbers on the side. "Five hundred per crate, and twenty crates."

The vampire grunted. "Considering the dwindling size of our army, I'd say that's enough."

"Oh, and you can color code yourself, set up friend or foe IDs, and more." Max double-tapped the top of the medallion and then dragged his finger around it. The armor phased through the entire spectrum of colors.

"Impressive." Kassallandra took a medallion and activated her armor. She shaded it red to match her hair. I didn't tell her it would make for an easier target on the battlefield.

Fashion first!

Thomas consulted an arctablet. "Let's get these distributed to the troops."

Komad and the other faction leaders took medallions for themselves. I was ecstatic to finally not have to strip down to my underwear if I wanted to spawn. I grabbed armor for Shelton and the others as well.

Time ticked down to the final hours before the truce ended. My appetite dwindled. My stomach twisted into knots and I had to visit the bathroom more times than I wanted. While the others plotted the final details of the attack, I imagined all the ways this could go wrong or right.

And where the hell is Emily?

Thomas called a final meeting in the war room as the final hour struck. "I contacted Xanos's people and inquired about extending the truce or signing a permanent peace accord."

"Sounds pointless." McCloud said.

Captain Takei shook his head. "It's brilliant. Makes them think we're desperate."

Thomas continued speaking as if no one interrupted him. "They sent me a single demand: Surrender. I told them we would consider it."

Elyssa projected an image of Thunder Rock in the middle of the table. Forests and rocky ridges surrounded the large crater. The scars of our battle against Daelissa still heavily marred the surroundings. "We ran some portal tests to probe the boundaries. Nothing opens within this perimeter." She circled the forest area around the crater. "The devices they use to detect supers also block portals."

"Will our new armor stop their electro-bullets?" Kassallandra asked.

"Unknown," Thomas said.

"Nothing like uncertainty to start a battle," Komad said dryly.

Elyssa continued marking the map, showing weapon emplacements and attack vectors.

Xander Tiberius entered, wearing golden robes and a crown. He'd abdicated his role as Overlord when we made a treaty with him, but apparently still liked to play make believe. "I apologize for my tardiness, but important matters of state interfered."

His twin sons, Devon and Rhys followed close behind, self-important smirks on their faces.

Max groaned. "Do you mean Faria made you do your chores?"

"Quiet, brother." Devon held up a fist. "As an Arcane, you are under our jurisdiction."

"Max, I'd like you to come over here," Xander said. "We need to discuss something."

"Really, Father?" Rhys rolled his eyes. "I'd prefer he stay right where he is."

Xander put on an air of confidence, but something about the way his eyes darted back and forth and the slight tremble in his hands made me think he was a lot more nervous about the impending battle than he wanted to let on.

"Max, come here." Xander stared across the room at his son.

But Max shook his head. "Whatever you have to say to me, you can say to everyone in the room."

Thomas watched them in stony silence, his ice-blue eyes as penetrating as the arctic cold. "Xander, why haven't your people reported for duty?"

"I recruited an entire army of noms," Xander said. "But you refused to train them."

"An army can't be trained in a week." Thomas raised an eyebrow. "When can we expect your Arcanes to report for duty?"

Xander tapped a finger on his chin. "I want no part of this mad plan of yours. I will hold my people in reserve so when your plan fails, Queens Gate will have defenders."

I noticed Devon holding his arcphone as if trying to take a picture of the room without anyone noticing. Since most Overworlders didn't have Facebook or Instagram, I didn't understand what his deal was. But in the brief time since I'd met Xander and family, I'd learned they were snakes. Max was the only decent one out of the bunch.

I acted on pure instinct and blurred across the room just as Devon tapped on his phone screen and smirked.

I almost reached him in time.

A portal slashed open in the crowded room, shoving everyone around it to the side. Xander and the twins looked rather smug as they walked toward the open portal. A purple-skinned giant glowered at us from the other side.

"Zon!" I shouted.

He tossed through a metal canister the size of a beer can. It smacked into Xander's chest and rolled on the floor. The portal snapped shut in Xander's face.

"What the bloody hell?" Devon swiped at empty air where the portal had been.

"Zon!" Xander looked around wildly, as if the portal had simply relocated somewhere else in the room.

The canister hummed louder and louder.

"Bloody betrayer!" Colin shouted.

"Everyone, get out!" I shouted. "Go, go, go!"

But the room was too crowded. Bodies packed the doorway in their haste to escape. I channeled with everything I had and blasted a hole through the ceiling and all the way through the roof. Debris crashed down on the table. I didn't think I could grab the canister and hurl it out in time. Plus, I didn't want to cause a massive cave-in outside. So I wove a Murk shield around the canister, forming a funnel up into the hole.

The canister detonated an instant later.

The explosion blasted up through my magical chimney, but it was too much for the shield to handle. Murk shattered and heat washed across me. My back slammed into stone and more of the ceiling caved in. The rumbling faded a moment later, leaving me in darkness. Dust filled my lungs. I felt as if I'd been sandwiched between two semi-trucks. I coughed and spat, trying to catch my breath in the claustrophobic space.

The ringing in my ears faded, replaced by distant shouts and screams. My night vision flickered on, but all I saw was stone and dust. The aphotic armor covered my arms and torso. It had apparently saved me from the brunt of the blow. But a slab of stone lay across my legs, pinning them.

I tried to shove it off me, but the awkward angle gave me no leverage. Though I felt the pressure on my legs, they didn't hurt. Since I wasn't lying in a lake of blood, it seemed the armor was keeping me from being crushed.

Well, that's one way to test it.

With all hell breaking loose, it seemed a good time to test the armor's flex. I unleashed Kalesh and spawned. My upper body swelled with muscle. My horns grew until they clinked against the stone. There was no room for wings, so I stopped before they made an appearance. Unfortunately, the sheer weight of the stone on my legs wouldn't allow them to grow, meaning I'd have to rely on increased upper body strength.

I braced a clawed hand on the floor and pushed with my other. The slab shifted just a fraction. I channeled a wedge of Murk from my eyes and used it to help me push. At last, I freed my legs. They looked ridiculously small compared to my demonic torso.

"Looks like I skipped every leg day for a hundred years." My little pocket of space wasn't large enough for me to grow my legs, so I'd have to make do. I adjusted myself until I was flat on my back, then braced my feet on the stone and pushed.

The slab lifted. I shifted it gradually in case there were other trapped people nearby, and soon I had enough space to squeeze out. When I climbed out of the rubble, I almost wished I hadn't. The war room was filled with stone. The walls and ceiling were gone. Arms, legs and even a head protruded from piles around the room. Thankfully, all of them were covered by the new armor.

Bloodstained stones near the former doorway told me not everyone had been wearing protective gear. I went to the person whose masked head jutted above the rubble. "Are you okay?"

"Aye, lad." The face wasn't visible, but the voice belonged to McCloud.

I carefully shifted stone until he was free. A loud growl startled us. Stone shifted, and a red-armored arm jutted from the pile. We heaved a slab to the side and helped Kassallandra crawl free. Her mask melted away to reveal a furious face. She looked down at me and did a double-take. "What is wrong with your legs?"

I realized I'd forgotten to manifest them. "Technical difficulties. Stand by." I concentrated and spawned them to proportionate size. Then the three of us went back to work.

Before long, Templars made a hole through the rubble blocking us off from the outside. Then the work began in earnest. Superhuman strength made shorter work of it, but the upper floors of the mansion looked ready to cave in at any moment, so we had to be careful.

"Curse those traitorous bastards!" McCloud bared his teeth as if ready to chomp his way through the mess.

"They will die when I find them." Kassallandra crushed a piece of rubble with her armored hand.

Elyssa, Thomas, and the others were freed next, followed by the other faction members. Thanks to the armor, none of them looked much worse for the wear. But that wasn't the case when we finally cleared the blood-stained area near the doorway.

Xander and Rhys had been crushed. Devon had been the lucky one, trapped in a small space beneath them. Then again, maybe he hadn't been so lucky. He was barely conscious, talking incoherently when Templars freed him. A healer loaded him on a flying carpet to take away.

Max stared at the bodies. I couldn't tell if he was sad, angry, or simply in shock.

I found Devon's phone not far from where he'd been. There was no question in my mind what had transpired, so the texts between Devon and someone named Pidge came as no surprise to me. The time stamps were from the day before.

Pidge: We received your communication. What do you wish to convey to the Overseer?

Devon: I am Devon Tiberius, authorized by Overlord Xander Tiberius to give you information in exchange for promises we will not be harmed and will be allowed to function as part of Xanos's new regime.

Pidge: Only very valuable information is worth that.

Devon: It's extremely valuable but will expire in twelve hours.

They went back and forth for a while, but finally settled on Devon's terms. In exchange, he told them about the surprise attack and offered to help them assassinate our leadership. I should have been furious—burning with rage. But I wasn't even surprised. If anything, I was numb. All our planning had been for nothing.

Despite the incredible mess, Thomas had turned a slab of rubble into a makeshift table and was already handing out assignments. Elyssa was right by his side, the two of them operating as if nothing had happened.

I shrank to human form and joined them. "What now?"

"Razor forces are in Queens Gate." Thomas projected images from the city on a new arctablet. Dozens of tanks and armored units poured from a giant portal right at the far end of the valley near the waystation. Behind them swarmed foot soldiers in full black armor. The ASE feeding the images dropped lower for a better look through the portal. The hulking forms of Zon and Xanos stood on the other side of the gateway.

Zon's face was stony. Xanos's shone with delight. She would soon have final victory over the pesky denizens of the Overworld.

CHAPTER 40

E mily and Tyler pushed through the crowd of Templars, eyes wide with horror.

I breathed a sigh of relief. "Thank god you're back."

"Justin, what happened?" Emily stared at the live-action invasion, mouth agape.

"A traitor sent Zon a picture so he could open a portal in the war room," I said. "They tossed through an explosive device, but our new armor protected us."

"Holy shit." Tyler shook his head. "We just stepped out for fish and chips and this happens?"

Max stood in the back of the room next to Conrad and Ambria, his eyes red from crying while his friends tried to comfort him. He caught my gaze and quickly looked down in shame. I walked over to him and put a hand on his shoulder. "Max, this isn't your fault."

He shuddered. "I should have known my father would try something like this."

"Why did they come here if they knew Zon planned to blow it up?" Ambria said.

"Because they were supposed to go through the portal," I said. "That's what they tried to do but Zon closed it in their faces."

A new portal sliced open where the hallway used to be. Neat rows of Templars and other factions waited in Moore's Vault on the other side.

"Everyone suit up and ready for battle," Thomas said. "We are now defending Queens Gate."

Kassallandra made a fist and held it up. "We will avenge this cowardly attack and send the dogs to their graves!"

"Aye!" McCloud raised a fist. "Kill the bastards."

Komad raised his fist and scowled. "We will dine on their blood."

Sabre nodded grimly but said nothing.

Captain Takei regarded them solemnly and lifted his fist. "May justice prevail."

They filed through the portal and joined their factions. I followed Elyssa through and took her aside. Her violet eyes glowed with anger.

"We should have known Xander would try something like this." She bared her fangs. "All the clues were there, but we were too caught up in our own affairs to see it."

"This was too much, even for Xander." I shook my head. "Something tells me there's more to it. Maybe Xanos influenced him somehow."

"Maybe." She looked doubtful. "We may lose today, but we're taking them with us."

"Don't think that way." I gripped her hands. "We still have a chance."

A wistful smile lifted her lips. She kissed my cheek. "I always loved your optimism, Justin."

"Don't speak in past tense either." I looked her in the eyes. "We *will* win." I didn't know how, but I'd pull a rabbit out of my ass and shove it up Xanos's nose if I had to.

"Okay, Captain Optimism." She kissed me again and went to join her father on the command platform.

Conrad and gang hopped on their flying brooms and assembled with the special operations division. Shelton and Adam hovered next to them. Judging from the looks on their faces, Ambria was telling them what had happened.

Emily grabbed my arm and took me well away from the others. "I need to talk to you."

My heart nearly stopped. "What's wrong? Are you not going to fight?"

She looked hurt. "Of course I am. But I need to tell you something."

"And it's a doozy." Tyler shook his head. "Just promise you won't be angry."

A lump of ice formed in my stomach. "Oh god. What is it?"

She told me, and I was angry—downright furious that she hadn't told me sooner. But what she said also gave me hope. I just prayed it wasn't too late.

The giant omniarch opened a new portal leading to the outskirts of town. Our army marched through and onto rolling fields and pastures. We lined up along the ridge of the highest point on the outskirts of town. The logistics crews guided our veiled war machines through and readied them.

Shelton and Adam glided over on their brooms.

"I just heard the news," Shelton growled. "How's Max?"

"He's not taking it well," I said, "but that's to be expected."

"Just leave it up to Xander to ruin our surprise attack." Adam threw up his hands. "Well, I guess this is it. Been nice knowing all of you."

"We got this." Shelton clapped the other man on the back. "Just unleash your unholy nerd rage on them."

The valley rose at a gentle incline all the way up to the entrance to the waystation, meaning Razor had the high ground and a clear view of us. Meanwhile, our troops dashed around like chickens with their heads cut off. Even the usually orderly Templars scrambled chaotically, as if they had no orders at all. Even in the direst conditions, Thomas and his Templars maintained order. Something was horribly wrong.

Razor marched ahead with all the organization of a military parade, neat lines of soldiers, tanks, and armored vehicles. What they saw of us had to fill them with confidence. Xanos was probably loving every minute of this.

I tapped my com badge. "Thomas, what's wrong with the troops?"

"Nothing." He sounded as calm and collected as ever even in the middle of pandemonium. "Even the best plans don't survive first contact with the enemy."

"Yeah, well the enemy tried to blow us up and our plans didn't survive."

"True, but the leadership survived. So the question is, whose plans didn't survive first contact?" Someone else spoke to Thomas. "Justin, be ready. Borathen out." The com badge went silent.

Tyler chuckled. "Clever man."

"Clever?" I still didn't understand how in the hell everything was okay if our troops looked like this was their first day in basic training.

Razor troops were only a few hundred yards away, far closer than they needed to be for their tanks to fire on us. "Jesus, are they planning to run us over?"

"No, they're overconfident," Tyler said. "Otherwise, they would've stopped about a mile out and started bombarding us with those tanks."

Shelton glanced back at the veil hiding our war machines. "Yeah, they're gonna be in range of our weapons soon."

The Razor tanks began to fan out, forming a line about two hundred yards away. They'd begin firing any minute now.

All our com badges activated at once and Thomas's voice came through. "End chaos exercise on my mark. Three, two, one, mark."

The scattered Templars abruptly filed into neat lines and the other factions assembled into orderly formations. Squadrons of Blue Cloaks on flying carpets and brooms shimmered into view from behind a veil.

"Activate aether pendants," Thomas said.

I twisted the circular badge on the left side of my armor. It lit green and emitted a low whine. More electrical hums charged the air. Veils dropped to reveal half a dozen towers shaped like Tesla coils. They fired into the air, and a crackling curtain of negatively charged aether collided with normal aether.

Daelissa had used magic interdictors against us in the war. Without an aether pendant filtering the magical energy, trying to use magic would cause nausea and intense pain. We'd planned to set up the interdictors near Thunder Rock to keep Xanos and Zon from using magic. But they and their army were just outside the interdiction field.

"Someone remind me how an interdiction field is going to help against tanks and guns," I said.

Adam grinned. "While we were gallivanting across the realms, Cinder continued researching Razor weapons. Apparently, they utilize advanced arcnology. The electro bullets aren't actually electrical. They're filled with something similar to Stasis. Same with the tank rounds."

The Razor tanks fired all at once. Thirty black spheres three feet in diameter streaked toward our army. Blue Cloaks intercepted several of them, stopping them with shields or blowing them out of the sky.

The ones that landed should have exploded on impact, electrocuting anyone within a hundred feet. Instead, they fizzled and popped briefly as the aether charges inside them were negated by the interdiction field.

I looked at Xanos through my spectacles and was not disappointed by the anger and surprise on her face. Zon looked as emotionless as the last time, but his eyes narrowed as a second volley of tank shells fizzled to no effect.

A series of clanks and thuds rang loud. Dozens of glasslike spheres filled with crackling energy sailed into the air from veiled catapults. Fueled by magical speed, the crucibles streaked toward their targets and smashed to earth before Razor could respond. Rows of enemy forces collapsed. Tanks melted to slag and armored cars exploded.

Cheers rose from our ranks.

Shelton barked a laugh. "Surprise, mother fuckers."

Xanos's fist glowed brilliant green. She fired a massive blast at vampires on the frontlines. Soldiers scattered, but the energy dissipated when it hit the interdiction field, unable to maintain cohesion.

Shelton blanched. "Holy shit, she's scary."

Emily gave me a look. "I have a bad feeling about this."

Xanos scowled and a portal flickered into existence just behind our front lines. But it winked away an instant later, another victim of the interdiction field.

"Hah, they can't even portal behind us," Shelton said. "This one's in the bag."

I turned the spectacles on Xanos. Wind whipped her flame-red hair around her face. She seemed to look right at me and bared her teeth. I gulped.

"Shit." Adam's eyes grew wide. "They're death-balling!"

"They're what?" I lowered the spectacles. Razor tanks, armored cars, and soldiers charged the center of our front lines. The vampire army there was more than capable of handling soldiers, but what could they do against tanks?

Crucibles sailed through the air, crashing down in front oncoming vehicles, but there were too many.

The magic-resistant armor on the tanks made them virtually immune to normal attacks. Only the extreme energy in the crucibles was enough to take them out. Add that to the mass and weight of the tanks, and I didn't know how vampires were supposed to stop them.

Daemos flanked by hellhounds raced toward the vampires, spawning into demon forms as they did. The first tank reached the line. Vampires swarmed over it. Kassallandra in her blazing red armor leapt on top and ripped off the hatch. She yanked out the hapless tank crew and hurled them to the vampires.

More tanks met the same fate, but there were too many to stop.

I aimed my broom for a tank that made it through. Emily grabbed my wrist. "Not yet, Justin. Not yet."

"But—"

She shook her head.

"We can't just let the damned tanks roll over us," Shelton said. "Let the man do his thing!"

"Trust me when I say it's not time." Emily held my gaze until I nodded.

A giant saber-toothed lion slammed into the tank. More felycans leapt lightly atop it and ripped off the hatch. One dropped inside and emerged a moment later, blood dripping from its claws.

Smoke trails filled the sky as nearly a hundred missiles streaked toward us. The whine of jet engines reached my ears and formations of drone jets soared out of the gateway behind Razor.

"They're using their air defense missiles," Adam said.

Shelton grimaced. "They won't explode, will they?"

Adam looked up and behind us. "They don't need to. They're going to slam into the interdictors."

Blue Cloaks were already moving on intercept courses, but we didn't have nearly enough people to deal with them.

Emily scowled. "I'll deal with them." She leapt into the air on golden flames and streaked toward them.

Tyler sighed. "Damn, she's magnificent."

"I should be up there helping her," I said.

Tyler shook his head. "You promised Emily you'd wait until she said to go."

Shelton gave me a crazy look. "Why in the hell would you make a promise like that?"

"Because I had to." I watched Emily streak through the sky to intercept the missiles. Golden rays blasted a dozen from the sky, but there were too many to stop. Two slammed into an interdictor. They didn't explode, but their kinetic energy snapped the tesla coil in half. Energy crackled and the device lost power. Two more interdictors met the same fate.

The protective net began to falter. Xanos fired another blast of green energy. This one penetrated further inside.

The bulk of the battle turned chaotic, Razor weapons began to work again. The tanks opened fire on the rest of the interdictors even as our army swarmed them. But the soldiers were the least of our worries.

Another volley of missiles came for the remaining interdictors. The tiny jet drones swarmed among the flying Blue Cloaks, blasting carpets and brooms out of the sky. Emily and the Blue Cloaks took out dozens of missiles and jets, but even if they'd had ten more just like Emily, they couldn't have stopped them all. In minutes, our last interdictor went down.

The Razor army was only a third of what it had been. Most of the drone jets were down and their soldiers weren't equipped to fight supers in hand-to-hand combat. Without weapons, Razor soldiers were just noms in fancy uniforms.

Then Xanos leveled her fists and unleashed hell. Jade beams speared through supers and Razor soldiers alike, eradicating anything living in its path. Nothing but ash floated in the wake of her fury. The glow around her fists vanished. Zon aimed a strike. A massive beam sliced through the vampires and Daemos. Anything caught in the middle just vanished.

"Sweet baby Jesus!" Shelton stood in his broom stirrups. "How in the hell are we supposed to fight that?"

Emily streaked down and hovered next to me. "Justin, it's time. Just don't show too early." She turned to Conrad. "Ready?"

He nodded grimly. "I'm ready."

Ambria kissed his cheek. "I love you, Conrad."

"I love you too." Then he spun his broom toward Emily. "Shall we?"

Emily's eyes flashed gold. "Indeed." She streaked toward Xanos and Zon, Conrad and I flying in her wake.

Xanos smiled and spoke in a booming voice that seemed to fill the valley from one end to another. "So it ends, children, as all things must end."

I magically amplified my voice. "The only thing ending today is you. Eve killed your siblings, and you're next."

Her eyes flared. "Impossible. Eve would never do such a thing."

"She used Unmaker. Araxos, Posthanied, and Couriondral are dead."

Zon's brow furrowed. "If this is true, why has she not come for us?"

Xanos shook her head. "Because he lies."

I didn't care if they believed me or not. I just needed to distract them long enough so we could get closer. When we got to within fifty yards, I unleashed a torrent of Brilliance. Conrad fired bolts of azure blue. A jade shield intercepted our attacks with ease.

"There is nothing you can do to harm me." Xanos smirked. "Join me and live. Fight me and die."

Xanos believed she had the upper hand. And in that, she was wrong. Dead wrong.

Emily veered closer to me and touched my arm. "Good luck."

When she touched me, she activated our secret weapon. Intense heat surged inside me like a pressure cooker ready to explode. I flew straight between the Apocryphan, knowing this desperate attack might be our last chance.

Emily attacked Xanos, and Conrad fired at Zon. When both Apocryphan ignored me, I knew this would work.

About thirty feet from Zon, I leapt off my broom and channeled all that bottled up energy into the biggest blast of my life. I aimed my fists at Zon. He looked bored. Like someone who had to fight a one-legged man in an ass-kicking contest. He thought he could win without an ounce of effort.

But at the last instant, something like fear lit in Xanos's eyes. *She knows.*

"Zon, your shield!" She cried.

But it was too late. "Shazam, mother fucker!" Jade energy erupted from my fists. Zon's shield would have stopped my normal attacks easily. But

I was way beyond normal now. I punched through Zon's half-assed shield and skewered his brain. The giant toppled, smoke drifting from the hole in his head. "Hey, buddy, I went for the head this time!"

I turned a blast on Xanos, but she bolstered her shield to full strength. The blast drove her back, feet digging furrows in the ground. I manifested into demon form, surging ten feet tall and landed in front of Xanos.

"How?" She cried.

"Like I said, Eve killed your siblings." I shrugged. "Couriondral left us a nice gift."

Emily hovered next to me. "I gave Justin her powers."

Conrad guided his broom to my other side. "Perhaps you should consider surrender, Xanos."

I could practically see the gears turning behind her head. "Opening a portal will take too much energy." I motioned toward the remnants of her army. "You're all alone, Xanos, and out of options."

She smiled. "Not entirely." In an instant, she dropped her shield and leapt. But she didn't come for me, she went for Emily. A black portal opened and swallowed them whole. I dove for it, but it closed before I got through.

Xanos had Emily.

CHAPTER 41

"You've got to be kidding me!" I roared in my guttural, demonic voice. I held up a fist in anger but became distracted by pulsating green veins beneath my blue skin. Emily told me that my body could handle Apocryphan power only in short bursts, or I risked burning myself to a crisp.

"They went to the Abyss," Conrad said.

"Shit." I glared at empty air where the gateway had been. "There's nothing we can do."

Conrad tilted his head. "Um, you've got the same powers as Xanos."

I snapped my big blue fingers. "Oh yeah." But there was another problem. "I don't know the symbols for the Abyss."

Conrad produced his arcphone and projected Vitania's list. He scrolled to the correct one. "Here they are."

I did as I'd done days ago and willed a rift to open. But this time I didn't go weak in the knees. This time it felt as easy as opening a door. An inky black portal sliced open. Bracing against the awful feeling, I stepped in and let it swallow me. Probably due to my godlike powers, I stepped through it as easily as any other portal, feeling only the slightest resistance.

The Abyss snapped into view around me, but Emily and Xanos were nowhere in sight. I waited for Conrad to join me then said, "We didn't portal to the same location they did."

"Then we'd better gain some altitude." Conrad pulled up on his broom and went higher.

I still didn't know how to fly but I gave it a shot anyway. I leapt into the air and willed myself to fly. "Up, up, and away!" I landed back on my feet. "Son of a biscuit eater!"

"Just levitate yourself," Conrad said. "Or maybe use your energy like a rocket engine."

I tapped a finger on my chin. "I really need to ask Emily how she does it." I imagined energy channeling from my feet and propelling me up into the sky. Then I leapt and willed it to happen. Green flames flared from my armored feet and shot me into the air. I gained control by blasting the same energy from my hands.

In other words, I flew about as well as drunk and blindfolded Superman.

"Yeah!" Conrad raised a fist over his head when I joined him high in the sky.

A few hundred feet in the air, I spotted flashes of light at the infernal fount. "Over there!"

"Xanos is going to kill Emily if we don't help," Conrad said. "Justin, I think you're the only one powerful enough to do it."

I took a deep breath. "Let's do it."

We dove toward Xanos and Emily.

Emily flitted back and forth in the air, dodging massive blasts of energy, but not returning fire of her own. She was barely surviving. All I had to do was swoop in and save the day.

"Annoying bug!" Xanos pump-faked in one direction and blasted in the other. Emily dodged right into it.

Her back arched and a horrific scream cut off as her body exploded into green mist.

"No!" I screamed. "Xanos, you fucking bitch!"

Xanos bared her teeth and glared at me. "You might have abilities like mine, but I am far stronger, boy. Your body cannot handle the strain as mine can."

"Maybe not, but I'm willing to try!" I streaked toward her, arms outstretched. Even if I completely burned myself out, I had to kill Xanos once and for all.

A portal opened behind Xanos and Emily leapt onto her head. Golden energy exploded around the Apocryphan's ears. Xanos stumbled to her knees, stunned and disoriented. Emily gripped the giant's head, face straining as if she were trying to squeeze rocks out of her ass. She cried out, red and sweating, and then leapt free, hovering above Xanos with a triumphant smile on her face.

Xanos staggered to her feet, eyes wild with surprise. "How are you not… dead?" She looked at her hands, and back up at Emily. "No. No!"

Emily held a glowing jade orb about the size of a beach ball in her palm. "Those who seek great power do not deserve it." The orb faded and dissipated like mist.

Xanos dropped to her knees and screamed to the heavens. "No!"

I thought my eardrums might burst.

"Wow." Conrad's mouth dropped open. "I thought Emily died."

We landed a few feet behind Xanos, but the Apocryphan slumped, wailing in agony.

Emily landed in front of her. "You proved yourself unworthy like so many before you. Live your life, Xanos, and leave us alone."

"I would have united all the realms." Xanos wiped tears from her face. "I was the only one who could stop Baal. Now he will win."

"No, he won't," Emily said. "We'll stop him."

"You fools." Xanos sneered up at her. "Do you even know who he is? Who he was before the Sundering?"

I offered a guess. "Hades?"

She scoffed. "That speck?" Xanos rose to her feet and rounded on me. "There are few ancients as old as Eve. Most left long before the Sundering. One god remained, hoping Eve would also leave. He despised her work and wished to mold creation as he saw fit. He was a jealous god and wished to be the only one."

I didn't feel like playing games. "And he is?"

"Some call him God or Allah. We knew him as Elohim." Xanos bared her teeth. "There are few physical forms that can contain his power. He believes combining the realms will return him to physical form."

Her words literally drove me back a few steps. I could barely wrap my mind around what she'd said. "Baal is the devil. He can't be God."

"Oh, but he is." Xanos clenched her fists. "He fathered many failed creations and was insanely jealous at how easily Eve birthed new life."

I noticed Xanos's many-voices still lurked beneath her normal one. They seemed more muted than usual. Apparently, taking her Apocryphan power hadn't removed that skill. "How do we know you're not lying?"

"Because you've knocked me from the chessboard, you fools!" She wiped more tears from her face. "I have no reason to lie, for I will share the same fate as anyone else in the realms unless Baal is stopped."

"Well, I guess you'll just have to help us, then." I tried not to smirk.

Rubbing salt in fresh wounds would only fuel hatred. Xanos didn't have all her powers, but she still had enough to be useful.

Xanos's chin quivered and fresh tears pooled in her huge eyes. "You will never stop him. There is no point in even trying." And then she raced for the infernal fount. Without her powers, it would burn her alive.

As she leapt over the edge, a black portal opened and swallowed her slowly.

"No!" Her arms flailed helplessly as she sank into the inky pitch. "Let me die! Let me die!"

And then she was gone.

I gave Emily a concerned look. "Where'd you send her?"

"To spend quality time with her mother." A pleased grin spread across Emily's face. "It's time for Eve to hear the truth from her daughter."

I whistled. "Savage."

Conrad landed next to Emily. "I thought Xanos killed you."

"I learned a little trick from Lumia." Emily sprinkled golden dust on her head. Another Emily split from her and stood before us. "This is a dust golem. It's physical, so it feels real." She touched it to demonstrate. "I blinded Xanos for an instant and dropped one of these. Then I relocated with a portal. I was going to just escape, but then you and Conrad showed up and it seemed like the perfect chance to execute my plan."

"That gave you the chance to stun her and steal her powers." Conrad blew out a breath. "Brilliant."

Emily sighed. "We're going to have to be more than brilliant to beat Baal. He's only got a few more pieces of the Saila puzzle to complete before everything is beyond our control." She looked me up and down. "How do you feel, Justin?"

I showed her the green pulses in my veins. "I tried not to use too much power, but I don't know what this means."

She frowned and traced a finger along my arm. "Your skin feels okay. Maybe this is just a side-effect of holding in so much energy."

I stopped channeling the flight power and settled onto the ground. The light beneath my skin faded, but I could still feel it deep inside, a nuclear core powering a go-kart. "What happens if I channel too much power?"

"Worst case, you burn up or explode in a ball of green fire." Emily put a hand to my chest and her forehead creased. "Perhaps I should mute the power for the time being."

I put a hand over hers. "No, please. I need it for Baal. Maybe if I practice, my body will adjust."

"If you overextend yourself, you risk annihilating yourself." Emily sighed. "And to be honest, I don't know if using the power will actually acclimate your body. Xanos and the others were built differently. Their bodies and souls could handle it."

"I'm part demon and part Seraphim." I shrugged. "That's got to count for something."

Conrad frowned. "Isn't your body human, Emily?"

"I'm also one generation removed from Eve." Eve shrugged. "My body and soul are quite similar to hers."

"Why didn't you keep Xanos's powers?" Conrad asked. "Can't you handle using their power?"

"Because it's too much bloody power." She shook her head. "I won't risk Eve taking it and returning it to Xanos." Emily's eyes rested on me. "Justin is also quite a magical brawler. I thought he would be the best candidate to wield Couriondral's power for the time being."

I raised an eyebrow. "The time being?"

She nodded. "If we defeat Baal, I will purge his power and Couriondral's from this world. If I have another chance, I'll do the same to Eve." Emily's lips pressed into a flat line. "Eve, Baal, and the Apocryphan have proven over and over again that no one deserves to be a god."

I raised my hands in praise. "Amen and hallelujah!" Then I tempered it with a request. "But if you let me keep Couriondral's power, I promise to be super good."

Emily's lips pursed. "Perhaps. But let's take one step at a time, shall we?"

Conrad tilted his head slightly. "Is there any way I can fly and have powers like yours, Emily?"

"Perhaps one day. You have a depth of willpower unheard of in children your age." Emily put a hand on his chest and closed her eyes. "Beyond the bright aura of the primal fount, I see something else inside you—an aura of great power." Her forehead tightened. "Like Eve said, you do have dragon fire inside you."

Conrad's eyes flared. "Dragon fire?"

I grimaced. "Did a human mate with a dragon back in the day?"

Emily's nose wrinkled. "I'd prefer not to imagine that. But what it means is that Conrad does have great potential. If he's somehow descended from Altash, then I don't see why he couldn't draw more power from the primal fount."

Conrad nodded somberly. "If only I could talk to Altash. Maybe he could help me."

I scoffed. "That dragon is the worst when it comes to communicating and helping, believe me."

Emily took a deep breath as if steeling herself. "I suppose we should return to Queens Gate." She shuddered. "I'm not looking forward to seeing the carnage."

"Neither am I." Xanos and Zon had wiped out dozens of lives in one brutal strike. Maybe Emily was right. No one should have that kind of power.

Emily slashed a hand and a dark portal opened. She stepped through and vanished without a word. Conrad and I exchanged a glance and followed her.

Black furrows cut through hundreds of yards of field. A breeze swirled the ashes of those caught in the path of Zon's and Xanos's attacks. Hundreds of soldiers in Razor uniforms sprawled between us and the waystation, mingled with those in aphotic armor. Slagged tanks, destroyed drones, and other armored vehicles littered the field.

The death toll from this battle wasn't as staggering as what I'd witnessed during battles with Daelissa, but it was tragic and horrible nonetheless. Our sacrifices had likely prevented thousands more. Xanos had likely planned to take over nom governments with subterfuge, but when she openly declared herself ruler, that would have surely triggered even more wars.

With her incredible powers, she would have annihilated nom armies and brought humans to heel with wholesale slaughter.

I saw the Templar command platform hovering not far away. I leapt into the air and flew on jade flames to reach it.

Elyssa's eyes flared when I landed in front of her. "Uh, is there something you're not telling me, Justin? Since when did you learn to fly like that?"

I took her into my arms and kissed her, wishing her lips could make me forget about the death toll. Wishing we could just leave this dimension and find one where mad gods didn't try to take over the world every few years.

While it didn't make the terrible day any more bearable, it reminded me why we fought, why we sacrificed and put our lives in danger all the time. It was so we could enjoy moments like these. It was so one day we might have as many of these moments as we wanted without worrying about the next jackass who wanted to rule the world.

Shelton, Adam, Max, and Ambria landed their brooms on the platform.

"Oh, Conrad!" Ambria squeezed him so hard his back popped.

Conrad smiled so wide I couldn't believe it was the same guy. Apparently, he needed Ambria as much as I needed Elyssa.

"Where's Xanos?" Shelton looked at us with wild eyes. "And how in the hell did Justin headshot Zon?"

"This woman amazes me." Tyler put an arm around Emily's shoulders.

She leaned against him and sighed. "Do I, now?"

"Oh yes, Miss Glass." He kissed her forehead. "In many ways."

Shelton groaned. "Uh, are you guys about to do the deed or tell us what in the hell happened?"

Tyler chuckled. "Both, if you'd like."

Emily pinched his cheek. "Tyler Rock, behave."

"As you wish." Tyler cleared his throat. "Emily stole Couriondral's powers and gave them to me right before Couriondral died. Emily had to distract Eve, because she would've known the moment the powers were gone."

"And that's why you asked Eve to get that poultice," Conrad said. "So she wouldn't be there when Emily stole the powers."

Tyler snapped his fingers. "Bingo. And then she portaled me far away so Eve wouldn't see the Apocryphan aura in me when she came back out."

"I guess I missed that part," I said.

He nodded. "Yeah, you ran off into the woods before we could stop you."

"Why didn't Tyler use the Apocryphan power?" Ambria said. "We could have ended everything without so much bloodshed."

"Tyler's body can't handle that much power, so I had to mute the aura." Emily shrugged. "The only person I trusted who could handle them was Justin."

Elyssa frowned. "Why not just use them yourself?"

"Because I have my own powers," Emily said. "I may not be as strong as an Apocryphan, but having Justin help me seemed far more effective than going at it alone."

"And she still beat Xanos by herself," I said. "Totally schooled her."

"Not quite by myself," Emily said. "You were a crucial distraction."

"Yeah?" Shelton said. "Well, tell us everything already!"

I told them how Emily tricked Xanos and the fate of the powerless Apocryphan.

Shelton burst into laughter. "Man, talk about karma!"

Elyssa looked worried. "What if Eve gives her powers again?"

"She can't just make powers out of thin air," Emily said. "She'd have to birth another demigod or take the powers from someone else."

"What's to stop Eve from killing Xanos?" Adam said.

"I don't think she will." Emily shrugged. "Then again, she's somewhat unpredictable."

"That's for damned sure," Shelton said.

"If Eve can take powers, why kill the other Apocryphan?" Max asked. "She could have taken their powers and set them free."

Emily sighed. "She seemed to think that stripping them of their powers was a fate worse than death."

"Yikes." Shelton grimaced. "So there's a chance she might put Xanos out of her misery."

Emily's lips twisted. "There's no telling with Eve."

"I can't imagine how cold-blooded you have to be to fucking stab three of your kids to death," Tyler said. "She probably portaled in behind them and stabbed them with Unmaker before they could react. Then the magical blight from the sword finished them off."

"And that woman is the mother of all humanity." Shelton shuddered. "Talk about mommy dearest."

Adam nodded enthusiastically. "Amen!"

Thomas, who'd listened quietly until now, spoke. "We're indebted to you, Emily." He looked out at the battlefield. "Unfortunately, we lost hundreds today. It will take some time before we can rebuild and face Baal."

"Speaking of which—" I sighed. "Turns out Baal was a god before the Sundering—and not just any old god."

"Hades, right?" Shelton said.

"The opposite." I pointed up. "That god. Elohim."

They went silent, faces white with shock. Even Thomas's forehead creased.

"So if he finds enough relics to finish Saila, the theory is that the realms will recombine, and he'll get his body back," Tyler said. "And he'll be supreme ruler of whatever is left."

"Unmaker was Saila's sword," Emily said. "I think Baal will have a hard time taking it from Eve."

"What about the relics hidden in the Abyss?" I said. "With the Apocryphan dead, what's to stop Baal from flooding the place with his minions?"

"Baal doesn't know they're dead yet, but he will soon." Emily bit the inside of her bottom lip. "Our only choice is to find the relic, whatever it is, and find another safe place for it."

Shelton grunted. "We can only play keep away for so long. What's the long-term plan?"

"Good question." Elyssa blew out a breath. "Emily, do you have any idea what relics Baal needs?"

"Not an exact list," she said. "There are several major relics that have been lost for ages—the dagger, the heart, the eye, and the nose."

"The nose?" Shelton snorted. "What's that do, sniff farts from a mile away?"

Ambria gave Conrad a look. "It so happens that we know where most of those are."

Conrad scratched the back of his neck. "The dagger and the nose are in the Glimmer. Underborn has the heart, the map, and the key. He probably has others as well."

Tyler raised his eyebrows. "Man, you kids have been busy. How in the world do you know so much about the relics?"

Max grinned. "Oh boy, have we got some stories about those."

"I guess we do." Conrad sighed. "I lost one mother but resurrected another in the search for the heart."

"It seems we have a war on two fronts," Thomas said. "Keeping the relics from Baal and defeating his army. The endgame is almost here, and Baal has the high ground."

We definitely had a rocky road ahead of us. There was no telling how close Baal was to finishing Saila and his dragon army would be formidable even with Emily and my nifty new powers.

But we'd overcome the odds. We'd defeated Xanos and Razor Echelon.

Gird your loins, Baal, because we're coming for you.

BOOKS BY JOHN CORWIN

THE OVERWORLD CHRONICLES

Sweet Blood of Mine

Dark Light of Mine

Fallen Angel of Mine

Dread Nemesis of Mine

Twisted Sister of Mine

Dearest Mother of Mine

Infernal Father of Mine

Sinister Seraphim of Mine

Wicked War of Mine

Dire Destiny of Ours

Aetherial Annihilation

Baleful Betrayal

Ominous Odyssey

Insidious Insurrection

Utopia Undone

Overworld Apocalypse

Apocryphan Rising

Assignment Zero (An Elyssa Short Story)

OVERWORLD UNDERGROUND

Soul Seer

Demonicus

Infernal Blade

OVERWORLD ARCANUM

Conrad Edison and the Living Curse

Conrad Edison and the Anchored World

Conrad Edison and the Broken Relic

Conrad Edison and the Infernal Design

Conrad Edison and the First Power

STAND ALONE NOVELS

Mars Rising

No Darker Fate

The Next Thing I Knew

Outsourced

For the latest on new releases, free ebooks, and more, join John Corwin's Newsletter at www.johncorwin.net!

ABOUT THE AUTHOR

John Corwin is the bestselling author of the Overworld Chronicles. He enjoys long walks on the beach and is a firm believer in puppies and kittens.

After years of getting into trouble thanks to his overactive imagination, John abandoned his male modeling career to write books.

He resides in Atlanta.

Connect with John Corwin online:
Facebook: http://www.facebook.com/johnhcorwinauthor
Website: http://www.johncorwin.net
Twitter: http://twitter.com/#!/John_Corwin

www.johncorwin.net
john@johncorwin.net

www.ingramcontent.com/pod-product-compliance
Lightning Source LLC
Chambersburg PA
CBHW030802260626
47169CB00001B/154